INTO A RAGING BLAZE

INTO A RAGING BLAZE

ANDREAS NORMAN

TRANSLATED BY IAN GILES

Quercus

New York • London

Quercus

New York • London

This book is a work of fiction. Names, characters, institutions, places, and events are
either the product of the author's imagination or are used fictitiously. Any resemblance
to actual persons—living or dead—events, or locales is entirely coincidental.

To Anna K.

1

Brussels, Friday, September 23

The man came out of the entrance to the EU Commission, went around the building, and started to walk down Archimedesstraat. Dark hair, gray suit, and a blue shirt. For a moment he disappeared out of sight. Team two radioed in a few seconds later—they were posted a hundred meters down the street and could see him clearly.

The target had been under surveillance for three months, and nothing suggested that he would change his plans today. He was regular in his habits: worked long days at the office but always finished at the same time, around seven, and would drive home in his car. Today he was leaving the office at five, since it was a Friday. As expected.

He and his wife had a weekend place they had rented for the last two years. The cottage was located by a lake in the Doornendijk nature reserve in the Flemish fenlands of Meetjesland, about ten kilometers north of Ghent—an area rich in birdlife and with excellent fishing waters.

The target got into his car—a metallic green Audi that was parked a hundred meters further along the street, close to the crossroads with Rue Stevin—started it and pulled away from the curb.

The traffic flowed along. The Audi was a few cars ahead and moved quickly through the city via Rue de la Loi, Kunstlaan, and Avenue Charles-Quint, heading northward. After fifteen minutes it was on the A10 freeway. Team two was three hundred meters further ahead, in the inside lane. The target maintained a high and steady speed and showed no signs of being conscious of their presence.

After forty kilometers he turned off at the junction for Merelbeke and joined the R4 going north. They remained in formation. At this speed, expected time of arrival was in thirty minutes.

But on the way toward Ghent's industrial quarter the target slowed and, instead of continuing along the R4, he turned off toward the port. Team two, which was ahead of the target, missed the turn and had to stop on the shoulder to wait. The Audi drove past the warehouses along the quay, rounded the docks for the cargo barges, and pulled over into a gas station. Team one stopped in a neighboring parking lot and observed the target.

He got out, filled up the car, paid, and then drove out of the port and back on to the northbound R4—the anticipated route.

Team two rejoined after a few minutes. They were preparing now: they took out the vials, loaded three hundred units of insulin, and made sure that the insulin pen and backup were both working. Three hundred units was ten times the daily dose that the target took for his diabetes—it was enough. The main thing was that nothing suspicious should be detected during the autopsy.

At the junction for Bruges, he joined the A11 and, a few kilometers later, as expected, he turned on to the N448. When everything was going smoothly it could seem like the target had been involved in the planning of the operation: everything happened as if by agreement. But, naturally, no such agreement existed. The target was unaware.

They passed through Assenede, which was the nearest town. Team two had taken the faster route, avoiding the center, and were already halfway to the cottage.

He was driving slowly now and would not leave their sight. He stopped at a tobacconist's, got out of the car, leaving the engine running, and hurried in, returning a moment later with a newspaper and what looked like a few packs of cigarettes, then drove on. They had prepared for a longer stop in the village, but he continued along a country road without stopping again.

There was no traffic here. Their vehicle and that of the target were the only cars to be seen in the avenue they had just turned into, which stretched ahead for a kilometer. The cottage was secluded, on a wooded spit of land, accessible only by the bumpy road that ran through the woodland and ended by the house. The plot looked out on to one of the small lakes—a lawn ran all the way to the water's edge—and it was completely hidden from view, unless you stood on the opposite shore with binoculars. There was a small risk of birdwatchers, but it would all go so quickly. If anyone happened to see what was going on, they wouldn't understand what they had witnessed anyway.

They slowed down and let the target turn on to the road through the woods to the cottage. Once the Audi was out of sight, they slowly followed it, parked the car halfway up the road to the house, and got out.

They moved quickly on foot along the edge of the wood. It was densely wooded with low visibility. They had to be careful; the target wasn't more than ten or so meters away. There was the house: a vacation cottage with a low fence, gate, and bushes. The metallic green car was parked on the edge of the road. There was the target, standing in the living room of the cottage, still wearing his coat, with his back turned to them.

They rounded the corner just as he came down the front door steps on to the lawn. He was on his way to the water's edge but only managed two or three steps before something made him turn his head—perhaps the noise of their sneakers as they ran toward him. No visible signs of violence was the critical thing. He tensed up, but he didn't really understand what was happening; he was barely afraid when two of them pressed him down onto the grass and gripped his arms while number three stuck the insulin pen into the hairline on his neck. They quickly carried him down toward the water's edge and waited until his body had stopped fighting, checked his pulse, and then they left him.

2

Stockholm, Wednesday, September 21

It was just after eight in the morning and Carina Dymek had already managed two hours of work. The first of her colleagues were beginning to turn up now—she heard the clicking of ceiling lights being switched on, the low scramble of chairs being pulled toward desks, and then the familiar motif played by computers during start-up. Carina was not a morning person. She hated early mornings and wasn't really mentally with it before ten, but on this Wednesday morning she couldn't worry about that. She had been forced to come in early to have, even theoretically, a chance of getting through the threateningly long to-do list that filled a brightly colored Post-it note on the side of her computer screen.

There were 8,634 messages in her inbox. At the top of the screen there glowed seventy-five new, unread, blazing red e-mails. Many were just informational in nature—reports and newsletters—things that didn't require any action. Those could wait to be read, if she read them at all. But, mixed into the flood of messages like those, there were e-mails she couldn't afford to miss. Red-flagged e-mails, e-mails titled *Thanks in advance for quick response,* orders with short deadlines, questions from the department head that required immediate responses, or e-mails like the one she had just brought up, which bore an urgent subject line of *ORDER—Data for UM in Berlin, deadline 22nd Sep. 16:00.*

Even among the priority e-mails she was obliged to prioritize. The night before, she had lain in bed and gone through everything she had to do the next day. Anxious thoughts kept revolving in a meaningless circle. After hours of unsuccessful attempts to fall asleep, she had come to the conclusion that everything was important: everything had to be prioritized. There was only one solution—the only solution that the MFA had taught her for these situations: to deny oneself a good night's sleep. She got up.

The windows were still dark, the corridors dim and silent when she arrived at the department, hours before everyone else.

As it got light, the government buildings in the district around Drottninggatan in central Stockholm were filled by approximately four thousand civil servants, all of whom sat down at their computers, just as she had, in well-lit, uniformly furnished office landscapes and started the day's work. They worked in the shadows of ministers, served the government, and were tasked with giving the nation's political leaders the best possible understanding of myriad issues that ministers needed to grasp in order to better rule the country and decide on its foreign policy. They were the government's support as it ruled. Some might say that they used a friendly but determined hand to control the government. They explained developments in unfamiliar countries; they gave ministers their view of the situation. They produced facts and gave opinions. They made assessments and took decisions that affected people and entire societies. Even decisions that had no effect whatsoever were taken—that happened every day. They gave advice and the politicians listened. The government ruled Sweden, but in the shadow of the government there were those who managed the levers and controls and the organization: the Government Offices of Sweden.

The Government Offices of Sweden was something of which normal people, without the right to be in its corridors, only had a vague understanding. Those who worked at the Government Offices obviously knew that it comprised the Prime Minister's own staff, called the Prime Minister's Office, and then the Office for Administrative Affairs, which managed all the resource issues that constantly flooded the organization: IT, security, salaries, and other administrative matters. Beneath this pair there were eleven departments. One of them was the Ministry of Foreign Affairs—the MFA.

Of all the ministries, the MFA was the largest and most secretive. With its two-and-a-half thousand staff, one hundred embassies, four hundred consulates, and permanent representations to the UN, EU, and delegations in other international organizations, it was a gargantuan machine, a leviathan greater than all the other ministries combined. Civil servants in the rest of Government Offices always regarded the MFA and its diplomats with envious admiration, a mixture of longing to be one of them and hatred because they never would be.

The Ministry's four buildings in the government district were closed addresses. Within their walls, the nation's foreign policy was formed. Internally, the Ministry was called the House and was divided into twenty-five departments. Out of all the departments, the Security Policy Department was the largest and quietly considered to be the most important, the one that had the foreign minister's ear. The Security Policy Department—or SP, as it was called—stretched across two stories of the office block at Fredsgatan 6. Down its long, winding corridors and past the rows of offices, close to the stairs between floors five and four, was room 1523. In its depths sat Carina Dymek at a height-adjustable desk, writing with speed and concentration on a computer.

She was satisfied. Soon she would be able to tick off the biggest order on her list—the foreign minister's file. The foreign minister was going to Ukraine the next day for a meeting with President Yanukovych, talks with the Enlargement Commissioner, Štefan Füle, and a swathe of other meetings. Yalta, Crimea. The EU's relations with the large, splintered post-Soviet nation were on the agenda. Central Asia. The Tymoshenko case, energy security. It was important to continue applying pressure to the leaders of Ukraine while at the same time intimating that the country had EU prospects if it chose to develop in a democratic direction—everything to avoid forcing it east into the arms of the Kremlin and Gazprom. The country's economy was in crisis and its politics were heading in an increasingly authoritarian direction. The EU's instrument, in the shape of the European Neighborhood Policy with its various development and support programs, was the soft power that the Union could exercise. The foreign minister was committed to the issues. The Ukraine desk officer at the Department for Eastern Europe and Central Asia was currently working on some analyses of Ukrainian domestic policies and relationships with Russia, while Carina's focus was on the EU and security policy.

As always, it wasn't the formal, agenda-driven talks that were most interesting, it was those on the sidelines. The foreign minister's coordinator had already indicated that the minister wanted bilateral meetings with several of Ukraine's advisers and a meeting with Tony Blair, who for some reason was in the Crimea; the foreign minister also wanted to meet a security adviser at RAND who worked as a consultant for the Ukrainian defense ministry, as well as a handful of others. Carina needed to draft the outline of a short speech for the dinner in the evening. It was also to be expected that certain current and sensitive EU issues would come up, even if they didn't directly affect Ukraine.

The foreign minister's file was the collective result of the work of, on average, five to ten desk officers in at least two departments and a collection of embassies around the world. Before every trip a unique file was compiled with analyses and reports, Swedish messages and talking points for media contact, CVs of important people, and practical information about the trip. Ideally, the file was meant to reflect all political aspects and eventualities, and meet all requirements for facts that the minister might possibly have.

Carina took a deep breath and glanced through what she had written. The key messages were good, cogent. She knew the Swedish positions and didn't need to shuffle through old strategic documents to know what a foreign minister should and shouldn't say. Just two or three more talking points—in bullet points—then she would choose a bunch of analyses before going to see her new unit head, Anders Wahlund, to check the texts with him: she had fifteen minutes after lunch to go through the most sensitive parts of the material with him. Hopefully the file would then be done, barring a few minor changes. She would send over her contribution to the

Ukraine desk officer, who would have a secretary in the unit make three copies of everything before running over to the minister's office, so that the minister would have the file in the car the next morning, allowing him to look through it on the way to the airport.

The foreign minister had a photographic memory. Everyone knew that he preferred statistics to reasoning, data rather than a desk officer's fumbling analyses. He often liked incredibly technical details about nuclear power plants, Russian combat vehicles, and other things that a foreign minister apparently had a use for. According to those who worked closest to him, he read everything. The Foreign Service produced hundreds of reports every day. Apparently he read all embassy reports, all major news, blogs, research—everything. Carina couldn't understand how it was possible, but that was what they said. Orders from the foreign minister's office often came with a slightly condescending reminder to the desk officer not to include "the normal" embassy reports, just facts and "the most relevant things."

In her eight years at the Ministry, she had sat eye to eye with the foreign minister on four occasions. He was unquestionably brilliant, but basically uninterested in people who weren't foreign ministers.

It occurred to her that the minister might not even be in Stockholm. If not, she would be forced to send the whole file as an encrypted e-mail to Kiev, call them, and get someone to drive it down to the Crimea to hand it over personally.

She dug out her phone from under the papers and called the minister's press secretary, but that diverted to a cell-phone voicemail. She pulled up the electronic phone directory and found the extension for one of the assistants.

Call forwarded. Then some scraping noises and a whispering voice that answered: "Marianne."

Carina introduced herself. She explained briefly that she was preparing the minister's file for Ukraine. Was the foreign minister in Stockholm today?

"I don't actually know."

"Okay."

"He's going to the Congo later this week—for the Dag Hammar-skjöld ceremony. But I don't know anything about Ukraine. Can I get back to you? Or maybe try Elisabeth?" the assistant whispered in a stressed tone.

Carina hung up.

Assistant number two didn't answer. The foreign minister's adviser, some young upstart straight out of the Young Conservatives, did pick up his cell. Wasn't the minister in New York? He clearly had no idea. Carina ended the call quickly, leaned back in the chair, and thought through the options. He would be in Yalta within eighteen hours if he wasn't there already. Then Africa, then New York and the UN.

She really did need to know where the foreign minister was. Then the obvious solution occurred to her: check his blog. She went to the site and, naturally, he had already had time to blog in the morning. He was in parliament today—so still in Stockholm for at least another five hours.

She wrote for half an hour uninterrupted. Her fingers rattled across the keyboard in a series of rapid movements. Points for a possible press conference: The Eastern partnership was of key importance to relations between the EU and Ukraine, she wrote, before adding a few sentences about the importance of a long-term relationship and about the country as part of Europe. General formulations. The EU had trading relations and aid as its two greatest weapons but it was the Russians who had true geopolitical power—they controlled access to oil and gas. It was vital that the message about the rule of law and human rights was clear, while not punching the Ukrainians in the nose and hurting their pride, which would make Yanukovych turn to Moscow. The Kremlin was already talking about discounted oil prices. In a few months it would be winter in Kiev and then political loyalty would be counted in dollars per barrel. She read through what she'd written, rapidly making additions and amendments until she had a decent draft. It was a quarter past nine.

As the Security Policy Department's EU coordinator, it was she who had to get the department's seventy-five diplomats to sing from the same song sheet on everything to do with EU security policy. She was the one who had to keep up with EU procedures, put together negotiation instructions for Brussels and make sure that ministers and junior ministers had the right information. She was the one who sent out stern reminders to colleagues about keeping to deadlines and she was responsible for ensuring that everyone affected was informed and ready to react.

The last few months had been hectic. The Arab Spring and the Libyan campaign, Kosovo, the Horn of Africa, and more generally the EU's more or less fulfilled ambition of becoming a military security policy operator meant, in practice, a myriad of meetings and decisions, informal contacts, and thousands of papers with proposals flitting between the capitals of Europe. All this went through the encrypted European communication system, Coreu. There was a database where all member states and the Council of Europe secretariat could post messages—a never-ending noticeboard where thousands of messages, agendas, and minutes were published every day. It was Carina's responsibility to keep track of this flow of information and make sure that the department didn't drop any balls. There were those who hated Coreu. When Sweden had joined the EU and connected to the information system, the volume of mail and messages had increased by fifty percent overnight. Carina liked the tempo. She enjoyed having direct contact with other European foreign ministries and the feeling of being a part of real politics. Fifty or sixty hours a week were a prerequisite to do the job, but that was generally okay. This morning, however, the sheer volume of new messages on Coreu made her draw breath. Dealing with the stream of Coreu data was sometimes like playing an unending tennis match against an inexhaustible Agassi.

She stood up and stretched her arms. Her back creaked. Tiredness washed across her like an anesthetic and made her stagger. She needed coffee.

Carina looked around. Her room was narrow, a little smaller than the others on the corridor. There had been a possibility that she might get the office next door to the Head of Department, at the top end of the corridor—a light room with a view toward Strömmen. It had been the last EU coordinator's office. But, instead of Carina, the DPKO desk officer, responsible for contact with New York about Swedish contributions to UN troop activities, had gotten the room. He was of a higher rank. But he was going to Santiago soon, and then perhaps it would be her turn.

She really ought to tidy up, she realized. It was one of the things she never prioritized. She had never been good at physical order. Deep down, she didn't quite understand what the point was of constantly tidying up—always gathering things into neat piles, putting them in drawers and boxes—when the order was there in her head all along. She was in full control. She prioritized. She was completely fulfilled by her work—what did it matter if there were a few papers here or an apple core there? Everyone knew that she had a fully equipped intellect, but no one believed her when she said she had a system in her office. People visiting her office would often stop short in the doorway as if confronted by a natural phenomenon. Johan Eriksson called her room "the Batcave." The deputy Head of Department had started to drop small hints, so sooner or later she would have to tidy up. Why on earth couldn't she be left in peace in her room as it was? She was one of the best analysts in the department. She knew it, even if no one ever said so in as many words. Johan and others would constantly bombard her with various texts for her consideration, and she would usually take pity and quickly glance through their documents, dead calm and absorbed, before leaving a few comments. And the fact was that she was rarely wrong. Despite this, she knew that the office of a civil servant at the MFA shouldn't look like this.

The desk was a jumbled landscape of crusty coffee cups, fruit peelings, tubs of paper clips, reference works, handbooks, and an avalanche of papers that had slipped down toward the computer screen. Somewhere or other there ought to be a cactus, but she didn't take care of it. The shelves along one wall were brimming with books, papers, and files. She contemplated the stacks of paper lying on the floor. The elegant, sheepskin-clad Lammhult armchair was beside the table. It actually belonged in the UNHCR desk officer's room, but she had discreetly carried it to her office the day he left on paternity leave and nobody could remember whose it actually was. It was comfy, but couldn't be sat in because towering off it was a stack of reports from all the past year's summit meetings at the EU. That pile was a problem—from time to time it extended to the floor. Sometimes she would find classifieds in it—which was not good. The security guards patrolling the building at night were always checking if there was any classified material lying around in offices. If you forgot to lock up classified material, you received a warning in the form of an angry red note on your chair in the morning. Three warnings and you would be called in to the department head.

The best way to keep a secret was never to divulge it, so they said. But in practice that was impossible. The greater part of the work at the MFA was done under cover of secrecy stamps. The House was bulging with secrets. They were collected, discussed; some built their entire careers on having access to the right classified material. The encrypted mail system delivered a flood of classified reports and analyses depicting reality in its true, complex and raw form. Everyone was careless with secrets. Classifieds were always lying around because no one could be bothered to adhere to the strict rules concerning the handling of secret material. But chucking classifieds on the floor was probably a little too nonchalant. She spotted a report from a NATO meeting in Kabul littering the floor, bent down, and picked it up. In all likelihood there were even more classified reports in the piles. She quickly shuffled through the armchair pile. She wouldn't forgive herself if she made the beginner's mistake of getting caught being careless about secrecy. She couldn't become a problem to the department, not now.

As EU coordinator, Carina had to work like a slave, but if she stuck it out for another year she would be within reach of a promotion. Her predecessor had been a deputy director. Every EU coordinator before her had been. But not her, she was still a desk officer. It wasn't something that she dwelled on, but those were the facts, and a poisonous suspicion had begun to spread through her that she wasn't quite as good as the others. The department head seemed to like her. But she knew how it was: she hadn't taken the Ministry's Diplomat Program—she wasn't a "dipper"; she had come the long way around to become a diplomat, and that made all the difference.

Carina had started as a temp in the Press, Information, and Communication Department, the least prestigious place to work in the entire building, but had quickly demonstrated an aptitude for analysis and had gone on to short temporary roles at the Department for Eastern Europe and Central Asia and then the Americas Department. Finally, after six years, she got a permanent job at the Security Policy Department. Thank goodness. "Dippers" were guaranteed a permanent position; they were guaranteed a career. She and they were not the same Homo sapiens. She had to fight every week to show her worth. She had considered applying to the Diplomat Program but the thought of rejection had held her back. There were twelve hundred applicants every year and just a handful were accepted after written examinations, stress tests, intelligence tests, and ten interviews. Everyone at the department would know if she didn't make it and it would be proof that she was second-rate. So instead she had thrown herself into her work and now it was beginning to pay off. As of a few months ago, reports would appear in her pigeonhole every now and then with a Post-it saying, *Swedish options?* Or, *Carina, your views appreciated. Nils.* The department head had caught sight of her and begun to use her as a kind of informal sounding board. She would read through and quickly send her assessment. And now there was the rumor of her promotion. Small signs. You made your own luck. How she could be so sure, she didn't know, but all the same . . .

It had started as a rumor in the department. Johan Eriksson knew one of the unit heads at Human Resources and had heard that her name had been discussed at a meeting. After that it had quickly become the accepted truth that Carina Dymek was going to become a deputy director next year. But no one really knew whether it was true, not even the department heads, because no one understood the Byzantine procedures in place at the Human Resources Department. Sometimes one could sense a deeper meaning, a pattern in the way posts were filled and who was promoted. But then those patterns would be broken by unfathomable placements that once again meant the MFA's personnel policies reverted to being the mystery that kept the entire diplomatic corps on tenterhooks and filled the House with rumor and speculation. Like when a deputy was recalled from Rome under suspicion of housing allowance abuse and suspended, only to turn up as the ambassador in Rabat a year later. Or when one of the country's most prominent political figures was left to wither away on a pointless inquiry, only to be brought back into the fold and made ambassador to Hong Kong. Unpredictable turns like that sent shock waves throughout the building and generated endless speculation. It enchanted and frightened in equal measure. One thing, however, was clear—loyalty paid off. If you stayed in the House, you made your career. The former Marshal of the Court was a warning to all. He had worked at the royal court for over ten years when he returned to the MFA from his leave of absence. He was promptly dispatched to Islamabad in the midst of the worst terror bombings for years. Everyone got the message: opt out of the Ministry and you can go to hell when you come back.

In reality, the career ladder was perfectly clear and straightforward. Administrative staff had zero career development; they remained assistants their whole lives and could only hope for postings to embassies in decent capital cities. Then there were the political appointments, those working around ministers: junior ministers, press secretaries, and senior advisers—the political experts. They came from the parties, had broken through the youth organizations and political meetings—they belonged to another world. There was deep mistrust between them and the civil servants. Carina felt it herself. As a civil servant she and her colleagues were loyal to the

House: it was *their* House; the politicos were just temporary visitors. The day after changes in government, moving boxes would be sitting outside the offices of junior ministers and political appointees, and then they were gone. But the civil servants stayed. They knew their House and they knew their government—they knew how to get a minister to see the light and grant approval to their proposals.

For the civil servants and diplomats, a career at the MFA was ostensibly simple. You started as a desk officer, then became a deputy director, then perhaps you became a director and, finally, maybe, an ambassador. The thing that had made her fight for a career at the Ministry was the chance of working in embassies, in the closed rooms of Brussels or Washington. This opportunity was available once a year in the autumn with the commencement of the so-called Grand Call. All vacant positions were published on an internal database, graded by rank, and anyone who wanted to could apply. The Grand Call was the cause of a storm of rumors and intrigue on an annual basis, with everyone trying to get on the good side of bosses and ambassadors in the hope of a good word, while horse-trading with the Human Resources Department. Diplomats had free reign to use the tactics they had been trained in to drive forward their own ambitions rather than to run Swedish politics. It was a time for hopes, dreams, alliances, and razor-sharp rivalries—but with a smile. The last day for applications was the beginning of a four-month game of negotiation in the arena of personnel administration that few saw, but, according to what Carina had heard, reached such a level of complexity that in the end no one was even able to guess who might get which job. Everything disappeared into the labyrinth that was the Human Resources Department. She had heard that the HR administrators would have huge, secret, marathon meetings to which no one else had access, and during which they would draw up lists that no one had ever seen but everyone had heard of, ranking personnel by means of an intricate system. Finally, applicants found out which position they were being offered, or not offered, whereupon an enormous logistical apparatus was set in motion. Hundreds of moves between capital cities and embassies, as well as between floors in the House back in Stockholm, would take place. Next year she was going to apply to an outside position—an embassy. Beijing, perhaps. Or maybe something completely different—Nairobi. She shivered with anticipation.

Carina stepped out into the corridor and put the classifieds into a burn trolley—a large, locked wastepaper basket on wheels into which civil servants dumped sensitive papers through a small flap after they had been read. The trolleys were taken regularly to a location outside of Stockholm where everything was burned in a secure manner. Often the trolley in her corridor was overflowing by the middle of the week, with secrets sticking out of the flap.

She went into the bathroom and splashed water across her face, dried off, and looked critically at herself in the mirror. Four hours' sleep wasn't enough, but she didn't look as hollow-eyed as she felt. Her face, with its prominent chin, always became furrowed and wolflike when she hadn't slept well. But you could hide the dark rings under the eyes with a little makeup. Simply because she was so tired, she had dressed extra formally in a black suit, crimson top, and black shoes. She had glossy polished nails. It didn't do to wander around the Ministry yawning—no one here wanted to know about your weaknesses. It was important to appear sharp. She always wore a suit to work. In her private life, she never wore a suit, but at the MFA she was in the service of the state. The suit provided her with a steadiness of character—like a piece of armor. Casual clothes were not accepted, something which she had learned quickly the hard way when she had started eight years ago. On her first day, she had come to work in a stylish denim jacket. A man, who she later discovered was the Head of the Press Department, had stopped her in the corridor and said, "Oh, nonuniform day, is it?"

She hadn't understood what he meant and had said that they were her normal clothes.

"You won't come back from lunch in those clothes," she had been told.

At lunch she had gone, with a lump in her throat, to the NK department store and returned with a navy blue suit, white blouse and black shoes. She had worn a suit ever since.

Her hair was pulled back tightly in a ponytail. It made her face look more open and alert. She was proud of her straight, dark-blond hair, and liked the freckles that populated the bridge of her nose and spilled on to her cheeks. An early boyfriend had lovingly said that she looked like Jodie Foster. She had a straight nose and gray-green eyes with a gaze that had wavered six or seven years ago but could now be directed at anybody without any sign of a tremor. She had learned; she had grown up. She had never been one of the best-looking girls at school; instead, she had been a member of the gray mass of quiet, clever pupils. But she was here. The hotties worked at 7-Eleven and she worked at the MFA. She adjusted her jacket. She was pleased about how fit she was. Swimming had kept her in shape; she liked the feeling of her shoulders filling the suit. She was thirty-two years old and never thought about what she ate; it was as if a fast-spinning machine inside her burned all the energy. She combed back a strand of hair that had fallen across her forehead. No one would believe that this was someone who preferred to wear hoodies and sneakers in her free time, who lived in a pokey one-bedroom apartment with all her clothes strewn everywhere, who left dishes and wine bottles for weeks, who liked to lie in until one on weekends, who liked to provoke people by using the word "cock" inappropriately, who loved Depeche Mode, and sometimes—when she hated her job—dreamed of becoming a computer-games programmer. Who knew that below this controlled exterior there lay an uncontrollable temper? She could have such outbursts of rage. Sometimes she was driven by a rage from some unknown place that made her throw glasses at the wall when she was drunk and scream in such a way that she frightened herself, and which only swimming, furious swimming, length after length, could calm down. None of this Carina Dymek was visible. She was a diplomat; she knew how to maintain her mask. You were sociable, but not intimate. You were happy and lively and clever—you were not a big mouth and didn't act out.

She had always wanted to be a diplomat. She had fought to get here, first as a student and a research assistant at the Department of

Law in Uppsala, then as an unpaid volunteer at Amnesty in Stockholm, followed by a short internship at the embassy in the Hague, and finally as a summer temp at the MFA, before a longer-term temporary position. Now she was here. She was in. Sometimes she would think on her way to work, Here I am, walking along, a diplomat. One of the key people at the Security Policy Department of the MFA.

And then she had Jamal: a new man.

She smiled, got out her makeup and applied concealer using her fingertips, then a little rouge, added a little more mascara to her eyelashes, glanced into the mirror—approved—and stepped out into the department again.

In the kitchen she got a large coffee from the machine. There was no milk in the fridge. Then it occurred to her that there hadn't been any milk in the fridge for months. The ministry had been the subject of a draconian 200 million–kronor cutback, and all departments had been forced to cut costs. Most had cut travel, blocked acquisitions, and stopped using consultants and contractors. The deputy Head of the Security Policy Department had gone one step further. Apart from making the expected savings, she had also written a two-page memo banning the purchase of milk and cookies. Carina laughed to herself as she remembered the department meeting where they had been informed of the decision. No more departmental milk and, with great seriousness, they were informed that anyone who wished to offer guests coffee would have to source the accompaniments themselves— under no circumstances was the department's account to be charged. By now the memo was a classic—mocked extensively. But who needed milk? She only needed the coffee.

The Head of Department's personal secretary, Birgitta, was in the mail room using the photocopier. They smiled at one another.

"Here you go." Birgitta handed over a small bundle of papers. "They're from Nils. He wants to know what you think. Aren't you clever, helping him out? I'll make an appointment for you," she said, before patting Carina amiably on the arm, collecting her papers from the photocopier, and disappearing.

On paper, Birgitta was merely one of many administrative resources in the Ministry, but in practice she held much of the real power. The small, old fashioned but very elegant woman, who wore tweed suits, scarves, and little brooches, was the one who ruled over the appointment calendar of the Head of Department. She refused to keep it electronically; instead, everything was entered into a large leather-bound book that only she had access to and which always accompanied her to meetings. Those who didn't stay on good terms with the department head's secretary never got an appointment with the head, were never informed about meetings until the last second possible, and were generally vilified by the administrative personnel. Birgitta was very probably quite terrible to have as an enemy, but for some reason she seemed to like Carina.

The mail slot was half empty. She hadn't bothered emptying it for a couple of days. At the top there was a report about the latest developments in Mazar-e Sharif, then a report about the troubles in Nigeria, embassy reports from Pristina, London, and a special report about an attack in Kabul, as well as details of meetings with the Russian interior ministry. Over twenty reports—all interesting reading—but nothing that required her immediate attention.

Even the driest documents gave the impression that you were treading through hidden rooms, ready for exploration: grand halls, underground vaults. To read an embassy report was to come close to the low-key, confidential conversations taking place in Brussels, Paris, Washington, and Moscow. Carina always read quickly but accurately. Sometimes she would stop on a well-formulated sentence about al-Qaida's worldview, about the intrigues of the Russian Duma, fitted into a conversation over lunch at Quai d'Orsay. When she found a really interesting report, she would feel quietly excited and discreetly happy. Reports with titles such as *Afghanistan— Monthly threat assessment, August 2011* or *The "single narrative" of European home-grown terrorism: a British perspective* had an irresistible appeal. To read and analyze reports like that was an important part of why she loved her job. Her ability to peel away the layers to reveal the underlying structures, expose implied opinions and find meaning between the lines had made her a respected member of the department. She enjoyed being able to skim through a report and split it up into its component parts. Even crusty dry reports from a Directorate General of the European Commission could generate a sort of glow. They were real to her. There were whole worlds hidden within their cool and formal, meandering and lengthy sentences. They weren't just words, they were the secrets that formed the future.

She gathered together a pile of papers and slammed the mail room door to make sure it locked. On the way back, she swung by Johan Eriksson's office, but he was on the phone so she went on, stopping in the kitchen to fill her coffee cup.

At lunchtime, she hurried to the nearby shopping mall and ate quickly at one of the oval salad bars. She had managed to finish writing up the material for the foreign minister and felt jittery due to low blood sugar. The mall was full of people milling from shop to shop around her. She let her thoughts wander. On the way out of the office, she had put her head around Anders Wahlund's door—her new unit head. A new boss was always a cause for worry, which was precisely why she wanted to show that she was friendly, as well as get her first impression of him. But his office had been empty.

A hand brushed her shoulder, making her come to.

"Hi, darling."

It was Jamal—her Jamal, standing there in the sea of people, smiling his beautiful, wide smile at her.

"Hi." She slid off the bar stool and embraced him.

She was once again struck by how good-looking he was. Jamal was tall, thin, and had dark, curly hair that he tried to comb down into a normal hairstyle. He was wearing a dark suit, white shirt and a wine-red tie, and looked every part the Ministry of Justice civil servant that he was, but better-looking than the others. The slender face and the dark, serious eyes that always seemed to be pondering his surroundings made him appear almost noble, like a young prince. Beautiful people always had the upper hand, and Jamal was beautiful, even if he appeared not to realize it.

"How are things?" he asked.

"Good. Give me a kiss."

Jamal smiled and kissed her lightly on the mouth. His lips were so soft—she wished he hadn't leaned back so quickly instead of letting her kiss him longer. But Jamal was careful. He looked at her tantalizingly. She had noticed how reserved, almost distant, he could be with people he didn't know. Far too many colleagues were in the mall at lunchtime—someone might see them kissing and then the whispering would start. She was still surprised that she had gotten together with this reclusive, earnest man who didn't miss any nuances. Jamal was so radically different from her last boyfriend, she reflected with satisfaction, that there were no similarities whatsoever.

"Are you catching the crack-of-dawn flight tomorrow?"

She nodded. The morning flight to Brussels at seven was notorious. She pulled him in toward her, slid her hand into his jacket, and stroked his back. She would have liked to slide her hand under his shirt to feel his skin, but she knew that Jamal wouldn't like her doing that in a place like this, among people.

"Do you have time for a coffee?"

"Sorry." He gestured vaguely over his shoulder toward the government district. As a legal adviser at Justice, he was constantly bombarded by different demands and orders from the justice minister. Carina had told him that he worked too much. Even by her standards, he worked too much. She had never seen anyone who was as thorough as Jamal—it was as if he thought that the smallest error might cost him his job. "I have to finish writing some things. The minister's going to the Hague tomorrow and the deadline for her portfolio is this evening."

"Oh, love." She carefully placed a hand on his leg.

"It's the usual," he said. "See you on Friday?"

She nodded. He smelled so good—she could breathe in the scent of him when he stood close to her. It wasn't long until the weekend; just a trip to Brussels and then they could finally be together. She leaned forward and kissed him on the mouth. He laughed, as if taken by surprise, and kissed her back.

*   *   *

She had almost stopped caring about men. It made life so simple. She lived alone in a one-bed on Luntmakargatan, right in the heart of Stockholm, worked at the Ministry and, during her free time, swam, read, watched horror films, and sometimes grabbed a drink with colleagues—it was an uncomplicated life. Especially since her ex-husband Peter had finally stopped calling her, which he had been doing for the last few months. Her life had a new sense of ease. For the first time, she was being left in peace and starting to feel like herself again.

The relationship with Peter had been a big mistake and, as is so often the case with big mistakes, it had been committed gradually, in small steps. With hindsight, it was impossible to understand how she had put up with it. Ten years of her life, with the last two or three blurring into a gray haze. She should never have stayed so long.

Peter had been studying medicine when they met. He had impressed her. He told her about how absurd, yet fantastic it was to dissect a human being, described how beautiful the human body was on the inside. He pondered ethical dilemmas, issues about the final stages of life, because he wanted to make a difference for patients who were in the most difficult, irrevocable situations. She fell in love. She was studying law, but she rarely socialized with her own classmates; Peter preferred to socialize with his and she had nothing against that, as most of hers were tedious eager beavers. When he started to earn a living, Carina still had a year of her studies remaining, which was when something happened. He complained that she wasn't earning any money. That was holding him back, he said. He felt he was paying for everything. When she started working as a volunteer for a human rights organization, he would often point out that she could make much more if she took a job in a law firm. When they had gotten together, he had claimed he was bohemian and "cool," but over time he became more irritated by her. He thought she was careless, and that her temper was annoying. She was so over the top—couldn't she just calm down? She never understood his need for calm. Why should she calm down? With time she came to understand that he didn't really mean "calm." He meant quiet and controlled—controlled by him. He would be irritated if she talked politics too much. "Stop lecturing," he would say. She dominated conversations and didn't give him space—she stole the limelight, he would complain. They got married anyway. Perhaps she had thought things would change—that marriage would lift everything to a new level. They had a big church wedding in one of the oldest churches in the city, followed by dinner for one hundred and fifty guests. They planned and saved for over a year. It was hard to grasp that she was the woman in the photos with the extravagant hairdo and the enormous wedding dress.

When she got the job at the Ministry, Peter was happy at first, but he wouldn't even contemplate moving abroad. They moved to a larger apartment. He had very clear views on the decor and would hide or throw out anything not to his liking. He was a food lover and liked to decide what they were going to eat and drink. He thought that she drank a little too much wine. He said things about her body— that she was unfeminine, that she should work out more—so she joined a gym. She met her old friends less and less. At dinners and in the company of his friends, Peter was delightful and charming; sometimes she caught sight of the man she had fallen in love with. She thought she was happy, in the grand scheme of things. Bored, perhaps, but happy. It was ten years before she realized late one evening how far things had gone.

They had been invited to a dinner. The host was a close friend and colleague of Peter's and everyone present, apart from her and the hostess, were physicians. That was how they socialized—with Peter's colleagues. A substantial portion of the dinner was dedicated to gossiping about people at the hospital and talking about vacant positions. Late in the evening they had gotten into a long-winded discussion about a senior physician that Peter hated. When one of his colleagues suggested that female senior physicians could never be as good as male ones, Carina became angry and began to disagree, and it was then that it happened. Peter was very embarrassed and just stared at her as if she were vermin. That was how she remembered it. There was a tense silence around the dinner table. Nobody agreed with her, not even the women present. Peter tried to laugh away her angry questions, but when she didn't give up he hissed at her to come with him to the kitchen. There, he asked her what the hell she was doing. She should hold her tongue, he said. The dinner continued. Afterward she couldn't understand what she was doing there, didn't understand what these people had to do with her and, above all, she didn't know who the man was who later sat beside her in the taxi home. He had slowly worn her down and made her weak, undermined her with his little rules and prohibitions, his sharp comments and silences, threats and pleading, a never-ending range of restrictions that made her start to consider her every action through his critical eyes. The Peter she had fallen in love with was gone. But the sterling Carina who wanted to eat, drink, discuss, fuck, and laugh had also disappeared. She didn't recognize herself, and that frightened her.

At home, she had, as Peter put it, made a scene. Years of self-control evaporated when Peter began to complain about her behavior during dinner. She broke some of their china on the black marble kitchen counter that Peter had insisted upon, screamed at him that he was an asshole, that he had always been an asshole, and that it was over. She got him to retreat to the bedroom, whereupon she tore through their wardrobes, gathered a few clothes that she shoved into a bag, and left. Sofie, the NATO desk officer, had let her sleep on her couch. A month later Carina and Peter were divorced.

They had lived together for ten years and when it ended it was liberating. A part of her, the real Carina, had been waiting all these years to reclaim her body again. Just six months later, she could no longer understand how she had been able to live with that man.

She became skeptical of men—most were uninteresting, to her eyes. She had slept with a few, but quickly became bored. But Jamal surprised her. They had met by chance. One Friday, two months after she had left Peter, she had allowed a few colleagues to persuade her to join them for a drink. In the bar, she ended up next to an unobtrusive, pleasant guy who was utterly beautiful. They spent three hours talking about books, international law—about things she liked. She couldn't explain what it was about him that fascinated her, but he moved her deeply, on a fundamental level. She fantasized about kissing him, embracing him. That night, she couldn't sleep for the first time in a long time. She wanted to carry on talking with him and she wanted to fuck him.

A few days later he called. Under the pretext that Jamal needed to borrow a book, they met in Stockholm's Old Town for a coffee, which became an endless walk that neither of them wanted to finish. They roamed through the inner city down to Stureplan, continued to Söder and meandered through the district over Västerbron to Kungsholmen, and they talked. Finally, they ended up in a blustery beer garden down by Norr Mälarstrand, drinking wine. She had never talked so much to anyone in her whole life. His parents were from Cairo, but fled when the regime began to threaten his father, who was a lawyer. He had grown up in Sweden. She told him about herself and her family, about Poland, the diffuse wonderland, as her relatives called their homeland. They understood each other.

He was careful to begin with. Then they had sex for a whole weekend, over and over until, sweaty, they got up to make spaghetti, naked in his kitchen in Hammarby Sjöstad. For one summer week, she completely lost track of time. She wanted to eat him; she had never felt like that with any man. She absorbed him, making him an irreplaceable part of her biochemistry.

Around three she heard a mass of voices approaching in the corridor. She had been sending e-mails back and forth to the Ministry of Defense and Ministry of Finance for two hours, concerning an EU conference about security policy that the MFA was to organize, but a problem had arisen as to which budget should be used to pay for it. Now a budgetary paper was being sent back and forth between ministries with various amendments. During the last hour she had begun calling around, trying to calm everyone down so they could reach a decision. She needed certification from them, that was how it worked: when a text or a proposal was okay, each affected ministry gave its certification, which meant that the ministry had read the document and accepted the text as it stood. It usually worked well but, for some reason, Finance didn't want to accept the reasoning by Defense that some of the money could be taken from aid funds. Involving other ministries and gathering opinions so that all expert resources were used and everyone was in agreement was the Swedish model—in the Government Offices it was called "joint preparation." But there was nothing more trying than preparations that ran amok like this, or ran aground in a storm of e-mails.

A group of civil servants in dark suits thronged past in the corridor. She recognized Johan Eriksson's familiar laugh and smiled at a half-caught remark about not all Danes having horses in their gardens. A woman paused and loitered in the doorway.

"Hi, Carina." Her penetrating voice filled the room. Deputy department head, Marina Steinhofer, was a burly woman with her hair tied up in a knot like a strict, old-fashioned schoolteacher. "We're having a department meeting now." Steinhofer cast a disapproving glance around the room. "You're coming?"

"Absolutely."

Carina had completely forgotten about the meeting. Really, she needed every last minute to finish responding to the questions from Finance, but, whatever, she would have to work half the evening anyway. She dug up her calendar and the small black oilcloth notebook she used to take notes, and followed Steinhofer out into the corridor.

Those who participate in meetings at the Ministry must know their place. Anyone who sits in the wrong place is without exception admonished with a smile and a wave of the hand, revealing by way of their mistake that they do not belong and should not be present.

In the outer ring, on the chairs lined up against the walls, sat the assistants, interns, temps, and others who didn't belong to the core group. Around the table, in the inner circle, sat the diplomats, according to rank. The department head always sat at the end with the deputy department head beside him and the rest of the civil servants in descending order of rank to the other end of the table. An outsider would probably marvel at the fact that everyone managed to be seated like this, but it was something you learned to do quickly and soon it seemed natural. It was barely a rule—more a frame of mind.

The Security Policy Department was the largest department in the MFA. They were responsible for policies concerning war and peace, security, terrorism, and disasters.

Conversations ended abruptly when the department head, a tall man with a serious face, entered the room. As if a signal had been emitted, all faces turned in unison toward the end of the table where he sat down. Carina took her usual seat close to the middle of the table.

The room was silent. Only the sound of papers could be heard, as the department head leafed through a few documents before looking up and, in a muted voice, saying, "Well."

The meeting had begun.

It started with a welcome for a new colleague, the new unit head who had joined the department. Anders Wahlund got up. So that was what her new boss looked like, she thought. He was about the same age as Carina. A sandy-haired, pale man in a pinstriped suit that was a little too stylish. The newcomer looked around with a broad smile and said a few words about how happy he was to return home to the Ministry and especially to the Security Policy Department. Everyone knew that he was one of the rising stars in the MFA. He was young, and had already distinguished himself in Kiev, Moscow, and Damascus. He seemed lively and perhaps a little aggressive. The dim room and rows of motionless faces looking back at him seemed only to give him more energy, as he feasted on their gazes.

"Once again, a warm welcome to Anders," said the department head.

Everyone quietly noted the familiar way his first name was used. Her new boss sat down and, at that moment, their eyes met and he seemed to understand who she was. He nodded at her with a smile.

"Let's continue. G1, if you please."

The unit head for G1 took the floor. He was a lieutenant colonel and filled the room with the baritone of one who had spent a lifetime training his voice to bellow across barrack yards. He and the four suits sitting around him dealt with troop contributions to UN forces. They were the nucleus of the department, officers who spent every day working within the framework of a global military system, waging war on various continents and creating peace and stability on others. When the lieutenant colonel spoke, everyone in the room pricked up their ears. They were currently extremely busy with the Libya campaign, he explained. The budget was too small to guarantee more than two months of Swedish involvement, but the Ministry of Finance was refusing to increase it. Negotiations were also ongoing with the UN about a peacekeeping force in South Sudan. Operations were scheduled to begin before the end of the year. But the government in Khartoum was making impossible demands. It was a moving target, said the lieutenant colonel.

"And will we stay on budget with the UN operation?"

"Short answer: yes. Two hundred and seventy million. Plus or minus ten."

"Thank you." The department head looked around the table. "G2—any relevant matters?"

That was Carina's unit. According to protocol, the unit head always had the first word but, since he was new, he merely shook his head with a smile and gestured toward her.

"You have the floor, Dymek," said the department head.

Everyone turned toward her, rows of faces and dark suits. She cleared her throat. Even though she had sat in these meetings many times and set out EU security policy, her mouth was always a little dry the second she was put on the spot. But only for a second. She rarely doubted herself. The fact was that she had gotten by just fine without a boss and suspected she could do without this one too.

"Discussions," said Carina in a businesslike manner, "are currently ongoing in the EU about the joint military headquarters for operations in the Horn of Africa." Then she continued, point by point: the circumstances surrounding the EU's new security strategy; negotiations concerning Bosnia's EU candidature. She was calm, presenting sentences like chains of logic, the words coming to her just as she wanted them. Everyone listened. She finished by mentioning the foreign minister's visit to Ukraine and by reminding everyone that she would be in Brussels the next day for the usual meeting.

"Great. Thanks," said the department head.

She leaned back. The entire time she had been speaking, Anders Wahlund had been leaning forward, listening keenly. Now he smiled at her and jotted something in a small notebook.

The final unit to report was responsible for humanitarian aid and disaster assistance. Their unit head was away in Geneva, so Johan Eriksson had the floor. Carina didn't have many close friends, but Johan Eriksson was one of the closest. He was different from the others; he didn't do low-key irony, that slightly playful cynicism so prevalent among staff at the Ministry. Johan Eriksson was keen and forthright in a way that she had immediately liked. A farmer's son from Skövde, he had become a diplomat and actually wasn't joking when he said he wanted to change the world. His ultimate dream was a posting to New York. He often talked about the Big Apple. Everyone, except him, knew he would never get there. *Johan Eriksson will never get to New York*—it was practically an expression. He was too good for departmental management in Stockholm to let him go, and not sufficiently well liked by the UN ambassador in New York to get the post. How many times had he applied to New York? At least five. Rejected every time. Now he was a few chairs down from Carina, explaining current UN operations in Pakistan, which had been hit by flooding. Thousands of villages under water. Immense bureaucracy. India causing trouble at the UN, but aid getting through, in spite of it.

"Good," said the department head without further comment. The meeting had already run over by five minutes. "Thank you, all."

Afterward, a small group stayed behind, surrounding the new unit head. The room was full of Carina's colleagues flocking to the coffee cart, engrossed in quiet but lively conversations. She approached and greeted him.

"Ah, Dymek," said her new boss exuberantly as they shook hands. "I've heard a lot of great things about you. Good to meet you. Your presentation was perfect."

She smiled broadly and nodded. That slightly patronizing tone that some men used toward her—she hated it. It didn't bode well. She said something about looking forward to working with him and hurried away. By the elevators, she caught up with Johan Eriksson and a group of colleagues.

"Hey, Johan—you look tired."

He grunted in response and rubbed his eyes.

"How's it going?"

"To hell."

A well-groomed older gentleman beside them, the Head of Disarmament and Non-Proliferation, looked at his younger colleague with amusement.

"I've been with Finance all morning," muttered Johan Eriksson, unaware of the other's smile. "There's nothing more tiring than trying to convince those damn bean-counters. They don't get that disasters cost money. It doesn't matter what we say. They don't care—we might as well send some rubber ducks to Pakistan. Jesus Christ—that's Swedish foreign policy in a nutshell. *Completely* absurd."

They got out of the apartment and promised to do a long lunch soon. But not this week; this week, neither of them had time.

3

Brussels, Thursday, September 22

There was dense traffic on the freeway into Brussels, but it was moving quickly and smoothly, as if every vehicle around the taxi knew that each and every minute counted for Carina and that they were escorting her into the city center in a high-speed convoy. It was nine thirty in the morning. The flight had landed on time and, if everything continued the way it was, she would arrive, as usual, just before the meeting began at ten o'clock in one of the spacious rooms inside the Justus Lipsius building.

She had nodded off on the plane and slept all the way to Brussels. As usual, she'd half-jogged along the moving sidewalk toward the Brussels international arrivals hall and got a taxi.

The large cube of mirrored glass that was the EU Council's headquarters, the Justus Lipsius building, towered above them further up the Rue de la Loi. It was where the Council's working groups held their meetings. Approximately three hundred working groups and almost three thousand committees met every other week to hammer out decisions through negotiations between representatives of member states. These formed the foundations of the EU organization. Policy issues that couldn't be resolved by working groups were escalated to the next level and dealt with every Thursday when the Brussels ambassadors of member states met. Anything that still needed to be negotiated after those kinds of wranglings normally ended up on the ministers' table at the next top meeting.

She was going to spend the day behind the Swedish flag at the Committee for Security, COSEC, a working group dealing with issues of importance concerning joint European security policy. Today's meeting was to be about security in the Mediterranean. She glanced at the agenda. Mostly points of information, no particularly significant decisions to be taken, nothing that would lead to drawn-out discussions as far as she could tell. She would make the plane home at eight.

Security in the Mediterranean was a vague concept. Everyone could look at it from their own perspective. Countries like Italy and France saw regional security as a question of migration—i.e., stopping the flow of migration. Spain's line was that it was also a matter of fighting terrorism, and was supported in that respect by several countries, including the United Kingdom, the Netherlands, and Germany. Other EU delegates kept a low profile.

Her instructions for the meeting were summarized into four points and jointly prepared with a number of departments at the MFA, Justice, and the Ministry of Enterprise. They were brief. She was to observe the southern member states and, if necessary, intervene if discussions turned toward asylum policies. Otherwise there were no other lines in the sand to defend. It was important to emphasize that security was a part of the wider neighborhood relations with the Mediterranean nations—that was the first point. If necessary, she was also to highlight that security matters ought to be seen against the background of the dramatic political developments in North Africa and the Arab Spring, and could not limit the EU's commitment to democracy in the region. Also, if necessary, she should argue that security could not limit shipping. Reforms to the Schengen Agreement, outlining the EU visa regime and border control regulations, were not to be discussed at the meeting—Justice didn't want things like that being handled by the wrong working groups. There were already around twenty working groups in existence dealing with issues of migration and asylum with Swedish representatives from the police and Justice at the negotiating table: it was none of COSEC's business. Thus, kill any discussion of Schengen at the meeting.

She hurried across the expanse of carpet on the third floor. It always took ages to get your pass out and get through security down at the entrance, but she had made it through the door along with two other delegates, the Slovenian and the Bulgarian. They recognized her and gave a friendly nod.

The room arched over clusters of diplomats who were standing talking as they waited for the meeting to begin. Slowly, everyone began to take their seats. The table was a huge oval that filled the room, with at least ten meters of empty space in the middle that was filled by a floral arrangement dominated by red flowers. Delegates continued to hurry through the door, primarily gray-haired men in reasonably well-fitting jackets. Out of twenty-seven delegates, only she, the Spaniard, and the Finn weren't members of the old guard. But she rarely spoke to the Finn—he usually sat engrossed in a sullen silence as if he had just tumbled out of the Karelian forest and was wondering where on earth he was. The Spaniard, who had the seat next to her, was a pleasant fellow. You always sat in alphabetical order according to country at these things, so she always had a Spanish colleague to her left, and at COSEC it was Alejandro who was standing by his seat drinking coffee.

"We must stop meeting like this." They shook hands.

Two weeks ago they had been at the same meeting in New York. The sense of déjà vu made her smile.

"We're the Marriott caravan," he said and laughed softly.

It was true; they were the traveling salesmen of international politics.

The murmur became subdued and a concentrated silence followed. The chairman smiled jauntily at the delegates around the table and leaned toward the microphone.

Two hours later, Carina came out from the room, trembling with anger. It was lunchtime and the wide corridor was filled with diplomats. The entire EU building hummed with people. She normally liked being in Brussels, but this morning had been unbearable. They had discussed cooperation with countries around the Mediterranean. The French proposed cooperation for stronger security. The French delegate had, unsurprisingly, spoken at length about the importance of security and about the threats from across the Mediterranean. Human trafficking, drugs, terrorism. North Africa was a problem. The Frenchman was good—he spoke skillfully— but she could not tolerate his words. She had heard it all before, so quite why she had reacted so strongly now she wasn't sure, but she just wanted to disagree. She thought about Jamal. What would he have said? she wondered. The British and several others sup- ported the Frenchman. A united front, they said. A joint policy to ensure Europe's security. Shortly before lunch, she had requested the floor. She leaned forward to the microphone and spoke about the importance of human rights, she reminded them all of the ref- ugee convention and queried, sarcastically, since when had there been similarities between refugees and terrorists? She spoke far too loudly and for far too long, while the other delegates stared at her. She had overstepped the mark; she knew she had. Nothing in her instructions said that she should pursue matters as forcefully as she had, and they definitely didn't say that she should give the French- man a dressing-down, she thought guiltily. But that didn't matter; she simply couldn't allow statements like that to go uncontested. Eventually, she had fallen silent and leaned back into her chair. No one said anything.

She had already reached the elevators when a man caught up with her. She was still agitated and couldn't place the short, plump, plain man who had apparently been present and listening to the meeting.

"*Madame*, do you possibly have a moment?" he said. "I have something I would like to show you."

She merely shrugged her shoulders. She would have preferred to eat lunch alone but in Brussels it was common to be approached, or for someone to get in touch, and all you could do was go along with it. She was Sweden's representative in COSEC—her lunch would have to wait. They took the elevator down together.

The man was vaguely familiar. He wasn't a delegate, but rather one of the backbenchers: temporary guests, advisers and legal experts who sat in the back row, listening, observing. The man was around fifty, dark-haired, short, and dressed in a dark gray suit that was a little tight over the stomach. When they came out into the street, he apologized for intruding on her time but repeated that he had something that might interest her. Did she feel like taking a walk?

"Of course. But you'll have to tell me where you're from."

He smiled uncomfortably. He said he didn't represent any particular organization. "I ordinarily work for the EU Commission."

"I understand." She didn't really understand at all. But she noted that he didn't give his name. He was nervous.

"Shall we?" he said. He knew a small place nearby that did excellent shellfish. He recommended the oysters, if there was time for a longer lunch. They strolled along Rue de la Loi and turned into a side street.

"You really told them off." He laughed. "Nicely done."

"I don't know . . ."

"What you said, those were your personal views, no?"

"Yes," she sighed.

"You can hear the difference, you know, between personal views and when diplomats say what they have been told to say. You can tell." He smiled.

They reached a narrow park squeezed in between chunky office blocks. The restaurant was in one corner, no more than a little local eatery. They chose a table and she ordered a salad.

"I can understand if you're wondering what this is all about," said the man, once they had been left alone. He cut himself short and stared across her shoulder through the window. She couldn't help turning her head to look. There was nothing to see, just the street with parked cars and the dark greenery of the park.

"Are you familiar with EIS?" he asked.

She shook her head.

"European Intelligence Service. It's a federal authority. A European organization that will be formed next year. The decision is going to be taken at the next meeting of the Council of Ministers."

"So it doesn't exist?"

"No, not yet," he said. "But it will very much become real if no one puts a stop to it."

He waited while she received her salad and he a cup of coffee. She examined the man as he lit a cigarette and quickly thought through what she needed to know. So he wanted to tell her something about intelligence cooperation. It was probably information from GD Home, the Commission's general directorate for security of the interior. But a proposal from the Commission for a new security organization would surely not be news to Stockholm. Not if the decision was going to be taken at the next Council of Ministers in a month. She smiled at him. Why give her information that Justice probably already had? The whole situation was a little funny, yet irritating at the same time.

"There are those who want to give the EU a new role," he said in a tone so low she was obliged to lean forward. "Its own intelligence organization. You're probably familiar with the debate. Everyone is talking about new security and foreign policy. The EU as a superpower. They would like to see a United States of Europe. EIS is the first step—the creation of a joint spy organization."

"Who are 'they'?"

He waved the question away with a grimace. "People in Counterterrorism. Hawks. Please don't ask me to name names. I work at the Commission, I know what they're capable of. Look here: there is a proposal that is practically complete for the European Intelligence Service, but there are very few people who are familiar with the proposal in its entirety. EIS will be a secret authority, controlled directly by the EU's foreign minister, and its powers will be enormous. The right to conduct wiretapping and signals intelligence work within Schengen. The execution of operations not covered by the laws of member states. Special operations, things like that." He looked hard at her to let it sink in, before continuing. "I'm a European. I have always believed in the EU as something great. Do you know what I mean? But this . . . this is the Union rotting from the inside. It has to be stopped. Here." He produced a USB drive from his jacket and pressed it quickly into her hand. "Take it."

"What is it?"

"The proposal."

"But why give it to me? I don't have any . . ."

"You have a conscience." He looked at her seriously.

"But . . ." She lost her thread through sheer astonishment and shook her head. Conscience? It was a long time since she had heard someone use that word. Didn't he understand how it worked? She wasn't there as an individual; she was part of the Swedish diplomatic corps. What her conscience said wasn't always relevant to Swedish foreign policy.

"Read it. Then pass it on to the right people."

"But who do you think I am?" she burst out. "I don't have any powers . . ."

"I'm not talking about powers," he said sharply. "I'm talking about your sense of right and wrong. Use it. I've sat in on a number of the most recent meetings and I've heard how you speak. What you said today was not the Swedish position," he said with a smile. "You spoke from the heart. That's a very unusual quality in Brussels, let me tell you."

She squirmed. He was right—sometimes she went a little too far in discussions. There was something about his agitation that was genuine, personal. He meant what he was saying.

"Okay. But, just so the picture is clear, you want me to leak a proposal from the Commission."

"It's an unfortunate word. But, if you want to put it like that, then . . . then . . . yes."

She was sorely tempted to tell him that, unfortunately, she couldn't help. She knew there would be trouble if she returned with a draft from the Commission about a new European intelligence organization. There was a lot of prestige and a lot of sensitivity in matters of high secrecy like intelligence cooperation. Justice and Defense were the ministries responsible for the issues; it would be important to navigate carefully from early on to ensure it didn't look like the MFA was trying to muscle in. She would need to talk to Anders Wahlund, even if the thought of explaining to him how she had gotten the report made her feel unhappy. Justice would presumably react—they were suspicious of all outsiders and intelligence was not something a diplomat should be getting involved in. Admittedly, she was in the Security Policy Department, but some kind of explanation would be necessary to account for why she had turned up with a text like this. At the same time, she felt a childlike excitement at the prospect of taking a top secret, sensitive document back to Sweden. She opened her palm and looked at the memory stick.

"I don't know . . ."

"Take it. You'll regret it otherwise."

"Will you give it to anyone else?"

"I don't know. Perhaps."

She fingered the little piece of black plastic. A secret report from the Commission. She knew that she shouldn't accept it. Everything would be simpler if she didn't. She put the USB in her inside pocket and slowly started to eat her salad. The man regarded her in silence. There was something a touch pathetic about him. He looked friendly enough. His brown eyes and soft face, the beard and the thin hair made her feel a little sorry for him.

"I don't even know your name."

"You can call me Jean."

"Jean. It doesn't make a difference."

"True." He smiled sheepishly and gulped down his coffee.

She didn't know him, she reminded herself. People could appear to be as pleasant as anything and actually be completely untrustworthy. She didn't know whether he was actually operating alone, as he claimed, or whether he had a taskmaster—the Commission, or someone else. She glanced at him and smiled when he met her gaze.

"Aren't you going to eat something?"

He shook his head. "I'm not hungry, I'm afraid. How's the salad?"

"Just fine," she said and wondered what they would talk about now that he had persuaded her to take the document. When she looked up from her plate she saw that he was staring across the restaurant with a curious pursed grimace on his face, not taking any notice of her. She looked down at her salad, chasing one of the pieces of crispy bacon with her fork while trying to work out what was wrong with him. He was frightened, it occurred to her. Scared, for real.

She speared a salad leaf with her fork. "I can't promise anything."

"I know. But you will try, won't you?" The man looked at her quietly. Then he rose from the table, nodded furtively, and left her with a silent goodbye.

4

Stockholm, Friday, September 23

Four hundred and twenty pages. She waited by the printer in the mail room while the pages were spat out, one at a time. Back in her office, she sat down to look at the document. High up on the first page was a row of code designations, serial numbers, and stamps. She studied them for a while and noted that they were genuine. The report was in the second-highest top secret classification. She had never handled documents with the highest classification. The serial number said that it had been written by DG XI, the Directorate General for Home Affairs at the European Commission, just as she had thought. There were no sender details—no names. The title caught her attention: *Security Across Borders—A New European Intelligence Service.* They had always been ambitious at the Commission, had always had ideas about how the European Union should grow and become a superpower. But she hadn't heard of this initiative. On the other hand, there were probably lots of initiatives to reinforce cooperation between security services in the EU that she knew nothing of. The Swedish Armed Forces, Justice, or the Swedish Security Service took care of things like that, while diplomats were rarely let into the conversation. Everything ran on a strictly need-to-know basis and diplomats didn't really need to know anything about operational security work in order to do their jobs. Furthermore, MFA was seen to be a leaky bucket. There had been incidents when desk officers had opened their windows during the summer and whole piles of sensitive papers had been blown right out on cross-breezes, before fluttering to the ground all over

Fredsgatan outside. The mistrust toward people like her was dense. It was therefore not surprising that she wasn't familiar with this. Maybe she shouldn't even be reading the text. But the report had been given to her and she wasn't going to pass up the chance.

She turned the pages, quickly skimming the introductory paragraphs that primarily contained standard formulations about European security that she had heard many times before. She glanced through the table of contents and turned to a description of how a contact network would be established.

The phone rang. It was the desk officer at Finance.

"Did you get my proposal?"

"Yes, of course . . ."

She threw the report aside and brought up her inbox. She had no idea what proposal he was talking about, but she opened his e-mail and quickly read it while her colleague on the line cleared his dry throat impatiently as he waited.

"Can you reconcile it?" he said. "We might be able to get this signed off before twelve. We need it by then at the latest. Otherwise we won't have time to run through it with the junior minister, and then it won't fly."

"Okay. Absolutely." She looked at the clock: one hour.

She didn't have time to read the report now. It seemed to be interesting, but it wasn't her problem. All she could do was forward it to Justice. She pulled herself together and wrote a brief message describing how she had come by the report: she had been approached, she wrote, by a civil servant from the Commission and she believed the material should be dealt with by Justice. She was therefore attaching it, both for reference and so measures could be taken. Then she plugged in the memory stick, uploaded the report and entered the addresses of two people at the Ministry of Justice's unit for international cooperation. It occurred to her that she could also send it to Jamal—she added him to the list of recipients.

Jamal called just after lunch. He was stressed and hadn't had time to eat lunch. Yes, he had received the report that she had sent but he hadn't had time to read it. He was talking in his civil-servant voice.

She didn't know how to talk to him when he sounded so formal, as if she was just any old colleague. Maybe Jamal felt it too, because suddenly he said, in his normal voice, "Do you want to meet this evening?"

"Yes," she said. "Definitely." She wanted to say something big—something that could express what she felt for him—when Jamal disappeared from the receiver.

"I'm coming!" she heard him shout across the room, and the sober, stressed tone of voice was back. He had a meeting shortly.

At half past six, Johan Eriksson stood in her doorway and swore that she must either be insane or very close to a promotion to be working overtime for such a poor wage. He insisted that it was time for a drink at Pickwick's. Jamal had called again during the afternoon; he had to stay for a little longer, so she was in no rush. She quickly finished an e-mail to the desk officer at Finance while Johan shifted impatiently from foot to foot, then she gathered a few sensitive documents and threw them into the safe, locked it, switched on her phone's voicemail, got up, and yawned. Okay: one drink.

A lively murmur met them at the door to Pickwick's. Most of the Swedish civil service appeared to have found their way there already and were now stood in a dark gray mass of suits, drinking their Friday beers. It was at Pickwick's that servants of the government gathered. This was where they ate lunch, where they had a beer after work as they loosened their ties. At the bar there was a throng of assistants, deputy directors, ministers and junior ministers, investigators and experts; there were gatherings of experts in road taxation, fishing quotas, and the Middle East peace process, along with a few tourists. The pub was a copy of a Pickwick's in London and, like all perfect copies, it was more authentic than the original; there was a long dark wooden bar with small Guinness napkins, windows with crocheted curtains, wooden panels, and chairs with creaking, moss-green leather cushions, while colorful engravings depicting scenes of fox hunting adorned the walls. The same sandy-haired women were always behind the bar, accustomed to drawing off draft beer for the employees of the civil service. The only thing that hinted at its Swedish address was the stuffed elk head gazing gloomily across the room from its spot just inside the door. She would always remember Pickwick's for this, and because it was where she first met Jamal.

They squeezed up to the bar between a dozen other civil servants from the Ministry of Defense. Johan managed to order a glass of white for her and a beer for himself.

"Seriously?"

"Yes—a guy from the Commission gave me a report and wanted me to leak it."

"When was this?"

"Yesterday, after the meeting in Brussels."

Johan listened with a smile while she told him how the man had sought her out, how they had gone to a café nearby, and how he had given her a USB stick.

"Sexy."

She laughed. Sexy?

"It's objectively sexy to be approached," said Johan. "It means that you are someone. *Une personne très importante*," he said in his dreadful French, reaching for his beer glass. "Look at Hans Blix: he was big game before the Iraq invasion. It's a sure sign that you're about to be promoted."

"Being approached? Or getting a bigger room?"

Johan laughed loudly. Exactly. People who got promoted often got to move into one of the larger, brighter offices on the boss's corridor that overlooked the street and Gustav Adolf Square. Everyone knew that was how it worked. The converse also applied: a better office was a sign that you were close to a promotion. If you kept an eye on the distribution of rooms, you knew who counted, whom the departmental management liked, and in whom they had no interest. When a colleague who had one of the better offices left the department, intense speculation would always arise about who would move in. The guessing game had already begun and many indications suggested that it would be Carina.

"Patrick is leaving in the New Year."

Everyone already knew that the DPKO desk officer was going to Santiago, despite the job not having been formally advertised yet. This was Johan's favorite subject—who was going to be promoted and who was going to get which overseas posting. He was quite adept at gathering this kind of information.

"Have you heard anything more?"

She shook her head. "No, nothing."

Johan leaned closer with a delighted smile. He knew a little, he said. He knew one of the unit heads at the Human Resources Department. They had lunch from time to time, and the most recent time this acquaintance happened to say that someone with a Polish name was on the list.

"Are you sure?"

"There's only one Dymek at the MFA, surely?"

She smiled. Nothing was certain until you got the phone call from the HR department. But it was lovely of him to say it. She wouldn't mind being promoted. They clinked glasses.

She leaned against the bar and looked across the noisy room. It felt good to have left the office, good to feel a little inebriated. She was in no hurry to get home to her quiet apartment, if Jamal would be working late.

"I'm thinking of applying for a transfer out," she said after a while. It was a secret that she hadn't even told Jamal. But it felt right to tell Johan. The opportunity to talk about it with him made it seem more real.

"Oh?" Johan lit up. He loved this kind of information. "Which embassies will you apply to, then?"

"I'm thinking about Shanghai. Or Nairobi, or Bangkok." She enjoyed saying those words. Each and every one contained a new life, which could soon be a reality for her. "I want to get away. You know, do something completely radical."

"You go, girl," said Johan cheerfully, adding, "And what does your man say about it?"

"I'm going to tell him. He shouldn't be too bothered by the idea."

It would be wonderful to go to a posting, far, far away with Jamal. Just throw themselves into a new environment that they could discover together. At embassies, you got direct contact with ministers and politicians. You lived large—and for free—and, even if you had to work around the clock, the salary was still better than the twenty-eight thousand a month you got at home. In Stockholm, work was so regulated. Everyone was tied to all the deadlines, all the ministerial requirements, and other ministries. Out in the field, the work was more relaxed. You were probably forced to arrange St. *Lucia's Day* events in mid-December, and advertise dismal glass art exhibitions, but that didn't matter. She just wanted to get out—it didn't matter where. You probably weren't supposed to think like that when applying for posts. Everyone at the Ministry was so strategic and careful—her colleagues in the Security Policy Department built their careers with almost ridiculous care. The ideal was a first posting at a small embassy so that you could learn the diplomatic crafts of issuing emergency passports, writing reports, and developing contacts in a host country. Then you were meant to do a few years in Brussels to get a feel for the EU, then some time at home to make sure the bosses in Stockholm weren't forgetting you, and then back out into the world for a bigger job at a larger embassy or the UN representation. That was how everyone methodically climbed up the career ladder, rung by rung. But she didn't want to think like that. She was happy; she felt stronger than she had been in years. She wanted to throw herself out into the world, thunder along in a jeep in the mountains north of Nairobi, wander through glittering Shanghai, look out across Bangkok in the misty morning from the thirtieth floor and say, "Here I am. Jamal and me. This is my life."

"Don't apply to Nairobi."

"Why not?"

"They can never get people for the embassies in Africa. If you write down Nairobi, they'll see nothing but that and just go on and on about Africa." Johan leaned against the bar. "Apply for Shanghai and Bangkok. If the job in Nairobi is still available at Christmas, you can fire off an application for that too."

"To Shanghai then."

She raised her glass. Johan was probably right; he was good at these kinds of tactics. She would talk to Jamal about it this evening. He was probably still at work, she thought, with a pang of guilty conscience. He worked too much. He seemed to never say no— perhaps that was the problem. He was so thorough, in a way that surprised her and would probably irritate her someday. He never let anything go until he was completely satisfied. "It's just work, Jamal," she had said to him. "You're wearing yourself out." "Working at the Ministry of Justice isn't just a job," he had said. "It's a responsibility." She had laughed, until she realized that he meant it. He was a part of the legislative process. He created laws, and he was one of the people who had to ensure that laws were balanced and proportional—that they led to a better society. For him, it was personal. In Egypt, there hadn't been any proper laws—just a state of emergency and a corrupt judiciary—just power. There, the law was just a text—nothing but empty words. There, all that existed was Mubarak and the army. But in Sweden the system worked, he had said. There was a law and it applied to everyone, no matter who they were.

"Jesus, there're a lot of people," Johan exclaimed contentedly, as if it was he who had invited everyone. "Look, there she is, the new junior minister." He pointed at a group of people with his glass. "I don't understand how politicians work," said Johan and shook his head as if it was a concern he had borne for a long time. The stupidity of politicians and their lack of basic competence was a subject Johan would return to, without fail, after a few beers. "Do you want another?" he asked.

Carina shook her head. She was already fairly tipsy; if she drank any more she would only get sleepy. Some colleagues from the Security Policy Department streamed in through the door, spotted her and Johan, and pushed their way toward them. People from the department filled the bar. One of the newly arrived colleagues offered to buy a round for everyone. "Okay," she said, "one more drink." They toasted the end of the week. She and her colleagues were currently dealing with the most important issues of foreign policy, and they knew it. Everyone talked at one another about everything they had heard in the last twenty-four hours from Brussels. The noise enveloped her.

These were her colleagues. Safe, intelligent, professional people who really cared about international policy and worked fifty hours a week to make sure that Sweden continued to be a player in the game of foreign policy. For eight years she had struggled to get here, to stand here and belong to this small group of people who had the opportunity to work at the MFA, brokering war and peace, dealing with security issues that everyone else only ever read about in the papers. And she had done it: she was one of them.

5

Stockholm, Friday, September 23

The first bars of *Stabat Mater* floated out of the speakers: soft strings and then the song flowing out in dark tones. Pergolesi. Beautiful music.

"Is the volume okay?"

She nodded. No one she knew listened to classical music as much as Jamal did. In the beginning, she had thought that he was trying to impress her, but it wasn't like that. Each time she came to his house, he would play classical music or Arab folk music. He thought that pop music was too loud, which she had tried to disprove by playing Depeche Mode, but he hadn't been convinced. They would probably quarrel about it in the future, she thought with a smile.

Finally she was here, at Jamal's. The week lay behind her. Friday evenings always had something glimmering and beautiful about them. It was the part of the weekend furthest away from the next working week, the time when everything was still possible. The weekend felt at its most free on that evening, when she could finally be with Jamal. She could barely remember everything she had done during the week. She had managed—by the finest margin—to finish putting together the travel folder for the foreign minister's visit to Ukraine and, practically at the end of the long Friday, she had—just before the deadline—managed to finish joint preparation with an agreement from all ministries. Like this, looking back, the hundreds of e-mails, hours of phone calls, meetings, and hasty lunches all formed a flickering haze. Somehow, she had crossed off every item on her Post-it note.

She had left Johan at Pickwick's with the others and come straight to Jamal's when he called to say he had finished work. Their Friday nights together had become a comfortable routine that they had established carefully between themselves. She loved it. They hadn't been together more than a few months and already they had a joint life with small moments of beauty, like this Friday evening.

During the last month they had started to see each other more often. She had taken a few changes of clothes and makeup to his place and been given her own shelf in his medicine chest. These were the small steps toward moving in together. She noticed that he liked this, and that made her so happy. At the same time, there was something reserved about him—a kind of withdrawal, an inward movement, away from her. In many ways, he was more secretive than she had first believed, she thought, contemplating him as he went into the kitchen to check the food on the stove.

She took a sip of the wine. It was good. Cold and dry.

Jamal lived on the top floor of one of the apartment blocks in the Sjöstad district. The open-plan apartment was expansive, with panoramic windows offering a striking view of Stockholm's southern suburbs, above which the dark night sky was filled with towering rain clouds. It was a quiet place. A lookout. The vaguely minimalist style reminded her of a business hotel. Jamal liked hotels, he had said. He liked it when things left little trace after themselves. The feeling of anonymity made him calm. It said BADAWI on his front door. His family came from Cairo. You couldn't get further from Cairo than this peaceful suburb in south Stockholm.

"You never need as many trinkets as you think," he said once, when she'd asked why he had so little furniture. Half joking, half serious, he added that you should never own more than you could pack and carry away in three hours.

Jamal's cell rang. He disappeared into the bedroom and pulled the door shut behind him. She stayed sitting in the living room and looked out of the windows. He sounded agitated. She could hear him speaking low and fast, as if he feared being overheard. Sometimes he raised his voice in small outbursts that she didn't understand a word of. He sounded different when he spoke Arabic, or perhaps it was just the person he was speaking to who made him sound like that—angry and sharp in a way she had never heard before. The conversation dragged on and eventually she became restless and got up. She heard his terse answers and then what sounded like an attempt at reassurance. Jamal didn't normally leave the room when talking on the phone. But this didn't seem to be any ordinary phone call. At the other end was someone who belonged in the other part of his life, the part he never mentioned and that they never talked about.

Shamefully aware that she was eavesdropping, she moved toward the windows. Jamal never talked about Egypt. It was as if it was a dark secret within him, so hidden away that she almost forgot it existed. It struck her how little she actually knew about this part of his life. He had only mentioned his parents once. His father had had a legal practice in Cairo, he had said. But the father didn't seem to be alive any longer, because Jamal had talked about him in the past tense. He never mentioned his mother; he said little about growing up in Cairo. Normally, she liked people to have a secret, something of their own. But, right now, all she felt was vague unease.

She dropped into the sofa again and waited. The morning paper was lying on the coffee table. She leafed through the first part distractedly but nothing caught her interest and she put it down. It was then she caught sight of the small book: a thin volume with a yellow cover—worn and well used, as if it had been in someone's coat pocket for many years.

She picked it up, opening it carefully. A collection of poems, she thought with a smile. How lovely to think of Jamal sitting and reading Arabic poetry. What a shame that she didn't understand what they said. All she could do was look at the rows of ornate characters that flowed into each other in beautiful, yet incomprehensible patterns. Perhaps they were religious texts. The thought that Jamal might be religious had never occurred to her. Perhaps he was a Muslim. To her, religion was something so alien that she hadn't even considered the possibility. Although, presumably, he wasn't all that religious, she reflected immediately, because he drank wine. Then she felt ashamed of her anxious train of thought—as if it was a problem if he were a Muslim. The small, prejudiced worry that had pushed its way forward irritated her. She didn't want to feel like that, didn't want to be someone who thought like that.

One section, in particular, was heavily read. The book opened by itself at a certain point. It was a long poem that stretched across several pages. The paper was well thumbed, discolored and a little glossy from the hands that had turned the pages so many times. Jamal's hands had turned the pages specifically to this poem. She looked at the rows of foreign characters and a strong affection for the fragile pages grew within her. Her beloved Jamal, who read poetry.

Two of the final verses in the poem were marked with a blurred, vertical line in pencil. She had done just the same when she was younger and wanted to remember beautiful passages in books by Camus or Mayakovsky, or other authors that she worshipped at the time. One particular line was also underlined. She looked hard at its wavy ornamented characters and small dots, as if the meaning would become apparent if she stared at the Arabic for long enough.

The door opened.

Jamal sank down beside her on the sofa. He looked tense, rubbing his face without saying anything. He barely seemed to acknowledge that she was sitting next to him.

"Sorry," he said finally. "I had to take that."

"Who was it?"

"No one in particular."

He shook his head and immediately looked more resolute. No one in particular. It was obvious that he didn't want her to ask more questions. He was sitting next to her but looked like he was far away in his thoughts. She could only guess. She stretched out her hand to gently touch his, as if bringing him back to life.

"How are you?"

"Okay." He looked at her. His gaze was completely empty for an entire second. Then he gathered himself and focused. "I'm fine."

Seeing the book that she was still holding in her hand, he said, "Where did you find that?"

"It was lying here."

He took the book from her. "Where?"

"On the table." She waited and watched. What was up with him?

As if he understood her thoughts, he said in entirely different tone of voice, "I was just wondering. Sorry, I'm tired. Stressed." He took a deep breath and sighed. Now he had his ordinary smile back. "Sorry, darling."

They kissed. It felt good when he held her; to be close to him again subdued the unpleasant feeling she had just had. She noticed how he relaxed.

"How was Brussels?"

"Hard work."

He looked at her in surprise.

"Difficult discussion about cooperation on north Africa. Security in the region. Mediterranean cooperation. You know. It was so . . . racist." She sighed. She really shouldn't have gone at them so hard at the meeting the day before, even if, at the same time, she was rather satisfied that she hadn't let all those distasteful statements from the French and the others go unopposed. "They talked about refugees from north Africa as if they were all criminals. Terrorists." She sighed. "So I talked about human rights. I gave them all a telling off."

He laughed.

"I was so angry. I've never been so angry before."

"I know how it is," he said. "Just ignore them. There's no point trying to change them." He shook his head slowly.

She put her arms around him and kissed him.

"You know the report I sent to you? There was a man from the Commission who asked me to leak it."

"Seriously?"

"Yes," she said. "He popped up like some jack-in-the-box and gave me a draft directive about intelligence cooperation in the EU. Some secret organization. He said it had to be stopped. It was strange." It occurred to her that Jamal could pull the report up on his e-mail so that they could look at it together. "Get your laptop; I'll show you."

Jamal fetched his computer and plugged it in. He found the e-mail from Carina and opened the attachment. It was a scanned copy of the EU report. *Security Across Borders—A New European Intelligence Service.*

"Have you read it?"

"Not all of it. I haven't had time."

Jamal scrolled down through a few pages of the document. "Looks genuine. European Intelligence Service. Never heard of them."

"He said that it would launch next year. They're going to take the decision at the next council meeting."

"What was this man called?"

"Jean."

"Jean?"

"That's what he called himself."

They read together in silence. Jamal examined a few pages a little longer, then scrolled to the end. "Typical Brussels prose," he noted. "Why did he give this to you?"

"Because I'm Swedish, I think."

Presumably Jean had given her the proposal because he thought that Sweden should get in on it early and exert an influence. He was probably just a normal civil servant at the Commission who wanted Swedish points of view on a coming proposal. He had expressed himself rather dramatically, but that was probably what he had meant. Sweden was notoriously bad at entering EU processes early. The Swedish foreign policy machine rarely managed to find things out in time to contribute with ideas and form legislative work in the EU before all the texts were locked and ready. The EU's back-door diplomacy was entirely dominated by Britain, Spain, France, and Italy. They reigned in the corridors of Brussels. The man probably wanted to give Sweden the chance to react, pull the emergency brake before this new security cooperation was fact.

But he had also given the report to *her*, personally. He had talked about conscience, whatever he meant by that. In hindsight, it all seemed a bit daft.

"I sent the report to Justice, L3. This is their headache."

They refilled their wine glasses and went out on to the balcony to smoke. Carina only smoked occasionally, preferably with Jamal. She inhaled deeply and a cold gust made her shudder. He was standing close to her, with his arm around her waist and looking out into the darkness. They said nothing. It was a beautiful silence, an affinity. She could talk with Jamal like she could with no one else, but the last few times they had also been silent together. It felt good, to be silent with someone. It had been years since she'd been able to do that without feeling lonely.

"Where should we go on vacation then?" she said lightly.

"I don't know," he said in the same tone, playfully. "Any suggestions?"

"Somewhere warm, I think. Maybe Egypt?"

She glanced at him. She paused. Perhaps she was going too quickly. She should be more careful, but she couldn't help herself. The silence surrounding his Egyptian background was like an annoying scab that she couldn't help but pick. "I mean, especially now," she added quickly. "It would be interesting—after the Arab Spring."

Jamal snorted. "Arab Spring."

She paused.

"Nothing has happened!" he burst out in the same loud voice. "People thought they would get freedom but it's just the same shit as before. Same damn military hanging on to power, like the fucking parasites they are." He angrily blew cigarette smoke into the darkness. "Mubarak's old friends. Same gang. You have to burn them off, like leeches. It's the only way."

She remained silent.

"And the EU, with its promises of support. Where is that support? They don't want to provide support; they just want to buy up all of Egypt. They don't care. They don't give a damn about the Egyptians."

"But surely the EU is supporting development . . ." she began, carefully.

He looked hard at her. She had been going to say something about Egypt, its colonial history that certainly cast a shadow over relations in the Mediterranean, but that there was also an honest will to ensure Egypt became democratic, but she said nothing. This wasn't just about international policy for Jamal. Her bird's-eye perspective was too distant from the events. She was looking at it like an analyst, but for him it was his other home country at stake. She had never before seen him so upset. Maybe he knew people who had taken part in the demonstrations—friends and family who had been badly treated.

"I don't trust them one bit," he said angrily. "The EU doesn't want democracy. The EU wants stable, calm regional neighbors. They don't care about people, or about Egypt. Not really. For the EU, it would almost be better if the military regime came back. More stable. And the Americans are even worse. They bought Mubarak to protect Israel. They're scared to death of Arabs. It's not surprising that people turn to terrorism, because they're all Arabs already."

They stood silently beside one another at the balcony rail.

"Europe is afraid of the Islamists," he said after a while in a softer, more thoughtful voice. "They are afraid of Islam. Deep down, they hope that all Egyptians wake up one morning and forget everything to do with the Qur'an, forget everything about where they come from, and just go out and shop for a bunch of crap shipped there by the West. I can understand why some people want to blow them into the sky."

She shrank back—how could he say that? Jamal's outburst surprised her and made her want to argue, while at the same time being stimulating. He was no ordinary civil servant; he sounded more like an activist.

She didn't reply, just nodded and sipped her wine. She decided that it was best to change the subject, and, after a while, said, "What would you say if I applied for a foreign posting?"

He looked at her in surprise.

"The big call for applications has gone out."

Jamal nodded and seemed to slowly release his gloomy thoughts. "Where would you like to go?"

"I don't know. Not Europe. Somewhere far away. I've almost forgotten that I can actually work anywhere around the world. I work at the MFA. And now, with a permanent contract . . . If I apply for a posting abroad," she finally dared to finish, "do you want to come with me?"

Jamal laughed and shrugged his shoulders. "Why not?"

She leaned forward and kissed him. For the first time in a long time she began to feel how her life was coming together. It was Friday evening and she was standing here, a little tipsy, together with this beautiful man, and dreaming about working out in the wide world. Two years ago this had just been a dream. A tingling sensation of happiness swept through her. She was free.

"Let's go in." Jamal was freezing. He took a last puff and flicked away the cigarette, which flew away in a glowing arc through the darkness.

He began so carefully, as she had noticed that Jamal often did. He undressed her, first her blouse, then the bra, pants, and panties. They kissed. He kissed her on the breast and the neck and the collarbone. She tore his clothes off him, his erection standing straight up in the air. They made love on the sofa. Afterward, they hurried into the bedroom and got into bed, sinking into the quiet companionship that she had begun to like so much. She thought about Cairo. A pleasant intoxication hummed in her body. Jamal went to the kitchen to fill their wine glasses.

"That report . . ." she heard him say through the wall. "I'll read it. Then we'll work out what you should do with it. Maybe you should tell your unit head as well."

"Yes." She was still in a warm, indolent state and it was very reluctantly that she began to think about the report again. The last person she wanted to think about right now was her arrogant new boss. "No more work," she said. "It's Friday."

Jamal would still be beautiful when he grew old—the thought drifted through her consciousness while she contemplated him with a smile as he returned to the bedroom with their refilled wine glasses.

6

Stockholm, Monday, September 26

On Monday morning she woke alone in the apartment. Jamal was already in Vienna. He would be away all week, together with a delegation from the Ministry of Justice. The two of them had stayed in his apartment all weekend, with a few brief interruptions to drowsily go and buy takeout. They had made love and talked about the future, about her applying for Shanghai, about traveling to Cairo, about books, international law, and a thousand other things.

There was a note from Jamal on the kitchen table, wishing her a good morning. She missed him already. They had fallen asleep late and she hadn't even noticed when Jamal had gotten up and left.

She got ready quickly. The day brightened under a chilly, blue sky. On the subway into town, people thronged around her, but she barely noticed them. She was happy and exhausted. The air was cool and fresh when she emerged on the escalators, pushed through the crowds, and walked the last stretch to the office.

The Security Policy Department was a hive of activity. Two desk officers from the task force greeted her hastily as they rushed past her in the corridor, probably on the way to a new meeting about the Libyan mission, which was going to be discussed in parliament later in the day. A group of colleagues was standing outside of the department head's office, talking through a memo, while the Head of the International Civilian and Military Operations Unit was pacing back and forth in the midst of a serious conversation on his cell. She passed Johan's office and said hello, threw off her coat and bag in her own office, carried on down toward the kitchen, and got a cup

of coffee before collecting the latest crop of reports from the mail
room. The energetic atmosphere was contagious and put her in a
good mood. It was mornings like these when she felt that together
they could change the world.

She had been working at her computer for an hour when the
department head's secretary appeared. She winked at Carina and
raised a mother-of-pearl-painted nail in an I-want-a-word-with-
you-for-just-a-second gesture while she continued giving rapid
answers into her cell. She ended the call with a few polite words,
snapped her cell shut, and shook her head.

"Nils wants to see you."

"Okay. About anything in particular?"

"He didn't say. You have an appointment at eleven o'clock. In his
office."

The Head of Department's secretary disappeared down the corridor before there was time to ask more. Carina could hear her cell
ringing again, a strange chirruping. She smiled. The boss wanted to
see her. Perhaps it was finally her turn.

It was a few minutes before eleven when she hurried down the corridor. It was good manners to be on time; you couldn't keep the
Head of the Security Policy Department waiting. The door to his
office was shut. A closed door meant a meeting was in progress and
that the next person should sit down to wait on the sofa outside.
Antechambered, as they said. The Head of Department's secretary,
who was sitting in the room next door, nodded at her. She could go
in; they were waiting.

They?

Carina arranged her facial expression, knocked, and opened the
door.

The Head of Department's large, light office always engendered
respect. It had a high ceiling, with a panoramic view across Gustav
Adolf Square to the Opera, the Palace, and the Baltic Sea, which
penetrated right into the heart of Stockholm. In the room were the
department head, Nils Bergh, the new unit head, Anders Wahlund,

and someone she only knew vaguely. They stood up when she entered. The man she had not met before introduced himself as Henrik Langer from the Ministry of Justice. She got the impression that they had been sitting in silence for some time before she had knocked. They all looked at her with serious expressions.

"Please close the door."

She knew what she was expected to do. A chair beside the small sofa suite where Anders and Henrik were sitting was free—she shut the door and sat down.

The department head remained standing. He was tense. She had been in so many meetings with him that she knew how he behaved. He had a particular way of clearing his throat.

For a moment she thought something serious had happened that they needed her to assess. Or that someone in the department had committed misconduct and they wanted to consult her on the matter. But then she noticed that it was something else.

The department head leaned back against the table, adjusted his tie for the second time and cleared his throat. Then he finally sat and said briskly, "I have another meeting in a few minutes. But I wanted to do this right away."

She waited. Her attention was suddenly focused; she noted details, wrinkles in the Head of Department's face, the reflection of the sun glittering on the small coffee table, that the new guy, Wahlund, was holding his breath. She looked quickly at Henrik Langer; his face was completely expressionless. Nils Bergh cleared his throat again.

"We have received information from Justice that worries us."

"Oh?"

"Are you familiar with this?" He held up a bundle of paper: it was the report she had been given by the man in Brussels. "It is in your possession. Is that correct?"

She nodded. Slowly, a worry began to form and sink through her like a cold drop of silver. The Ministry of Justice. They had contacted her bosses—who were now sitting here and looking at her gravely—about Brussels. About the contact.

"I asked whether that is correct."

"Yes. That's right."

Instinctively, she kept a low profile—asked no questions, offered no defense. She didn't know what had been said before she had come in or before that, but it was not about a promotion. The department head had a way of getting annoyed if he perceived that he was being mouthed off at. His background was military and he didn't tolerate opposition. The men looked at each other, as gravely as judges who had already decided upon the death penalty but did not know who would pronounce the sentence.

The MFA had taught her never to hesitate. To continue talking, continue using full sentences. She said, "I was given the report by someone from the EU Commission. He approached me in connection with the meeting."

The department head's gray-blue gaze rested on her. They were listening now, with immobile expressions.

"Why were you in Brussels?" said Langer, the man from the Ministry of Justice.

"I was at the normal working-group meeting. COSEC."

"And you say you were given the report by someone in Brussels."

"Yes. He sought me out."

"What was he called?"

"He . . ." She stopped when it occurred to her that she didn't know. "He said he was called Jean."

"Just 'Jean'?"

"Yes. He didn't give his full name. But he was from the Commission."

The three men stared expressionlessly at her while she told them how the man had approached her in Brussels, how they had gone to the restaurant, and she recounted their conversation there. They contemplated her the whole time she was speaking, as if they were thinking intensely, or as if there was not a thought in their heads whatsoever.

"You're saying that this Jean . . . gave you the report," said Nils Bergh with a skeptical pause. "Why would someone give you a document like this?"

"I don't know," she said. "He just turned up."

"We have been in touch with the Commission. According to them, no one has released the report in an improper manner." The department head looked at her without blinking. "So why would the EU Commission lie?"

"I don't know."

She fell silent.

"Our friends in EU circles have confirmed what the Commission has said. I ought to say that we have made certain inquiries into what happened."

Friends. What friends?

"We're in a difficult position and will need to give answers to people in the EU. So I want you to tell us truthfully how you came across the document. It's not material that you normally deal with."

"But I've told you what happened." She looked at their disbelieving faces. "Why don't you believe me?"

Langer emitted a loud sigh.

The department head had a different sharpness to his voice when he said, "Carina, surely you understand how serious this is? If you don't tell us, we'll be forced to investigate this."

"I don't understand what this is about," she said.

The words hung in a cold silence.

They didn't believe her. They thought she was lying, that she was protecting herself.

She knew it was too late. But she couldn't sit there quietly. "Nils, listen to me," she said in a last throw of the dice. "I got a report. It was *given* to me—by a man who said he was from the Commission. I sent the report to the affected party at Justice. That's the truth."

Nils Bergh looked at her for a long time before saying, "But the Commission hasn't got a leak. We've talked to them. They've gone through their systems and now they want us to investigate the whole thing. Sweden's friends in the EU want us to investigate this. So we need to know more. If you really did get the material from someone at the Commission, as you claim, then you must be able to say who it is."

She nodded. Jean.

"But I haven't done anything wrong," she said. "I'll prove it. I can find him, if you want."

He interrupted her with an irritated gesture of his hand. "We don't need to discuss this any further, Carina. You do not enter a house where you are not invited. Do you understand? As a civil servant at the MFA, you have no right to deal with issues as you see fit."

She remained silent as he continued.

"I'm disappointed, Carina. You're the last person I would have expected to do something like this."

He looked at her with his cool eyes. Then he sank back into his chair; the dejected movement made her shudder.

The room was silent. They had finished and no one moved.

"Don't you understand? You've put us in a very difficult position through your self-indulgent behavior. We'll be looked at in a different way. Seen as less reliable."

"Who will see us like that?"

"That's none of your business," Langer cut in.

The department head sighed and said solemnly, as if he had now reached a decision and wanted to conclude with a judgment, "You will be placed under investigation, Carina. We will therefore have to suspend you from your duties."

The others sat in silence.

"Effective immediately."

She could no longer hold back a sharp pain that forced itself to the surface. "What is this?" she burst out. "I was sought out by someone from the Commission. How was I supposed to know what he wanted? I was there; he came to me. Why don't you believe me?"

"You clearly haven't been listening to what we have said," said the department head tersely.

No, apparently she hadn't listened properly. She didn't understand what they were talking about. For a second, she fumbled in the darkness, all her thoughts running away in a chattering jumble. She didn't understand. What had she done wrong? They didn't believe her, and she couldn't make them change their minds. She had an almost irresistible urge to slap their faces. She wanted to say more, but her mouth couldn't form the right sounds.

"You are relieved of your duties, but will remain on full pay until the investigation is concluded. Then we'll see."

There was a strained silence.

"You're wrong," she mumbled.

They remained silent, staring at her.

"Where's the original?" said Wahlund, who had been quiet throughout.

"In my office. In the safe."

"Is that it?" Henrik Langer looked at her sharply. "You sent the report by e-mail to my colleagues at Justice."

"I scanned it," she said quickly.

Something made her keep quiet about the USB stick. She no longer knew what was happening; all she had to go on was her gut feeling.

"Who exactly did you send the report to?"

"Per Lennerbrandt. And you," she said, nodding at Henrik Langer, who didn't respond in the slightest. "You were the only ones I sent it to."

"And Jamal Badawi."

She nodded.

"Why didn't you say so?" Langer said brusquely.

She mumbled that she had forgotten.

"Have you given the report to anyone else?"

"No."

"Are you sure?" said Langer, with poorly disguised sarcasm.

She remained silent.

"It's a shame it had to turn out like this," said Nils Bergh. He cleared his throat. "I'm very disappointed, Carina."

He was disappointed? She could only look at him—every possible word had dissolved into spittle. Wahlund and Langer were gazing emptily into the air and seemed mostly to be waiting for this embarrassing, concluding part of the meeting to be over. She said nothing. The department head nodded and got up.

Wahlund led her down the corridor after the meeting. Halfway, he turned around and said in a strangely businesslike tone, as if it was a mere practical detail, "You can give me your pass and ID card." She fumbled for the cards and handed them over. They continued down the corridor, Carina a few steps behind.

There weren't many people in on her floor; lots of them were away working, like usual, with their offices empty. They reached her office. At her door was a security guard. She recognized him; he was normally down by the entrance.

"What's he doing here?"

"It's standard procedure," said Wahlund, who clearly also thought the situation was awkward. The guard looked at them sullenly and fingered his belt—he was restless and tense.

"What should I do?" she said.

"Get your things and he will escort you out. Don't touch any work papers." For the first time, Wahlund looked concerned; his eyes flickered. When she didn't say anything, he merely nodded briefly and apologetically, turned around, and disappeared along the corridor, clearly relieved that it was over and done with.

She went into her office. Everything looked as it should: the desk lamp was still on; her coffee mug where she had left it, still half full; her notepad, filled with scribbled notes; all the reports, papers, Post-it notes. It was her office, here was years of her work. She had been in a hurry earlier this morning; her coat was still cast across the back of the office chair. Just as she came in, the computer pinged—she must still be receiving e-mail; people were expecting her to be there to reply. Suddenly she had an impulse to sit down at the computer and just keep working, as if nothing had happened, but the guard reminded her of the reality. She tried to gather her thoughts and remember what she should do. But her skull was filled with a vast vacuum that could implode at any moment, pulling Drottninggatan and the ministries around her into a black hole. She saw herself standing there in her office on the fifth floor of the MFA building at Fredsgatan 6. The building enveloped her with its layers of corridors, offices, conference rooms, storerooms, mail rooms, and elevators—all in the middle of a gray and autumnal Stockholm, that small, well-organized, cold city that hated her. She felt faint; she wanted to throw up.

"Come on; get your stuff," said the guard.

She only had a minute. Every small action acquired a decisive significance and was simultaneously so meaningless. She began to gather together some papers at random, but didn't know where among the piles to begin. She took a script from the bookcase, *UNDP Human Development Report 2009*, weighing it in her hands. What did she need it for? She put it down.

"What should I do about the books?" Carina gestured vaguely at the bookcases that covered one of the walls. "All of these?"

The guard looked at the bookcases with uninterest. "I've not been told anything about that. You'll have to ask them to send them to you."

She looked around the room. She remembered what she needed. At random, she selected Joseph Nye's *Understanding International Conflicts* and pretended to search through a bundle of papers, to gain time. She couldn't find it and swore through her teeth. When you needed something it was never there.

"That's enough. Let's go." The guard was standing right beside her.

"I'm looking for my house keys, okay?" she said in such a sharp, authoritative tone that, for a second, the guard actually understood that she was really a diplomat, and backed away.

She had put it somewhere near the computer. It was there; she knew it must be. She groped frantically in the mess that was her desk. The guard wouldn't let her have more than another minute, then it would be too late. She no longer had her pass and she wouldn't be able to get back into the building: this was her only chance. Worst case, she could ask Johan to come in during the evening and look, but they would probably lock her office door. Where was it? She was sure she had left it near the computer, but that had been several days ago. She pushed aside the pile of reports, the writing pad.

There, next to the keyboard, was the memory stick.

She grabbed it and slipped it into her pocket. On one of the piles close by was a copy of the report. Wahlund, in spite of it all, had gotten so nervous that he hadn't taken the report from her immediately. She took it.

"What are you doing?" The guard was in the middle of the room. "Are you done?"

Yes, she was done.

Colleagues had stopped in the corridor and were now standing silently in a group, looking on with curiosity while the guard locked the door to her office. Why couldn't they just leave her alone? The whole situation was so absurd and degrading. She was an intruder. No one moved, no one left, everyone looked at her nervously as if she had a contagious disease.

"What's happened?" Johan Eriksson pushed forward and worriedly looked at her and then the guard. "What the hell are you doing?"

"Step aside," hissed the guard.

"What's happened, Carina?"

She tried to smile, but her face was stiff. "I have to go," she said.

"What do you mean?"

She didn't reply. The guard had put a hand on her arm and started to walk her toward the elevators. Johan followed them.

"I'll call you," he shouted after her.

Something in his words made her snap. She needed to get out before she began to cry. They hurried down the stairs; she had enough presence of mind not to take the elevator, in order to avoid colleagues. The guard trotted behind her to the ground floor. It was all so absurd, like a pathetic comedy in which she hurried through the building followed by a security guard with rattling keys and a gun. At the entrance she carried on out of the doors without looking back. She passed the green-tinted window of the guard post, pushed past two desk officers from the Department for Asia and the Pacific Region whom she recognized, and came out into the blinding light on the street.

7

Brussels, Monday, September 26

Bente Jensen had left the office without telling anyone. In no rush, she had then driven to the northern end of the port.

She liked driving. She was good at it, she drove quickly and could read the traffic effortlessly—it came naturally. When she had started at Säpo many years ago, she had always been able to impress the guys in Dignitary Protection with how safe she was behind the wheel. She had been in the business for almost eighteen years. Eighteen years was a long time. But unlike many others, she rarely thought about it; she couldn't understand people who were nostalgic. The years passed by and would never come back, and then, sooner or later, death came and then life was over. She didn't see the point in brooding over things that couldn't be changed.

Nevertheless, there were occasions when even she reflected on the past. The meeting she was on the way to brought back memories of when she had been in the car on the way to an identical meeting, almost two years ago, with the same man. That time it had been about a request for Sweden's support in getting into a terrorist group with bases in the Sahelian region of western Chad, by infiltrating a Swedish-Norwegian network of al-Shabaab supporters. She hadn't seen him since then. There was no reason why she should have. Meeting face to face was a clumsy method that involved risk of discovery; she preferred to keep that kind of contact to a minimum. But the last time they had met, Green had chosen to meet her outdoors, not in a hotel or in a safe house, and it was the same this time. Presumably the result of a healthy mistrust of her. MI6 was a professional partner; she didn't have to worry about contacting them. Their operations were well prepared. All meetings, even tiny working meetings like this, were arranged so that neither she nor they had to expose themselves to any unnecessary risks.

She turned off, toward the port, through an industrial area where the offices were still dark and silent, past a large warehouse with trucks lined up outside, quietly waiting to be filled before rolling away to their destinations. A gray sky covered Brussels. The morning was still young.

The white oil tanks in Neder-Over-Heembeek were visible from afar. Bente was on time. There was a genuine satisfaction to be had from being on time. It gave a sense of order, of peace, of being systematic. In her line of work, that kind of precision was crucial—in the worst situations, lives might depend on it. A colleague had told her that fighter pilots often took pride in getting into formation in the air at exactly the time stated. She liked the thought of it: she had done the same.

The car jolted when she rolled across the deserted plot beside the tanks. She parked next to a fence and turned off the engine. Not a soul was visible. She glanced in the rearview mirror and, for a moment, met her own eyes before turning away. She didn't like mirrors; she always got the impression that they were staring back at her. She had a factual relationship with her appearance and had never been one to look in the mirror for pleasure, mostly because she wasn't particularly coquettish and was suspicious of that kind of vanity. There was something pathetic about people who were obsessed by their own appearance. Personally, she had never cared what others thought about how she looked; she knew that her appearance was little more than a part of her personality, and furthermore it was the part that lapsed most quickly. She knew that she wasn't beautiful in the stereotypical sense that models were. She had a square and strong body that required a certain amount of exercise if it wasn't to accumulate body fat. It served her well; it was her fortress and she liked being in it. It had a density that commanded respect. She was strong—stronger than many men—and had never heard the comments that women in her field often had to put up with. When she had started at the Security Service, she had spent her first five years at Counterespionage before moving to Counter-terrorism, quickly becoming the deputy, then the liaison officer in Vienna, and now she was head of the new office in Brussels—the Section.

She couldn't remember when she had realized she was differ-ent from other people. That her face was different. Apparently it was unusually still—it lacked expression. It had been some time before she had understood what people meant, but gradually she had noticed that she didn't smile when others did, that she didn't make the expressions they did and that were expected in order to demonstrate that you were listening or liked something. She always listened attentively; it was odd that people didn't understand that without her having to grimace and posture. Naturally, she had understood the value of it in time. She could smile warmly and arrange her face in a number of ways that suited the context, but if it was up to her then she preferred to avoid that particular art and instead look on to the world with her normal, unmanipulated face. It had high cheekbones, clear eyebrows, and a small, round chin—a good-looking face, so she had been told, but she had no opinion on the matter. Two brown eyes looked straight and piercingly back at her in the rearview mirror. She was forty-four years old and knew who she was; she didn't need the approval of others. She pulled back her pageboy hair and took off her pearl earrings—a precau-tion; she didn't want to drop any jewelry—checked under the seat to ensure her service weapon was where it should be and reached for her coat.

It was a minute or two before half past six when she got out of the car and walked along the fence that ran around the tank area, down toward the quay. And there he was, on the quayside, approaching on foot, as if he had appeared from thin air.

"Good morning, Bentie," he said in clipped, British English.

Jonathan Green: he looked ordinary. A normal Brit with a boy-ish appearance, strawberry-blond, short hair, glasses. MI6's chief in Brussels had spent most of his life not being seen, and invisibility was now a part of his personality, his appearance. People didn't notice him. Even Bente, who was accustomed to memorizing faces, found it difficult to remember what he looked like—apart from his eyes; she remembered those. Completely clear blue eyes—neutral, almost glassy—a gaze that didn't do what the rest of his face did but continued to intently study her face and continuously make assessments as they talked.

Green was a rising star in the British spy world. A possible candidate for the top jobs back in London. Two daughters, married, his home was to the south of Brussels. She didn't know much more. The way he spoke gave away his background: an intonation that breathed Eton and Cambridge.

They wandered along the quay.

"It could be a mistake."

"This is no mistake," said Jonathan Green drily. "She's a clean skin. Someone is controlling her. I'm just saying that this leak is not a mistake."

Bente shrugged her shoulders. "But the report has ended up at the Swedish MFA. It's not as if it's on the web."

"But didn't you say that she—"

"Dymek."

"Yes. That she had distributed the material?"

"To our Ministry of Justice, yes."

She glanced at Green. He had an unmoving, inscrutable face. This was a man who took no risks. Presumably he was, right now, thinking through what effects the incident might have, which courses of action there were—what he would tell London.

"Jonathan, let's not make this bigger than it is. It's a storm in a teacup."

"It's not a storm in a teacup. It's a leak. It's a crack in the system and if you don't take it seriously we'll be facing a fucking tsunami." He looked straight at her. "Let me be completely honest. I don't trust Swedish diplomats. Okay? That girl has no business with that report. Yet she distributes it—all over the place, if I understand you correctly, Bente. You have to take control of the situation, before it all goes to hell. We're not going to wait for some damn politician to get hold of the report and ruin everything. And, by the way, the report contains critical, operational data. Washington, and many others, would go through the roof if it came out. That report could do a lot of harm in the wrong hands."

"Okay. I hear what you're saying."

"Good."

A barge moved slowly past in the channel. She looked at it while she gathered herself. She hated being lectured like this but she had no desire to irritate him any further. He was Her Majesty's Secret Service in Brussels. And he was right. If the Commission's report came out, the proposal that the Brits had spent years fighting for would be blown to smithereens.

"I've talked to Stockholm," she lied. "We're looking into it."

"Good." He relaxed.

"So you don't think she was alone?"

"I don't think anything. I just want to be one hundred percent certain that she isn't leaking. That no one is leaking."

"And if she's cooperating with someone?"

He looked across the channel. "Then we'll have to take care of it."

Back at the office, Bente called Stockholm. It was a routine matter, but the Brits were worried and it was no good waiting. It rang twice before the receiver was picked up at the other end and a dry voice said, "Kempell."

She outlined the conversation with Jonathan Green. There was silence at the other end for a while. Gustav Kempell never spoke cold, she remembered. He was quiet, a listening person, who could seem deferential to those who didn't know him. As the longest-serving Head of Counterespionage, he knew every methodological trick in the book, every technique for contact, recruitment, and assessment of sources. For two decades he had cultivated a wide-spread network of sources and he was intimately familiar with the temperament of every foreign security service out there. He was one of the people who had recommended her for her current post as Head of the Section.

"We ought to take the Brits seriously," Bente finished.

"Yes," said Kempell, slowly.

"Or?"

"Yes, yes," he said and tried to sound more enthusiastic. "Of course." He had received a call from the Government Offices earlier that morning. The woman had been suspended until further notice. Until they knew more. He fell silent.

Bente knew how Kempell felt about the Brits. He was always unwilling to work too closely with other security services. As Head of Counterespionage it was his job to be skeptical, but sometimes Kempell and his people irritated her. They were so careful, suspicious at such a deep level. After all, it was the Brits they were talking about—close partners—not some Colombians, dumping people out of army helicopters. She told him that it was worth showing that they were taking them seriously. This Dymek, perhaps it was best to look into her.

Yes, that was probably worth it. Kempell would talk to the MFA and take a closer look at what had happened.

She promised to call him when she arrived at Stockholm Arlanda airport.

A smell of paint still lingered in the corridor. The Section for Special Intelligence, SSI, or just the Section, as it was called, was in newly refurbished premises in central Brussels. The Section had been installed discreetly, in line with the usual procedures, and to the rest of the world it was a small and seemingly unknown IT consultancy—an obscure company with stable finances and a global client base. The other nine stories of the building were home to a European children's fund, a Belgian accountancy practice, and a branch of Crédit Lyonnais. Every morning the foyer was filled with normal people who commuted in from the leafy suburbs of Brussels. None of them knew that, beyond the unmanned reception on the twelfth floor, behind gates made from frosted, armored glass, there was a whole office filled with technicians from the National

Defense Radio Establishment, FRA, along with source controllers and analysts from the Swedish Security Service, Säpo.

The Section was the secret branch of Sweden's presence in Brussels. An experiment, some said. Six months in, the cooperation between FRA and Säpo was working better than expected. They were all in the same line of business. Bente Jensen had recruited with care, along with her deputy, an officer from FRA. The job description comprised one sentence: to combine targeted signals intelligence with human intelligence gathering abroad.

Officially, Säpo wasn't allowed to operate outside of Sweden. According to Swedish law, the Security Service was not permitted to make use of signals intelligence. Everyone knew that was completely stupid. The modern world required targeted intelligence gathering, even abroad. Bente had hated the feeling that had spread throughout Counterterrorism in the years before the formation of the Section—that it was impossible to tell where the enemy was; that you were just waiting for the next catastrophe. The blindness had spread, they had lost focus, started to miss things. Enemies had moved around like gray shadows in the field of vision, but they hadn't been able to distinguish them. Wahhabi terrorists had been able to strike, undetected until the explosive was primed. They had been lucky. Abdulwahab's failed attack in a street filled with Christmas shoppers in Stockholm was the only disaster that had actually hit. But there had been more, things that the media and parliamentary populists never got to hear about, like the white-supremacy movement that was constantly growing and becoming better organized, or the extremist groups within the environmental movements planning attacks against storage sites for highly enriched uranium. They were out there, but the politicians refused to listen. Without signals intelligence it was impossible to track them. It was like slowly getting cataracts. Säpo had long been fumbling in the dark. She had been at Counterterrorism when the laws banning them from using material gathered by FRA had come into force, and it had been mere months before their grasp on reality had been lost. In the future, they would probably describe them as the blind years. Several failed counterterrorism initiatives and the Abdulwahab fiasco had made people in the field begin to say that the Security Service should only be brought on board if you wanted to get shot in the leg. It was humiliating.

The solution had been found a year ago. It was so simple and elegant that it was surprising no one had thought of it before. After a period of dialogue between FRA and Säpo, SSI was created—a joint office with FRA personnel on indefinite secondment to the Security Service. Officially, a collocation, but in practice a joint effort to combine specialist intelligence gathering and signals intelligence, in the heart of Europe. The Section had been operational for nearly six months, and what had seemed like a house of cards was still standing. It had taken longer than the leadership team had hoped to produce usable information. But Bente was not worried. Targeting intelligence gathering so that they could really track the radical Muslim networks or right-wing extremists in Europe took time; they were forced to take each step carefully. Calibrating signals intelligence so that you really were listening to the right cell phones, actually intercepting the right e-mails and monitoring the right online forums—that all took time. She was still satisfied work had moved forward. Infiltration required patience; you couldn't force it. But the signals intelligence work was already delivering useful data. Recently, they had received several parallel orders from Counterterrorism and Counterespionage. They monitored thousands of websites, hundreds of phones and IP addresses, around the clock. They were supporting an American operation in northern Afghanistan. They were infiltrating discussions within a Swedish-Somali network, had the precise locations of fifteen Swedish al-Shabaab members, were monitoring a Chinese engineer at Ericsson, and carrying out joint surveillance with the Danish PET. They had regained their sight. The landscape was back in full focus.

SSI's deputy head, Mikael Reuterberg, looked up from the computer when Bente entered his office and shut the door. He was one of the young veterans from the National Defense Radio Establishment,

understood Arabic, and had a special ability to piece together fragments, to spot patterns—an intuition that surprised her. He understood things quicker than anyone else.

"I'm going to Stockholm for a few days," Bente said.

Mikael nodded, as if it didn't surprise him in the least, and passed
her the morning report.

Bente leafed through it. "Anything important?"

"No. A group of al-Awlaki supporters are on the move. Their number three passed through Damascus yesterday and landed in Frankfurt
this morning. The Germans picked him up; he claimed that he was
going to visit family. Nothing concrete. The new sources at the Commission that we contacted during the spring are ready for assignments."

She glanced through the report: new al-Shabaab training camp
traced via cell phone calls in Oslo; Islamist groups in Frankfurt; two
Swedish-Moroccans gone to Karachi—converts, probably; a list of
new websites under investigation. Under the heading *Counterespionage* there was nothing.

"We have an incident involving the EU Commission," Bente
said. "A report has leaked."

"Oh?"

"A Swedish diplomat is mixed up in it." She briefly outlined the
information she had received during meeting with Green without
explicitly mentioning his name.

Mikael's forehead creased slightly; he nodded. He promised to
check it. "When are you going?"

"I'll take the lunchtime flight. You'll have to take over the
command."

She asked Mikael to contact people at the Commission and see if
it was possible to find out more about the leak. They agreed to direct
some surveillance against EU institutions and social media—trawl
the traffic, see if they caught anything.

She stood by the window. From there she could see the city center, the Luxembourg station, the EU district, and the Commission
rising above the surrounding roofs. The Belgian capital vanishing
in the drizzle.

A Swedish leak. A diplomat. Presumably just a small mistake, negligence. But you never knew. Green was unusually worried, at least for Green. Normally he was as cool as a fish. Whatever had happened in Brussels was no coincidence. Leaks rarely were and, what was more, she didn't believe in coincidences. She wasn't religious, didn't believe in God or any other magical powers. Belief was for others. She saw facts. Facts were the only thing that held the world together, and the facts she worked with were about people— their behavior, their inner logic.

People were creatures of habit. Habit formed routines, patterns, and a history. The young diplomat was no exception. Everyone's behavior was driven by logic. It might be a crazy logic, developed from an extreme ideology or a sick mind. But there was always some form of order. It just meant you had to see the world through the target's eyes. If you understood how a person thought, you also knew whether he or she was to be considered a threat.

London was always prioritized. When it came to European security services, the British were the most important. The relationship with MI6's imposing headquarters on the banks of the Thames at Vauxhall was crucial. Bente could think of over a dozen operations in recent years that had gone ahead after signals had come from the British setup. The triad of the domestic security service, MI5, the foreign espionage service, MI6, and the home of signals intelligence at GCHQ— Government Communications Headquarters—comprised one of the strongest spy networks in the world, and Sweden was fortunate to be their partner. London was the source of the data that changed the game plan—that made operational decisions in Stockholm possible.

Surveillance, interception, arrest, prosecution.

Only the British crown had a global presence. British surveillance resources could reach all corners of the earth, they had agents on every continent and it was only natural to be dependent on them. Without the Brits, Säpo—as well as the Swedish Military and Intelligence Service—would have huge blind spots. It wasn't something that was expressed out loud; politicians didn't like to hear things like that.

Three summers ago Bente had been in Rabat for confidential talks with the American embassy and the Moroccan authorities, and at a small reception in the evening, organized by the Americans, she met an official from MI6's office. He was drunk, and had flirted with her. He had said that Sweden was so conscientious. It was probably true. Sweden was a conscientious little brother. London had faith in Stockholm, and faith was a rare and valuable resource in their business. The British supplied their conscientious partner in the North with data and intelligence. In return, Stockholm listened attentively to British wishes and desires. British projects were supported; Sweden was sensitive to their statements at the UN and within the EU. The new European security service was a project that had received support. The European Intelligence Service—a hopeless initiative. To get twenty-seven member nations to agree to something like that was complete madness. They couldn't even agree to bomb Libya. But the Brits weren't giving up. And now, against all the odds, the organization was close to realization. Bente would never have believed that they would succeed in forcing it through. She couldn't help but envy them sometimes. Their machinery. Their influence. They were competent; they had an ability to take control of situations, run operations across the world. Was it possible to admire machinery? Well, she did. Behind every British operative was an enormous resource, an apparatus that could shine through everything with a blinding, revealing light. The Brits had the means to sieve through a global flow of information for data; they had sufficient presence on the ground in the form of infiltrators and field personnel that they knew exactly what was being said in African governments, they knew what the Pakistani ISI was thinking, knew which orders were passed across crackly cell phone connections in the Yemeni branch of al-Qaida. Only the Americans could manage the same level of clarity. They knew their enemy.

The rain streamed across the car as she pulled out of the underground parking lot on to Rue de Luxembourg. Brussels was a gray and shadowy city, full of umbrellas and heavy façades. She coaxed the car around Square de Meeûs. After just one hundred meters, she was in a stationary row of angry, red rear lights. Roadwork ahead had stopped the traffic. In one of the cars in front, a driver lost his patience and began to honk his horn—long and drawn out. Shortly after, a second horn chimed in, now more staccato, a furious exhortation.

The traffic had come to a complete standstill. Workers in bright yellow reflective vests were stood gesticulating and trying to redirect the traffic. On the radio they were playing a noisy rock song. She bent down and got out her personal cell. She had one for work and one for the rest of her life, the life that her friends and family, and everyone outside of the business, knew about. How simple it was for people who only lived one life! Bente was forced to live two: a normal one and, encapsulated into that like dark matter, a hidden life.

"Darling, I have to go away for a few days."

Her husband didn't seem surprised. "Oh? Okay," was all he said. He was at work. She had hoped he might sound more disappointed. They had invited a couple to dinner that evening—the Rothmans, who lived in the same block and with whom they had carefully begun to socialize after a local gathering. The Rothmans had two children the same age as her own sons, ten and twelve years old. Fredrik didn't ask where she was going, or when exactly she would be back, and she was grateful for that. Her husband wasn't to know where she was—couldn't know. No one could. That was work. It was a way of life.

She knew that Fredrik had been looking forward to dinner with the Rothmans. They had interesting jobs: he was a doctor and had worked in Asia several times, while she was a professor at the university in Bruges. They were chatty and lively—too talkative for her liking.

She was used to dividing up her existence, breaking it down into what was visible, and what others could never see. She rarely thought about it. Fredrik was also used to it. They had been married for almost thirteen years. They worked well together. Good parents.

A good team. She was careful and kept an eye on everything; he was careless but better at making contacts. She didn't understand how he could have such a messy wardrobe and yet be so well dressed when he left for work. On the other hand, he occasionally got tired of her attention to detail, she had noticed, her habit of doing things the way she thought was best. He worked in mergers and acquisitions of companies in the automotive industry; she was the head of a small IT consultancy—or so they said when they met others. She needed it to sound so boring that no one asked any more questions. They never talked about her real job—never. Fredrik knew—he was the only person who knew the truth—that she worked for the Security Service. Naturally, he couldn't know what she did with her days. They had a silent agreement that he wasn't to ask and she wasn't to tell. In the beginning he had refused to accept it; he wanted to know, had been curious. Counterterrorism! Couldn't she tell him something exciting? Was she hunting anyone in particular? He promised to keep quiet. He was jealous if she traveled. Who was she going to meet? Why couldn't she just answer her cell? But in time he had stopped asking questions. She almost missed them.

Starting at SSI was taking it another step. The post at the Section was a protected position and was surrounded by the highest level of secrecy. SSI was of such a nature that, outwardly, it did not exist. There were no operational reports and the budget was secret. No one, apart from a handful of people at the top of Sweden's intelligence operations, knew about them. She still remembered the March day when she had come home and told him that she had gotten the job; she could barely tell him anything about it—just that it was in Brussels, nothing else. But Fredrik was used to this. All he said was, "Good; then we'll move to Brussels." More than that had never passed between them with regard to her job. The kids thought their mom worked in IT and her husband didn't even know that something by the name of SSI or the Section existed. If he wanted to reach her at work, he had to follow a specific procedure. Each morning she disappeared, before returning in the evening. Sometimes she could see him wondering, pondering an unspoken thought. There was nothing unusual about that; he had a right to be curious. But there wasn't much to tell, either. It suited her down to the ground not to have to tell him what she had done during her day, like other couples; she liked being left alone. The silence around her was such that it deepened over the years, it became entrenched. The silence was their marriage covenant.

She crawled past the roadwork. The workers had dug a large hole in the road and were moving to and fro in the rain. She drove carefully past the row of hectically blinking yellow lights. Then the queue was gone. She turned on to Belliardstraat, passed the EU district and entered the Belliard Tunnel, sweeping onward into the Kortenberg tunnel. Soon she was on the freeway.

The flight from Zaventem was an hour late. She sat at the edge of the transit hall, at a comfortable distance from a family with children, as several businessmen circled around the rows of seats with cells glued to their ears. As usual, she couldn't help reading her environment. She noted that no one could see her screen. The security mindset never left her. It was an old habit, an occupational hazard. Fredrik would laugh at her and say that she was paranoid, but that wasn't true—she was never worried. She just couldn't help but interpret faces, body movements, which way gazes were looking and all the other small everyday situations that took place around her, reading them all, seeing threats and risks, seeing security. It was part of her vision; over time it had become just as natural as it was for others to distinguish colors. At airports she always noted the deficiencies in security, noted where the CCTV cameras were located, which angles weren't being covered, observed the behavior of passersby. She particularly paid attention to people who were different from the crowd; she always noticed if someone was watching her.

Sitting at the far end of the row of seats, close to the gate, with the enormous curved glass window looking out on to the runway, she was undisturbed. It felt good to be immersed in work. There was always a pleasant sensation of increased concentration when she was approaching a new case, a new task. A lot of human existence appeared to be hopelessly messy and irrelevant, but when you got up close in order to distinguish threats, risks, then it all took on a new sharpness. The smallest detail might be the bearer of interesting meanings or implications. Chaos became meaningful, the complexity a part of the challenge. Discerning a threat and understanding its implications, its orientation and gravity, the underlying motives and, somewhere among all these parameters, spotting the outlines of individuals, actors, targets—that was to understand reality better.

Mikael had given her a USB with information about the Swedish diplomat. She cast an eye around and opened the files.

The first was a photo. A young girl, looking into the camera without smiling. A determined gaze. Straight, dark blond hair; no distinguishing marks. The second file was her CV. She had the profile typical of a young civil servant: degree at Uppsala University, some work abroad, temporary role at the MFA, then eight years in different departments—the Department for Eastern Europe and now the Security Policy Department. There was even a short précis of her personal history. Born in Sweden—Stockholm; Polish father, Swedish mother. Divorced.

A normal person, by all accounts. No hits on her criminal record; no unusual financial goings-on, according to checks with the Swedish Tax Agency and the Enforcement Authority. She wasn't on the radar of Counterespionage in Stockholm. Carina Dymek was the kind of person Bente would have filtered out if looking for potential threats.

The third file was a summary of what was known about the leak. So far, that wasn't much. A report from the EU Commission had, in some unknown way, gotten out of the system and, by another unknown way, ended up in the possession of Carina Dymek. There were many unknowns. In all likelihood, there would be someone among Dymek's colleagues or friends, someone who had the same or a higher security clearance than her, who had provided her with the report. That couldn't encompass more than about fifty people.

Mikael had contacted the EU Commission; naturally, they knew of the leak at this stage—the Brits had already spoken to them.

Around twenty interviews had been conducted with employees
at the Commission and anyone who might have had access to the
report was to undergo in-depth security checks. The system was
comprehensive. Documents, even those with high secrecy classifica-
tions, passed through many hands—there were probably hundreds
of people who had come into contact with the report. The Commission, which comprised twenty-five thousand employees and tons of
documents flowing back and forth on a daily basis, would essentially
need to trace precisely how this document had moved through the
organization, following its route between employees, through photocopiers, fax machines, and e-mails. They needed to find out exactly
who had read the text, how many copies there were, who still had
copies and which copies had been lost. Then they would have to com-
pile it all carefully in order to see where the leak had occurred. It was
like wandering around with a small hammer and banging on the
pipes of a huge oil refinery to try and find a small crack that might
blow the entire establishment to smithereens. It was a Sisyphean
task, a hopeless task. It was fairly surprising that the Commission,
after just three days, was claiming they had made no errors, as their
Head of Security had insisted when Mikael called her, just as Bente
was leaving the office. So pathetic, and so typical of larger bureaucra-
cies. They wanted to prevent a larger investigation, avoid inspectors
rooting around in their stacks of paperwork, and were protecting
themselves by denying responsibility. Most likely the EU Commission had misplaced the report and had no idea where it was. It was
convenient to have a young Swedish diplomat to blame.

Whatever the case, the fact was that a report from the EU Commission had leaked, and a Swedish civil servant, Carina Dymek,
was mixed up in something that affected national security.

The last file that Mikael had included was the leaked EU report.
A draft. Classified as *secrète*, the second highest level of classification. The text was about four hundred pages long; she didn't feel up
to reading it now.

She clicked back to the photo of Dymek again. Steady gaze. Was
this someone who leaked top secret material, who committed a

serious crime? Had she been tricked? Perhaps. It remained to be seen. Bente shut her computer and leaned back.

The flight was delayed by yet another ten minutes. She reflected for a while about the reasons why a plane could be delayed. Small, incorrect decisions during the loading of baggage or a slightly slow deicing of the wings could then cause a small delay that got quickly worse due to the increasing frequency of landings per minute. That was how collisions of time hit aviation schedules, with the result that yet more planes were delayed. When the situation became sufficiently critical, there was always the risk that procedures began to fall aside while they tried to bring things back under control. It was situations like those that a criminal could take advantage of. A terrorist. A spy. That was how risks were created—through chains of errors in the small details, through failed procedures. It was always about people. It was human error, the human element, which caused threats to come into being, leaks to occur.

She awakened from her thoughts. A businessman lost it, marched across to the gate, and began to argue with the woman behind the counter while the others stayed where they were, fiddling with their cell phones.

Mikael had written a brief list of actions for the Dymek case. Before she had left the office, Bente had detailed two men to listen in on the Commission's data stream. The Section was now carrying out some targeted searches on the Internet—using open sources. They were also going into Coreu and the other encrypted e-mail systems used by the EU, and making a handful of careful intrusions on to the servers of some embassies. It was important to have time to understand whether there were signs that the leak had spread through the diplomats of other countries.

The proposal for a European intelligence service was sensitive. She hadn't followed all the political twists and turns, but knew it was the darling of the Brits. For the report to have gone astray now was embarrassing. If Green was right, there was a risk that the project would be pulled apart by the media and various national parliaments who would start asking questions, demanding investigations. It could be a scandal that brought down ministers—if Green was right. So far, only one civil servant had crossed the line.

She looked at the time. One and a half hours late now.

She hated delayed flights. For someone with a robust psyche, she found the tedium of being forced to sit among the jumble of luggage and other bored, waiting travelers unusually difficult. The whole point of airports was that you were supposed to leave them. It could be guaranteed that there was a corner of hell that was a transit hall of endless waiting.

8

Stockholm, Monday, September 26

Carina took a deep breath, pushed away, and struck downward into the pool. The water flowed along her body. She brought her head to the surface and drove her arms down through the mass of water, kicking and steaming forward in a violent front crawl. She was fast. Her muscles worked well together. She reached the tiled end quickly, turned and pushed again. She swam another length, turned and pushed. Everything around her was a kaleidoscope of blue swimming-pool water, glimmers of lights, and echoing voices. The roar of her own breathing grew. The rhythm came to her arms and legs after two lengths. Everything around her vanished.

She hadn't been able to stay at home for a second. The silence in the apartment choked her; all she wanted to do was lie down and stop breathing. It had been several months since she had felt like that: an empty feeling, a struggle to breathe, to swallow. When she had lived with Peter, there had been periods when she had felt like that every day. It was a horrible feeling that had crept into entirely everyday situations—at dinner, on a walk—toward the end of their marriage, even when they had sex. A sucking feeling that made her feel like she ceased to be Carina, made her lose her footing and, deep down, left her empty. She could only describe it to herself as being consumed from within—as if Carina was disappearing. She never told anyone, but the emptiness was there. The risk of losing herself, of ceasing to be who she was and letting the emptiness spread, was always there. That emptiness was her inner enemy. Swimming was the only thing that helped—swimming fast, for a long time, until the limits of exhaustion, until the body was just a body and everything was reduced to beats of the heart.

She had called Jamal several times, but his cell was switched off. She had left several messages, but couldn't manage to say on the phone what had happened. Just call me as soon as you hear this. Call me, darling. The prospect that it might all be a mistake kept revisiting her thoughts; she just wanted what had happened not to be real. Over and over, she looked at her cell—in the subway, on the street, in the changing rooms at the swimming pool—just in case the Ministry had called to say it was all a misunderstanding.

She swam at a fast pace, as if a torpedo was chasing her, then switched to butterfly after fifteen lengths and beat furiously through the water. After twenty lengths, her thoughts finally cleared. They began to lose weight and finally there was nothing holding them back. They eased, dissolved. All there was left was rushing water, breathing and the movements of her body. The large blue mass of chlorinated water calmed her. She swam forty lengths without stopping. The last five lengths she floated along doing backstroke, counting the lights hanging from the ceiling.

When she finally reached the handrail at the edge of the pool and pulled herself out of the water, she had been swimming for over an hour. She was panting. Daylight streamed through the large windows to the swimming pool. The air echoed with lapping water and high-pitched children's voices. The worry and emptiness was still there, but it wasn't as strong any longer.

The changing room was quiet. The only people there were a woman with her daughter, and a group of older ladies. Carina's body felt heavy after swimming. She showered and spent a long time in the sauna. Sweat flowed from her pores and ran down her back, across her face, formed small drops on her eyebrows. Her thoughts were clearer now, there was space in her head to think things through. She was able to pick things apart again, piece by piece like she normally did, and analyze them. Why hadn't they believed her? They had always trusted her judgment previously. That a man had approached her in Brussels was a fact, so why didn't they believe her? The EU Commission claimed the opposite, that there was no leak. But that didn't have to mean anything. They were probably trying to avoid a scandal, avoid the blame—protecting themselves. Of course, it was entirely possible the man had lied, that he wasn't really from the EU Commission, but she hadn't gotten the impression he was a liar—quite the opposite. Perhaps it was a misunderstanding. Was someone else supposed to have received the report? No, the man had known her name, he hadn't hesitated—it hadn't been a mistake. Everything had happened for a reason.

She had told the truth, and yet they didn't believe her. She constantly thought back to the meeting that morning, their skeptical, contemptuous expressions; she returned to the same thought, crashing into it like a solid wall, and each time her rage grew.

Why?

Why did she have to go?

She hadn't done anything wrong. She had done everything by the book. It wasn't right. She was right, not them.

She looked in a mirror while she brushed her hair. She had to find the man in Brussels. Jean. Yes—that was the only way.

She was hungry like a beast when she came out on to Medborgarplatsen. She needed something to eat. Trembling due to low blood sugar, she staggered around, unable to decide where to go, but finally ended up in a small sushi place next to the subway station entrance, by the pedestrian crossing to Folkungagatan. It was empty, as all restaurants were in the post-lunch lull. She ordered nori wraps, miso soup, and green tea, and sat on one of the small stools by the window. She called Jamal again, but his cell was switched off.

She had a missed call. It was from Greger Karlberg. They had agreed to meet for lunch today, she remembered. She had completely forgotten; how embarrassing. She listened to his message. He had called twice; the second time, he had hung up. That had been three hours ago.

Greger was an old school friend, the only one from high school she still saw. They had grown up on the same street in Ängby and attended the same school. After high school, their paths had gone different ways and they hadn't seen each other for over ten years. By complete coincidence, they had met in the cafeteria in the Rosenbad building one day. It transpired that he worked as a developer in the Government Offices IT Department. They had started to spend time together again and, funnily enough, it was as if almost no time had passed at all. They knew each other; they were similar. Greger still had unhappy love affairs, which they discussed. His boyfriend had recently ended it for the third, and probably final time. He was down and needed to talk.

Greger answered the second time she called his cell. It didn't matter that she had forgotten about lunch, absolutely not. Apparently he could hear that her voice sounded different, because he asked if something had happened.

Yes, she said. Something has happened. She didn't feel up to saying it on the phone. Did he have time to meet? Greger promised to come as quickly as possible. She sat for a long time, drinking green tea and looking at the crossing as people and traffic streamed past. No one asked her to leave, even though she stayed for over an hour.

Eight years she had been at the Ministry. Eight years. She had given it her all. She loved her job, despite the stress, despite the bureaucracy, despite the men and their pacts. She had never doubted that she had made the right decision applying for foreign policy instead of commercial law, like many of her classmates at college. Despite the low salary and the hundreds of hours spent working overtime, in spite of all of it, it was worth it. It was the feeling of being part of something important that drove her. She gave her all for the ministry. Even when she didn't believe in what she was doing, she did her job. She was loyal and her managers had always liked her. She was analytical and had good judgment. She delivered. International policy was a part of her life, and now they wanted to take it away from her. How could they think she was lying? She was an asset, yet they still wanted her gone.

Then she thought about her parents—what would she say to them? They were so proud of her. Especially her father, she thought bitterly. What would she say to him? He had been so happy for her; when she had gotten into the Foreign Service it was as if all his hard work had been for something. She had succeeded in a way he never had been able to in Sweden. Andrzej Dymek, the officer forced to bury his dreams when he left the army and fled from Poland in the seventies. In Sweden he was just a fucking Pole. He had been a taxi driver for a number of years before retraining as a secondary school teacher. That she, his daughter, had gotten into the Ministry of Foreign Affairs was like a victory over the Sweden that had received him with so much suspicion and disdain. They would never get to her, because she was a diplomat, she worked for the government. She knew that was how he thought.

She could barely contemplate how they would react to the bad news. Her father would be so disappointed, or—more than that—something great would be lost. Perhaps she didn't have to tell them. Never let them know. For a second she considered the idea and saw immediately how impossible that was. She swore to herself. You should never become bitter, her father had taught her. Bitterness consumed you like a corrosive poison if you gave in. But just then, that afternoon, everything was bitter. It couldn't end like this. It wasn't fair. She looked at the crossing, where cars were sat in a large group at a red light outside the restaurant. If she found the man in Brussels, perhaps she could sort everything. It had to be done.

"Carina!"

Absorbed in her gloomy thoughts, she hadn't noticed Greger, who was standing and waving at her through the restaurant window. After a day surrounded by alien and hostile faces, it was such a relief to see him out there in the crowds on Folkungagatan. Same old Greger, with his shaved head and his black down coat spanning his massive, well-set figure. He looked like an old skinhead and might have seemed dangerous, had it not been for the almond-shaped eyes that were surprisingly friendly.

She began to cry. It happened as soon as she caught sight of Greger. She stroked back her hair and tried in vain to stop the tears flowing. Then she collected herself, rose and stepped out on to the street, where Greger waited, worried.

"What the fuck has happened?"

They walked toward Slussen. It felt good to walk alongside him. She wasn't alone any longer. Radiant afternoon light covered the street and cut around people in the crowd, turning them into black silhouettes.

"Have you broken up with your boyfriend?"

Greger was direct—she liked that. Honest. She didn't have to pretend. The first time she had shown him a picture of Jamal, he had said, right away, that he was a hot guy, that it was unusual to see a straight guy that good looking.

"It's work," she said. "I've been suspended."

She hadn't intended to tell him everything. But she did. She needed to talk to someone who could listen, who she trusted. She needed to know that she wasn't imagining it all. As they wandered around Söder-malm, she told him what had happened, how she had met the man in Brussels and been given the memory stick, and then how the Head of Department had called her in and interrogated her, accused her. Why hadn't they believed her?

"And what about now? What happens now?"

"I don't know," she said.

They had reached Mariatorget, and wandered slowly between the trees while the wave of rush-hour traffic moved past them in a boisterous current along Hornsgatan.

"Do you still have the USB?"

She got out the small object and gave it to him. According to the laws governing the distribution of secret information, she wasn't really allowed to say a word to Greger about the report, let alone give him access to it. But she let him hold the USB stick. She didn't care. He clasped it between his fingers, like a rare insect.

"So it was this that he gave you? This USB stick?"

She nodded.

"What does the secret report say?"

"It was a proposal for a European security service. I've only skimmed it."

He nodded and looked skeptically at the memory stick before returning it.

They went into the cava bar on Swedenborgsgatan, just opposite the subway station in Mariatorget, from which people were streaming out now that it was the rush hour. It was her favorite place, full of people on Friday evenings. Right now the bar was deserted; they were only just opening and the staff were moving around and lighting candles, getting ready for the evening. Greger bought two glasses of wine.

She watched him and smiled. How unlikely it was that she was sitting here, just thrown out of her job, and that it was Greger who was here and listening to her. But it was right. In a way, it was just like in high school, years ago, when they had gone to the *konditori* at Brommaplansrondellen and talked every lunch break. Greger was her friend. He was completely uninterested in her physically; everyone who knew him knew that he was gay. He had been able to talk about feelings, unlike all the other pimply Neanderthals who had surrounded her at the time. They used to talk about the world's problems: whaling, nuclear weapons, how sick it was that there were people who could press a button and destroy all life on earth within fifteen minutes. She was tired of all the idiots at school, frustrated by all the unfairness in the world. They agreed that *Blade Runner* was a great film—as was *The Terminator* and *Terminator 2*, but definitely not *Terminator 3*. Greger got her to listen to Depeche Mode and strange old bands like the Sisters of Mercy. He was chubby and hopeless, unhappily in love with the school's district champion in gymnastics.

And here they were now—grown up. He was a computer technician and she was a diplomat. She had been convinced it was possible to change the world. But was it truly possible? She wasn't so sure anymore. The ministry was a machine, within which she was clearly just a cog.

"So your bosses don't believe that you were contacted in Brussels? They think you're lying." Greger sat down and passed her a glass.

"Exactly."

"Why? I don't understand."

"I don't understand either. Apparently the Commission denied they had a leak, and said the leak was someone else. So they presumably think it's me. They said I had damaged their faith in Sweden." She threw up her hands. She didn't know herself how to explain it. It was incomprehensible.

"It all sounds so stupid," said Greger. "You're one of the hardest-working people I know."

"Maybe they're right. Maybe I did something wrong."

"I don't think so."

"They said that important friends in the EU had lost faith in Sweden because of my actions. That I was a leak. But I don't understand what I've done."

"You've done nothing wrong," said Greger. "It sounds like you did everything right. Perhaps that's what the problem is. Perhaps they need someone to blame."

She shrugged her shoulders. Yes, perhaps. In that case, she was in real trouble.

"What do you know about this 'Jean'?" said Greger after a while.

"Nothing. I don't even know if 'Jean' is his real name. He said he worked at the EU Commission."

"But you know what he looks like?"

She thought about it. Yes, she remembered him clearly.

"It's not as hard to trace people as you'd think." Greger gave her a wry smile. "I know some people who can do this kind of thing. No one would notice anything. But they would find him, I promise."

"And it's illegal, I presume."

"Not particularly."

"Greger, I don't know . . . I'm a civil servant. I have to obey the law . . ."

"Of course. But you're suspended. And they're going to investigate you. From what I'm hearing, it sounds like, if you don't do something pretty drastic, you won't be a civil servant or on the right side of the law for much longer." He looked at her seriously. "Listen to me. Do you want them to be right?"

"No . . ."

"So what are you going to do?"

She didn't answer. What could she do? She just felt incredibly tired; she didn't know how she should handle this. Perhaps they were right. Perhaps she had taken an inexcusable risk meeting the man and accepting the report. Perhaps it was reasonable for them to suspend her, pull her in for a disciplinary hearing, and, once they were done, leave her behind, stricken like a wounded animal. No, she couldn't let that happen.

"Carina."

She looked up from her wine glass.

"You've done nothing wrong." Greger leaned forward and put a hand on her shoulder. No, she hadn't done anything wrong. But the more time passed, the more her guilt would grow. She was the accused. Unless she could prove what had really happened, that a different chain of events had taken place, she would be guilty. He was right, but that was little consolation.

"You have to fight back," he said. "Otherwise they'll find you guilty, even though you're innocent."

"I don't have a chance, Greger!" she burst out. She wanted to fight, but right now she couldn't see how, or whether it was even possible. The ministry loomed above her like a massive, impenetrable fortress.

"Yes, you do."

She looked out of the window.

"Okay," she said without any conviction.

"You have to find him—the guy you met."

"But what do I do if I don't find him?"

"Start looking. Then we'll see."

9

Stockholm,
Monday, September 26–
Wednesday, September 28

The apartment was dark when Carina woke up. She looked around drowsily but couldn't understand where the fly was that was buzzing around the room.

Her cell.

She heard it somewhere in the apartment. For a second she had forgotten what had happened that day. The only thing she felt in that moment was the warm, dark apartment enveloping her, and the humming, buzzing sound. Her body was heavy; she pulled herself up, groped her way to the door, and finally found her cell in her handbag in the hallway. It had stopped vibrating before she reached it.

It was Jamal. She looked at the time: almost midnight.

They had stayed in the bar for several hours—she and Greger. She didn't want to be alone and had needed to talk about what had happened, needed to feel that there was someone who cared about her. She was drunk when she got home and had fallen asleep on the sofa.

"Hi, darling."

Jamal sounded worried, happy, and irritated, all at the same time, when she called him back. He had gotten her messages and had been trying to get hold of her all evening. He had called the office, had been close to looking up the number of her parents and calling them too. What had happened?

She told it like it was. Telling Jamal about it felt unreal. Jamal became deadly silent at the other end. He didn't try to comfort her, didn't try to belittle her or say that everything would sort itself out, that it was just a mistake, and she was grateful for that. It was serious, and he understood that.

"My God," he said, finally.

"I don't know what to do," she said. "But I think I have to find him, the man who gave me the report."

"I'm coming home."

"No, Jamal."

"Yes. I can catch a flight first thing tomorrow."

"You can't just leave Vienna," she protested, although what she wanted most of all was him there, beside her, with his arms around her, close—wanted it so much that tears formed in her eyes. "Stay in Vienna. You can't just leave the negotiations."

"Screw the negotiations."

"My love, I'll be fine."

She changed her mind almost right away after he had reluctantly given in. They would see each other on Thursday, in three days. It was for the best; she needed to sort this out for herself.

Talking to Jamal calmed her down. She missed him. Just hearing his voice on the telephone made her feel that things were possible. He wanted to know everything they had said at the meeting, all the details. It was completely wrong, he said over and over. Finally, she no longer had the strength to talk about the MFA; she felt ill just thinking about it. How was Vienna? How were the negotiations? He told her about the Americans who wanted to cut the UN budget, about a lunch with a completely manic UN chief. He had just returned from dinner with people at the Swedish embassy and was going to bed shortly. He was staying in a small hotel with horrid rooms and good breakfasts, close to the UN building. She knew where it was, remembered the heavy brown wardrobes in front of the windows; she too had stayed there.

Could they go out for a meal when he came back? He was longing to sit with her in a decent restaurant, just the two of them. Then they could talk everything through, together.

"I'm beginning to hate the MFA," he said. "How can they do this to you?"

Jamal was so loyal, it surprised her. Men rarely supported her, and she didn't expect it, either. She always thought that she, when it came down to it, was alone. But Jamal was on her side.

She only slept for four hours that night and woke to a gray dawn outside her window. Thoughts of the report, the Ministry and Brussels all rushed through her head. She knew right away that she wouldn't be able to fall back asleep and got up, took a shower, made breakfast—a more substantial breakfast than usual, with egg sandwiches, some fruit salad, and coffee—and ate on the living room sofa.

Her body ached. The day before had left her bruised. It was barely a day since the terrible meeting with the unit head and a part of her still couldn't quite understand what had happened. But some of her just wanted to give up and accept defeat, unconditionally. Deep inside her, a treacherous little voice whispered that it was probably all her own fault. She felt faint and shut her eyes. No, she thought.

No.

She was Carina Dymek, one of the best people at the Security Policy Department, and what she had done wasn't wrong. They wouldn't judge her; they wouldn't get her to admit a mistake she hadn't made. Never. She poured another cup of coffee. Slowly, the anxiety passed in a gloomy and stubborn train of thought.

Greger was right. She was innocent. She would fight. But she needed facts—meat hooks to hang this shapeless reality on.

It was half past six. She got out her laptop and, as it got light outside, she started to search the EU Commission's website. If she assumed that Jean had told the truth, that he was from the Commission, then he was probably there.

She had been in contact with the Commission hundreds of times, by e-mail and phone, with different civil servants in different parts of this widespread organization. But she had never before been in a situation where she needed to find a stranger she didn't even know the name of but who had unexpectedly capsized her entire existence. She had to find Jean, but, as she sat in her apartment, she had no idea how. The organization was divided into eleven so-called directorates, expansive departments that handled a myriad of political matters that coursed through the European Union's veins on a daily basis. The text on the memory stick had come from one of those departments. There, among thousands of officials, somewhere in the bowels of the Commission, the man who had contacted her had to exist. Given the contents of the report, it was most probable that it had come from GD Home, the Directorate General for Home Affairs, covering security of the interior, migration, and police matters. Directorate A handled terrorism, organized crime, migration and police matters in the EU. He would never have gotten hold of the report unless he was in Directorate A. That was where Jean had to be. The head of that department, she saw on the website, was Joaquim Nunes de Almeida.

Just after nine, when she was sure people would be in their offices, she got out her cell and called the switchboard at the EU Commission in Brussels.

"*Bienvenue à la Commission européenne,*" said a soft, automated voice, which informed her that her call was in a queue and asked for her patience.

It took a few minutes.

"*La Commission européenne, bonjour?*" said a very crisp and professional switchboard operator.

"*Bonjour,*" began Carina and quickly explained that she was calling from the Ministry of Foreign Affairs in Stockholm for de Almeida.

She was connected.

Strings music filled her phone. The same exuberant music that reverberated through all EU telephone systems. After a pause of a second or so, which felt like an abyss, the music began from the start again. She was about to hang up when there was a rattle. Someone picked up.

A woman said abruptly, "*Oui?*"

Carina quickly brought the phone back up to her ear and introduced herself, explaining that she needed to speak to de Almeida.

"What does your call concern?"

She had clearly come through to a secretary who wasn't going to let just anyone talk to the boss.

"It's about a report. Registration number KOM(2011)790."

"Oh . . ." said the woman, sounding slightly more cooperative. "Monsieur de Almeida is away on official business. Can I take your name?"

She shouldn't have called. If de Almeida found out a Swedish diplomat had called and mentioned the report, he would naturally begin to wonder. The slightest suspicion that it had fallen into the wrong hands would lead him to contact Stockholm.

"Hello?" said the woman impatiently.

"I'm actually looking for someone called Jean."

"Jean who? Do you have a surname?"

"No . . ." she said and strung the seconds out while she frantically thought about what to say. "It's about the report I mentioned."

"I'm sorry, but I don't think I can help you," said the woman with all the cordiality necessary to disguise her irritation. "Jean is a common name. Perhaps you should try your embassy; maybe they can help you."

Carina thanked her and hung up.

There was no point in carrying on making calls if she didn't know his name. The risk that someone would be suspicious and raise the alarm with Stockholm, or another capital, was far too high. She had moved too quickly. Stay calm, she thought. Focus.

She made some new coffee and rewound her thoughts to the day in Brussels when the man had turned up. Jean. She remembered clearly what he had looked like. How he had sat opposite her and talked. His voice had rasped a little, probably because he smoked. Yes, he had been fingering a cigarette pack. She closed her eyes, squinted hard, and tried to remember—to truly see all the details. She did what they taught her at army headquarters on the intelligence courses, tried to see the details as a connected system of associations, without getting hung up on any of them. They were sitting in a restaurant. Dark wood; leather seats. She was sitting opposite him. He had a small, round face. Beard. Dark, natural curls. Gray hair at the temples; clear wrinkles around the eyes. He was probably around fifty years of age, maybe a little older. Close-set eyes filled with worry that searched their surroundings. She scoured her memory, trying to find even the smallest detail that could give her a clue.

Several times he had glanced across her shoulder, toward the entrance to the restaurant. Toward the park outside. What was he looking for? She had noticed it even at the time, the way he was looking around. Perhaps he was being followed, or maybe he was just scared. That wasn't unlikely. Leaking secrets like the ones he had was almost certainly a sure way to make enemies. Now she could see his frightened-but-determined face before her quite clearly. She saw the eyes, the furrows, the wrinkles, his little, stubborn mouth.

Conscience, he had said. At least she had a conscience. She needed a picture of him—a photo. Something that tied him to reality, that connected him to a name, an address, something.

She returned to the EU Commission's website again. There were hundreds, if not thousands, of subpages—the website substructure vanished into an unfathomable deep. She began looking for photographs, first at random, then more systematically. Each time she found one she would stop and study it. Pictures of smiling people, people in discussion, young and old, in suits and jackets, advertising pictures of youths cooperating across national borders, all with smiling faces.

The Commission works closely with the European Parliament and national governments to run the Union in the overall interests of its 455 million citizens . . .

So many officials. They all looked so stunningly similar. Sometimes she would reach a page that required a password and she would have to retreat. For hours she trawled through the EU Commission's website before beginning to search other websites, looking at French and American sites, stumbling across various politics blogs, news sites, sites on Google she had never heard of. It was like a never-ending excavation, where she dug deeper and deeper into the mass of information with the help of new search keywords and new combinations of those words. He was not allowed to hide; she would find him. She was working like one obsessed. He must have been caught in a picture somewhere. One picture—just one—that was all she needed. It would mean he was recorded, stored, visible, possible to reach. Outside the window, the day passed and turned into a blue twilight. A first small success came late in the afternoon. A website for journalists featured a list of the Commission's staff. There were lots of Jeans here—but only names, no pictures. She noted the names and started searching for them, clicking her way from page to page. But there were several thousand people working for the EU called Jean; it was impossible to say which was the right one. On one occasion she was certain she had found him. She had found a picture of people at what looked like a reception, and she paused, examining a short man with a beard, but was forced to accept that it was just someone who looked like him. He had to be somewhere. Somewhere. She forced herself to think like that so she wouldn't scream out loud. She couldn't lose heart.

Where are you Jean? Where, where?

It was late in the evening when she called the Italian restaurant on the ground floor of the building next door, to order takeout. She had searched hundreds of websites and needed a break. She moved around the apartment, turning on the lights.

Continuing to search without a plan wasn't going to work. She couldn't go through every possible webpage where there might possibly be a picture of Jean—it would be better to go to Brussels and stand outside the entrance to the Commission and hope he turned up sooner or later. She swore loudly. She needed to rethink.

She spent the rest of the evening going through a photo service where she had found pictures of people from the EU at different conferences, summits, inaugurations—endlessly monotonous pictures. Thousands of pictures, thousands of faces, but no Jean.

It was almost one o'clock when she decided to stop searching. Yet she remained sitting and staring at the pictures without getting anywhere. She stood up and went into the kitchen to pour a glass of wine. She had been sat at the computer for almost twenty hours and she was dead tired, but she knew she wouldn't be able to fall asleep.

There was a remake of a Japanese horror flick running on one of the cable channels. A man had just been found dead in an apartment, scared to death, his mouth grotesque and wide open, his face contorted. Everyone who watched a particular video died seven days later. In the film, everyone knew they were going to die and tried in vain to prevent it from happening. Death was a demon girl with lank, dripping hair that crept toward her victims out of the television. Carina could understand exactly why she wanted to kill everyone. They had done her wrong and now she wanted revenge.

The morning after, she carried on searching the Internet. She felt a growing anger. The anger ran through her, scratching the inside of her gut. She should really stop roving around all these websites; it wasn't working, she knew that. Yet she couldn't help herself. She clicked from one page to another, searching restlessly for pictures, a name, anything that might provide her with a clue. Over and over she googled different search keywords, but she had already visited many of the hits the day before. It felt like she was going around in circles, and it pissed her off a lot. At lunchtime, she was close to throwing the computer to the floor in despair.

It couldn't carry on like this. She wouldn't find him. Not like this.

She needed to get out. She pulled on her coat, pushed her feet into her shoes, and took a brisk, furious walk down toward the city center. Everything irritated her. Everyone was in the way. When she crossed a road near Hötorget, she was inches from being run over. Startled by the car's horn, she stuck a finger up at the driver, who grimaced at her in his rearview mirror. She marched into the PUB store. Department stores were full of things to look at and she needed distractions. She went up and down between the floors on the escalators, wandered around the clothing departments. Slowly, she regained her calm.

She still had the report. If there was anywhere that she might find a clue about what had happened, something about Jean and their meeting, it was bound to be there, in amongst the hundreds of pages of the Commission's report.

Back at home, she made some sandwiches and ate them at the kitchen table. A dog was howling somewhere in the building. The sound—a muted complaint—penetrated into the stairwell and was audible through her front door.

She sat down in an armchair with the report. The pile of paper rested heavily on her lap. An EU report. Four hundred and twenty pages of Brussels prose. It was because of this that she had lost her job. She had never thought that something like this would be of such significance to her. It was lucky she was quick-witted. If she hadn't remembered the report and smuggled it out of her office she would never have gotten her hands on it again. She carefully turned to the first page.

Security Across Borders—A New European Intelligence Service

She settled down and began to read.

The report was introduced by a sweeping description of the present-day situation. The text talked about the threat to our societies—terrorism, organized crime, floods of refugees—and how these threats were only growing in a globalized world. It was no longer possible to distinguish between civilian and military threats, said the report. And this required closer cooperation between military and civilian security services.

The Union had a common strategy against terrorism and other serious crime in Europe. The so-called Stockholm Program had been a success, but now the battle for a free and open Europe needed to be taken to a new level. There was a need for a central organization at a European level. An organization that could function as a central operator, a meeting place for the nations' security services.

The hours passed by without her noticing while she worked through the heavy, bureaucratic text. It whispered, threatened, argued, reasoned. It wanted to persuade, convince, make her think like the person who had written the report. It wanted her to say yes. The entire text was dripping with the same racist assumptions about the EU and the surrounding world that had been a source of provocation for her so many times previously. Border controls, illegal immigrants as potential threats. Terrorism and Muslims.

The text was constantly getting at a basic idea, which only became apparent after a couple of hundred pages. It was time to go one step further, said the report—it was time to develop, "a European, transnational ability to defend the freedom and security of the European Union and its member states. For this purpose, we propose the creation of a federal European security organization, with the purpose of promoting and coordinating the fight against terrorism and organized crime, both within the Union and throughout the world."

She read on. There were then several chapters that outlined how the security service would work, what mandate it would have, which assignments it would undertake. The text became more and more detailed and technical. The new organization was described, its methods for gathering intelligence in EU countries, its direction. During the first two years a "platform" would be developed containing sources, informants, and whistleblowers throughout Europe. Parallel to this, a network of sources and infiltrators outside of Schengen would also be developed. She shuddered—these were real secrets. Long paragraphs outlined how to efficiently connect "resources" to the global fight against terrorism. Two long chapters described how operations outside of Europe's borders would be carried out in order to, as it said, "prevent threats to the Union." The next chapter explained how the EU would develop a closer collaborative relationship with Mossad, the CIA, and other agencies. The report then continued, section by section, by detailing how effective exchanges of information and operational resources would be facilitated between the security services of European nations, including MI6 and MI5 of Britain, the French DGSE, the German BND, the

Spanish CNI, and many others. Within three years, the organization would have "independent operational abilities."

Operational abilities.

Jean was right. This was the groundwork for a European spy organization.

The final pages included a budget. At first she thought she had misread. The estimated cost for the EIS, it said, quite matter of fact, was 1.1 billion Euros.

Stockholm city center stretched out beneath a gray sky. She stood at the window and looked toward Sveavägen, where people passed by on their way home from work; it was already afternoon. The day had flown by while she read, without her noticing. Somewhere, deep down in the pages of the report, there were clues that would lead her to Jean. He would be able to explain what this was about. She shouldn't be in possession of this information. But now she was, she couldn't pretend it didn't exist. She felt a strange, sucking sensation in her stomach and got up to pace around the room. A new European intelligence service. She worked in the Security Policy Department, she had worked day in, day out on European foreign policy, yet she hadn't heard anything about this. Not even a hint. It didn't make sense. A giant like that couldn't just slip under the radar. Secrets always spread through Brussels. The biggest secrets got to be known by everyone, sooner or later—it was a city of whispers. Somewhere there had to be more information: minuted conversations, notes, preliminary studies. Jean knew more. But where could she find him?

The reference number.

She checked herself. It was a chance, but it might just work. Reference numbers were unique. Each EU document had one, and all documents that referenced a report also referred to the same number, creating a link back to the first document. This way, each and every EU document created its own winding paper trail in a complicated series of numbers. With the reference number, she would be able to, with a little luck, trace the documents associated with the report and the spy organization hidden within it.

KOM(2011)790. The characteristic EU number was printed in the top right-hand corner of the first page. If there were more documents connected to the report, they were probably at the Ministry of Justice archives; this was their area of responsibility. She sent a text message to Jamal asking him to call.

After dinner, she made a fresh attempt to find Jean online. Yet more smiling faces and horrid pictures of people in office settings. At around nine it occurred to her that she had read something in the report about a meeting in London that had apparently fired the starting gun for the entire EIS project. She leafed through the document to the right page. An informal conference in London, it said, where an agreement had been reached concerning the foundations of the organization. When she searched online, she found nothing. Naturally, the meeting had been secret. Instead, she found several hits for a lecture on EC law and jurisprudence underpinning the fight against terror. The link was two years old. She clicked and was taken to a PDF from the Harvard Law School.

She scrolled quickly through the text. At the end was a series of pictures, somewhat amateurish photographs of men in suits on a panel, talking, smiling at the camera in a reception.

She leaned closer to the screen. She knew one of the men. It was Stefano Manservisi, the Head of the EU Commission's Directorate General for Internal Security. Next to him were two women, posing with huge smiles. Behind them a group of people were chatting.

There.

It was him: Jean.

10

Stockholm, Monday, September 26

Intelligence was the art of formulating accurate guesses about the future. Anyone looking for threats also had to be able to imagine a future where that threat might become a reality. Not all possible futures were of equal interest; it was only a certain type that was worthy of attention: the one that bore a threat against the safety of the nation. It was important to be careful when putting together fragments of information and trying to distinguish these potential futures, scenarios. Not an exact science, obviously—rather, it was a question of probabilities, risks.

Bente dropped these thoughts as she slowed her car, pulled into a parking space and grabbed her handbag. The flight had been delayed further. She had come straight from Arlanda airport, but she was still late.

A secretary from Counterespionage met her in the bright entrance to the Security Service building and quickly led her up to the eighth floor. They were waiting for her in a cold conference room. Gustav Kempell, who was Head of Counterespionage, two investigators from the branch, and a technician.

They shook hands, introducing themselves by their first names. Gustav, Joakim, Lars, Jakob. No one needed to know more.

Kempell was the same as always: same square glasses and still, gray gaze; same calm manner as he went right to the point as soon as they sat down.

In the first stage, Dymek was to be profiled—her friends, family, networks, her travel and meetings, whether anyone had spotted any unusual behavior, contact outside of what was expected. They briefly discussed if she could be considered to have a motive, and if so how it was to be investigated. But it was still too early to contact her. First they needed to know more. They needed to go through Dymek's work computer—it would be confiscated from the MFA.

The question was how she had gotten hold of the material. She had told her bosses that she had met a man from the EU Commission, but the Commission denied any such contact.

The incident was serious, but could be contained. Civil servants mismanaging secret documents, causing cracks in the wall of secrecy, had happened before. But this was about a diplomat at the Ministry of Foreign Affairs—close to the government. It was connected to the EU Commission, to the Brits, and a sensitive project. The information was highly classified. It was therefore important to deal with it quickly, tidily, and without a whisper of the affair reaching the media. The damage was potentially extensive if the report was distributed any further. Everyone agreed that it was vital to secure all copies—physical and especially digital. The distribution of the report digitally involved far greater damage; to stem it was crucial but would involve significantly more detective work.

Perhaps Carina Dymek had just been in the wrong place at the wrong time. But they couldn't count on that. If she wasn't alone, who was her contact?

"Probably someone that Dymek trusted," said one of the investigators. "Someone she was willing to take risks for."

"Not necessarily. Someone may be putting pressure on her."

Perhaps.

"We'll postpone discussing motives," said Kempell. "First we need a comprehensive profile—relations, networks, everything—then we can see if we can get under her skin. I want to know if this is an isolated case, if it only concerns this civil servant—Dymek. We'll have to hope so," he added without any conviction. Skepticism was the watchword in Counterespionage and Kempell was the branch's chief skeptic.

For now, they were only to observe and document.

"What does the Commission say?" Kempell asked, turning to Bente.

"Nothing new. They claim that they have no leak." She briefly explained what Mikael had heard in Brussels. The Commission had clammed up—it was a reflex reaction. They were afraid of scandal and wanted to avoid an investigation.

"That's just as well. We'll focus on Dymek and leave the Commission alone." Kempell adjusted his glasses and said, as if in passing, "I gather you were in contact with the Brits this morning."

"That's correct."

The question took her by surprise. She hadn't thought that Kempell would bring up her meeting with Green in front of the others. She had told him about it in confidence and had believed it would remain between the two of them. Had she known that Kempell would be so open about her contact, she would probably not have told him about Green.

"And what did they say?"

"They're worried."

Kempell looked intently at her. His perseverance irritated her.

"The Brits are keen to limit the damage," she said quickly. "They see a greater risk than we do, I would say. Perhaps they know more than we do. They're prepared to support our investigation. I think we can form a decent partnership on this."

Kempell nodded. "So your judgment is that the Brits know more than us. Did you get any impression of what it might all be about?"

She thought back to what Green had said in the morning—that there might be a tsunami. She looked at the others. What could she say that wouldn't immediately leak into the rest of the building?

She shrugged her shoulders. "They think this is bigger than just Dymek."

Kempell looked at her quizzically. Then he turned to the others.

"Remember," he said, "it is important that we cooperate with London. No matter what, we must cooperate. This is a serious incident, but damaging the Brits' trust in us would be far more serious. Our relationship with London has taken decades to build; it is an old friendship. It must endure, even after this fucking Dymek is gone."

I I

Stockholm, Tuesday, September 27

The peace and quiet of the Secretariat for Intelligence Coordination was always a pleasant surprise to Bente. An unexpected calm ruled here, as if the rest of the world was far away. A wine-red carpet muffled all footsteps. Broad fields of sharp, white daylight spilled through the windows.

A woman appeared, noiselessly, nodded at them, and disappeared through a door. The Secretariat was different from all the other parts of the Government Offices. Here there were no stressed civil servants, no one stood in a doorway talking to a colleague, and it was silent. No telephones ringing, no rumbling photocopiers. A row of closed doors lined the corridor.

An intelligence officer waited politely while Bente and Kempell took apart their cells. It was routine security; modern cells were easy to infiltrate. As long as there was electricity in a cell, the enemy could, with the right technology, transform the telephone into a bugging device.

The Secretariat for Intelligence Coordination, otherwise known as SUND, was the government's very own spy center. It was through the SUND offices, on the top floor of the Ministry of Defense, that all intelligence for the various ministries flowed. It was here that discreet contact with the security services of other nations of significance to the government took place; this was where all intelligence from the Western embassies reached the Government Offices; this was where the focus of Swedish intelligence work was determined; this was the command center. It was also here that it was decided who in other ministries would have access to the highest-classified materials—materials to which Dymek and a group of trusted individuals had access—information vital to the security of the nation.

Along the corridor hung paintings of different warships. At the end of the corridor, two crossed sabers were mounted on the wall above a Swedish flag. The military was a different species. Bente couldn't help but wonder about their rituals, their orders and ceremonies. But they were easy to work with.

At the end of the corridor was the Green Room, one of the few government conference rooms that was completely secured against all forms of surveillance and bugging. Behind the green door there were three men, sitting and waiting.

The trio stood up when Bente and Kempell entered the room. The Head of the Security Policy Department, Nils Bergh, was opposite them, straight backed, fingering some papers and noticeably worried. There were dark circles around his eyes; his gaze wandered now and then across the empty table. Next to him was Carl Mellqvist, the Head of SUND, and a little to the side was the administrative director of the MFA.

It was amazing how easy it was for everything to go to hell. One miss and decades of earnest work was overshadowed by a single incident. For, without a doubt, that was how it was: the thin, austere man who headed the Security Police Department would have to shoulder the blame. The Foreign Service had never had a leak like this, and sooner or later someone would demand a head on a silver platter.

Bente nodded at them and made an effort to smile. It worked, people relaxed. She usually thought of it as her professional smile: we're working together; we're in the same family.

There was silence. Mellqvist entered the airspace with a low voice that was accustomed to being heard and obeyed. He welcomed them.

"So . . . Perhaps we should start with a situation report?"

Everyone around the table looked at her expectantly. These men didn't know her and wondered who she was—she could see it in their faces. Of the three of them, it was probably only Mellqvist who knew that she was from the Section rather than Counterespionage. None of them wanted to hear what she had to say because whatever she said would be a problem. Their dark suits made them look like glum funeral directors.

"We can say that Dymek came across a document on the 22nd of September and that she then passed it on. It concerns, as you all know, an unofficial document from the EU Commission. What we are now looking at is how the document fell into her hands and what Dymek's motives are. And, naturally, how we can limit the damage, as far as possible." She turned to the Head of the Security Policy Department. "Has she been suspended from her duties?"

"Yes."

"Good."

The administrative director leaned forward. "So what do we do now?"

"We need to get a clearer picture of what happened—circle in on Dymek. There are basically three plausible scenarios at present. The first is that she came across the information on someone else's behalf, someone close to her, someone putting her under pressure, or someone she wants to help. The second scenario is that she is acting by herself. The third is that some sort of mixup has taken place. The last of those is, as you may understand, less likely."

She paused and let this sink in.

"We still don't know how Carina Dymek acquired the material," she continued. "We are now profiling her contacts—anyone who has been in touch with her. First we need to understand how the document has been spread. I dare say there is a good chance of dealing with this incident quickly." She looked at them for a moment. "However, we still don't know whether there is anyone behind Dymek." She quietly noted the tense expressions on their faces. "If that is the case, and we can't rule it out, we have a far more serious situation on our hands. Depending on who is behind her, and their motive, the situation may change quickly."

These were not reassuring words, but she hadn't come to reassure anyone. They needed to hear the truth. There was a vulnerability, a potentially serious threat to the nation, and it was her job to deal with that threat.

She turned to the Head of the Security Policy Department. "I gather you've talked to her."

"That's right."

"Can you tell us what she said?"

"Yes . . ." Bergh cleared his throat. "Dymek didn't seem to understand that she had done something wrong. She claimed that all she had done was meet with a man in Brussels who had given her the document."

"Was she any more specific about who gave her the report?"

He paused. "She claimed he was called Jean."

"Just 'Jean'?"

"Yes. She said she didn't know his surname."

"But she knew he came from the EU Commission, didn't she, Nils?" Mellqvist interrupted. "So she must have known something. Probably withholding something. And the answer is probably at the EU Commission."

Mellqvist's tone was insistent. He looked at Nils Bergh, who was fidgeting.

"Yes, absolutely."

They had clearly talked through what they would say before the meeting. There was a script and Nils Bergh was obviously not adhering to it. Mellqvist glared irritably at Bente and Kempell. He was suspicious. He looked stiffly at the others around the table, as if to remind them of certain agreements. Naturally, they didn't want people from Counterespionage snooping around the Ministry of Foreign Affairs. The Security Service always meant trouble for people like them: it was bad press and put things in flux, upsetting a carefully maintained order. These men had built their careers on avoiding things like this.

"Can you describe how she handled the report?" said Bente after a pause, pretending to ignore Mellqvist.

"She sent it to Justice."

"Just to them?"

He smiled self-consciously. "As far as I know."

"We are investigating in the utmost detail, of course." Mellqvist interrupted again, worried by all the questions. "But the idea that there are others behind Dymek seems far-fetched at present."

"I'm not so sure," said Kempell slowly.

"Oh." Mellqvist stopped in surprise.

Kempell turned back to the Head of the Security Policy Department again. "Do you remember anything unusual about her behavior, before her trip?" he said.

"No . . ." The department head thought about it. "No, she was doing her job. There was nothing that . . ." He then shook his head as if to underline what he had said. "Dymek went to Brussels on a regular basis. But when Justice contacted us . . . we understood that things weren't right. So we took action." He looked at the others, worried, and cleared his throat.

Kempell let this gloomy train of thought hang in the air a moment.

"Can you describe Carina Dymek?"

"How do you mean?"

"As a person."

"Um . . . she was good. Thorough. She did an excellent job, I would say. There were no issues with her."

"Does she work for anyone else?" said Kempell.

At first Bergh looked at Kempell uncomprehendingly. When the implication of the question dawned on him, his face froze. His gaze wandered off. "No, it . . ." He cleared his throat and fell silent.

"Sorry?"

"I don't think so."

His face was now formed into a tense, unhappy grimace. It was as if the words sucked the air out of him. That the Security Policy Department at the MFA had, by mistake, leaked such a sensitive report was a minor catastrophe, but to have been infiltrated would be an outright nightmare. Bente didn't envy him, but they couldn't take his wellbeing into account. They needed answers, and it was the painfully honest answers that mattered.

"Do you think she is a spy?" Bergh burst out and stared at them. "Is that it?"

He looked pale, as if awaiting a death sentence.

"No," said Kempell. "It is one scenario. One of several potentials."

The poor man fell back into his chair. Everyone looked uncomfortably at him and waited until he had gathered himself.

"What should we do with the Brits?" said the administrative director, who had been sitting in silence throughout.

Kempell sat quietly for a second. Bente knew what he was thinking. They couldn't say too much about the Brits, not at this stage. Contact with Green and MI6 would be dealt with through Bente's channels of communication, no one else's. Everyone waited for Kempell to say something, but he just looked placidly at the others and nodded. "The most important thing now is to stop the spread of the information. We will probably have a better picture in a few days."

"Good," said Mellqvist acidly. "Because we don't want the foreign minister to have to stand up in front of the media and explain this one."

"I don't think anyone wants that," said Kempell.

Kempell needed to smoke after the meeting. Bente walked with him down to Strömmen. Hadn't he quit? she asked. He looked at her in surprise, as if wondering silently which of his other habits she was familiar with. No, no, it was just that the Service had become smoke free, not that he had.

Her cell rang. It was Mikael, in Brussels.

"Green has been in touch," he said. "They're sending people to Stockholm."

"Wilson?"

"Probably."

Green had promised to get back to her. Presumably the Brits would be flying their people in within a day. He didn't know more. He hung up.

"They're sending Wilson."

She noticed how Kempell stiffened; he didn't like surprises. No one had expected the Brits to react so quickly and send people to Stockholm at this early stage, not even Kempell.

They looked across the flowing water rushing between them and the parliament building. Roger Wilson. That meant that London was taking the incident seriously. With a little luck it also meant more help from the British apparatus.

Bente had met Wilson on two occasions: once at the base in Bagram, five years ago, and once in London, shortly after the notorious operation in Hamburg, carried out by his team. She was familiar with his methods.

"This is going to get messy," said Kempell.

"But it's good that we have London on our side."

"I'll never trust them. You know that." He blew smoke. "MI6 does what it likes, and to hell with us." He smiled. Kempell's skepticism of all foreign security services was so firmly rooted that it had become part of his personality. "And I'd take care around that Wilson. You remember what happened in Hamburg," said Kempell.

Yes, she remembered. Marienstrasse. It had taken the Germans six months to clear up after that infamous insertion. Those who knew Roger Wilson at all, which was a very narrow circle of people, respected him but knew that it was wise to keep a certain healthy distance. He worked with his own team. He moved through gray areas.

12

Stockholm, Thursday, September 29

Carina leaned forward toward the screen and zoomed in. The resolution was poor, the picture was grainy. She wasn't sure. Was it really him? Jean?

He was standing in the background, a few meters behind the Director General, and to the left of the picture. He was dressed in a suit, like everyone else, and standing with his hands in his pockets, talking to a woman who was turned away from the camera. He didn't seem aware that he was in the photo; it was the Director General and his smiling colleagues in the foreground who were being photographed, but the focus had also fallen further back so that Jean's face stood out in the background. She brightened the picture slightly and examined his face, then zoomed in on that part of the photo until a strange, grainy picture of a ghost filled half the screen.

Yes, it was him. Jean.

Greger had suggested they should meet at a bar in Kornhamnstorg in the Old Town. Late in the afternoon on a weekday like this, the place was half empty. Here they could talk in peace.

Her head still felt heavy. After finding the picture, she had fallen asleep, exhausted, and had slept like the dead for fifteen hours. She had been so light-headed when she woke up that, for a second, she'd thought she had dreamed the picture and was forced to check it was still there, that she hadn't been mistaken, after all. But there he was—Jean.

Jamal had called her several times from Vienna without her noticing. She was almost angry with him for not coming straight home to Stockholm, despite the fact that she had personally persuaded him to stay. She knew it was childish. When she'd called back, his cell had been switched off. She'd left a message. Then she had texted Greger a link to the picture of Jean. *I've found him.*

Greger turned up just as she was buying a latte. He embraced her and they sat down at one of the tables by the window.

"I didn't think you would be in touch so soon," he said. Greger was noticeably happy. He hurried to the bar and ordered an espresso before returning, knocking back his coffee, and then saying, "So you've found him."

"Yes. I think so."

She brought up the picture on her cell and zoomed in.

"And you're sure it's him?"

"As sure as I can be."

Greger leaned forward and studied the picture. He noted the web address of the link, typing it into his own phone, then looked at her, impressed. "Good work." He examined the picture again. "Okay. But you don't know what he's called."

"Like I said, he said he was called Jean. And that he worked for the EU Commission. That's all I know. I'm guessing he works for the Directorate General that looks after interior security and police matters in the EU."

Greger looked at her uncomprehendingly.

"GD Home," she said.

"Okay?"

"That's what it's called. Here . . ." She handed over a list of names and EU abbreviations—words she guessed were useful when looking for a civil servant at GD Home. "That's the reference number for the report he gave me."

Greger noted it on his cell.

"Aren't you going to show it to your bosses?" he said.

Show them the picture? Oddly enough, the thought hadn't even crossed her mind. Yes, perhaps. Then she felt the doubt forcing its way through. No, not just a picture—that wouldn't be enough. They wouldn't believe her. Look, here's the man who contacted me in Brussels. So what? She needed more facts.

"I have to find him first. Do you think that it's possible?"

"Shouldn't be a problem."

Greger sounded so sure that, at once, she felt worried. It occurred to her that she hadn't asked him the obvious question about what he intended to do. "I don't want to do anything illegal, Greger."

He laughed and made a dismissive gesture. "Don't worry. I'm just going to talk to some people I know. They're cool."

Johan Eriksson leaned forward over her cell and looked at the photograph. He had called her and asked how she was, whether she wanted to meet. He was the only person at the department who had been in touch.

"Yes, that's the Head of GD Home," he said and pointed at Man-servisi. "And she's his adviser; she's worked on police coordination a lot. I met her in Brussels once, at a conference," he said and smiled so broadly that Carina refrained from asking more.

"And him?"

She enlarged the picture so that Jean's face filled the small screen of the cell. He creased his forehead. Carina didn't know anyone with as many contacts and acquaintances in the business as Johan Eriksson. Regardless of whether they were in Brussels or Stockholm, people would approach him to say hello all the time, people she knew nothing about. For a few seconds Johan seemed to be turning through a huge, internal Rolodex. No, he said finally. Not someone he knew.

"Are you sure?"

He looked at the picture again, and shook his head. "Why do you want to know?"

"He was the one who contacted me in Brussels."

Johan Eriksson examined the picture again. No, he didn't recognize him.

"Quite sure?"

He shook his head once again. "Sorry."

She put away her cell and looked across Gärdet. An Irish set-ter was running around on the wide expanse of grass and sniffing at things. It was Johan's dog, sorrowfully looking for a tennis ball that he had thrown. Carina struggled to rein in her disappointment. Deep down, she had hoped Johan Eriksson would exclaim, "Oh, him!" Like he normally did.

"So it's him who has caused all this trouble for you?"

She nodded.

There was a cold wind. After a while, the dog rushed back with the ball in his mouth. Johan threw it again. What was she going to do, then? he wondered. Was she going to contact him?

"I have to get hold of him," she said.

"And then what will you do?"

"We'll see."

"People are talking about you," he said, after a while.

"What are they saying?"

Johan Eriksson sighed. "You know. Bullshit. Like, that you were working on behalf of someone else."

"What? For who?"

"A foreign power." He laughed uncomfortably.

"Who thinks that?"

"The management."

They looked at the dog in silence, a distant dot on the grass.

"It's not true. You know that, don't you?"

"I know," he said slowly. "You don't make mistakes like that."

Johan was probably her last friend at the department. Most peo-ple would eventually see her as guilty. But Johan Eriksson knew her too well; they'd worked together closely. He would never distrust her.

"You might not know this," he said after a pause, "but I almost got sacked four years ago."

He had been in Kosovo with a Swedish delegation. They'd had meetings with KFOR, with the EU, and with the new government. The entire delegation was staying at the old Grand Hotel in Pristina and the hotel was ice cold. Every day they'd spend half the night in the bar, because it was the only place in the whole hotel that was heated, possibly the only place in all of Pristina. One evening, a guy showed up there and had a few beers with them. He was an American—aid worker; nice guy; talkative—had been in Kosovo for three years. Before he left, he gave them a report.

"It was a CIA product. It showed that several ministries in Kosovo were involved in drug smuggling and that people at the EU office were acting as middlemen."

"What did you do?"

"I showed the report to the management back at home. They told me to forget about it and threatened me with suspension. Do you understand what I'm saying?" He looked at her seriously. "Bad timing. The EU had taken over after the UN's failure in Kosovo. Everything was a fucking mess and it was crucial for the EU to show it was possible to change the country. A disclosure like that would have destroyed all confidence in the EU. It would have been a catastrophe."

"They probably deserved it."

"Of course." He shrugged his shoulders. "But who cares about justice? That's never been a priority."

13

Stockholm, Thursday, September 29

A concentrated calm prevailed over the technical unit of the Security Service in Stockholm. Bente had brought dinner, which she had eaten in one of the computer labs, sitting at a computer in the chilly room. Occasionally someone would pass by on the other side of the frosted glass, which looked into the corridor.

The benches held measuring instruments, and some computers hummed. On one trolley was Carina Dymek's computer. The technicians had removed the hard-disk casing and exposed the electronics; the machine was a mere tangle of wires and circuit boards.

They had gone to the MFA at lunchtime and the contents of Dymek's office had now been sorted into around twenty plastic bags, which were standing in the room next door. The report was no longer there; they had quickly established that. Not the original or any copies.

After taking apart Dymek's computer, the technicians had brought up all the raw data; they sorted her files, retrieved her Internet history, recreated deleted documents, and searched the hard drive for encrypted information, hidden codes in picture and sound files.

Carina Dymek's hard drive was very messy. The overwhelming impression was that she was an unstructured person. Thousands of documents were sorted in what was, presumably, a unique order that only Dymek knew, under a range of different subjects, in hundreds of folders, dating back years. Bente clicked back and forth through the documents, opening and closing files at a brisk pace, occasionally stopping to read a paragraph in a memo written by Dymek. She had a driven, exacting style—straight to the point, no funny business. These were the traces of a hard-working young diplomat.

It was almost nine when she stopped for a break. The corridors lay empty. Two technicians were still in the room next door, running an analysis on Dymek's Internet history. Bente got a coffee and joined them.

She liked technicians. They had the kind of practical skills that analysts lacked. They could sift for fresh information that moved an operation forward. What they did was disentangle names, times, IP addresses, and hundreds of other parameters, before doing a huge jigsaw puzzle to find out how it was all connected. With the help of the technicians, you could see a pattern, identify relationships, habits, risky behavior, and threats.

"Here's Dymek's web traffic. At least the traffic that was on the government's port eighty," one of them explained.

The logs were there—every occasion that Carina Dymek had gone online, neatly recorded. The screen was filled with rows of Internet addresses and technical data, dates and times, movement through pages. This was Dymek's digital existence for the past six months, everything she had visited on the Internet from her work computer. The rows ran down the screen, quickly, like a manic demon knitting a furious stream of characters. She could distinguish different addresses: Stratfor, Hotmail, BBC, state.gov.

Dymek had regular habits; tracking her behavior was like following an even diurnal cycle. Every morning, she logged in at the same time, plus or minus fifteen minutes. Almost no casual browsing; no unusual addresses. She usually checked her private e-mail account between ten and twenty minutes before starting work. During the day, she spent half an hour on different news sites, both Swedish and international. In the afternoon, she would log in briefly on various websites for think tanks. Foreign affairs, Stratfor, Crisis group. All work related. Every day, there were constant log-ins to EU pages.

Bente leaned forward. It ought to be quick to discern any deviations. All organizations checked their employees, and the Government Offices were stricter than most. They ran automated checks
on civil servants' computers and, when they discovered suspicious
behavior, it was standard procedure to observe the employee to
establish whether there was a threat. Deviations were always visible.
But Dymek's Internet history showed no signs of abnormal activity,
nothing that shouldn't be there. Just like her hard drive. The government's servers had also been intact throughout the entire period,
explained one of the technicians. The detectors on the outside of the
network's firewalls and in what was referred to as the demilitarized
zone—for example, the router circuitry—were all working properly.
The encryption system for documents had not raised any alarms
about intrusions; the firewalls were all up. The report had not been
downloaded.

The technician pointed at the screen. They had discovered something that was possibly of interest. About a week ago, she had visited
various websites for hotels in Cairo.

Cairo.

It might just be a holiday. A desk officer spending an hour at
work organizing their vacation was no crime.

Two investigators from Counterespionage had interviewed
Dymek's line manager, Anders Wahlund. According to him, Dymek
appeared not to have understood why she was being suspended. So
what was Carina Dymek up to? All Bente could see was the blank
and uninteresting image of a proficient civil servant doing nothing
other than her job. She didn't believe in coincidences—there were
always intentions and motives behind even the most seemingly coincidental events. Why had someone like Carina Dymek made such
a rudimentary error as handling unauthorized classified material?
How could she have messed up so badly that she was suspended?
Either she was misguided, which didn't seem very likely—Dymek
had been well appraised and described as an analytical person—or,
more worryingly, she was being driven by a conviction that she
was right. An ideology. But what ideology, in her case? Nothing in

Dymek's profile suggested she was the extreme type. Engaged, certainly, but not a person with extreme views. Nothing in her history suggested criminality. Green had called her a "clean skin," beyond all suspicion, but that of being in the service of a foreign power. An anomaly; a hidden threat. Several of the investigators at Counterespionage believed the same thing. But it seemed far-fetched that Dymek would work for a foreign power. Then again, who knew? Perhaps she was living a double life. People had a tremendous ability to hide things.

Dymek had told of a contact in Brussels, but it had not yet been possible to verify the story. It could be an outright lie, or at least a distortion of what had really happened in Brussels. Sticking close to the truth was a common way to lie convincingly. But why would Dymek lie? She thought about Green and his concerns about the leak, and was once against reminded that, of all people, London had decided to send Roger Wilson. Why send Wilson? He was a bulldozer . . .

Something in the overall picture didn't make sense. But Bente couldn't grasp what it was that was disturbing her; like a vague itch, it was impossible to pinpoint where the problem lay. She called Kempell and left a message on his cell. They needed to bring Dymek in for a chat. Then she called Mikael; he was still at the office.

"We need to find the man in Brussels," she said. "The one who was in contact with Dymek."

14

Stockholm, Friday, September 30

A hesitant drizzle was falling on Stockholm when Bente hurried out of the gateway from her temporary, protected address, close to Karlaplan. She was normally accommodated here on her longer visits to Stockholm. She had stayed with the technicians until midnight and needed coffee. On the drive to the Security Service headquarters, she pulled up at a convenience store on Karlavägen and bought a cappuccino and bagel.

It was early on a Friday morning and the streets were still deserted. The day would start soon, but right now there was not a soul to be seen. The bars down on Stureplan had closed just a few hours ago and had turned the square into an empty, gaping hole. The odd taxi rolled slowly past the pedestrian crossings.

Stockholm was her home city, but nowadays she felt more at home in Brussels. Stockholm didn't have the same finesse or elegance as the Belgian capital. Not to mention Vienna. She loved Vienna. That was truly a city of style and good taste. Her time there as liaison officer had been wonderful.

She drove up Kungsgatan, past the dark shops and bars, and continued to Kungsholmen and the looming police building with its somewhat suburban style that she always thought looked so very ugly.

Kempell and his team were waiting for her on the eighth floor.

"Is he here?" Bente asked.

"He's arriving at nine twenty. Traveling under the name of Oliver Hollington."

Roger Wilson was on the morning flight via Copenhagen. She hadn't expected him to come so soon, but it was just as well. The earlier, the better. That Wilson was traveling under the name of Hollington was a good sign. Hollington was one of his aliases that they were familiar with. That meant he wanted them to discover him. London had even notified them, earlier in the morning, of the flight on which he was arriving. The Brits were coming to cooperate.

In Counterespionage, they did a quick rundown of what they knew. The flight time had been confirmed with Arlanda airport and they had confirmed that Wilson had checked in. He wasn't traveling alone—a further two people were reported to be accompanying him.

"What do we know about their intentions?"

The investigator, whom everyone simply called Joakim and who seemed to be the one managing contact with London, fidgeted. The British objectives for the meeting were no clearer now than they had been twenty-four hours previously. They probably wanted to cooperate, he said feebly.

Kempell muttered into his coffee cup. "Probably?" He needed facts, not supposition.

He was in a bad mood, and Bente could understand why. Wilson wasn't coming to Stockholm to listen to them. He was coming to Stockholm because the British security services were on to something, and a visit to Stockholm was one stage in an operation being controlled from London. They couldn't do anything except sit nicely and wait until Her Majesty's envoy deigned to meet them. The Brits were in charge. That annoyed her, too.

Of course the Brits were directing their attention at Stockholm. The FRA had received a request from the British to conduct signals intelligence on Swedish networks. Perhaps London had discovered something.

Government Communications Headquarters in Britain was the leader in signals intelligence. They had the ability to search the global flow of information in a way that only the Americans could match. GCHQ often worked closely with British foreign intelligence, MI6, and with the British security service, MI5, particularly in counter-terrorism matters. The Brits had a wealth of experience in filtering through massive quantities of data as part of their operations. It produced results. They had the capacity to follow thousands of jihadists around the globe like a shadow; they could make millions of simultaneous intrusions; they could process data from surveillance footage, cells and cable traffic from millions of sources so quickly that action could be taken within mere hours of the initial discovery of a watched individual at a border control, on the subway, in a café.

"They want to listen in on Sweden."

"Are they looking for targets?" Joakim asked.

"I recommend everyone to take a sensitive approach to Wilson. And also listen to what he doesn't say," said Kempell, as if he hadn't heard the question. He looked at the time. "They'll be here in two hours."

The meeting dispersed; everyone disappeared into the corridors. Bente accompanied Kempell in the elevator to the top floor. They exited on to the roof through a fire door.

From here, there was an expansive view stretching for miles across the treetops of Kronobergsparken. It had stopped raining but there was a cold breeze. High cumulus clouds were racing across the Stockholm sky.

"I'm looking forward to meeting him," she said.

Kempell was silent and lit a cigarette. The ventilation ducts around them hummed quietly. To him, Wilson was just a concern, but for her he was an equal, one who went unseen. Wilson was one of the truly hidden operatives in this industry, one of MI6's special resources.

The Brits were good at masking their agents—it had taken Swedish Counterespionage several years to ascertain who Wilson actually was. He had turned up four years earlier, in Denmark, as a consultant to the Danish International Development Agency. That was where he first crossed their radar. PET, the Danish security service, had tipped them off about the Brit. But then he had disappeared and it had been around a year before they had another chance to study him at close quarters, this time in Hamburg, a few years after the Madison Garden bomber. Wilson followed a trail that led to a logistical cell with connections to al-Qaida in Saudi Arabia and Pakistan. For the first time, they understood what he was. In hindsight, they also came to realize that MI6 had let them understand who he was. London had let them in on a small secret because it suited them, because they wanted to involve their Scandinavian siblings.

Roger Wilson was a man hunter. He worked globally, and was one of the toughest out there. As far as she knew, he had previously had a key role in domestic counterterrorism at MI5, as part of Operation Kratos, in which operations used lethal force. There were unconfirmed reports that Wilson and his team were responsible for the botched operation that ended with the Brazilian, Menezes, having his head blown off on the London underground in 2005—an operation that SO19 had taken the blame for. The rest of his background was unclear. Welsh descent. Military background in the Special Air Service. Spent four years in Peshawar and completed several tours of duty in southern Afghanistan as the coordinator for British counterterrorism. Before that, Indonesia, Kenya, Sierra Leone, the Falklands.

Kempell inhaled deeply. "I don't understand what his business is here."

Just before eleven, a loud voice could be heard in the corridor. Kempell and the two investigators from Counterespionage, Joakim and Lars, who were sitting and talking with Bente in low voices, fell silent and stood up. The security doors clicked open and Roger Wilson marched into the conference room, followed by a young woman with her blond hair held up in a French twist. She was new; perhaps she was an operative.

"Good morning, madam!" he burst out and threw his arms wide open. "Great to see you again."

"Good morning, Roger." Bente introduced him to Kempell, who looked like a piece of dry driftwood next to the full-bodied Brit.

She had forgotten how enormous he was. Not particularly tall, but wide-shouldered and thickset like a bull, with a broad, fairly handsome face and a powerful jaw that looked like it could bite through a saucepan. He was wearing a moss-green oilskin coat with a corduroy collar, chinos, and sturdy shoes; he looked like he had come to Sweden to go walking in the wilderness. In another life, he might have become a certified forester. He shrugged off his coat and threw it on to a chair.

"Welcome to Stockholm," Bente said and she offered them something to drink—tea, coffee, water.

An assistant poured coffee for everyone. The new woman merely nodded at them and sat down on a chair, waiting. She had an unmoving, tough face. Wilson briefly introduced her as Sarah, and the woman, whose name was almost certainly not Sarah, flashed a smile at them.

Wilson was far more exuberant. He greeted everyone with brisk, hearty handshakes. Lovely to be in Stockholm. Yes, thanks, the flight had been fine. He laughed, as if someone had said something funny.

"You really do have some fancy digs here," said Wilson, straightening his ill-fitting blazer and looking around with a wide smile while stirring his coffee. The Security Service headquarters on Kungsholmen had been refurbished the month before, at the same time as undergoing a security upgrade. The Brits probably knew that.

Bente nodded and agreed. "Once again, welcome," she said once everyone was seated. "It's good that we can meet."

"Wasn't the last time in Hamburg?" interrupted Wilson cheerfully.

"Yes, that's right."

"And now Stockholm."

Everyone waited. Wilson stroked his chin and observed the Swedes surrounding him with an empty smile.

Wilson was no office worker. He wore the jacket like a foreign object. He was tanned and his hands, which lay quite still on the table, were rough and had thick nails. It was easy to imagine him in the rugged mountains of northern Pakistan in khaki camouflage fatigues, an assault rifle slung over his shoulder, surrounded by Pashto-speaking guides and fellow commandos.

"Okay. You probably know why I'm here," he said, almost apologetically.

"Due to the incident: the leak," said Bente.

"Leak?"

For a long moment dead silence fell on the room. Everyone around the table stopped what they were doing. Wilson was sitting opposite them with his eyebrows raised in surprise; he didn't seem to have understood what she meant. The woman introduced as Sarah stopped taking notes. Wilson turned to Kempell and said, with a smile, "I don't understand . . ."

"Well . . ." For a fraction of a second, Kempell lost his thread completely, before quickly regaining his composure. "The report concerning EIS that the Commission was working on, which has now leaked to one of our diplomats," he said.

"Yes, yes! Of course," Wilson exclaimed and nodded forcefully. "That story. I assume you have started to look more closely at . . ." He stopped and looked down at his papers. "Dymek. Carina Dymek. Is that right?"

"Yes," said Kempell. "We're investigating her."

"Good, good." Wilson smiled.

Something wasn't right. Wilson was too restless. He seemed strangely distanced, as if he simply didn't care what they were talking about.

"Are you looking into anyone else as part of this?"

"No, not yet."

"I understand."

Everyone now looked at Wilson, who was nodding slowly to himself.

"It's a good idea to deal with the leak, naturally," he said languidly. "But let's leave it at that for a while. That diplomat, Dymek— she isn't the real problem. She's just a girl who's fallen in with the wrong crowd."

Dead silence fell on the room. He *didn't* want to talk about Dymek? A scurrying sensation ran across Bente's back. They had missed something.

Wilson leafed through his papers and then said in a businesslike tone, "What do you have on Jamal Badawi?"

"Badawi?" Bente looked at Kempell, then back to Wilson. "He's Dymek's boyfriend. Works for the Ministry of Justice." She hadn't expected questions about the boyfriend.

"Yes, that's one side of him."

The investigators from Counterespionage glanced anxiously at her and Kempell. Wilson turned to the woman beside him, who had sat silently throughout so far, and nodded. She opened a file and read rapidly from the document.

"This is Jamal Badawi." She placed an enlarged passport photo of him on the table. "Jamal Badawi: thirty-two years old; Swedish citizen of Egyptian origin. Left Egypt at ten years old and was granted asylum in Sweden together with his parents. Lives in Stockholm and currently employed at your Ministry of Justice. All of this you are aware of."

Wilson interjected with a smile. "We almost missed him too, at first. But we wanted to be sure there was no Islamist connection. I mean, he is an Arab. It's standard procedure. But what we discovered was far more than we had imagined."

The woman from MI6 resumed her presentation. "Jamal Badawi's family were part of the opposition to Hosni Mubarak. His father and uncle had close ties to the Muslim Brotherhood for decades. It's worth mentioning that the father, who was a lawyer, represented several of the best-known critics of the regime in various trials in the years before the family left Cairo and Egypt. He and Jamal Badawi's uncle were close friends with key persons in the Muslim Brotherhood—for example, Aboul-Fotouh and Mahdi Akef—people at the top of the organization. For many years, Badawi's uncle was even a contact for Hezbollah. Then the Badawi family fled—all of them, except the uncle, Akim Badawi, who stayed in Cairo. After the Badawi family arrived in Sweden, the father died. But Jamal Badawi stayed in touch with his uncle Akim."

She produced a new photograph and put it on the table next to the one of Jamal Badawi. Akim Badawi was a fat man with a small, well-groomed beard around his chin.

"At the same time as Jamal Badawi came to Sweden, Akim Badawi was appointed as the trustee of a number of foundations. The Brotherhood has hundreds of foundations that receive funds through donations, collections, and certain property deals in Europe and North America. As you know, it's difficult to tell which of these are for entirely legitimate purposes and which provide funds for terrorism. Transactions in cases like these often occur through a long chain of middlemen, companies, temporary offices, or in cash. We have been able to trace funds from several of the foundations that Akim Badawi looked after to groups in the UK—Luton; Birmingham. The money also appears to have been used for training camps. It was through our financial analysis of the Brotherhood that our attention was drawn to Akim Badawi."

"Appears to have?" said Bente.

The woman looked up from her papers and gazed at her coolly. "We have evidence to suggest that. The contacts Akim Badawi had were all people from groups on watch lists—contacts he continues to maintain to this day."

"Excuse me," interrupted Kempell. "Is this not a matter for Counterterrorism?" He looked around at Bente and the British visitors. "So far I haven't heard anything that directly affects the operations I am responsible for, anything to do with Counterespionage."

Wilson nodded and spread out his hands. "I'm sorry. I got the impression that London had already spoken to you. Mea culpa, I guess. But I hope that you will pass on the relevant information to your colleagues working in the fight against terror?"

"Yes. Of course."

Kempell looked around in annoyance. Lars stood up and left the room to call someone in from the Counterterrorism branch.

For a while there was a tense silence during which no one seemed to know whether the meeting should continue. This was an unexpected and embarrassing turn of events. Kempell had no right to deal with the case alone. In the new division of responsibilities in the Security Service, he was obligated to coordinate with Counterterrorism and hand over jurisdiction to them if an investigation took the direction that this one appeared to be taking.

Wilson leaned toward Sarah and said something into her ear. Kempell and Joakim, the investigator who had stayed behind, sat still, as if carved from stone, surreptitiously watching the exchange between the Brits in silence. Finally, Kempell made a small gesture toward the visitors and muttered that they should continue.

"Okay," said Wilson with gusto. "Absolutely."

The MI6 woman sat up and straightened her papers. "We have been monitoring Akim Badawi and those around him for some time. It wouldn't affect you or Sweden if it weren't for one thing: this man appears in several of our terrorism investigations. And, about three months ago, Akim Badawi contacted his nephew, Jamal. We intercepted an e-mail."

"An e-mail?"

"Yes. A message to Jamal Badawi."

Wilson leaned forward and passed a piece of paper to Kempell, who glanced through it and passed it to Joakim.

"We should probably go through this letter more thoroughly later," said Wilson, "when your colleagues from Counterterrorism are present."

"And this . . . letter," said Kempell, looking skeptically and the two Brits, "has made you suspicious of Jamal Badawi. Is that right?"

"Yes," said Wilson. "That's about right."

Everyone stared at the two Brits.

"You mean that the leaked report . . . that it was on the orders of certain individuals in the Muslim Brotherhood? Is that what you mean?"

"There's a lot to suggest that."

Good God. Bente shut her eyes for a moment and rubbed her face.

She had wondered why London had sent one of their counter-terrorism specialists, but now she understood. She observed the MI6 woman, who straightened some papers in front of her. Wilson leaned back and looked at the Swedes opposite. It was clear that the Brits knew what they were talking about. Dymek wasn't the target—she was just a courier—the person of interest was Jamal Badawi.

"Why would Akim contact his nephew?" she said.

"Jamal Badawi is well placed, I assume."

"So he's meant to be an infiltrator?"

"We don't know," said Wilson. "But he's in your system."

"We check all employees close to the government," interrupted Kempell.

"We're not suggesting you've failed in your security checks. We're just telling it as it is." Wilson shrugged his shoulders.

There was quiet. For a moment, the far-away traffic was audible, even through the dirt-speckled bulletproof windows.

"This is very . . . dramatic information," said Kempell slowly. At first it seemed as if he was about to add something, but then he stopped and a sharp crease formed on his forehead. An intense thought process seemed to occupy him. He looked to the ceiling, first to the right, then to the left, while everyone waited.

This wasn't okay; Bente hated it when meetings ground to a halt. Kempell just sat in his chair, fingering the investigation the Brits had handed them. He was quiet; he seemed to have withdrawn into his own thoughts. She turned to Wilson.

"What you're saying paints a whole new picture of the threat. It means that we're potentially dealing with terrorism, right?"

They looked at her.

"We're grateful for this information," she continued. "But we need to take it to our chiefs."

Wilson raised his hand. Absolutely, absolutely.

"How long will you be in Sweden for?"

"As long as is necessary. You can contact me on this number." He held out a card.

She envied the British and their way of controlling events. Being able to give and take, being able to enforce their will. They created the weather of tomorrow, while the Swedes were forced to guess the forecast.

"And your signals intelligence is actionable?"

"Yes," said Wilson in a surprised tone, as if it was a dumb question. "We're listening to everything being said in Cairo."

Bente smiled. And in Stockholm, but out of politeness he didn't say that.

"I would like to provide you with access to our signals intelligence. Can you let us know how we can contact you in Brussels?"

Bente wrote down a number for the Section in Brussels and handed the note over to Sarah. The number would lead to the Section's inbox—an answering machine with no recorded greeting. Anyone who called it was, after a number of security checks, permitted to speak to Mikael, or another coordinator, who returned the call.

Wilson nodded with a smile. "And if I might make a suggestion . . . ?"

"Naturally."

"Dymek. She's Badawi's little girlfriend. Use her. Let her lead us to the bigger fish. Then we'll bring her in. We can always get her to talk."

"I'm not sure what you mean, Wilson."

"A conversation, Bente. Just a conversation. Jesus Christ, I'm not proposing that we give her suppositories and fly her to Damascus."

"Okay."

"I suggest that we prioritize the Arab. Focus on Jamal Badawi, study him, and see what he does. He's just a little shit in the grand scheme of things. Akim is the target. If we handle this right, his nephew can lead us into the Brotherhood. And our primary way in to him is through this diplomat, Carina Dymek."

Wilson was right. Carina Dymek was useful, if she played along. They needed to talk to her and get her to understand the threat, appeal to her loyalty and sense of duty; she did, after all, work for the Swedish Ministry of Foreign Affairs—for Sweden. Now she was suspended, and probably worried and angry; perhaps they could offer a solution to the suspension and arrange a promotion, if she cooperated. Anything was possible. Bente thought for a moment. There would be ways in to Dymek, ways to get her to understand the threat, ways to make her willing to cooperate; what mattered was making contact with her and getting her to act under their orders so that Badawi didn't suspect anything. Then bring Badawi in when they knew more, when he was surrounded and had no other options, and get him to talk, sing to them all he knew. It was elegant. She caught herself smiling and immediately pulled her face together.

The Brits already had the case in hand; they would be forced to let them in on this. In reality, it was already a British operation. But they didn't have much choice in the matter; they needed London's intelligence. And Stockholm needed good relations with London, as Kempell had pointed out earlier. This story was just a fraction of a decades-long conversation.

"We welcome your cooperation. But we need to be on the same page."

"You mean the two Badawis?"

"Yes."

"Certainly. We'll give you what we have."

Wilson looked cheerfully at her and then at Kempell. The woman, Sarah, made a small note. "Excellent!" Wilson slapped his broad hands together. "Let's get to work."

15

Stockholm, Friday, September 30

They had agreed to meet at Mäster Anders and Carina was five minutes late. The spacious, warm bistro was booming with the sound of the many guests trying to drown out each other's voices.

She looked around the room and spotted Jamal at a table in a far corner with a glass of wine. He was always punctual. She couldn't help but stop and look at him for a moment. There he was, sitting and waiting for *her*. He had come to mean so much to her that she could barely believe that they had only met by coincidence.

They had had their first proper date here, at Mäster Anders. She would always associate the bistro, its egg-yolk yellow tiled walls and large mirrors, with Jamal—with a time of happiness. For a moment, the Ministry, the report, and everything else meant nothing.

She made her way to the table. When he caught sight of her he stood up, like a gentleman of the old school, and she liked it—a little against her own will. She hugged him and kissed him for a long time. They hadn't seen each other for several days and a funny kind of shyness came over them when they let go of each other. There was so much to say that they didn't quite know how to start talking about what had happened; instead, they merely smiled at each other and engrossed themselves in the menus. After they had ordered food, he asked her carefully how she felt, if she had heard anything from the MFA.

"No, nothing." There wasn't much to tell. She didn't really want to think about it now; she just wanted a break from it all for a bit and to be there, in the moment, with him.

Jamal sat before her, looking handsome, dressed formally, as always, in a shirt and dark suit with a dark-colored Italian tie. He looked so calm. Mäster Anders was somewhere he felt able to relax, he had said. If you were well dressed then, here, you were just one among the many, and that was exactly what he wanted. She absorbed him with her eyes and decided to remember this picture forever. For a second, she considered saying nothing more about the report, but she could see that Jamal was curious. He knew that she was thinking about something she didn't want to say; he was like that—he noticed these things. There was no point in pretending, either; there was nothing that would make her change her mind now. She was going to Brussels to look for the man who called himself Jean, to make him understand what sort of position he had put her in by giving her that damn report, to persuade him, get him to understand that it had been wrong to pull her into this, even if she did have a conscience. She needed to make him understand that she was just a normal civil servant. As if it was quite unimportant, she said, finally, "I've decided what I'm going to do."

"Oh?"

"I'm going to go to Brussels and talk to the man who gave me the report."

Jamal looked at her thoughtfully but said nothing.

"He's the only one who can prove I'm telling the truth," she continued. "What's more, I want to know what this proposal is really all about."

Jamal pursed his lips. They sat in silence and drank wine, watching other guests around the room. Finally, after the food had arrived, he said, "But if you go to Brussels . . . don't you risk looking more suspicious?"

"I don't think I can be under any more suspicion, Jamal."

He looked down at his plate and carried on eating.

"I requested those documents from the archives, by the way," he said after a while.

"Did you? Thank you, darling." She leaned forward and stroked his hand.

"It's sensitive material." He sighed.

"I know."

"You have to be careful, my love."

Yes, she would be careful. But at the same time, what did she have to lose? If she didn't do something, they would never believe her.

Jamal looked at her with concern.

"I asked a friend to help me find him."

"A friend?"

"Greger."

"Greger?" For the first time the steady, calm expression on Jamal's face fell away. "The computer guy?"

"Apparently, he knows someone who . . ." She stopped herself, because what she was about to say sounded strange to her ears. "Well, he can do stuff like that."

Jamal looked at her with raised eyebrows.

"He said he can find him—Jean."

"But tracking someone down . . . That's illegal." Jamal shook his head and said through clenched teeth, in a low voice, "Carina—think."

Think. As if she hadn't already done so. He had no right to rebuke her. She was almost tempted, out of pure spite, just to provoke him, to say she was going to give Greger a copy of the report. But she stopped herself. She needed Jamal; he couldn't turn his back on her. She knew how careful he was. They were similar, had both studied law. Breaking the law wasn't in their nature. The difference was that she was fighting not to be left in the cold. And she had read the report, and something in it had made her recoil.

"I have to get hold of him, Jamal."

"I understand. But doing things like that . . . doesn't help."

"You mean illegal things."

"Yes."

She hesitated. She wanted to believe him, but she knew that he was wrong. She reached for her wine glass and drank deeply. They sat in silence.

"What are you thinking about?"

"About Brussels." She looked around the noisy room. She was thinking about what the man, Jean, had said—that she had a conscience. It had annoyed her that he had inferred things about her; it was meddlesome. But he had been right: she did have a conscience.

"When I read the report . . . It's such an awful proposal. He was right," she said, "the guy who gave me the report. It's not something the EU should accept."

"Carina"—Jamal leaned forward, took her hands in his—"think carefully. Don't bring emotion into this. What you feel may be right, but take it easy."

"I know what I'm doing."

"But if you don't want to burn all your bridges, at least keep Greger out of it."

"Why?"

"Tracking people . . ."

"He's a friend and I trust him."

"More than me?" Jamal's dark eyes were looking straight at her. He was sitting quite still, as if trapped in his suit. She could have just reached forward with her hand and said something, something small to make him calm down. But she didn't want to ask for forgiveness; it wasn't her turn to say sorry. A bitter sadness stung her insides. Wasn't he listening? He shook his head.

"Don't be silly," Carina said.

Jamal took an angry swig of wine. He tapped the table hard with his index finger. "You should've talked to me."

"I did. I am right now."

He wasn't listening. "That report," Jamal continued irritably, "it's green-stamped, isn't it? Your pal, Greger, doesn't have that level of security clearance, right?" He looked straight at her. "He doesn't even have the right to hear you whisper about material like that. And you know it."

She was silent.

"I think it's really very unwise to look for this man in Brussels. There must be other ways. It's confused enough already—"

"It's not me who has confused matters," she interrupted him. "Okay?"

The sadness and anger heaved out of her. She didn't want to feel like that. She wanted to be happy with Jamal, but couldn't deny the anger welling up inside her.

"I just tried to do the right thing. I can't help it that he gave me that fucking report. I was *approached*. And for some reason that leaves me out in the cold. I was just trying to do my fucking job."

The people at the next table glanced at them, Jamal turned toward them and they immediately looked away. "I know," he said in a low voice.

She wasn't so sure he did. But she had no desire to hurt him; he meant well, even if he didn't understand.

"I have to get hold of that man. That's just how it is. And"—she looked around the lovely dining room—"that report has no business masquerading as a part of European democracy." It had been said. She took a deep gulp of her wine. "Greger can help me."

"I can too."

"Can you?"

Jamal looked right at her. He didn't answer the question but instead said seriously, "There are lots of other ways to deal with this situation, Carina. And I care about you a lot. You know that."

They were lying in Jamal's bed; it was just after midnight. They had made love, hard—more intensely than for a long time. He had gotten so far inside her in a way that made her scream and want to bite him. She felt calm and serious, as if a deep sadness had only now come to the surface.

They kissed. Then he got up to fetch them each a glass of wine. He went to the kitchen, took the bottle out of the fridge, and returned with two glasses.

"What's that book?" Carina asked.

It was the small, worn yellow book that she had found next to the sofa a week ago. Now it was on his bedside table. She snatched it up and flipped through the pages.

"That?" He gave an embarrassed smile. "A poetry anthology. I got it a long time ago." He took the book from Carina and turned its pages; he seemed unable to decide whether he liked talking about it or not. "They're poems by Ibn 'Arabi. Do you know him?"

She had to say no, she didn't know who that was.

"Muhyiddin Ibn 'Arabi—an old Sufi master."

She nodded. He carried on turning the book's pages, casting an eye at her, cautiously, as if trying to decide whether she thought he was silly. Or as if he was in some way worried. She stayed silent. Something told her that she was, quite unexpectedly, very close to a hidden part of Jamal, a part that had lain buried within him behind rows of closed doors. Every word she uttered now would make him stop and shake off the situation, laugh—bat everything away in a heartbeat. She sat quite still and waited.

"My uncle likes the Sufis," he said with an empty laugh.

She nodded. So he had an uncle.

"I got it as a birthday present when I turned ten. Give a ten-year-old a poetry anthology by a medieval Sufi poet." Jamal laughed again in the same dry way, like a snort, and became serious. He fingered the book. "He said it was a book I would find useful as I got older . . . and lived far away," he continued quietly. "He was right."

Jamal turned the pages slowly, quietly, as if swathes of thoughts were passing through his mind, unsaid. "It's a special book." He looked at her with an oddly sorrowful gaze. "I've never shown it to anyone."

She nodded. "Sorry, I—"

"No," he interrupted. "It's fine. You don't have to apologize. You weren't to know. And, as it's you, it's fine anyway. You're not just anyone. You mean so much to me."

Could he read her something from it?

At first he was embarrassed by the question. No, he laughed, he was terrible at reading aloud. "It's in Arabic. You won't understand any of it."

"Read it anyway. I want to hear it."

He looked at her, as if weighing her up with his eyes, judging whether he could trust her. Then he shrugged his shoulders and turned the pages of the book. Finally, he settled on a poem. He chose the one that was underlined at the end.

"I don't know what it's called in Swedish," he muttered. "Doesn't matter."

He sat quietly and gathered himself. Then he began to read. The words and sounds that came from his lips were completely alien to her. He read slowly to begin with, clearing his throat and seeming to struggle. But after a while he got into the rhythm of the poem and words flowed out in waves of beautiful rhyming sounds, braided together intricately, the meaning of which she could only guess. It was so strange and so beautiful to hear the melodic Arabic coming from his mouth. It was his language; it had been there inside him all along. He read with a concentrated gravity, an intense glow she had never seen before and she loved him for it. There was so much about him she wanted to know.

He stopped. The poem was finished. He shut the book, laughed self-consciously again and put it to one side, reaching for his glass.

"You read so beautifully."

"Do you think so?"

He was sweet when he was embarrassed. Reading the poem had put him in a good mood. The subdued, strange atmosphere between them was gone.

"It's a beautiful poem," he said. "A love poem. It's about always finding home, if you carry love with you. It's obviously the love of God he's talking about, but also that of the woman he loves. It's written as a story about a man who travels through the desert, missing home and remembering his loved one. Here." Jamal pointed at the book, trying to translate. "'When you see the campfires, your desire will grow into a raging blaze. Do not be afraid of their lions. Your desire will show them to be cubs.' Something like that. I can't translate it properly; it's much better in Arabic," he said and put his wine glass down. He read the lines again in Arabic.

"You read well."

Once again she felt happy to be lying next to a beautiful man who read Arabic love poems. Suddenly, she turned toward Jamal and kissed him.

Carina stretched out an arm and felt Jamal's warm body next to her. The room was dark but she didn't need to see him, just feel him close by and hear his breathing. He smelled so good. It was a calm smell of skin, a little salty.

They were lying beside each other and couldn't sleep. Not yet. Neither wanted to glide away from the other and let the tranquil hours of the night disappear in the blink of an eye. Instead, they lay there and talked, quietly, with long pauses, in the darkness.

He told her about Egypt, about Cairo. Things she had never heard him say before, perhaps things he had never told anyone before. She almost hoped so—hoped she was the first to have reached his secrets.

In Cairo, he had lived with his mother and father, his sister and his grandmother in a spacious apartment in the suburbs—Masr el-Gedida. He remembered the apartment and the fine, old building, built in a European style—a large, shadowy apartment, where his ancient grandmother, now long since passed away, wandered around closing the shutters in the middle of the day to keep out the heat and dust. When the shutters were closed, you had to talk quietly so as not to disturb Grandmother, who was sleeping. During those afternoon hours, he would creep around by himself, pretending he was in a labyrinth, sliding around the parquet floor, or he would lie in his room and read. He liked *Robinson Crusoe*. They had a lot of books at home, he remembered. He went to school in Cairo before he came to Sweden. But he didn't remember much about school. There were only boys in his class, and one of his best friends was a little boy called Alaa, but everyone called him the Sparrow. They had white school uniforms and his sister used to tell him off when he got his dirty. They played a lot, ran around the neighborhood surrounding the school, knew every tiny street and alleyway off the large avenue that ran alongside of the wall that surrounded the school. In the summer, the air between the houses was always perfectly still. The sun was so strong in the middle of the day that no one went outside, only Jamal and his friends: the Sparrow, Hossam, and some others whose names he couldn't remember. In the older blocks, in the alleys, you could get lost and find the strangest things. The city was never-ending.

Carina shut her eyes and listened. Jamal told her about his father. Sometimes he was allowed to accompany him to the law firm at the weekends. He was just a little boy, ten years old, and he would sit in an armchair and wait while his father worked at his desk or spoke on the phone. When he got bored, he would wander around the quiet, cool rooms in the small office and examine things. He remembered that difference between inside and out, the cool rooms and the white midday heat pressing against the shutters. They didn't leave Egypt until three years later. In the afternoons, they would normally run errands in the city center. Sometimes his father would meet colleagues at Al-Azhar University and drink coffee with them while Jamal sat and listened or played nearby. His father was kind, but apparently a lot of people didn't like him because, as a lawyer, he had taken on several clients who criticized Mubarak. The phone began to ring at night. One day his father found his office had been torn apart. They stopped going to the university and drinking coffee—it was too dangerous, they explained to him. Even his uncle, Akim, was threatened; after a gang of militiamen broke in at night and assaulted him and his wife, he went into hiding. Everyone was afraid. Jamal remembered how his parents sat up late at night talking, how his mother told him to come straight home from school, how she cried when she thought he wasn't watching. It became dangerous to remain in Cairo. Few came to visit.

Early one morning, they had gone to the coast. They stayed in their uncle's house for a few days. Jamal remembered vacation by the coast; he remembered the sea. But this was no vacation. Everyone was subdued; they didn't say much to each other. Then, without really understanding what was going on, Jamal traveled to another country with his parents—Sweden. It snowed. He remembered the snow and the little apartment they lived in, which was close to a forest, and how quiet and dark it was.

"I'm looking forward to going to Cairo with you," he said into the darkness.

They could wander around the Khan el-Khalili bazaar, he said, sit in the cafés on the west bank of the Nile, visit a restaurant that he knew did fantastic grilled lamb. He would take her to Tahrir Square.

She thought about the boys playing in the heat.

He held her in a way he hadn't done before. She shut her eyes and let herself be overcome by sleep. She was looking across Cairo; it spread out before her as far as the horizon—the long wide avenues, the tall buildings, the bridges, the bustle of people. She could see the Nile. She heard the rumble of traffic.

Carina stroked Jamal's back. She just needed to feel him there, beside her. Things felt more possible when they were naked together and she could feel his thin, strong arms around her. She just wanted to throw everything aside and make love with him, wipe out everything except for them. The room was dark but it was enough to hear his calm breathing.

16

Stockholm, Friday, September 30

Bente pushed open the glass door and stepped into the office. At this time on any normal Friday, the entire floor would have been dark—workstations empty, desks tidy. But the Counterterrorism branch was simmering with hustle and bustle—buzzing voices, ringing phones, chattering keyboards. Around her were colleagues working at computers, standing in groups and talking, or on the phone. The room was shrouded in an atmosphere of concentration. It was just after eight in the evening. Counterterrorism was planning several operations within the next twenty-four hours and was also working at top speed to analyze the intelligence, assess the threat.

One of the chief analysts, an expert on the Salafist movement, hurried past her, breathless. "I'll be right there!" he shouted. "Two minutes."

She moved past a group of people standing and examining surveillance footage on a screen and hurried to the frosted-glass door behind which Kempell and some other men and women had just disappeared. Twelve hours earlier, no one had known who Jamal Badawi was. According to Swedish records, he was a civil servant at the Ministry of Justice, with an address and phone number in the Stockholm area. He had undergone background checks, like all government officials; he was on the tax register, like all Swedish citizens. He barely existed.

They had missed him. The truth that would never reach the Swedish media was that they would never have seen the threat in time if it hadn't been for the Brits.

Kempell had informed management right after the meeting with Wilson, and the Head of the Security Service had given the go-ahead just hours later for Counterterrorism to direct all necessary resources at Jamal Badawi and Carina Dymek. The message was clear: management saw a threat against the government. They saw a media meltdown, headlines screaming that the Security Service had missed a terrorist threat against Sweden once again. The smallest hesitation would be interpreted as weakness. It was necessary to act.

A liaison had already been set up with London, with Wilson. Certain British resources had also been put on standby in Cairo and Brussels, MI6 had informed them. During the day, intelligence had begun to stream in from GCHQ, the Joint Terrorism Analysis Center, MI5, and other parts of the British counterterrorism apparatus. It was good raw data that immediately gave them a detailed overview of Badawi's contacts in Cairo.

Green had called her in the afternoon. He was happy to see the prompt Swedish response. He looked forward to their successful cooperation. She could hear his thoughts: What did I tell you? I was right.

Green had a team ready to strike, if necessary, he had said. She politely declined the offer and thanked him for the generous British support.

They're small fry, Green had continued. Let them lead you to Cairo. She promised to bear it in mind.

Roland Hamrén, Head of Counterterrorism, was young and energetic, someone who had enjoyed a stratospheric rise through the organization. Management had given him operational responsibility for the Dymek/Badawi case and asked Counterespionage to provide support. Kempell was sat beside him, silent, alert. This had been a bad day for him. Counterterrorism was in charge now; they owned Badawi and wouldn't be giving him back any time soon. The Salafist analyst slipped through the door just behind Bente and slid into a chair.

Hamrén cast an eye toward the door to reassure himself that it was closed. He began in Swedish. "Okay. Welcome." He looked around the table. "We'll shortly review the situation. Lots of new information is coming in constantly. Our objective during the next few hours is to develop a clearer assessment of the threat. Thanks to the valuable help we have received from our British friends"—he nodded briefly toward Wilson, who was sitting a few chairs away and smiled back, presumably without having understood a word that was being said—"we have better intelligence to work with. Hopefully, we can stop any potential criminal acts."

He stopped, and switched into rapid English with a strong Swedish lilt. "Some of us are well acquainted with the Muslim Brotherhood; others here may be less familiar with the organization. I therefore want us to spend a few minutes looking at the background of the threat scenario we have. We have a guest here from London." He turned, smiling briefly, to an older man with dark, curly hair. The man had been sitting quietly, leaning back, throughout everything, but now appeared to come to life. "I gather you are an expert on the Muslim Brotherhood and have studied the organization for several decades. We're glad you could come in from London at such short notice. George, you have the floor."

The stocky man rose smoothly to his feet and moved toward the projector screen at the end of the room. According to what Hamrén had told Bente earlier, he was one of MI6's authorities on pro-violence Islamism. She had never seen him before.

"Thank you," he said with a wide and relaxed smile. "Okay." He leaned over an open laptop on the table and brought up his presentation. "I'm going to try and give you a brief overview of the Muslim Brotherhood and, in particular, a collection of people within the Brotherhood that we now call the Ahwa group, which is our current focus."

A presentation appeared on the projector screen behind him: *Jihadist network within the Muslim Brotherhood—threat assessment.*

He sat down in the empty seat closest to the screen.

"You're all familiar with the Muslim Brotherhood. But, put simply, for those of you with less experience of working on this organization, the Brotherhood was founded in 1928 in Egypt by Hassan al-Banna, and is currently the group that has been in existence and active for the longest out of all Islamist groups. It wasn't originally founded as a political party; it was a *dawah*, a missionary organization. Their goal was to recruit and cultivate orthodox, committed Muslims, and they did that through preaching, helping the poor, and performing other community services, and through its followers constantly striving to lead by example, as good Muslims. They saw their own conservative interpretation of Islam as the only true one, and their fight for Islam as a liberation struggle against the British and against Judaism. During the first half of the twentieth century, the Brotherhood was an organization which used peaceful methods to recruit members, even as they used violence and guerrilla tactics against what they perceived as a Western oppressor. The organization at this time was therefore"—he clicked and brought up a new slide—"accepting of violence, anti-Western, anti-imperialism, anti-Semitic, and pro-sharia."

He stopped for a moment so that everyone could take this in.

"I'll come back to that in just a moment."

New slide: an old black-and-white photograph, taken seconds after the attack on Nasser, the then president of Egypt.

"This is 1954. The Brotherhood had grown over the years into a movement of the people, but came into conflict with the Egyptian elite and the country's president, Gamal Abdel Nasser. Nasser was a military man and saw the Brotherhood as a rival power. He wasn't interested in sharia law but wanted support from the Soviets instead, which upset large parts of the Islamic elite, including the Muslim Brotherhood. In October 1954, the organization attempted to murder Nasser, but the attack failed. Instead, the assassination attempt led to the organization being crushed by the Nasser regime. Thousands of members of the Brotherhood were executed or forced underground or into exile. I'm mentioning this because it is crucial to how the Brotherhood developed and makes it possible to understand why there is a threat today."

New slide: a black-and-white photograph of a man with a serious face and large, slightly bulging eyes, dressed in traditional Egyptian kaftan and fez.

"Sayyid Qutb. The Brotherhood's leaders drew completely different conclusions from their experiences under Nasser. Some started to suggest that the organization had made a mistake in its use of violence, and thought that they should proceed with caution in a more considered manner. Others," he raised his hand and pointed at the picture, "like Sayyid Qutb, were radicalized, and drew the conclusion that the only way to respond to non-Muslim society was through jihad. Qutb, as I'm sure you know, is one of the main ideologues responsible for the militant Islamism that inspires al-Qaida and other similar terrorist groups."

He changed the slide.

"Throughout the twentieth century, the development of the Brotherhood increasingly became that of a political organization. During the latter part of the twentieth century, you can see how the Brotherhood was clearly split in two: the radical, jihadist faction, inspired by Qutb, and the more moderate, conservative wing that wanted to reform the Brotherhood into a purely political organization. In 1984, they put up their first candidates in Egyptian parliamentary elections. Those encouraging a cautious nonviolent approach were the leaders of the organization at the time and enjoyed success in the elections. But they gained many opponents. So, to summarize, we can see a clear development of the Brotherhood. Firstly, their interpretation of Islam, from rigid and militant to rather more flexible and open to changes in society. Secondly, the organization's methods, from violent opposition to colonial powers to a peaceful political struggle in the Egyptian parliament. You can even see how the Brotherhood developed from its early organizational form, with underground cells, into a political party in opposition to the controlling power. The group also grew from existing only on a national level in Egypt to become an international organization with branches and mosques across the world. Most jihadists, however, thought the organization had betrayed its founders, and so they broke away. Several of the groups that have emerged from that branch are the ones we know of today."

He looked across at Hamrén, who nodded. New slide.

"Today the Brotherhood consists mostly of conservative members who think the organization should primarily involve itself in missionary work. These people are clear in their anti-Western sentiment. Then there are liberal politicians who want to modernize the Brotherhood. Beyond those two groups, there is a small, but significantly more militant, Salafist group that explicitly supports armed jihad. The Brotherhood contains all these different movements and, as you'll understand, there has been deep internal schism for a long time. When the Arab Spring brought the revolution in Egypt in February this year, the Muslim Brotherhood was thrown into an entirely new political situation. Their archenemy, Mubarak, and his regime were gone from power and the ban against the organization was lifted. The conditions for the organization to achieve political power were dramatically improved. There was a possibility for them to take on a dominant role in Egyptian politics. But, to get there, they also began, at least outwardly, to speak the same language as the West. The Brotherhood's leaders started to talk about democracy and human rights and so on, and said little or nothing about Islam and sharia. This caused outrage among their radical members. They believed the Brotherhood was going in completely the wrong direction—that it had lost its soul, that it had sold out to Western imperialists."

"Okay. And the threat assessment?" said Hamrén.

"A growing band of members are rejecting the increasingly pro-Western policies adopted by the organization. Several of them have left the organization for the Islamist al-Nour party and other similar groupings in Egypt. But some have chosen to stay within the Brotherhood, and it is this group that especially interests us. We have spent quite some time studying them, trying to understand their motives and how they behave compared to the rest of the organization. This group is completely different from the rest of the Brotherhood," continued the MI6 analyst. "Those people we have been able to tie to the group have a clear Salafist orientation, inspired by Qutb and pro-violence Islamism. These people believe the current development of the Brotherhood to be a betrayal of Islam. They are radical in their faith and see violent resistance as the only effective way to protect the Muslim world from Western influence. But they are careful. They work in the long term and only through personal recommendations, all to keep strangers out and protect themselves from infiltration. This is a case of a loose network within the Brotherhood. But what is interesting is that, unlike other jihadists, these people haven't left the Brotherhood; rather, they want to use the organization like parasites. The circle consists of people who began organizing themselves within the Brotherhood at the start of the millennium. There has been a secret, parallel organization in existence since 9/11 and the invasion of Iraq. The network has no official name, but we call it the Ahwa group." He looked around and quickly added, when it appeared that no one understood why MI6 called the group that, "They're named after the word for a traditional Egyptian café—an *ahwa*. We know that several of them meet in an apartment associated with a café in the older part of Cairo. We can get you some coordinates later."

"But surely it has to be assumed that the leaders of the Brotherhood are aware of these people," said the Salafist expert from the other end of the table.

"They are indeed aware of these people. But it's not as certain that they know these people are connected together in a network, or that they understand the scope of the network. The Brotherhood's head office and shura council outwardly deny that they have members who are jihadists, while simultaneously trying to deal with them internally. The most vocal individuals have been excluded. But most of those we have identified as being connected to the Ahwa group are careful. By not standing out too much, these people have been able to work undisturbed. It's important to understand that what we are talking about isn't a separate organization, but rather a group of people brought together because they believe in the same thing, which is that the Brotherhood in its current form is too weak and that they must return to Qutb's pro-violence ideology, encompassing an armed struggle against the West and unbelievers, the reinstatement of sharia, and so on. They've been able to take advantage of the organization's network and resources. They've even managed to avoid our notice. As recently as a year ago, we considered them to be little more than a debating society—an extreme wing of the Brotherhood, but not a real threat. Now we see things differently."

New slide: a schematic picture of a figure split in half. One half was shaded in dark green.

"What we now know is that individuals connected to the Ahwa group live a kind of double life. On the one hand, they are members of the Brotherhood. On the other hand, they have another, secret loyalty to the network. There are even members of the circle who talk outwardly of democracy, of understanding between religions, and other things that liberal members want to hear, but who we know are part of the network, where they are open about their values. Several of those that can be said to belong to the Ahwa group work within the Brotherhood's missionary activities, which also gives them the opportunity to come into contact with young people and influence them. We have also identified individuals from the network who are active abroad—in Houston, London, Hamburg, and Leeds."

"How many people are we actually talking about?" interrupted Hamrén.

"We're currently looking at around ten individuals in Egypt. Our people in London have also identified around a hundred people in the EU who are of interest. It's estimated that around the same number again are part of the group in North America, according to reports. But of course the network may have even more members, possibly as many as five or six hundred people, all with connections to the Ahwa group itself in Cairo. And in Sweden. We have, among other things, started from Akim Badawi. He's part of the periphery of the Ahwa group, but has a clear connection to some of its leaders. Presumably, he is important to their jihadist goals; we have discovered instances of transactions from foundations controlled by him to individuals in these circles."

"These people are difficult to map," Wilson filled in, "but we're seeing an increase in secret activity. They hold regular meetings.

We see them diverting money from the foundations in a way that worries us. There are similarities between what they're up to and the kind of attack planning that we saw before the bombing of the American embassy in Dar es Salaam, for example."

The analyst waited for him to continue, but Wilson just leaned back. Hamrén, Bente saw, was taking notes feverishly.

"There are grounds to believe that this network is undergoing rapid radicalization."

"Don't be shy. Don't say, 'there are grounds to believe.' We *know* that's how it is," Wilson growled. "It's just a matter of time. They want to destroy us."

The analyst gave a strained smile and seemed to want to object to this, but kept his teeth gritted. "Yes. It's not unlikely." He cleared his throat.

"But why now?" said Hamrén. "Jihadists have always hated the West."

"Exactly. Good question. I was going to get to it."

The analyst clicked to bring up a new slide. Enraged, screaming faces; a city by night: Tahrir Square, in the middle of the Egyptian revolution in February.

"We think that the revolution and the Western and EU responses to it have been triggers for a rapid radicalization of the Ahwa group. The revolution in Egypt in February was a turning point for everyone. The regime imploded, the old tyrant, Mubarak, disappeared and everyone, even the Brotherhood, saw their chance to form a new Egypt. We followed their activities closely during the spring and could see how the entire organization began an intensive effort to take pole position and regain the political power they had lost during the Mubarak years. The movement's leaders began to build political alliances with other, new politicians—liberal, pro-Western people. The more radical brothers were furious. They had also welcomed the revolution, but thought it would pave the way for an Islamic state, an Egyptian caliphate free of all Western influences. Many were also angry at the way in which the EU and the West quickly approached Egypt with requirements for democracy and changes according to the Western model. The radical wing perceived this as a new form of Western imperialism and an attempt to colonize Egypt with non-Muslim values. We've followed conversations between some of these people. They speak about how their values as Muslims have been violated, that it's time to respond more forcefully."

"Respond how?"

"We don't know. We have, however, seen clear indications that the network is playing host to activities, as of two years ago, that pose a threat to countries in the EU. Western countries—particularly northern Europe. We know that several of the individuals we are interested in gathered for a secret meeting in Cairo nine months ago. Akim Badawi was at that meeting. What we have found out is that they talked about trying to recruit followers at the Brotherhood's centers around Europe."

He brought up an organizational chart.

"Here is a bit more detail about the methods used by the Ahwa group. Basically, they utilize the Brotherhood's resources. The Brotherhood's organization is simple but very effective. They have established offices in over one hundred locations around the world and have a presence in most Western capitals. Their most common branches are so-called Dawah centers—a combination of library, mosque, and classroom—entirely legitimate enterprises. Overall, it is an efficient system of logistics and communication on a global level. Several of these centers are used by the jihadist network to recruit novices. The Ahwa group also makes use of the Brotherhood's financial resources, foundations, and funds to finance its activities and, so we believe, to finance acts of terror carried out by other, more visible, groups. As I said, we're talking about a network living in secrecy within a parent organization. A parasitic growth." The analyst looked at them, then said, "I think I'll stop there. Any questions?"

Everyone around the table sat in silence.

Wilson stood up. He lumbered to the screen and brought up a new slide—photographs of three Arab men. Two had large, uncut beards; one had a more groomed Newgate fringe.

"This man," he said with voice that filled the room, and pointed at the man with the groomed beard, "is Akim Badawi. He is our primary target. He is the one we believe is instructing Jamal Badawi, your civil servant. He's the one who gave the order to Jamal to recruit a Swedish diplomat and gain access to a particular report."

He stopped.

"These people are smart. They understand how to undermine their enemies. How to undermine us. By exposing our intelligence contacts, they can cause far more damage to us than by using a bomb. We believe that this is only the beginning; we can expect more violent forms of behavior to come. This business with the report is just preparation—for what, we don't know. That's what we want to find out, and we think the answer may be here, in Stockholm."

He turned to the screen. Bente looked at the picture. The man was about seventy. He had heavy eyelids; a round, pleasant face. His eyes bore a distant resemblance to the thin, beautiful Jamal.

"Akim Badawi is Jamal Badawi's uncle. Seventy-two years old; lives in Cairo; retired lecturer at the Al-Azhar University. He's a veteran in the Brotherhood—a member since the fifties. He started out as a young activist, went underground after the purge against the organization in the mid-fifties. At the end of the eighties, he spent four years in prison. He was, for a long time, part of the militant wing of the Brotherhood, propagating political Islam and revolutionary methods. But he's old now. He's no longer on the barricades—he finances them instead. Akim Badawi is the manager of a string of Brotherhood foundations. He's part of the group of trusted individuals who have access to the organization's economic resources. The majority of the foundations finance literary courses, Qur'an schools. But some funding goes to entirely different activities. We know that significant sums used to go to Hamas, and now they are being directed to European groups."

Wilson looked around with a smile, as if he was enjoying holding the attention of the entire room. "I can tell you one thing: it was pure chance that we found these Ahwa people. Our colleagues were investigating the cargo-plane bomb in the autumn of 2010, which was when we discovered a connection to the Muslim Brotherhood. That surprised us. We hadn't expected anything like that. It all started when we managed to identify a guy in Qatar who was acting as a middleman for al-Qaida. His job was to map out DHL's cargo flights from Yemen to American destinations and act as a courier, flying into Yemen with small sums of money. Some of this money financed the printer bomb we discovered on DHL's cargo plane in October of last year. Advanced bomb technology, let me tell you. Pretty damn good. It would have blown the plane to kingdom come when it landed in Chicago. But the Saudis found the guy. That was how we traced the bomb and brought the plane down at East Midlands airport. Then we started to unravel it all; we discovered that the money coming into Yemen was from the Muslim Brotherhood. Isn't that right, George?"

The analyst nodded slowly. "The money came from one of the Brotherhood's foundations. Akim Badawi was one of the people with access to that foundation. When we followed that trail further, we discovered that money was also going to British accounts."

Wilson interrupted him with a broad smile. "Exactly. We can see that the foundation is financing a range of different activities that we deem to be threats, such as several radical websites like Islam4UK and IslamicAwakening. The common denominator of the people looking after the foundation is that they are all part of the most radical element of the Brotherhood."

New slide: five photographs of younger men of Arab appearance. One of them was Jamal Badawi.

"These are some of the latest recruits to the Brotherhood. All of them have come into contact with members of the Ahwa group and its network in various ways. The man on the far right is Jamal Badawi, Akim's nephew."

Kempell, who had been sitting quietly throughout, muttered loudly in Swedish, "That can't be right."

Several of the Swedish participants at the table turned toward him in surprise. But he said nothing further, just shook his head slowly with a worried expression.

Wilson, who, without understanding what Kempell had said, still understood the critical tone, looked across the table at his Swedish colleague with a smile. "Sorry, was there something you wanted to say?"

Kempell cleared his throat uncomfortably and shook his head.

Wilson continued, turning to face Kempell at the other end of the table, as if calmly explaining something to just him. "Consider the following: Akim Badawi has had no contact with his nephew since Jamal moved to Sweden. For several years, they didn't speak at all. But then, just a few months ago, he sent his nephew an e-mail. It was the first time in two years he had been in touch. It's interesting: two years, then he turns up again. Here's the message. George?"

Someone made sure the light in the room was turned down a little.

British signals intelligence had clearly been listening in to Swedish networks. Bente looked at Hamrén, who was waiting expressionlessly for the Brits to find the right slide. She noticed that the British analyst was tense and fumbled as he brought the document up on the screen. It was an Egyptian e-mail to a Swedish computer. She, Kempell and most of the people from Counterterrorism in the room were aware that London carried out surveillance on Swedish territory, but it was still embarrassing to be proven right, on a huge projector screen. The room was silent; only the analyst clearing his dry throat was audible.

"Right. As you can see, it's dated April 20th of this year."

She looked, together with the others in the room, at the message that appeared on the screen. The original had been written in Arabic and scanned on to the computer. Only the Salafist expert and the British analyst seemed to be able to read it. The analyst, George, brought up a new slide: an English translation.

My dear Jamal, the message began. Akim Badawi apologized profusely for not writing for so long; he had been ill, he said, the days were getting shorter; he didn't know where all the time went. She read on quickly, past the bit about how Enna was, how Gamal was getting along, that Seif had graduated from high school last summer. Enna was mentioned repeatedly; she had hip problems. Amr had moved to Alexandria and got a job at a bank. Relatives, presumably. Then he asked how Jamal was, how his mother was— was she still unwell? *You should know*, he then wrote, *that we think of you and pray for you and her every day. We are so happy that you have a good job. It's just like Enna says: you're smarter than the rest of us put together, and patient.* Then he wanted to know how things were in Sweden. He imagined it would be cold at this time of year. He had received the photos that Jamal had sent, by the way. It looked desolate, but clean. Sweden seemed to be good, he wrote; a country that handed out the Nobel Prize for Literature couldn't be all bad, although he did wonder why Adonis had never won it. Did Jamal have a companion? *A man*, he wrote, *should never live alone for too long.* He hoped that Jamal would meet someone—a woman who could look after him. He was bored; since retiring from the faculty, he had too much time on his hands. But a lot had happened recently; he had almost forgotten that he was old. *Perhaps I can look forward to living for a few years in a free Egypt, despite everything.* Egypt! Everything was different now. There was hope. If God's will were done, the country would regain its dignity. *If only we can get rid of the damned military then this God-fearing, beautiful country has a future.* But the armchairs of power were comfortable, he wrote. The opposition to change, real change, was still large. Then:

> We still have to organize ourselves to fight the old oppressors. The old generals are playing charades with the populace. They claim that they are the revolution, but they'll feel a new revolution if they aren't careful. I wish I was twenty and could be out there with the young people. I meet a few people from the movement occasionally, by the way. They are happy but worried. We thank God for giving us the power to pull free from the oppressors. We have all walked through the desert, but for the first time I think things are genuinely changing. We all need power to build a new Egypt that can awaken. You're still young, Jamal; perhaps this will be your home one day. You're Egyptian, Jamal, and this is also your revolution. No one would be happier than I to have you

here, but I also know that you have a life in Sweden. Perhaps I'm just an old man that misses you, Jami (do you remember that Enna always called you that?). Desire is a remarkable fire, is it not?

Bente stopped and read slowly. A poem.

Their stations will be near.
Their fire will loom before you,
kindling desire
into a raging blaze.

Kneel your camels there.
Don't fear their lions.
Yearning will reveal them to you
as whelps.

The message ended with a short, traditional greeting, and was signed *AB*.

The analyst waited for everyone to finish reading.

"As you can see, the e-mail takes the shape of a letter from home. The people mentioned are all in the Badawi family—we've confirmed that. But this is mostly a pretext to say certain things that can't be said outright. Certain things in the message interest us in particular. You can see that he mentions 'the movement,' which we assume to be either the Muslim Brotherhood or the Ahwa network. London is leaning toward the latter. Akim Badawi is evidently trying to persuade his nephew to return home. Home doesn't have to mean Egypt; instead, we think it means he wants to enlist his nephew, Jamal Badawi, into the group."

"Then there's the mention of the photographs." The mouse cursor appeared, and moved to the relevant sentence. "We have validated this with"—he mumbled in an anxious tone and cast an eye at Wilson—"certain, targeted operations. We know that Akim Badawi has received photographs sent by Jamal Badawi. A steganographic analysis of the pictures hasn't shown that they contained any hidden code, but London hasn't reached a final conclusion yet. I know that the pictures will be subjected to further processing."

Wilson turned to Hamrén and then looked at Bente. "This message," he said, pointing at the screen, "is a sign. A challenge. We know that Akim Badawi manages foundations that fund terrorism. We know that he is part of the Ahwa group. So why is he contacting Jamal Badawi now? What does he want his nephew to do? It's questions like that which we are posing."

Hamrén nodded silently.

"Adonis." One of the Counterterrorism officers pointed. "First paragraph. Who's that?"

"Adonis. Yes, of course. Good." The analyst brought the mouse cursor up.

"It sounds like a cover name."

"That's right. The individual behind the name is Ali Ahmad Said. A Syrian author. Member of the resistance. Lives in Paris," said the analyst.

"Member of the resistance?" said Hamrén.

"Yes, against the Syrian regime. General anti-Western antipathy."

"Part of this Ahwa?"

"Not so far as we know."

"But is he a threat?" said Hamrén impatiently. "Is he part of the threat? That's what we want to know."

"No," responded the analyst with a look at Wilson. "We don't deem him to be a threat." He continued after a brief pause, "If we go to the end of the message, we see what is possibly most interesting—the poem."

The analyst enlarged the text so that only the lines of the poem were visible. Bente read through the lines again, slowly. Flowery, exotic imagery. She had never understood poetry. It didn't go anywhere.

"It's an ancient poem. It was written by a poet called Muhyiddin Ibn 'Arabi, who lived during the twelfth and thirteenth centuries. Ibn 'Arabi is known throughout the Arab world as a poet and philosopher. He is one of the prominent figures in Sufism. Yes, you may be aware of dervishes and the more mythical interpretation of the Qur'an. In the Arab world, these texts are still read and used by people . . ."

The analyst stopped for a moment, clearly noting how people in the room were looking vacantly at him. Someone moved restlessly in their chair. Out of everyone, it was only really the Salafist expert who was listening.

"Well, anyway," he said briefly, and cut what was probably a long explanation that he had carefully prepared back in London, "the poem."

Bente was grateful; little was as annoying as specialists getting sidetracked on to their nerdy pet subjects.

"What's in the e-mail is the last two stanzas of a longer poem. I should say that we've done a cryptographic analysis of the poem, but without any results. What we are probably seeing here is a basic code—a hidden message that Jamal Badawi is approaching his goal: 'Their stations will be near.' It's a way for Akim Badawi to tell him that it's time to get ready. 'Their fire will loom before you, kindling desire into a raging blaze,'" the analyst read quickly. "It is those lines, in particular, that worry us. We know that Akim Badawi is educated—he is familiar with Arabic literature; he is familiar with the Qur'an—and he is using this to send a message. It's the line about the 'raging blaze' that is key, that is what we consider demonstrates a threat. The love of God makes desire grow into a raging blaze. It's a classic motif, even in the Qur'an. A raging blaze is mentioned in key passages in the Qur'an—it is the fire that burns when a believer is filled with the love of God, but it's also a concept in the Qur'an that represents the final day. Our assessment is that Jamal Badawi is being prepared for some kind of attack—an attack with high aspirations, with the intention of creating massive destruction. And that involves self-effacement for Jamal Badawi."

The room was dead quiet. Everyone stared at the text.

"Thank you, George," said Wilson. "So, preparations are afoot. We know that Jamal Badawi has already given his uncle an answer of sorts. He has built up a relationship with one of your diplomats. He has managed to get close to people involved in your foreign policy and within the EU who he wouldn't normally have access to. He has then discovered, through this diplomat, a report about European counterterrorism that contains sensitive information about our joint work against terrorism. And now we have a clear indication that Carina Dymek is a loyal recruit. Because, unless I'm mistaken, she did not leak the report to any of the parties one might have expected. Not the Russians, not the Chinese. No one, except Jamal Badawi. Now you've seen Akim's e-mail; now you know what I know. London believes we are facing a threat and I'm inclined to agree."

Silence.

"Are there any indications of what the target is?" said Hamrén.

Wilson shook his head.

"Okay," said Hamrén. "Thank you very much."

The meeting was over. Wilson and his analyst left the room while the Swedish investigation team stayed behind for a quick briefing. Bente followed the Brits to the elevator. She wanted to try and get Wilson to say a little more about how they had come across this group in Cairo. She smiled at him, jokingly taking his arm in hers.

"A very interesting presentation, Roger."

He nodded morosely. "Thanks. Not all of your colleagues seemed to appreciate it."

She let go of him as he shuffled into the elevator, followed by his analyst. He wasn't talkative. She said something about Swedish resources naturally being ready to cooperate. As soon as the elevator doors had slid shut, she pulled out her cell and called Mikael.

"The Ahwa group: ever heard of it? Do we have the name recorded at the Section?"

A short pause. "A group in Sweden?"

"No, international. Apparently it's based in Cairo."

He thought for a moment. "In Cairo? No, I don't think so. I can check."

"Wilson came in here with an analyst and talked about a secret group within the Muslim Brotherhood. There's a connection to Jamal

Badawi—the guy at the Ministry of Justice—and Dymek. I'll arrange for you to get the British intelligence. Check it. Go through it all."

When she returned to the conference room, Hamrén and the others in Counterterrorism management were in the middle of a discussion about the threat assessment. Was Jamal Badawi a threat? To what extent should they respond?

"We need to keep an eye on him. Where is he now?" said Hamrén. "Do we know?"

"Right now . . . ?" The Head of Directed Surveillance leafed through his papers. "Two hours ago he left a restaurant, here, on Kungsholmen—together with Carina Dymek. They took a taxi to Badawi's address and they are currently still there."

"Okay. I want Badawi watched, twenty-four seven. It's simply not good enough that the Brits know more about our government officials than we do."

The men around the table took notes.

"And as for Dymek—we need to speak to her. Bring her in."

Hamrén was moving fast, Bente thought. Counterterrorism worked differently from rest of the organization—more direct, no finesse. She appreciated it. Kempell, however, looked tense. If it had been his case, he would have waited for Dymek. Counterterrorism was taking a risk trying to contact her at such an early stage of the investigation, but Bente knew what they were thinking. Presumably, they were hoping that she would play along and become a Security Service informant, lead them to Jamal and then into the heart of the group in Cairo. In their eyes, this was no longer about a leak; this was the global fight against terrorism. It was about the Muslim Brotherhood, not a civil servant who had stepped off the straight and narrow.

"Okay. Protection?"

The Deputy Head of the Dignitary Protection branch had joined them after the presentation by MI6. He looked like a wrestler, with dark, cropped hair and a wide back. Personal protection of the Prime Minister had been increased as well as that of certain other ministers who might be subject to threats, he said briefly.

Heads nodded. Roland Hamrén adjusted his dark-blue tie self-consciously.

"Has the government been informed?" He turned back to Kempell.

"The MFA. And SUND. But they only know about Carina Dymek, not the Ahwa trail," Kempell said in a low voice.

"We'll leave it like that," said Hamrén. "Okay. The hypothesis we're working off is that Jamal Badawi, the nephew of Akim, is recruiting for a radical wing of the Muslim Brotherhood, and probably for this inner, secret group that the Brits called the Ahwa group. It is also therefore probable that the group poses a threat to Sweden, given its aggressive ideology and the capacity it is expected to have."

Kempell made a noise, as if to disagree. A few around the table turned their heads but Hamrén pretended he had not heard anything.

"I agree with Wilson's analysis. Badawi and Dymek are threats to the government. Given they are in a relationship, it is likely that what Dymek has done isn't by chance but has to do with the Ahwa group. In that case, she is a threat—to the government and to national security."

Kempell muttered something.

"Sorry?" Hamrén stopped himself.

"How do we know that?" Kempell burst out. "How do we actually know that this group has anything to do with Jamal Badawi? He received a letter from his uncle. With a poem. It's pretty thin, Roland."

"It's enough."

"We checked Badawi out when he was appointed. Nothing suggested connections to any sort of militant Islamist organization."

"I believe you. And I believe British intelligence. You saw the e-mail from his uncle with your own eyes. We can't ignore that. Surely you understand?"

"Of course." Kempell shrugged his shoulders.

"The British intelligence is well founded," one of the chief analysts said.

"Of course, of course," said Kempell in annoyance. "But is it possible for us to verify it? No. That's all I'm saying."

"That's true. But their signals intelligence—"

"We have no sources of our own," Kempell interrupted sharply.

The analyst retreated. "No, not at the moment."

"So the intelligence that we are trusting is British," Kempell continued. "Just so that this is clear to everyone: we are using solely British data as a basis for operational decisions."

He turned to Roland Hamrén. The room was silent.

Everyone looked at the Head of Counterterrorism, who cleared his throat and said, "Yes. And that's good enough. For now."

"And we're placing blind trust in them," said Kempell.

"We're not trusting them blindly at all," said Hamrén sternly.

Others would have stopped here, but Kempell carried on. He was combative. Trusting British data like this was taking a big risk, he said. Did they have anything, anything at all, that could verify that Jamal Badawi was a threat? Apart from an e-mail and some speculation about radical groups in Cairo, fed to them by the British?

"In my branch," said Kempell, slowly, "we would require more. Facts."

"You say that." Hamrén bared his teeth with a small smile.

Bente looked down at the table and wished that Kempell would just shut up. He had gone too far. Of course he was right—in a perfect world they wouldn't trust the British so much—but he knew how it worked. Their world wasn't perfect. There was a potential terror threat against the government and they had orders to respond, quickly. Kempell was just an old man who, embittered, wanted to know best.

"What the Brits give us is top drawer," said Roland Hamrén.

"I'm sure. But it's British, just British. Perhaps I'm too suspicious, but I don't like it. You know just as well as I do, Roland, that reliable intelligence requires at least two or three sources. Otherwise it's not intelligence, it's just an opinion. Speculation."

Someone sighed loudly. If she had had a remote control for Kempell, Bente would have turned him off right away. She hated it when people made themselves a laughing stock. Kempell looked around the table with a furious expression; their gazes met. Be quiet, please, Kempell. She had never seen him like this before—so shrill in tone. He had had a bad day, management had taken his investigation away, and, for some reason, he now wanted to make his mark, but this was too much; this was pathetic. As Head of Counterespionage, he ought to welcome the apprehension of Jamal Badawi before disaster struck. But he seemed to be stuck.

"Gustav"—Hamrén put on an exaggerated tone of friendliness—"I understand your concerns. But we have a situation here, which means we can't wait. Okay?"

Kempell said nothing. Hamrén pursed his lips. An uncomfortable silence fell over the table until Hamrén thanked everyone, quickly, to indicate that the discussion was over.

17

Stockholm, Saturday, October 1

The homey sound of clinking crockery and the hum of the espresso machine reached Carina as she lay in bed. She yawned. The espresso machine was the only machine in the well-equipped kitchen that Jamal actually used. She stretched to pull back the curtains; a sharp, white daylight pierced through the windows.

Jamal appeared naked in the doorway with a tray. "Good morning." She sat up in bed. "Hello."

They drank lattes and ate toast and marmalade in bed. She wanted to say something, but she couldn't find the words. A tentative silence lay between them. It had been the first time they had quarreled seriously. But Jamal didn't seem to want to talk about what had happened at the restaurant the evening before, either. That was a relief; Carina was bad at sorting things out after the fact. It was usually better to look forward, she thought. Let what had already happened be. But their argument worried her. She just wanted everything to be good between them, for them to be close. She sought him out under the duvet. Jamal didn't seem to respond at first; he looked meditative and drank his coffee slowly.

"Do you want to go to Cairo?" He looked so serious that she pulled her hand back and sat up again.

"Yes, absolutely."

They looked at each other.

"Are you sure?"

"Yes." She embraced him, kissed him on the neck. "Quite sure."

They carried on drinking their coffees.

"I'm sorry about yesterday," she said after a while. "Sorry."

He shook his head. She shouldn't apologize. He understood that it was a difficult situation for her. He was stupid; he knew nothing about things like that.

"I got worried," he said. "I just don't want anything to happen to you."

He really meant it. It struck her how long it had been since someone had cared so much about her. "I love you," she whispered, or perhaps she only thought it.

Jamal's phone rang. It lay rattling on the bedside table. He kissed Carina and reached for his cell. She watched him as he sat on the edge of the bed, and noticed the change in his back, how tense he became when he saw the display.

"I have to take this," he said curtly and walked out of the room.

She stayed in bed and heard him answer in Arabic before he disappeared into the bathroom. The mumble of the telephone conversation continued inside. It bothered her that he shut himself away like that, completely unnecessarily. If the conversation was so private that he didn't want her to hear what it was about, it hardly mattered that she was listening—she couldn't understand a word of it, anyway. It annoyed her; it felt as if he didn't like her hearing him speak Arabic. It had happened a couple of times, and afterward he was always resolute but never said who had called or what it had been about—nothing. It was often a long time before his tense, somewhat absent manner disappeared and he became himself. Something was bothering him.

The murmur carried on in the bathroom.

She got up, pulled on Jamal's dressing gown, made a second cup of coffee using his espresso machine and waited. Finally, he came out of the bathroom.

"Sorry that took a while," he mumbled, putting down his cell. She chose to ask and say nothing. Curiosity had begun to turn into vague annoyance, which she knew she really had no right to feel. She kissed him fleetingly, swept past him into the bathroom and took a long shower.

When she came out, Jamal was sitting on the sofa with his computer on his lap. He had checked various travel agencies, he said.

She sat down next to him while he clicked around the web, comparing prices. Perhaps they could go as soon as the end of October? The weather was good then. There were tickets available that weren't too expensive. He would probably be able to take some time off. She nodded. She had all the time in the world, she thought gloomily. Quietly, she did the math; yes, she had enough money, she had savings. She would get by for six months, even if her salary from the Ministry stopped coming in.

As if Jamal had heard her thoughts, he said he would check with relatives to see if they could borrow somewhere to stay.

"My uncle has a house by the coast. I'll ask him. I'm sure he'll lend it to us."

"It'll be nice to meet him."

"You'll like him," said Jamal, without full conviction. "He's a fine man. And one of the most important people in my life. It's time you met him. He'll like you. I know that."

The thought of them together in Cairo finally broke into the slightly melancholic mood she had felt all morning. Finally she would get see something of where he had come from.

"So you do want to go, then?" he asked.

"*Yes*, I already said so." She laughed.

He put his laptop to one side and looked steadily at her. "It means a lot to me," he said. "You're the only person I've ever wanted to take a trip like this with."

Jamal went to an airline website. She sat next to him and saw him completing the various booking fields: fly in to Cairo, out of Sharm el-Sheikh. First, a few days in the capital, then a week by the coast in his uncle's house. Ms. Dymek. Mr. Badawi. The last week in October: out on Friday evening and then back ten days later. Flexible tickets, because you never know, said Jamal with a tone of voice that made her wonder if, despite everything, he had changed his mind. The tickets cost 8,500 kroner, but at least some of their accommodation would be free, she thought, and pushed her money worries to one side. She stroked Jamal's hair. Cairo.

18

Stockholm, Saturday, October 1

Bente stepped into the Security Service guest apartment and took off her coat. The air inside the late-nineteenth-century two-room apartment was still. Staff from the Protection branch would regularly enter to sweep rooms for bugs—it was standard procedure—but no one had been into the apartment since she arrived in Stockholm.

She had woken up early and hadn't been able to fall back to sleep, so she had taken a brisk walk around the block and bought a few apples from a corner shop before returning to the apartment. She shut the door and locked it behind her, took an apple out of the bag and bit into it before calling the Section.

Mikael answered right away. Yes, he had received her text message. He had that slightly thick voice he always got when he was excited. "I think we've found something."

"Okay?"

"You have to see for yourself. It's from a site for computer-game programmers, but they're discussing completely different things. I'll send you the link now. It's a discussion thread, almost at the bottom of the page. Number twenty three."

She went to the page. It was indeed a site for programmers, with various forums for different technical discussions about things she didn't understand. Computer nerds. There was a link to an Internet Relay Chat channel. It was encrypted, but the Section had managed to force the algorithm with the help of the FRA's processors. She only needed to read a few lines to know that it was a hit.

She called Hamrén, who was in a meeting. No, she couldn't call him back; she needed to talk to him. Now.

When she told him what SSI had found, he fell silent and listened to her. Then he began to speak quickly, almost in a staccato. Wonderful. Very, very good. Send it to the Directed Surveillance unit and the analysts. He would be back in the office within half an hour.

She sent an e-mail to Hamrén's chief analyst with a link to the channel, copying in the technical unit head, and leaned back. Perhaps the Brits were right, in spite of everything.

Two hours later, they were gathered in a semicircle—Hamrén and the Head of Directed Surveillance, together with four analysts and technicians from Counterterrorism. Wilson was also there with his adjutants, Sarah and George, and four new faces—anonymous young analysts who must have flown in from London during the last twenty-four hours. Wilson was leaning back in his chair and raised a limp hand in greeting when Bente came through the door. The blinds were closed; the pearl-white light of the projector screen cast an artificial glow over the walls and the faces of all present.

Hamrén waited until it was exactly half past eight before getting up. He momentarily found himself bathed in the white quadrant of light—squinted, was blinded—and took a step to the side.

"Good morning, everyone," he began. "You have all been sent the link. Magnus will go through the channel for us now. Okay, Magnus. Take it away."

The Salafist analyst began his presentation by cautiously opening a window on the screen. A functional, somewhat ugly, yet striking website appeared. The majority of the page was filled with a list of discussion threads. What they were looking at was a website for developers, he explained. Programmers, hackers.

"It is a meeting place for a community of roughly five to six thousand people. The common denominator is that they develop various programs together in open source code. Completely normal, legal activities." He clicked. "Here, for example: questions about graphical rendering in computer games, animation."

He opened a tab for a new subpage. Around twenty thematic discussion threads appeared in a list. He opened a new thread and scrolled down a seemingly unending string of posts. "For our purposes, this is an uninteresting discussion about programming online games," said the analyst, ending his guided tour. He clicked back to the homepage. "As you can see, nothing of interest to us. Except this."

The projector fan whirred. He brought up the IRC channel. A concentrated silence lay across the room while everyone stared at the projector screen.

The posts shone before them. What they said was markedly different from the technical subjects of the other threads. The most recent post was just two hours old, written by the user, Sala82. It contained a YouTube clip: a shaky video of the arrest of a black man. The police were British, judging by their uniforms. Bente glanced at Wilson, but he merely looked sullen; barely a flicker crossed his face. Several further YouTube clips were from the riots in London in August. Beneath them was a long string of heated posts about the British police state, about Big Brother society.

Magnus broke the silence: "As you can see, this is a far more political discussion. Unusual for a site like this, but not in itself worrying. However, if we go to the beginning of the discussion, we find things that are far more interesting."

He worked his way down the thread to an earlier post. The user, Redstripe, had posted it two days ago. It contained a photograph showing a man in a suit together with two younger colleagues. When Bente had first looked at the discussion thread, earlier that morning, it had taken her a second to recognize him: Stefano Manservisi, the Head of the EU Commission's Directorate General for Home Affairs—GD Home. The picture had been taken at some sort of conference venue with beige walls and gray stone floors—perhaps one of the rooms at the EU Commission in Brussels, with which she was vaguely familiar. Manservisi and his colleagues were smiling. Around them there were people standing and talking. The photo was poorly executed and amateurish, probably copied from the Internet because the resolution was poor; she could see the pixels on the edge of Manservisi's suit.

Under the picture it said, in English, *Need to ID the people in the picture. Anyone?*

Shortly afterward, on Thursday, September 29th, at 22:35, an answer had been logged from the user, Frontline: *Hi Red. What's up?*

Several other users promptly appeared in the thread. A dialogue developed. Bente could count almost twenty participants. The analyst scrolled slowly down the page so that everyone had time to read.

Wilson was leaning back in his chair with his arms crossed—immobile, inscrutable. It was Bente's signals intelligence at SSI that had discovered the IRC channel, not the Brits, and it didn't surprise her. She had good people at the Section, but the British outfit at Government Communications Headquarters had incomparably greater resources. They should have seen the threat long before SSI. She looked at Wilson through the gloom. His bushy eyebrows were drawn together over his blue eyes. Around him were his British colleagues, their faces attentive, reading the text on the screen. Wilson wasn't reading. He was looking straight ahead, lost in his own thoughts. Then he felt her gaze. He turned his head quickly and looked straight at her, expressionlessly. For a moment she felt like Wilson could read her thoughts, that he was judging them, trying to make out whether she posed a threat or not. Then there was a lightning-quick change in his facial expression. He blinked at her. A cold smile flashed across his face. A loyal glance between colleagues. She smiled back and turned to the front again. Of course the Brits had seen the IRC channel; she knew it the moment Wilson had met her gaze. His reaction had given it away: the stony stare, the exaggerated smile. He hadn't been reading what it said on the screen because he already knew what it said. Naturally, British signals intelligence had picked up on the ongoing discussion: it was on the Internet, with nothing more than some light encryption to prevent curious amateurs from finding it. The technicians at the Section had only needed a few hours to force their way past the encryption.

The question wasn't whether the British knew, but why they hadn't chosen to share it before.

> **REDSTRIPE:** Need to find them. All I know is they're EU. GD Home
> **FRONTLINE:** Ok
> **REDSTRIPE:** They're sick in the head
> **FRONTLINE:** lol
> [Sala82 logs in]
> **SALA82:** hello
> **FRONTLINE:** hi
> **SALA82:** whatareyoudoing
> **REDSTRIPE:** its no joke Seriously need to check them out. ID prefer-
>   ably asap. They're fucking with a friend
> **REDSTRIPE:** and with all of us
> **SALA82:** seriously
> **REDSTRIPE:** If you don't believe me look for KOM(2011)790
> [Darknite logs in]
> [Bando logs in]
> [Steph911 logs in]
> **FRONTLINE:** ???
> **DARKNITE:** agree. No hit
> **BANDO:** seems pretty classified
> **FRONTLINE:** not for too long I hope :D
> **REDSTRIPE:** My friend has it but don't talk about that. Spook stuff. CIA
>   stuff. The people on the picture wrote it. names, addresses, etc. is
>   what we need. then we can respond
> **SALA82:** sink some ships :)
> **DARKNITE:** agree
> **STEPH911:** readin u loud n clear

In the course of minutes, yet another ten users had logged in. And, throughout, it was right there: the mentioning of the EIS report. The reference number to the report was correct. It was odd to see it there, on a site like that. Everyone in the room read quietly. The atmosphere was close, concentrated. What was scrolling up before them

was a threat. The kind of threat they had spent their entire professional lives trying to eliminate. Magnus scrolled onward:

> **REDSTRIPE:** Focus on the guy in the corner. See pic here
> **ADAM:** What?
> **STEPH911:** Good morning N ;-)
> **REDSTRIPE:** Everyone. Need names & addresses before we can re-
> spond Particularly the guy on the left
> **GOLEM:** DDoS or what?
> **REDSTRIPE:** question for later
> **FRONTLINE:** They listen They watch you They are not your friends
> **REDSTRIPE:** word
> **STORM:** Do you mean this guy:

Underneath Storm's post was a grainy, enlarged picture of a face.
The face belonged to a man who was visible in the background of
the first picture. The picture was so well processed that the facial
features were clearly visible. The analyst scrolled back quickly, hovered over the fuzzy face of the man in the background with the
mouse, and zoomed in.

The man was in his fifties. Dark hair with streaks of gray. Set
figure, a slightly round face, beard, dark-gray suit. One of many
office employees to whom you wouldn't give a moment's notice if
you were next to them on the subway.

After that message, the posts came closer together. The analyst
scrolled slowly through the thread. A stream of comments. At first
mostly exclamations, jokes, admiration for the user, Redstripe, for
posting the link, rapid exchanges of this kind. They knew each other.
A close-knit group. Further on in the thread the tone changed and
became more serious. The discussion developed and became more
objective. Magnus scrolled forward twelve hours in the thread and
showed how the tone had become very much goal oriented. After
twenty-four hours, he said, it was clearly visible that the group had
started working as a structured and collaborative team. Led by
Redstripe, users like Frontline, Darknite, and Steph911 had gotten

organized. The posts were short and matter of fact, written with an almost military tone.

The analyst scrolled onward through the thread to a post on the morning of October 1st. "This is where we are now: Saturday. What we can see is in real time. Six people are logged in. All understanding each other perfectly."

The posts looked different, more like operational communications.

Check Belgian population register. URL anyone?

Number 2 is at the EU Commission, French guy. Check all employees. Does anyone have a list btw?

Dear friends and co-hunters, free face recog tool here: http://download .cnet.com/Face-Recognition-System/3000–2053_4–100000859.html.

Shit hot sources at www.silobreaker.com Maybe picasa or flickr are ways in Good work. Any I in Bxl who can check it out, how you get in, etc.?

WEAREBRINGINGTHEHOUSEDOWN

We know all info about their lan, all info welcome. Logins, etc., try to get access to everything!

Remember: no unnecessary entries, ok? No chitchat.

Here's the report's number KOM(2011)790. Search for that.

Keywords for those of you searching far and wide: Foreign Affairs Council, Justice & Home Affairs, Manservisi, de Kerchove, CTC, JAI, DG XI, surveillance, European Counterterrorism, intelligence coordination, etc.

Redstripe will be moving ftpn in 4hrs

Have a login for the EU intranet btw, kids stuff.

Sweet.

The analyst said, "You see, intensive communication, focused on gathering information about the report and the EIS and certain persons in that photo. We have counted twenty-eight different users active during the first two days, of which four are particularly active and leading the way."

The posts between the four users continued for hours, a rapid exchange of information, increasingly technical details revolving around how to find more data about the people in the picture, different ways of penetrating EU servers, EU networks, records, databases. Hundreds of posts—during certain periods, up to five or ten per minute. For hours, there had been an intense flow of chat between the four individuals. The closer they got to today's date, the more posts there were, the analyst noted. The reference number KOM(2011)790 was mentioned several times—the report that Dymek had leaked. The analyst pointed out a post that described, in detail, how to hack into the EU's document databases. Another listed all civil servants in section A3, the part of the EU Commission that worked on counterterrorism matters. This was where the photos, names and private addresses began to show up.

In silence, the analyst scrolled through the rows of posts. If they had missed this . . . Bente froze at the thought. But SSI had done its job, thank God. The system worked.

"We can also tell the participants have been in touch with each other through other platforms." The analyst pointed out a post that said, *I just talked to Steve, he might be on to something. Check this out.* He then quickly scrolled five minutes forward in the thread. Here was a discussion about names to be recorded.

"They've broken into the EU's servers. London's assessment is that this is in order to gain accreditation as journalists and, in that way, gain access to large parts of Justus Lipsius, the EU Council building where summits are held. That would give them great mobility and capacity to get close to the ministers and their delegations. The hypothesis we're working on now is that they are trying to get inside the perimeter security in order to get close to certain chosen individuals—targets. We're investigating how they've managed to access the accreditation system, and under which names." There was a range of ways—Trojans, secret doors. Magnus made a gesture at one of the technicians sitting beside him, who now cleared his throat uncomfortably. No, they didn't know precisely how they had gotten in. But they had gotten on to the EU Commission's intranet—that had been confirmed by Brussels.

"They're good," muttered Hamrén.

The analyst scrolled onward through the thread. "Let's look at their motive," he said. "The report mentioned here is the proposal for the creation of the EIS, a proposal that will be discussed at the summit on October 10th—the same report that Carina Dymek came into contact with. What the relationship is between Dymek and the individuals communicating here is not clear, but we're assuming there is a connection." He waved his laser pointer across the screen. "The group is quickly politicized. The rhetoric is the same as that among those leading protests against the FRA laws and supporting the people behind the Pirate Bay. The individuals in this group are probably among the upper echelons of the file-sharing world as well. We can also note certain anti-Western sentiment here, which tends to be common in autonomous groups."

He showed several posts talking about oppressor states. Here and there were video clips of police arrests, along with text about how the EU was increasingly becoming a military power, a violent machine.

The analyst stopped and let them read. It was the usual anarchist rhetoric: anti-system; anti-establishment.

Finally, Magnus turned to them and said, "To summarize, what we see is very probably some kind of attack being planned. The target is the Council of Ministers in Brussels on October 10th."

"What do you mean, 'probably'?" said Wilson's calm bass. "This *is* an attack being planned."

Everyone sat in silence.

Magnus scrolled down and stopped at one of the first posts: the user, Redstripe.

"We are dealing with a group with substantial technical expertise, who are infiltrating an EU summit and targeting individual EU officials in order to carry out some sort of action. By all indications, it is the people in the picture in particular that they are focusing on: Manservisi and the man here."

"I know who Manservisi is," said Hamrén, "but who's the other one?"

The analyst clicked back to the photograph. Hamrén pointed at the man in the background.

"He's called Jean Bernier. Works for the EU Commission. We've checked him out, because we couldn't see what the motive was for choosing him as a target, either. He's a civil servant, a lawyer."

"So why him?"

"We don't know."

"Because he works for the EU," said Wilson with a shrug of the shoulders. He pointed at the photograph. "This Ahwa group presumably wants to make an example of someone—kill an EU official—or use him to get into the summit."

Everyone sat quietly. Hamrén nodded. The analyst continued:

"We have begun to develop a profile, a preliminary profile, of this 'Redstripe' and the other users. What we are looking at is typically a man in his twenties, above average intelligence, comfortable background. Very knowledgeable about programming, but primarily self-taught. Almost ever-present in circles developing open code, and also involved in illegal file-sharing networks to some degree. He has antisocial, in some cases sociopathic tendencies. Most of his social interaction is via the Internet and he has a more-or-less global spread of contacts. He feels little or no affiliation with the society that surrounds him; it is this group that represents his values. Politically, it's harder to profile; the people in the group aren't generally interested in traditional politics or in parties. They have a more anarchistic approach to things. We think that, at some stage, agents of the Ahwa group have recruited them. Perhaps they don't even know that the group exists, they're just in contact with a middleman who doesn't reveal the organization behind it all. It's likely the people behind these usernames aren't familiar with the organization in Cairo; they're being used as instruments of terrorism."

After a brief pause, Magnus said, "MI6's assessment, which our colleagues at MI5 also share"—he nodded to Wilson—"is that this group has the will to carry out attacks that can damage vital societal functions. They have the ability to carry out an attack against a summit, the ability to damage key political institutions, and pose a direct threat to those participating in the meeting on October 10th. Finally, they have a motive and have plenty of opportunities to carry out attacks during the days of the summit. In short, these individuals pose a threat to national security."

"Where are they?" said Wilson in a low voice.

"We don't know."

"You don't know?"

"We haven't been able to locate the individuals physically. Not yet."

"Then it's probably best if you hurry up."

"Do we have anything on their method?" someone asked. "Of attack, I mean."

The analyst shook his head. "We still don't know what their course of action will be. But, given they are planning to get close to their targets, some kind of attack. Not in the building, as they appear to be targeting chosen individuals. We don't know; they may even be planning a bomb attack. It's most likely that these people"—he pointed at the discussion thread on the screen—"are not the same people who will carry out the actual attack. We are assuming that this group's task is to gather the necessary information for the planning of an attack. It would be in line with the way many Salafist groups are organized—as a network of isolated cells, where each cell has a specific function and operates without contact with others in the Ahwa group or the people who have been chosen to carry out the attack. Well, you are familiar with the structure."

"Suicide bomber?"

"Or, as I said, a more targeted attack. It's too early to say."

Hamrén got up and thanked the analyst. Magnus sat down.

"Okay," said Hamrén, "you know what the deal is. Track them down. Find them. I want names, addresses. Are we watching Badawi?" he said, and received an affirmative murmur in reply. "Good. Report back to Anders and me." He nodded at the Head of

Directed Surveillance. "We're also receiving reinforcements from London now," he added, looking at Wilson. "I want you all to cooperate fully with our British colleagues."

Everyone got up. On the way out, Bente caught up with Wilson.

"Roger."

He looked at her. "Yes?"

"That channel." She fell into step with him.

"Yes?"

"Do we have any more on it?"

"You mean more signals intelligence? At the moment there's nothing else."

"Are you sure?"

"What do you mean?"

"Well, is there anything else we ought to know?"

He stopped and looked at her. "What do you want, Bente?"

"You connect Jamal Badawi and this cell and their attack planning."

"Yes?"

"And Carina Dymek."

"Yes. And?"

"There are a lot of question marks hanging over these connections."

"Lots of question marks." He tasted the words. His lips were drawn into a joyless smile.

"Yes."

"Bente . . ."

He looked at her with an amused, almost pitiful expression. She thought it was probably the face he used in certain interrogations. It was simultaneously fatherly, caring and judgmental, which in stressful situations, extreme situations, brought about a deep sense of hopelessness in the person being interrogated.

"There are always lots of question marks," he said calmly. "What do you want us to do? Should we wait while these Arabs get organized and then hope they don't carry out their attack?"

She said nothing, waiting. A stream of people passed without noticing them.

"You know, Bente, if we had acted more quickly in July 2007, we would have stopped the bombs. A lot of Londoners would still be alive. But we were so preoccupied with question marks. We couldn't see the threat through all the bloody question marks. If there's one thing we've learned, it's that innocent people die when people like you and I hesitate. Don't hesitate."

"I didn't say that we should hesitate. But we need to have good reasons for our actions."

"Jamal Badawi is part of a Salafist organization," he said irritably. "I'm pretty sure he's building a network—and Dymek is one of the first recruits. The guy is a threat. That's reason enough for me. London is following this closely. Washington, too. There are a lot of people who want them off this earth. I don't intend to sit here and wait while the Ahwa group refines its bomb technology."

"If we act and it transpires we were mistaken, it'll be a damn mess."

"You sound like a politician."

"But am I wrong?"

"It doesn't matter. We don't let this Badawi out of our sight for a second. If he starts to make a move, we'll grab him. That's how it is."

He made an attempt to move on, but she said quickly, "Who's Jean Bernier?"

"Who?" He recognized the name but hadn't understood who she meant.

"Jean Bernier," she repeated. "The man in the picture."

"He's their target. Why are you asking?"

"Yes, but why him?"

"I don't know. Does it matter?"

"Do you know who he is?"

He looked at her in puzzlement. "Should I? London identified him for me." He shrugged his shoulders. "He's a civil servant, someone they want to kidnap, whose head they want to chop off as an example, I suppose. We'll have to see. Why are you focusing on him? Focus on the Arab and his stupid girlfriend instead."

Hamrén appeared.

Bente had almost pushed Wilson to the edge, almost made him roar. Another ten seconds and she would have had him on the ropes, would have made him say something he probably shouldn't have, something that showed what London was really thinking. But the moment was gone.

19

Stockholm, Monday, October 3

Medborgarplatsen was deserted on a Monday morning. Only a few early birds on the way to work could be seen hurrying by when Carina came out of the subway station. A cold, drizzling rain had fallen over Stockholm during the early hours of the morning. Droves of pigeons had sought shelter under the benches and ruffled their feathers in the wet, shaking the water from their wings. It was a quarter to seven.

Early morning was the best time of day to swim because you had the pool to yourself. Routine was important, especially now that she didn't have a job to go to. She had decided to do forty lengths and then go home and read the top secret documents that Jamal had gotten for her. The papers were in her apartment, waiting.

The swimming pool was empty apart from three other swimmers who swam silently to and fro in the lanes. Carina slipped into the chlorinated water, dipped her face in, and adjusted her goggles, then looked at the large clock face where the seconds slid by soundlessly. She pressed her heels against the tiles and pushed away from the edge of the pool.

Standing on the subway on the way home, she only heard too late that her cell was ringing in her pocket; she didn't manage to answer. It was Johan Eriksson. It surprised her that he was calling at nine on a weekday morning, and from his private cell, but she was happy to have a reason to talk to him. Luckily there was still a signal at this level. He answered right away when she called back.

"Hi, Carina."

The subway car went around a corner in the tunnel; the rails screamed. She covered one ear and pressed the cell harder against the other one.

"How are you?" he asked. He sounded tense.

"What can I say? I'm okay. Are you at work?"

"Yes." He paused. "Wait a second."

She heard him put the phone down, get up, and close the door to his office. Then he was back.

"Yes," he said in a more normal tone of voice. "I thought I would let you know. I don't know if I should, but . . . I'm doing it anyway." He stopped, and then said, "The department management had a meeting with Säpo this morning."

"Okay?"

The calm of swimming vanished immediately; worry crept back in. She moved quickly to the middle of the car, where there were fewer people, while she listened to Johan.

"I found out from Birgitta; a few of us were meant to have a breakfast meeting, but Birgitta called and said it was canceled because of an urgent meeting with Säpo. I went over to talk to her and she wasn't really allowed to say anything because it was about you—pretty serious stuff. Apparently they're going to take your case further."

"Further?"

"That's what she said."

"Further in what way?"

He didn't know. "The police were in here and emptied your office the other day. They took the computer and everything—a clean sweep." He hesitated. "You knew that, right?"

She swallowed. No, she hadn't heard that. And he was sure it was Säpo?

"They came out of the meeting a little while ago and I'm almost one hundred percent that it was the Head of the Counterterrorism branch who passed by in the corridor. What's he called? Hallén? No, Hamrén."

She closed her eyes.

"I thought you should know," he said when she didn't say anything.

"I'm glad you called." She looked around the car. Take her case further? Presumably some sort of investigation. They had emptied her office, so they were gathering evidence; the question was what the next step would be. She clenched her teeth and tried to stop the chill creeping along her spine.

Cupping her hand around her mouth, she said in a low voice, "What if they decide to arrest me?"

Johan sounded hesitant when he replied that he wasn't sure what she should do. The tone in his voice frightened her. For the first time since this had all begun, she was truly afraid; his voice was so lackluster, so quiet, he didn't sound at all like the cheerful Johan who could always find a solution. "I really don't know, Carina."

At home, she threw her swimming bag on the hall floor and opened the living room window. The fresh air surged through the apartment. The street below was empty; no one was visible—just parked cars by the pavements—nothing conspicuous. The anxiety made it hard to think. She had never imagined that the Security Service would be brought in; it meant they were taking what had happened extremely seriously. She didn't know how Säpo worked, not really; she could only guess. Perhaps it was the contact, the man in Brussels, who was the real problem? Or the report should not have been shared—not even within the Government Offices? The Security Service would take her case forward and she had no idea what that meant. They wouldn't believe her. Not if the department management team didn't believe her. She wasn't part of the House, not really. She hadn't taken the diplomat course; she was an upstart. They would never listen to her. She stood at the window until her arms were freezing. There was still no one visible on the street below.

Sitting on the sofa with a cup of coffee, she slowly turned the pages of the documents that Jamal had gotten for her. There were three short memos, all from the Ministry of Justice. She had asked Jamal what they were about, but he hadn't read them. She understood why—he wasn't really authorized to handle them. It had been a stroke of luck that Jamal had even managed to get the documents from the archives. Someone must have made a mistake. She couldn't involve him any further; he was already noted in the archive records as the person who had signed out the documents— that was enough.

The first memo was a record of a meeting held in Noordwijk, in the Netherlands, in June 2010. Ministers from all twenty-seven EU members had gathered at a spa hotel in the town and discussed a British proposal to reinforce Europe's fight against terrorism. The meeting was completely informal, it said in the report. The newly appointed British home secretary, Theresa May, was present. The atmosphere was good. She read on:

> The meeting was led by Great Britain's representative, Theresa May, who opened proceedings with a speech (see attached doc) about the British efforts to prevent and fight terrorism. May emphasized that the European Union now had a unique opportunity to become a key player in the fight against terror and organized crime. These threats were, by their very nature, global, and required a coordinated response to a far higher degree than was currently the case. The string of terrorist threats facing Europe showed how welcome and necessary such a reform was. The EU's Counterterrorism Coordinator, Gilles de Kerchove, praised the British initiative. It was a new level of European cooperation and a natural development of the Swedish initiative for improved exchanges of information and border controls that had been brought in under Commissioner Malmström. De Kerchove was of the opinion that it was possible to create "sharper European resources" that took better advantage of Europe's overall capacity to combat terrorism. "The threats are many. We shall face them as one."

Three pages followed, with a detailed description of the meeting. Several member states—Germany, Denmark, Sweden, the Netherlands—all supported the Brits, while France was more hesitant. Spain wanted to know more about how the coordination of operations and intelligence work abroad would function. Poland, the Czech Republic, Romania, and a few other eastern member states wanted assurances that the cooperation would not rule out bilateral contacts with the Americans. The overall impression, it said in the report, was that the EU sphere saw the British initiative in a positive light. A short comment concluded the report:

> The opportunity to operate transnationally, arrest and transport suspects, the use of lethal force, secret operations, etc. requires a number of changes to Swedish law. Given the political sensitivity, this demands the greatest caution in dealings with parliament and other authorities. The proposal also suggests that the EIS should have the right to conduct signals intelligence, using national resources, without explicit permission. This will require amendments to the so-called FRA laws and is technically complex. However, the Ministry of Justice is of the opinion that the British proposal is a natural development of the surveillance of data traffic already being carried out today. Proposals for a "sharp" resource as part of the EU's counterterrorism operations should be welcomed.

A number of changes to Swedish law. Carina found herself staring across the room. This couldn't be right. She read the text aloud to be sure she had understood it correctly. Without further authorization, without asking permission, using lethal force, carrying out secret operations, and cooperating with the FRA to use the data and surveillance resources of the authorities. Without having to ask parliament, without having to ask anyone at all except a small operational unit in the Government Offices.

At the back were two appendices: de Kerchove's speech in full and a list. The list was classified as top secret—for the protection of national security. It comprised fifty-four names, all numbered, presented in a long column. She read through them slowly; there was no Jean. Next to each name was the name of the organization to which they belonged. There were names listed for Sweden and, next to them, in parentheses, it said, Security Service, MUST, and the National Center for Terrorist Threat Assessment—NCT, respectively.

Security services. It was a list of contacts for a spy network within the EU. It merely confirmed what she had read in the report, but here it all was in black and white: a kind of European CIA with black ops, signals intelligence, all the apparatus required for an international spy organization.

Together with the other documents, there was one with the title *Annex*. It was some kind of legal agreement, which opened the way for potential cooperation. The text was extremely technical and referred to a number of international agreements on crime prevention, the Hague Convention, and other EU legislation. If she understood correctly, the agreement opened the way for foreign military and police to operate on European soil, but she wasn't sure. She would let Jamal read it; perhaps he would be able to explain it in more depth.

The final document was just a letter-headed page of A4 paper with the title *Guidelines for contacts with parliament and other authorities*:

All contact with parliament shall be kept to a minimum due to the sensitivity of the issue. The matter should not become known to any ministries except for the Ministry of Defense, the MFA, and the Ministry of Justice, and even within these ministries the information should only be shared with a very restricted, narrow group of people who are directly affected. Contact with other authorities concerning the matter, such as the Migration Board or the Swedish International Development Cooperation Agency, should only occur based upon the decision of the political leadership (justice minister or junior minister). As a rule, all such contact should be handled by the Security Service. Communication by e-mail or phone concerning the EIS should be, as far as is possible, kept to a minimum. Contact with the EU should take place informally in order to avoid the involvement of parliament.

She reread those lines. Avoid the involvement of parliament. A large part of the government was presumably also not to be informed about the project. By managing it "informally" it would probably not be necessary to tell elected politicians anything about it.

She pushed the papers away. It couldn't be right. Was it the same Ministry she worked for that had contributed to this? There was no doubt that the document was authentic; the text followed the typical guidelines signed by the junior minister for foreign affairs, setting out the rules. There was a short list of the people and departments at the MFA that had received a copy of the document—over twenty names and five departments—she recognized several of the names.

This was wrong. A government that did what it liked without listening to anyone was a monster. Parliament was elected by the people; they had a right to know. Jamal would have said it was the first step toward a dictatorship. It was against Swedish law. This was an enemy within speaking.

This was dangerous information. Merely being in possession of the document was a risk. She got up, determined to burn everything in her sink, but changed her mind right away. Don't burn them. Even if it was a risk to keep them, it was a risk worth taking. No one knew she had them; no one would look for them here. Furthermore, no one knew that she knew that parliament was being kept in the dark about the plans contained in the report. The report had caused nothing but trouble, but these documents were different—they couldn't be allowed to disappear. When the time came, they might be useful. If things went really badly, she could always send the lot to a newspaper; it would all go off like a bomb.

Greger should have been in touch, she thought. She hoped he had found something, but there were probably thousands of people in Brussels called Jean. Perhaps she shouldn't have involved Greger. Suddenly, waiting was unbearable. She was unable to control her anxiety; she felt it everywhere, like eczema on the inside. She called Greger, but all she got was his cell voicemail, so she sent him a text.

How's it going? Call me.

The website with Jean's picture looked just as it had done before. The photograph was still there. Seeing him in the picture made him seem more real and that calmed her. She looked at the photograph for a while then pushed the computer away. While lost in her thoughts, the doorbell rang.

20

Stockholm, Monday, October 3

Bente squinted into the sharp sunlight falling through the glass windows. The parking lot outside was bathed in bright daylight. White sky; parked cars.

Ten minutes to go. A young couple dressed in identical sweatpants appeared, pushing a shopping cart. They stopped by one of the cars, opened the trunk, and loaded their shopping. The woman said something to the man before they got into the front seats of the car and drove away. The cart was left in the middle of pavement.

The ICA supermarket in Sickla Strand was open from eight in the morning to nine at night, but at this time of morning it was almost deserted. The occasional pensioner could be spotted in the aisles, or perhaps a father on paternity leave, with a newborn strapped to his front. The cafeteria was mostly empty. A man in dirty clothes was sitting and muttering to himself. At another table, three builders were drinking coffee.

The target had left the apartment just after eight on Monday morning. No one had been seen coming or going since then.

Bente looked at her watch.

Three minutes.

If things were as the Brits said they were, and Badawi was a threat, it would rock the boat in Swedish counterterrorism circles. If they had missed a threat so close to the government, then something about the work of the Security Service was seriously wrong. She didn't know what to believe any longer. According to London, they were worryingly close to a disaster. If the British assessment of the situation was right, heads would roll at the Security Service, someone in the Swedish system would be held responsible for missing the threat. Kempell was presumably on a precipice. He had called her on Sunday evening, subdued. He had been informed that management wanted to review the handling of the case. Criticism had been directed at Counterespionage because they hadn't seen the connection to the Muslim Brotherhood. It had been a long time since she had heard him swear. He was worried about his budget, was pissed off at Hamrén, who he thought was moving forward too fast, without any caution. It wasn't even certain that this was a terrorist threat, he had argued. She had listened to him; sometimes that was all you could do when Kempell was really upset. She understood him. But it didn't matter; now it was all about Badawi. Late on Sunday evening, Counterterrorism had managed to arrive at an overall picture of the situation and had been able to take their first operational decisions. One of them was to go into Badawi's apartment.

At nine fifty on the dot, she drained what remained of her coffee and got up from the small café table at the entrance to the supermarket. She checked inside her coat—cell, wallet, service weapon—and headed toward the exit. Counterterrorism had told her to do some shopping first. Their attention to detail was meticulous, and they had even given her a shopping list. She was just a normal Swedish woman shopping at ICA, so in her left hand she had a shopping bag as she passed through the automatic doors and walked to the car. No one would remember that she had been there—just as it was meant to be.

Nine fifty-two. No rush.

She drove carefully through Hammarby Sjöstad, past new buildings overlooking a canal, and continued across a small square and along an avenue. There was barely anyone out. The people who lived in this area worked in the city during the day. Very few had criminal records. Well-behaved young office workers—that was the typical profile. A man with a stroller walked past; in a café, there were two youths with a laptop each.

She turned into a side street, noted the spotter in a green Golf. Okay. She parked and remained in her seat for a moment.

There: a small white van. It glided quietly along the street and turned the corner. She got out and began to walk toward the main door. The van had parked at the back, and, out of the corner of her eye, she saw one of the spotters in the café get up and move toward the exit. She walked calmly past an interior design store and a deserted restaurant, crossed a narrow side street that ran between the buildings and, for a moment, caught a glimpse of the area between the structures: a playground and a gravel yard, no people. Three more doors and she would be there.

The main entrance opened on to a dark stairwell with paint-spattered walls. It had been recently cleaned; a pungent smell of solvent lingered between the walls. She took a few brisk steps up into the stairwell and listened: someone was moving, probably two or three floors up; probably a cleaner, judging by the sweeping sounds, the rattle of a plastic bucket. Otherwise, nothing but silence.

She moved backward and got into the elevator where three technicians were waiting for her with their bags; they nodded at her. They went up in silence. The apartment was at the top, on the seventh floor. When she and the technicians reached the top floor, three operatives in plain clothes were already preparing for the intrusion. One of them carefully fed an optical cable cam under the door and was studying a small screen: an entry hall that opened on to a larger room. No movement; no sound.

The apartment had been under surveillance for the last twelve hours. All movements in and out of the main door had been noted. Badawi had arrived with Carina Dymek just after eleven on Friday evening and they had stayed in all weekend, apart from a short period, around seven in the evening on Saturday, when Badawi had gone to a Japanese takeout place on the same street to buy food. On Monday morning, Dymek had left the apartment at the same time as Badawi and gone home by way of the swimming pool.

Bente didn't like apartments. However much you prepared, you never quite knew what was on the other side. It was risky. Sometimes it went to hell, like last summer in Copenhagen when PET did a routine check on an address and found a guy in the bathroom with a Glock. That was probably worst—when someone was lying hidden and waiting.

A door opened a few floors below them. A bright, child's voice emanated up through the stairwell; a woman spoke to the child in a low voice. The elevator began to move. For goodness' sake, hurry up, she thought.

One of the technicians carefully unlocked the door and backed away. The plain-clothes operatives moved quickly through the open door, one after another. All were quiet. A dark hall opened out in front of them. Reflexes set in, a sudden sharpening of the senses as everyone moved through the apartment. They didn't expect to find anyone at home, but you never knew. Suspects who were hiding were risking in their lives in situations like that. The drill was to open fire if you couldn't clearly see someone's hands, if someone was deemed to be a threat by, for instance, making a sudden movement that might be an attempt to grab a weapon.

It was crucial to quickly take control of all spaces and ensure that anyone there was forced to surrender immediately; otherwise they were risking their lives.

But the apartment was empty. Bente put on gloves and moved slowly around the rooms, checking that no marks or damage from their intrusion were visible. It was a large two-room apartment, light, open plan, sparsely furnished. A surprisingly clean home— not a single speck of dust was visible. It was almost as if no one lived here, but the bed was unmade. In the sink were two wine glasses and a few plates. Magazines were stacked tidily on the coffee table; the dining table had been thoroughly wiped. There was a flat-screen TV on one wall, alongside a stereo and a computer. The kitchen was equipped with a brand-name fridge and an expensive-looking espresso machine. It fit the profile: young, competent civil servant with a decent income. This was the home of a meticulous person who would notice differences; they had to be careful. She stood in front of the small bookcase and read the titles. They were mostly crime-fiction novels and few of the usual classics, along with a lot of academic texts from the legal field and a few TV box sets.

A thin volume caught her attention. It stood out because of its tattered spine covered in Arabic characters, otherwise it would have been barely visible, wedged between two reference books. Being careful not to accidentally damage it, she worked the book out and slowly turned the pages. It had been read many times. Several pages were dog-eared and had been colored by the visiting fingers, some were crinkled due to water damage. Arabic poems, so far as she could tell. She stopped. In one of the poems, the final two stanzas had been marked with a pencil line. She showed it to one of technicians.

"Photograph this."

The technician put the book on a table and took several photos with his digital camera. Bente cautiously returned the volume to exactly the same location in the bookcase.

The plainclothes officers had waited for a while, bored, but had now disappeared. The apartment was quiet. All that could be heard were the technicians quickly and confidently working on their installations. One of them was squatting and installing a camera into a doorframe. In the kitchen, his colleague was attaching a microphone behind one of the halogen spotlights. There were now microphones in four locations in the room, he said; they would provide a perfect rendition of all conversations—the slightest sound.

"How long do you have left?" Bente asked.

"Fifteen minutes."

She flipped through a stack of films and CDs next to the stereo, carefully opening one case after another. A few Cronenberg films, some dramas. Nothing eye-catching. On the coffee table was Badawi's laptop. They would leave that. The technical unit had already infiltrated the hard drive with a Trojan and was running a spyware program that recorded everything: all e-mails and Internet logs, every keystroke, every click. Counterterrorism knew exactly what Badawi did on that computer. For example, they knew he had booked a trip to Cairo for two—now that was interesting.

On the fridge were a few bills, held up by a magnet. She glanced at them, mostly out of habit, then checked the sofa to see if anything was sewn into the cushions; she looked in the bathroom, searched the washing basket. Dymek was a regular visitor, judging by the panties in the laundry and the two toothbrushes by the sink.

One of the technicians appeared. "We're done."

Bente waited by the elevator while the technicians did a final once-over, putting everything in the apartment back to what it had been before. When they were finished, they turned off the lights and locked the door behind them, so casually that, for a moment, they looked like they lived there.

21

Stockholm, Monday, October 3

The noise made Carina jump. The doorbell made a long and aggressive sound, as if some brat was holding the button down. She got up and went into the hall. Through the peephole she saw three men standing in the crumbling stairwell.

They were waiting outside her door. Dark leather jackets, short hair, alert faces. They were clearly waiting outside her door. She had never seen them before. The one at the front reached forward and rang the bell again. Another piercing noise cut through the air and left a silence in its wake. Then there were heavy knocks on the door. She backed away.

"This is the police!" she heard from the other side of the door. "Open up!"

Her stomach did a somersault. She could have fallen to the floor and just stayed there. It was several seconds before she could move.

She ran through the apartment to the living room window and looked out. The street looked just as it always did, with one difference: right outside the main door to her building were two dark-blue double-parked Volvos. As she looked out, she saw three men standing and talking to each other and two others looking up at the window where she was standing. She moved back from the window hastily. For a protracted moment, she tried to understand what was happening.

They had come to arrest her.

She hadn't thought it would happen so quickly; it had only been a few hours since she talked to Johan. She tried to control her breathing. She couldn't be arrested. Not that.

The doorbell rang again.

No one would believe her. Not the Ministry, not the police—no one. If they brought charges, she didn't have a chance. If only the man who had given her the report knew what had happened . . . Only he could explain the situation to them. She had to find him before Säpo caught her. She had to get out.

The fear made her thoughts run through her mind like pure water. She moved quickly and purposefully, grabbing what she needed: computer, passport, wallet, keys, cell—and the report, the documents. She grabbed her swimming bag and threw everything into it, then pushed her feet into a pair of sneakers.

A heavy pounding could be heard through the door and then the doorbell rang again. Then a different sound: a low whining that quickly became a throbbing, scraping sound. They were drilling the lock out.

There was a small window in the bathroom, facing the yard. It was narrow, but she would be able to squeeze through. A bar of soap on the windowsill fell into the bathtub and bounced along making a dull clang like a church bell. She swore and pushed her way through the window with the bag in her arms; she leaned out with her feet on the windowsill, one arm holding the window frame. Next to the bathroom window was a ledge and, beyond that, a small balcony belonging to the next stairwell. There was about a meter between the two. For a second she almost changed her mind and climbed back into the apartment. She looked down and gasped.

The apartment block was four stories tall. Her legs felt limp as soon as she peered down the façade of the building. One slip and she would be dead. Perhaps it was completely crazy to do this; perhaps it would be better to go back inside and open up for the police . . . but the balcony was only two meters away. A few steps, just a few steps along a ledge on the façade and she would be there. She hung the bag out of the window and swung it through the air, throwing it toward the balcony. It landed with a thud on the inside of the rail. With her left hand she took a firm grip of the window frame and turned around slowly so that she had her back to the abyss. Carefully, she moved her right leg out into the air and put it down on the ledge. It couldn't have been wider than five or ten centimeters. She carefully moved backward out of the window and pressed down with her foot; it didn't give way. After a brief hesitation, she moved her weight to her right leg at the same time as she moved her left foot until she had just the tips of her toes on the window frame. There—a small lightning rod. She fumbled for it with her right hand and began to lose her balance. Nice and easy, she whispered to herself in between breaths. Nice and easy; nice and easy. Her legs shook. She pressed herself against the wall of the building, clasped the lightning rod with her right hand and slowly pulled herself away from the window, putting her left foot down on the ledge. Then she let go of the window. The ledge shook a little, but held. Don't look down, she thought. If she looked down, she would fall. She concentrated on the yellow plaster façade; its grainy pores were right by her face. Perhaps this was the last thing she would see in life, the dirty yellow plaster encasing the building in which she'd lived. This idea jolted through her body like an earthquake and for a moment she thought, I'm falling. But she was still there with both feet close together on the ledge, balancing on her toes like an odd ballerina. She wouldn't manage more than a minute or so; her calves were already trembling. Using small steps, she moved toward the balcony, first her right leg, then her left. Not too fast; nice and easy. A few centimeters at a time. She rested beside the lightning rod for a few seconds before continuing, holding the rod in her left hand now.

She had gotten about halfway when she heard a noise from the bathroom window. Perhaps it had blown shut, perhaps the police had gotten into her apartment—she didn't dare turn her head to find out, but just continued. Forward, one step at a time. The last bit was the worst. She needed to let go of the lightning rod and hurl herself toward the railing. If she slipped, she would fall precipitately on the outside of the balcony railing. Don't slip; nice and easy. She clenched her teeth and stared at the balcony. There was her bag, just a meter or so away. She bent her knees, tensed her thighs and with a violent exhalation she made a small leap to the side. For a brief moment she was floating in midair, four floors up, with her arms wildly outstretched. Then she hit the railing and grabbed hold. One arm slipped and she hit her face but managed to hang on, pull herself up and find a foothold. The disgusting taste of blood filled her mouth. A pulsing pain spread through her nose. Kicking, she fell over the railing and on to the balcony.

She got up and grabbed the balcony door, but it wouldn't open. The door was bolted; the latch was on. Without really thinking, she took her bag and used it to break the window. Then she stretched her arm through it and undid the bolt before pulling the door open.

She entered the stairwell and rushed up toward the attic. She couldn't risk coming out of the neighboring door on the street—she would be seen—she had to get away cleanly. A gray fire door led into the attic. She put down her bag and rooted through her swimming things and other possessions until she found her keys, and unlocked the door. At first she could see nothing and she groped around helplessly. It smelled of dust and damp. The dark was so dense that it was impossible to adjust her eyes to it. Then she spotted the small red dot in the darkness and rushed forward to press it. A row of pale light bulbs came on, revealing a narrow, winding passage between hundreds of storage units, all with small, numbered wooden doors. She knew that the attics in the apartment blocks were old and ran right across the top of the building. With a little luck, she would be able to make her way across the building and come out on the other side. There was a door that opened on to a small side street. She jogged into the storage area in the next attic, until the lights turned off and the darkness enveloped her in the blink of an eye. She groped her way to the next light switch, found the fire door to the next attic and continued along the lit passage. The storage units stood at attention in the gloomy light; small side passages led off to all sorts of dark places. Finally, she reached the end of the attic and crept through a fire door.

A stairwell. There was music playing somewhere.

She ought to be three doors down from her own stairwell, if she had calculated correctly. She heard nothing and caught her breath before hurrying down the stairs. On the penultimate floor, she paused to try and quell the sound of her panting while she listened.

No one was visible down by the door on to the street. The cold, fresh air hit her when she carefully opened the door. She was, as planned, three doors down, at the opposite end of the building from her own, the door that faced on to a narrow cul-de-sac. When she stepped on to the pavement and looked around the corner, she could see the dark-blue cars; they were still there. No one was visible on the street.

She crossed the road and walked, quickly, crouching down slightly behind a row of parked cars. She wanted to run, but someone might still be sitting in one of the cars and spot her.

At the corner of Tegnérgatan she couldn't stop herself any longer, she began to run, crossed to the other side, and ducked under some scaffolding, heading toward the crowds on Sveavägen. The whole time, she wanted to turn back and check no one was following her, but at the same time it was as if the action of looking over her shoulder would give her away, make her face stand out among the crowd. Every second, she was expecting the dark-blue cars to glide up alongside her, for firm hands to grab hold of her. Her legs shook. She felt unwell. She stopped at a pedestrian crossing by Sveavägen and was able to slow down and fall into the same leisurely pace as everyone else crossing the road when the light turned green. She hurried past a 7-Eleven and rushed up the hill, taking the steep steps up to the Observatorielunden park three at a time. She turned around the corner of one of the buildings belonging to the Stockholm School of Economics and almost knocked over a woman pushing a stroller when she reached the Observatory hill.

She ran up one of the small sets of steps. On the hill, just below the observatory, she had to stop to catch her breath. Her arms and legs were shaking and felt powerless. A couple of youths sitting on a bench looked at her. Why were they staring at her? Go to hell. Stop staring. She was sweaty, but shivering. Slowly, she carried on along the gravel path toward the viewing point next to the old, venerable observatory building that rested among the trees with its large, dark and shiny windows. She leaned against the railings that ran along the edge of the steep hill and looked out over Stockholm.

It had started to get dark. The darkness protected her and she relaxed a little. Her face hurt; she could feel it now the agitation was wearing off. It was all so unreal; the police had come to her home. Perhaps it was a mistake, she said to herself. Perhaps they were looking for someone else. But she knew that wasn't true. They had rung her doorbell; they had been looking for her, not anyone else. When she was sure she was out of sight from the street, she lay down on the grass. The damp chill pressed against her back right away.

22

Stockholm, Monday, October 3

An overcast sky loomed between the gaps in the trees, but in an hour it would be completely dark. Carina sat up and wiped her nose. The slight contact stung; tears filled her eyes. The back of her hand came away covered in blood. She got the towel out of her bag and held it carefully against her nose and waited.

The wet grass was soaking her pants so she stood up. There were no people here, just a grassy hill, trees. She took the towel away from her face. A deep red stain had formed on it. She rooted through her bag, found her cell, and called Jamal, but he didn't answer. He was in Vienna again this week, she remembered. She left a short message and asked him to call her. She didn't want to tell him what had happened; she had been the bearer of enough bad news lately. But she needed help. She wouldn't be able to return to her apartment; the police might still be there, and, even if they had left, she couldn't risk being there. They might come back tomorrow, or in just a few hours; it was impossible to know. She called Greger. He answered right away, as if he had been standing by with the phone in his hand.

"Hello, Carina," he said cheerfully.

"Greger, something has happened." She told him quickly.

He fell quite silent. Then he asked where she was.

"I'm in the Observatorielunden park."

"Wait there. I'm coming."

She went back to the viewing point and hung off the railings that ran along the park perimeter. The ground here fell downward in a steep slope, as if the hill had been cut with a large knife. From where she was standing, she had a panoramic view of the city. Far below was the evening rush hour on Sveavägen, while a mild light shone from the tall windows of the cylindrical main building of the city library into the dark evening. The people were small black dots, impossible to distinguish from one another. Traffic gathered at red lights. Carina shivered; goosebumps appeared on her arms. It was windy here. Plastic bags, stuck in the bushes, rustled and flapped. She looked around, but the only people nearby were some teenagers, smoking on a bench some distance away.

Why had Säpo come to her home? She didn't understand. She hadn't done anything wrong, she had merely responded in the way she had been trained to; perhaps she had made a mistake, but she was no criminal. Thoughts whirred around her mind like a dark mass of flies. She was a suspect, but for what? She knew how the MFA's procedures worked and she had expected to be called in for a disciplinary hearing. But Säpo . . . That was quite different. She had thought the matter could be sorted out, but instead she had quietly become a suspect—perhaps she was on a wanted list—and she didn't even understand why.

The sharp sensation of anxiety made her draw in the air through her teeth. Jamal. She needed to talk to Jamal. She went and sat on a bench, checking the time on her cell. It had been fifteen minutes since she called Greger; it would probably be a while before he arrived. At that moment, her cell began to vibrate. Incoming call. Number withheld.

"Hello?"

"Is this Carina Dymek?"

An unknown, businesslike voice.

"Yes."

"My name is Bente Jensen. I'm calling from the Security Service. I'm calling about a document that you've come into contact with— about the circumstances surrounding it."

Carina said nothing.

"This is a tough situation for you; I understand that. But it can be resolved—if you're prepared to talk to us."

The voice stopped, waiting for her answer.

"I haven't done anything," she said finally.

"I'd like to meet you. You don't need to worry. You know where the Security Service is based, on Kungsholmen. Come to the main entrance at ten o'clock tomorrow morning. I'll meet you there."

She heard how the woman waited a few seconds for an answer.

A sudden impulse made her hang up and put the phone down beside her. Perhaps it was stupid, but she couldn't stop herself. Her mouth was completely dry, and the knowing anxiety had returned. That woman, with her businesslike, calm voice, had tried to get inside her head. Säpo, she was just a case for Säpo. She got up from the bench and moved restlessly toward the old observatory. She really wanted to believe the woman, that things could be resolved. But how would she ever find Jean if they held her back, took her into custody?

A car appeared on the street. It drove past, made a right turn into a nearby residential street, and disappeared. Carina spied down through the trees. The street was empty.

Wait here, Greger had said. But for how long?

She threw her bag over her shoulder and began to wander toward the sloping lawns.

A grainy half-light lingered between the trees. The lawns were empty, dark surfaces. She was halfway through the park when a dark-blue Volvo appeared on the street. She stood completely still and watched as the car drove slowly along the edge of the park.

23

Stockholm, Monday, October 3

Bente reached out toward the conference phone in the middle of the table, lying there like a flying saucer at rest, and switched it off. The persistent sound of the cutoff phone line disappeared, and, in the silence that followed, she heard Hamrén swear quietly. Everyone else around the table said nothing. A few seconds later, the comms radio on the table in front of the Head of Operations came to life, crackling. One of the spotters was reporting in. No Dymek. They had left Dymek's apartment and done a few laps of the nearby area in search of her, but there had been no trace.

There were around thirty surveillance cameras in the area and Dymek's description had gone out to the command center. The patrol that had entered her apartment had been able to ascertain that she had left the apartment quickly: by all appearances, she hadn't packed anything and hadn't taken any outdoor clothing. A window was open; she had probably climbed out of it. She had not been seen leaving the building.

"I think we've lost her."

Hamrén looked up and nodded slowly.

Bente hurried down two stories and through the security doors in the corridor that led into the technical unit. Before Dymek had put down her cell, they were able to triangulate her exact coordinates by following her phone's GSM network communications through the base stations.

A technician passed Bente some headphones. She pulled them on and immediately all sound around her vanished. All she could hear was a kind of whistling, rustling. She took off the headphones. It was the silences in the conversation between her and Dymek, explained the technician. He made some adjustments with the computer—enlarged the sounds, purified the quality—and turned up the volume. Then she heard it: trees. The unmistakable rustling of treetops moving in the wind. But no voices; no one there except Dymek. She was moving on foot. She was probably therefore within a radius of no more than three kilometers, if she was moving at a high pace. If someone didn't help her to disappear, she might still be on the way out of town.

Dymek had fled. That surprised her. She hadn't thought Dymek would react so dramatically; it didn't fit her profile as a careful, conscientious civil servant. Perhaps Badawi was controlling her, like the Brits had said. In that case, this wasn't just an individual but a terror network responding, pulling together, regrouping.

When she returned to the top floor again, she found Hamrén and the Head of Directed Surveillance in the command room. Two teams had reached the park. They had found her cell—it had been lying on bench by the observatory—and they had done a sweep of the area. But no Dymek. Bente went to the window, where she had a view of central Stockholm and the railway tracks running toward the central station. She put her hand against the cool glass, drummed her fingers against the blank surface. Darkness was falling.

24

Stockholm, Monday, October 3

Carina crouched behind a tree and tensed each and every one of her muscles, ready to jump and flee. They had found her, despite everything, she managed to think, before the car moved slowly on.

She stayed behind the tree until she heard someone shouting. She recognized the voice but barely dared to believe it was actually him.

"Carina!" Greger appeared on the path. When he caught sight of her, he came to her and gave her a hug. "What have you done to your face?"

Blood had flowed; some had smeared across her cheek.

"Nothing to worry about. Just a nose bleed."

Greger looked at her in concern. "You look fucking awful."

They hurried down to a waiting taxi. She noticed the driver looking at her in the rearview mirror and brushed her hands over her face. Red flakes of dried blood stuck to her fingers. She sat and looked out of the window while they drove through the city center, looked at the people and traffic flowing by. Soon enough they were in the southbound half of the Söderled Tunnel. Splashes of yellow light pulsed through the car. They got on to the main road. Neither of them said a thing; she didn't want to talk while they were in the taxi. At Gullmarsplan, the taxi turned off and continued through the dark and deserted suburban streets of Årsta, before finally coming to a halt at the end of a long street in front of a tall apartment block.

She waited while Greger paid and then followed him through the main door. Standing in the elevator, she saw her reflection in the mirror for the first time. She looked terrible—blood smeared across her cheeks and around her mouth.

The tenth floor had paint-speckled walls and dark wooden doors. It smelled of fried fish. She had never visited Greger's before; they always met in town. Greger unlocked one of the doors at the end of the hallway and let them into a dark entrance hall, taking care to close and lock the door behind them.

For some reason, she had thought Greger would live a spartan existence. Perhaps because he was an IT technician, perhaps because he had never said a word about interior design. But this apartment was anything but a random assortment of furniture. The living room was dominated by a sofa suite that looked expensive and designer, with a fancy coffee table with chrome legs in the middle. A large portion of the walls was covered in framed photographs and old concert posters. The entire apartment gave her the bizarre feeling of having entered an exclusive rock club. Greger quickly folded up a few sweaters that were lying on the floor and put them in a wardrobe.

She remained standing still until Greger told her to sit down; it was as if she had stopped thinking. She sank on to the sofa.

"What's happened, Carina?"

"I told you—the police came."

He looked anxiously at her.

"They rang the doorbell while I was in the apartment—three plainclothes officers. Then I got a call from Säpo."

He shook his head. "Why would they call you?"

"I guess . . ." She broke off and thought about it. She hadn't really had time to think about why they had contacted her. Despite the fact that she worked at the Security Policy Department unit at the Ministry, she really knew very little about the Security Service and how it operated, how they worked. It was one of Sweden's most secretive authorities and the Ministry of Justice, not the MFA, ran it. Only those who had authority, who had working relationships with that part of the police, had any insight into the organization. But she knew that they dealt with cases to do with breaches of secrecy, stuff that could be categorized as the disclosure of secret documents, espionage.

"I guess they're investigating me." Her voice cracked and she felt sick. Was she a security risk?

"What did they say, then?"

"It was a woman who called and wanted to talk to me. She said that it would all get sorted out if I just cooperated with them, something like that." It occurred to her that she didn't know where her cell was. She rifled through her bag, felt in her pockets.

"Shit."

"What is it?"

"I left my cell in the park."

Greger watched as she rooted through her things again. But she knew she was right—the cell was lost. She had put it down on the bench, in the park. It was an expensive smartphone, full of apps, phone numbers, door codes, and her calendar that encompassed everything she needed to remember. She swore again.

"It'll be okay, Carina."

"No, it won't be okay. For fuck's sake."

"I promised to help you. So I've had a word with a few people that I know. Old friends. There are some people looking for Jean right now, and they know their stuff. I think we'll be able to find him."

"Are you sure?"

He shrugged his shoulders. "Ninety-nine percent."

It was possibly her only chance. She held her head in her hands. "I never thought it would be like this."

"I suppose they're in a bad mood at the MFA," said Greger.

"But *Säpo*. It's completely insane."

"They just called and wanted to talk, right? If you had really committed a crime, they wouldn't do that—they would have stormed your apartment with the sickest SWAT team they could."

She couldn't help but smile at the way Greger put it, as if they were in some action movie. But he did have a point. They would never have called her if they really saw her as a danger—as a threat, as Security Services liked to put it.

"Everything will sort itself out," Greger said with an emphasis that almost convinced her. "Now, this is what we're going to do. We'll have a bite to eat, then head to a friend's."

"This evening?"

"Yes. Alex is hosting the party. She's one of the people who have been helping to find Jean. It would be cool if you got to meet her. You'll like her." He shrugged his shoulders. "I'm going, anyway. I can't just sit at home. I need to get out, and I think you do too."

Going to a party was one of the last things she wanted to do right now, but it might be worth it if she got to meet someone who was looking for Jean. She needed to get a grip. She didn't want to go home yet and she couldn't just stay here in Greger's apartment.

"Okay," she said without any great enthusiasm.

"Wonderful."

He got up and fetched a well-thumbed pizza menu from the fridge. He threw it at her. Pick one; he would get it. He looked at her and shook his head. She was welcome to use the bathroom, take a shower if she liked. "You look like a fucking car crash," he said with a smile.

Perhaps Greger was right, perhaps she just needed to let go of everything for a bit. She chose a salami and arugula pizza. Greger pulled on his coat. He would be back soon. There were clean clothes in the wardrobe, he said with a nod to her bloodied T-shirt.

"Thank you for helping me, Greger."

"No problem. I'll be back before you know it."

When he had gone, she stayed sitting still for a long time in the quiet apartment. Finally, she was able to go to the window and look out. For a moment, she was convinced that there would be someone outside, looking up at her, but of course there wasn't. All that was out there was a normal Stockholm suburb. From the window she could see a traffic circle lit by streetlights. On the other side of the road was a cycle track that ran along a row of recently planted, fragile-looking trees. Further away were some lower residential buildings barely visible but for their rows of windows shining out into the gloom. A cyclist passed by and kept going into the dark.

She undressed and took a shower. The blood had dried on her face; her nose was tender but not broken and there wouldn't be any marks. She shuddered as she thought of how she had climbed out of the window. It was extremely dangerous; in hindsight, she couldn't comprehend that she had actually done it. Perhaps she had overreacted. The police had visited her and, as Greger said, they would never have done so if they truly believed she was a security risk. Presumably the Ministry had reported the matter to the police to establish what had actually happened and to get it off their backs. A couple of years ago, a guy at the UN Mission in New York had given a Coreu, a secret message intended for all EU capitals, to a Russian. There was an investigation, he had been recalled to Sweden and been put in the cooler. Everyone knew about the case.

It felt good to stand under the water and let it stream over her face and body. She yearned to swim, to feel the cool tiles against the soles of her feet and then push away from the edge, to be enveloped by the water. After forty lengths her head was always quiet, empty, and her thoughts more focused. She closed her eyes and imagined surging through the water, her arms flinging themselves into the weak opposition of the water, the regular movements of her body, blood roaring through her ears.

After the shower, she examined her body in the mirror. There were a couple of ugly bruises on her arms, as well as one under her left breast. What had she been thinking, jumping out of a fourth-floor window? She could have died. But she had panicked, she hadn't been able to stop herself. At least now she knew that Säpo was looking for her. She looked grimly at her own reflection, fixated by her own gaze. "Fix this now, Carina," she muttered aloud. "They will not be fucking right. *You* are right, remember that. You are right."

She pulled on her jeans and started to look in Greger's wardrobe for a top she could borrow. All his clothes were neatly folded. It was a bit embarrassing to rummage through his socks and underwear, so she quickly chose a sweater, which proved to be a little too large, and closed the wardrobe door.

Fully dressed, she lay down on the bed and shut her eyes. The fatigue after showering must have swept her away because she awoke with a start, with a feeling that it was the middle of the night. Only a minute or so had passed.

On the bedside table was a framed picture: a black-and-white photo of Greger, smiling, together with a beautiful man of Indian appearance. Carina picked it up and looked at it. Presumably it was Simon, Greger's now ex-boyfriend. They were lying together in a hammock, Simon with an arm around Greger in a tender gesture. A happy picture. She had never met Simon, but Greger had often spoken of him. He was an economist and trainer at SATS. He was Greger's great love but, from what Greger had said about him, Carina got the impression he was fairly mean and self-absorbed. Greger had been worried and angry many times when Simon had stayed out all night, refusing to say where he had been, and about Simon's rages, after which he would stay at one of his friend's. It pained Greger. But they always seemed to manage to solve their problems and they really were in love. Greger normally told her in detail about the trips they had planned—this summer they had intended to rent a cabriolet and drive through southern Italy. But that hadn't come off, she supposed. In the picture, Greger looked so happy, so relaxed, his face smooth as he lay in the arms of his man. They had been together for five years. She carefully put the photograph back.

25

Stockholm, Monday, October 3

A few hours had passed and everyone at Counterterrorism now knew that Dymek was gone. People without training rarely managed to disappear like this, but Dymek was out of sight. It was surprising, and ominous. It probably meant that she had help, that there were individuals around her who were trained to handle this kind of situation.

"Hi, Bente." Hamrén came up to her. "Come with us. We're going for coffee."

They went to a coffee machine. Despite being in the middle of an operation, the floor was in an evening lull. Only the people working on the Ahwa case, as it was now being called, were still working at their desks.

The team had searched the city center, swept the large thoroughfares, but even after just an hour it was clear they wouldn't find her. They decided to stop. Dymek was gone; it was better to quickly change tactics.

Bente pressed the button for a black coffee. A weak headache had begun to pulse above her right eyebrow. She needed caffeine.

"We lost Dymek," she said. "A shame."

Hamrén glanced at her, as if he thought she was trying to point the finger at him for a failed operation. He was on his guard. "We'll find her."

They needed Dymek. Dymek was their way in to Jamal Badawi. She was probably the only one who could give them a better understanding of the Ahwa group and the connection to Badawi. And a better understanding of herself, for that matter. Islamist groups were closed environments; it took a long time to get into them and win the trust of such people. As a non-Muslim, it was almost impossible. But Dymek was already there; she probably already had their trust. At the very least, she knew more than Counterterrorism did about Jamal Badawi.

"I don't like to ask you for this," Hamrén said.

"You mean you don't like using the Section's resources?"

"Yes, yes. The Section."

He was tense. She understood why: letting SSI into the investigation was acknowledging that his own branch couldn't manage the situation alone. But he had no choice. The Security Service had no right to request signals intelligence against Swedish targets. Signals intelligence was managed by the military and directed at external threats, abroad. That deficiency was the reason for the SSI's existence—to be a silent resource shared by the Security Service and the FRA, which made it possible for Säpo to listen in to Swedish data traffic.

She smiled at him. "Of course."

"Good. Good."

Hamrén nodded toward a chubby young technician who was sat spinning on his office chair while writing at his computer. She could talk to that guy over there; he would help her with the practical stuff. Hamrén downed his coffee and returned to the office area.

The Head of the Section's signals intelligence unit was at home. Bente could hear the noise of the TV in the background, then the abrupt silence as he hurried into an adjoining room. She explained the situation in brief. They needed targeted searches against Carina Dymek. "And Jamal Badawi," she added. "There will be data coming in from Stockholm, and possibly London. I don't quite know what, but names, technical parameters. Feed in everything you get. This is top priority, so call in as many people as you need."

When she had hung up, she sent a text message to Mikael giving him a three-sentence situation report, then refilled her coffee cup and approached the technician that Hamrén had pointed at. He was in deep concentration as he dissected Dymek's hard drive, and didn't notice Bente until she was right beside him. When he found out who she was, he quickly began to tell her which measures were currently being taken: IP numbers were being found, MAC addresses, routing tables, and hundreds of other technical parameters connected to Dymek's residential address, her work computer, and private Internet subscription. They had the work computer, but unfortunately not Dymek's private machine. The technician shook his head. A real shame. They had submitted requests to all the large telecoms operators to be notified if a new customer called Dymek turned up. They were already tracking her bank card. Similar measures were in place against Jamal Badawi.

"We're expecting a lot of information during the next twenty-four hours . . ."

"Excellent." Bente gave him a look to tell him that was fine for now. The technician nodded and looked at her uncertainly.

She handed over the contact number for the Head of Signals Intelligence at the Section. The technician looked at the number, taking it in carefully, as if it was an advanced algorithm. The Section was something different, something you hoped to become a part of but for which few were sufficiently qualified. It would be a pleasure, he said. He lifted the phone and made a brief call, instructed some colleagues and hung up. They were ready to begin.

He pushed a chair toward her. She sat down and watched in silence while he began to enter new selectors. There were special templates that were used to enter search terms in the databases for signals intelligence collection. They were stored there, together with millions upon millions of names of people, places, numbers, technical codes, and specifications that were, for various reasons, of interest to the military or the Security Service and were used to filter the flood of information that was sucked into the servers of the Armed Forces twenty-four seven. You could also search the digital and analog traffic flowing through cables across continents. Somewhere they would find a hit, it was just a matter of time.

When she got up from her seat, it was almost midnight. A group of technicians and analysts were still working at top speed on formulating selectors that they would then feed into the Section. She had spent a few hours reading the British intelligence reports, pointing out names and words that were relevant to the surveillance, but her presence was soon superfluous. Signals intelligence was heavy on the technology, and she was no technician. She knew nothing about software in cells or computers, had no idea how you created secret doors to enter other people's e-mail accounts or how you tracked a website log-in via cookies. Her speciality was the motivation and behavior of people.

Dymek was in flight. Perhaps she would stay still for the next forty-eight hours. Logistics were crucial in these situations. An individual with somewhere to hide and someone to arrange food, clothing, protection, perhaps even a new identity, had a far greater chance of getting away. Something told her that Dymek hadn't left the country. They would have known if she had tried.

It was sad, an intelligent young woman ruining her prospects like this. And Jamal Badawi, employed at the Ministry of Justice— diligent, good reports, no complaints. What made a young man like that fall in with a crowd of terrorists? There were models for understanding profiles like that, yet there was still something fundamentally incomprehensible about people, who had all the best opportunities, rejecting them, turning their backs on society, and throwing away their lives.

Bente passed a row of civil servants, all sitting at their computers, unmoving, and she couldn't help but stop. Different, grainy sequences of film flickered on their screens. Counterterrorism and parts of the National Bureau of Investigation were processing a mass of surveillance footage from central Stockholm. If Dymek had been caught on film, they would find her before morning. Stockholm wasn't big.

The fresh, humid air grabbed hold of her coat as she came out of the office. She took a deep breath. The October darkness lay tightly between the buildings. At the crossing outside the Security Service building, the traffic lights were blinking yellow. Only on a cold autumn night in Stockholm could city streets be this deserted.

Dymek was gone. But a person on the run was forced to hide every day, every hour and minute; the person hunting her only needed one moment to find her.

They needed so little: one word in a phone call, a transaction, a card payment, a brief visit to one of the web pages now being watched. It was time for the machines to do their work.

All that remained for Bente to do was one of the key occupations of her profession, which it had taken her a long time to master but which she had begun to appreciate more and more over time. She had to wait.

The ability to be still, in anticipation, waiting for the right moment and then knowing it was time to act—that was an art. It required calm, distance, and an ability to see the big picture. It required patience and an ability to endure uncertainty. But she was used to it. When the right moment came, she would know—and be ready.

26

Stockholm, Monday, October 3

The apartment thronged with people she didn't know. The loud music enveloped her in her chosen spot by one of the speakers. She looked around, sipping the beer someone had handed her. Greger had vanished. The last time she had glimpsed him, he had been in the kitchen, talking about something to do with computers to a guy with a clean-shaven head who was as fat as a Buddha.

She hadn't even met Alex, the host of the party. She and her friends were old hackers, Greger had told her on the way over in the taxi. They were different, lived an existence far from the nine-to-five of everyday life. Alex had done completely wild things. Greger had excitedly begun to tell her about when they had tried to get into NASA's systems. Carina had refrained from asking questions; she didn't want know.

In the middle of the floor, several people had begun to dance to the music. A heavy bass pulsed between the walls in the small apartment. There was an unbelievable crowd; the entire living room was a mass of bodies moving in the darkness. She watched them while she finished her beer, before forcing her way into the kitchen, getting a new one, and then changing her mind and pouring a large whiskey from one of the bottles on the counter. She still had no job to go to in the morning and might as well get a little drunk. Tomorrow, when she had slept and things looked clearer, she would call Jamal.

Around her in the small kitchen, people were pressed together, talking animatedly. She sat down at the kitchen table. The whiskey stung her throat. It was good, smoky. She got another.

"I'll have one, too, please."

She looked up. A guy with long blond bangs was standing next to her.

"There aren't enough girls who drink hard liquor. Girls should drink more hard liquor in general. Cheers."

"Cheers."

"What's your name?"

"Carina."

"Martin."

"Hi, Martin."

He swayed but regained his balance by leaning against a cupboard door. "How do you know Alex?"

"I don't know her. I came with Greger."

"Ah, Greger. I know him. We do stuff together." He grinned. "It's cool that so many of us are here, isn't it?"

"What?"

"Don't you know about Alex's site?" he burst out. "It's sick. I thought everyone knew about it."

"What's it about then?"

"Different projects. We build game environments. Things like that."

Alex, he explained, worked at EA but did fantastic things with open source code as well. EA? Yes, Electronic Arts. They made computer games. He looked at her in amusement. "You've no idea what I'm talking about, do you?"

"No."

He smiled.

"No, I know nothing about computers."

"But you drink whiskey; that's a good start." He reached for the bottle and sploshed a little more into his glass and then hers.

She ought to say no, but part of her wanted to get hammered. She held out her glass. It felt good to talk about something completely different; for a short time, she had gotten away from all the thoughts whirring in her head. For the first time in years, she had no idea what she should do and, right now, she didn't have the strength to think about it.

"What do you do, then?"

"I work at the MFA."

"Cool."

It just slipped out, an old habit. It wasn't even true any longer, she thought bitterly. Like so many others, he reacted with a mixture of curiosity and reverent distance, as if, in his eyes, she had been transformed into some other, alien being. The worst sort were the ones who began to ask her about current foreign affairs, as if she was a mouthpiece for the government, but he didn't seem to be one of them.

"So, what . . . ? You're an ambassador?"

She laughed. "No, no. I've been fired."

It was a silly thing to say and she regretted it immediately. The guy looked at her somewhat vacantly, unsure whether she was joking. He drained his whiskey.

"Oh. Fuck. What a drag."

She nodded and said it was all right. She asked what he did, in an attempt to change the subject. He was a developer at a company. Developed systems for logistics. He shrugged his shoulders and looked around; for a brief moment they hovered in a strained silence, surrounded by the roaring party.

She was grateful when a girl, who had been mixing a drink, leaned forward and said, "Are you Carina?"

"Yes."

"Hi. I'm Alex." She proffered a hand. "Join me; I'm going out for a smoke."

It felt good to get out on to the balcony. The tempo of the party had increased; the music was beating against the windows of the apartment. Sooner or later, someone would be knocking on the door to complain, she thought.

It was chilly outside. From the balcony, it was possible to see the center of the suburb of Fruängen, the darkened shops, and the subway station: a pale, neon installation with platforms that curved into the darkness. In the abrupt silence, she could hear the humming of a train in the station.

"Thanks for having me."

"Of course. Friends are always welcome."

Alex was a girl you took notice of. Short and toned, she was dressed in baggy jeans and a large gray T-shirt with a skull embroidered across the chest. She had a kind of serenity about her that Carina almost envied, a low-key assurance that demanded to be taken seriously. Alex dragged on the cigarette, moved her thick, dark hair to one side with an indolent head movement, and looked at Carina.

"So you want to find a dude in Brussels?"

"Yes. I need to meet him."

"What's so special about him?"

"He gave me a document," she said and stopped, unsure how she should summarize the last few days. What she'd experienced had been so unexpected that even now she occasionally felt like it had happened to someone else. "I had problems afterward. I need to find him and sort them out."

Alex nodded. "Greger said you'd been fired." She puffed on the cigarette. "I normally run a tight ship on my site. But he asked me, and I thought it sounded . . . interesting."

She began to thank Alex for her help, but Alex made a small, impatient gesture, brushing away the words.

"It's not entirely legal, but I'm sure you know that." Alex looked at her sternly, then laughed. "Not that I'm bothered. Just so you know."

"I understand."

She shivered; it was cold outside. Alex didn't seem affected by the chill.

"You really want to get hold of this guy."

"It's my only chance. They threw me out of my job, and this afternoon the police came to my house. But I haven't done anything. Only he can tell me what the hell is going on and explain to the people at the MFA that I haven't done anything wrong."

"We'll find him."

She met Alex's gaze; it was hard and clear.

"Politicians don't give a damn about normal people," Alex said. "Not really. I was part of the campaign against the FRA legislation and it was disgusting how much the politicians lied. They said that they cared about citizens' privacy and that was why they were voting for the FRA legislation. Do you understand? These people lie; it's their job. That report you got, the EU proposal, is just an example of how they try to control everything. So, no, if you're wondering—I don't have any problem helping you."

Alex stubbed out her cigarette against the balcony rail.

A tall, skinny girl danced up to them when they came back inside. She hugged Alex and said something Carina didn't hear through the music. It was past midnight; the party had begun in earnest.

"There you are."

Greger plodded across the room. "What's up?" He looked cheerfully at them.

"We're planning a world revolution."

"That's good." He laughed. "How are you? Do you feel better?"

She smiled, nodded. She did feel better. Something about the way Alex spoke had made her feel calm. She wasn't alone. She felt like things would be resolved, even if she didn't know how. She finished her whiskey.

Somewhere during the evening, a gap in time appeared. Carina clearly remembered standing and talking to Alex and Greger. Then she was offered another glass of whiskey, and spent a long time in the kitchen talking to three guys, but she couldn't remember what they looked like or what they had talked about. For the first time in several days, she forgot about the Ministry, the report, everything to do with her life. She danced for hours. Time disappeared. She didn't remember when everyone left; rather, she only noticed they had gone when the apartment was so empty that Alex was wandering around picking up empties, while a few guests lingered, talking. Greger was there, and a big guy with piercings. Carina was lying on the sofa and could hear their low voices while the apartment flew around above her in a slow spiral. She was so drunk. It was nice to lie there and close her eyes.

At some point—it must have been early morning—she awoke with her heart pounding and a feeling of desperation coursing through her body. The room was empty and dark. Around her, empty bottles and cans glimmered. Someone had thoughtfully put a blanket over her. When she tried to get up, the apartment capsized and threatened to overturn her, so she lay back down. She had shooting pains in her legs. What was the time? That thought and the thought of how she would feel the next day then appeared like small, sobering glimpses before everything vanished into a roaring, wordless blackout.

27

Stockholm, Tuesday, October 4

Carina squinted against the bright daylight streaming through the large windows. She had woken up a moment earlier with an unpleasant, floating feeling and she didn't know where she was. She was lying on a sofa and must have slept there for a long time, judging by how light it was. She was so dazed that she couldn't say with certainty what day it was. Tuesday, maybe—or Wednesday?

A garbage truck rumbled along the street below, making the windows rattle. She sat up painfully. The blanket had wriggled down around her; she pulled it away. The headache came like a slow pressure-point against the side of her skull. If felt like her head had shrunk two sizes during the night; the very smallest movement made her brain slide sideways and hurt.

It had been a long time since she had woken up in a strange apartment. The room looked completely different now: it was large and strangely peaceful. Someone had tidied up; the bottles were gone. A sudden feeling of shame came over her. At this time of the day, everyone was at work and she was here. When she tried to stand, she almost threw up. Cold sweat clung to her back. She sat stock-still until her stomach had calmed down.

The apartment was bigger than she had initially thought. Apart from the living room and the bedroom, there was also a study. In the kitchen, trash bags were lined up on the floor and a battery of bottles filled the counter, along with mountains of dirty dishes.

No one was home. She was grateful for that; she didn't want to talk to anyone right now; she just wanted to concentrate on forcing back the nausea and getting over the dreadful hangover. She hadn't had one like it for at least ten years. She had almost forgotten what it felt like the day after a real drinking session. She found the bathroom and took a quick, cold shower. She found a tube of toothpaste in the bathroom cabinet, squeezed some on to her finger and rinsed her mouth until she could only taste mint. She felt better already.

Standing in the bathroom, she heard the rattle of the apartment door. As if being discovered in the middle of a break-in, she held her breath and waited as the person in the hallway closed the door, took off their shoes, and withdrew into the apartment. She dried herself and dressed quickly.

In the kitchen, the girl, Alex, was making coffee in a Bodum French press. "Good morning," she said. "I thought you were gone."

"Hi. Yes, I . . ." Carina looked at the clock on the wall. "Is it half past three?"

Alex smiled at her. "It seemed like you really needed to sleep. Coffee?"

She nodded and stayed in the doorway to the kitchen, shy about being there, an unknown guest in an unknown apartment. Alex handed her a mug and looked at her with an amused smile.

"How do you feel?"

"Okay," she lied.

She sipped the coffee; it was so hot it tasted of metal. Outside the window, the pines swayed slowly. They looked alien.

"You look great."

"What?"

Alex held out her cell. On the screen was a picture taken late in the evening. Carina had an arm around Greger and was laughing with her mouth wide open. She was trashed. A girl she didn't know was hanging around in front of her and sticking out her tongue.

"I don't remember any of that."

Alex laughed.

They sat down and looked through the pictures from the party on Alex's cell. Carina didn't really feel like it, but was so weak that the mere thought of doing anything other than remaining seated and looking at the pictures seemed like an insurmountable effort. One of the last pictures was of her lying on the sofa with her head at a peculiar angle—she looked unconscious.

"Jesus Christ. I hope Greger doesn't put them online."

She hadn't thought about the report once since she had woken up, or the police, or the MFA; for a few hours, she had been free. But now it all came back. Reality regained its sharp contours. She needed to talk to Jamal. She finished her coffee.

"I think I need to go," she said. "Thanks for letting me sleep here."

"Already?" Alex looked at her in surprise. "You can stay, if you like. I'm just going to be working here for a bit." She nodded to a laptop on the kitchen counter.

"But . . ." The police, she wanted to say. But she was embarrassed; her tongue glued to her mouth. "I need to go home."

"Greger said that you probably shouldn't go home."

She looked up. Lively, brown eyes met her gaze.

"No, maybe not."

She leaned back and watched while Alex continued moving around the kitchen.

"Stay here for a few nights," said Alex with her back turned. "Then perhaps things will have sorted themselves out."

Alex reached into a cupboard, pulled out a box, rooted around, and handed her a small object. "Here." A plastic Mickey Mouse figure, and, dangling from its head on a chain, a key.

Alex wanted to show her something, and took the computer with her to the living room sofa. Carina watched while Alex opened her browser and logged in to a website—a forum with different discussion threads, as far as she could tell. Alex opened up a link and let her read it. It was in mid-thread and it was hard to understand what it was about. The posts were short, like telegrams. A number of usernames were throwing around different addresses and numbers.

"What is this?"

"This is our little secret," said Alex. She scrolled slowly through the thread. It was long, with hundreds of posts during the last two

days alone. This was what Greger had talked about. They were looking for Jean.

"My God," she whispered.

"This is Greger."

A photograph had been uploaded by the username Redstripe,
next to a post. *The* photograph.

He was there in the background—Jean. He had been circled and
Greger had uploaded an enlarged picture of his face.

Carina took the laptop and scrolled onward through the
thread. Around ten users were currently online and posting in
the thread, and the thread had a total of over five hundred posts.
New ones were appearing every minute.

She shook her head, as if she needed to jolt her brain to understand what it was that she was seeing. It was incredible.

"You see," said Alex. "You're not alone." Her cell rang. She got up
and left Carina with the computer.

She spent a long time reading the discussion thread and almost
hoped, for a second, that the posts would stop flowing in, but they
kept coming, each and every minute. Perhaps she had gone too
far; perhaps this was a mistake. But at the same time, what did she
have to lose? She went back to the most recent posts. Greger and
his friends were clearly getting close. This was bigger than she had
imagined possible.

"This is . . . impressive," she said when Alex came back. "But
do they know what this is about? I mean, do they know that the
police—"

"Oh, yes." Alex brushed away all further objections with a small,
dismissive gesture. "It's fine. This is no biggie for them. I know most
of them. They're good people and know what they're doing. What's
more," she added, as her phone chirped again, "the site is invite
only." She picked up her cell and vanished out of the room.

It was dark outside when Carina wandered down toward the center of Fruängen. It was a relief to get out; the apartment just made
her restless. An intense sense of unreality still lingered, as if it lay

between her and the rest of the world. She had slept most of the day and it still felt like she hadn't quite woken up.

It would be good to talk to Jamal; she missed him. Alex was kind to let her stay, but she wasn't sure she wanted to keep staying there—although going home was no option, not yet; she didn't dare. And she didn't have a key to Jamal's apartment. She sighed.

She cut across a residential parking lot between the apartment blocks and crossed a large playground. The streetlights had already begun to come on, and glowed with a weak pink hue. The day was already over. What was she doing here? she thought dismally. She was thirty-two years old and a diplomat—at least, until recently— and here she was, wandering around Fruängen, hungover.

The center of Fruängen in the late afternoon was deserted. All these suburban centers that had been built around the nodes of the underground network felt simultaneously pleasant and depressing. The dream of a good society, but all that was left was these low, barrack-like buildings filled with grocery shops and liquor stores. Some youths were passing the time outside the video store; an older man was in one of the chairs in the hairdresser's that had fading posters with the hottest styles from the last decade still in the window.

She found a pizzeria on the outskirts of the center. Three alkies were there, staring morosely at the street. An elderly couple was eating dinner in silence. No one noticed her. She picked a cola from the fridge in the corner and waited while the two guys in front of her ordered their pizzas.

"Yes, love—what can I get you?"

"Can I borrow your phone?"

The pizza baker shrugged his shoulders wearily. There was a phone next to the till, but it was apparently not for customers. He turned around, shouted something in Turkish to someone in the kitchen and got a short response. Yes, okay, he said. He pointed at the phone. Not too long.

It rang five times before Jamal answered.

"Badawi."

She exhaled. As soon as she heard his voice, it was as if her insides leapt. She leaned against the wall and felt warmth spreading through her body. Jamal was in Vienna, again. The delegation from the Ministry of Justice had entered a second round of negotiations about the budget for the UN agency, for which it controlled the Swedish contributions. Quietly, with one hand over the receiver so that the guy by the pizza oven wouldn't hear her, she told him what had happened. Vienna was so infinitely far away, but when she talked to Jamal he sounded like he was right beside her, as if he was at home in his apartment. It became quiet at the other end of the line. Where are you now? he wanted to know, his voice somber. She had thought he would shout loudly, get angry, but he sounded very serious, very matter of fact.

"In Fruängen." It sounded so odd when she said it, almost absurd; she laughed even though it wasn't in the least bit funny. A friend of Greger had let her sleep in her apartment, she explained, just for a night or two.

He wanted to come back to Stockholm. "I can catch the flight tonight," he said.

"No." She said it hard, almost too hard. She closed her eyes. How much she would have liked to say yes, come home, fly home. "It's not necessary," she said. "It'll sort itself out."

"I'm going to do it."

"But you might get involved in this."

"I'm already involved."

"You know what I mean."

He said nothing. Then he burst out with, "But it has to be possible to solve this!"

"Yes," she said, without any great conviction. "It must be."

She had shown him that damn report, and Jamal had gotten her the classified material from the archive: he was already an accessory. She definitely had to try not to involve him anymore, she thought to herself.

Jamal said that he had called her. He had gotten worried when she hadn't answered. She explained how she had forgotten her cell in the park. He wanted to know more detail about what had happened—had the police gotten into her apartment? Oh no, she said, not wanting to panic him. All they had done was ring the doorbell. But of course she had been frightened.

"I'm coming home on Thursday," he said. "See you then?"

"Yes, definitely."

They could go for a walk, he suggested. And then have dinner at his. "Things will be okay, Carina."

"Yes, I guess so." She sighed.

"They will. I'll help you."

She pressed the receiver against her ear and closed her eyes. He loved her. She could hear that he loved her.

"You're beautiful," she said quietly, and leaned her head against the wall.

One of the pizza bakers appeared behind her and took an order. He glared at her. She edged to one side.

"Jamal, I have to go. See you soon."

28

Stockholm, Tuesday, October 4

When she got back to the apartment, Alex was sitting on the sofa with the computer in her lap. Carina sank into a revolving armchair and looked at her. She felt completely empty after talking to Jamal. Standing there in the pizzeria and hearing his voice—a little stressed, a little distant—it had only made her feel more alone after hanging up. Would things really be fine? For the first time, she didn't think so.

"Are you okay?" Alex looked up while her fingers continued to clatter across the keyboard.

Carina nodded and looked at Alex as she continued to concentrate on her work. Now and then Alex would stop and—in a smooth, slightly absentminded movement—reach for her coffee mug, before continuing her rapid finger dance across the keys; she was clearly deeply engrossed in work that amused her, because she was smiling. After a while, she finished. She stretched, cracked her fingers, got up, and went to the stereo.

"There!" said Alex. She was in great spirits, and took a few small, happy dance steps on the floor as a heavy bass came out of the speakers. "We've found him."

Carina didn't understand at first. Jean? "Have you found Jean?"

"Greger called. They just need to double check a few things, but he was certain." Alex pulled out a cigarette and lit it. "He's coming over this evening."

A quiet jubilation grew inside her. Just a moment before, everything had been so hopeless. On the way back from Fruängen, she had decided she would call the Security Service and let them bring her in before things got worse. She laughed and got up.

Now there was once again a chance for her to prove who had given her the report, that it wasn't she who had leaked the report, but that she had done exactly the opposite—she had done the right thing all along and was innocent of all their accusations.

"Can I see?"

Alex logged in and brought up the thread. The latest post was only a few minutes old. Five usernames were connected and, while Carina was watching, the screen brought up a new post: *The Waterloo address—cross ref with other parameters. Running telephone reg again just for safetys sake. Ok, logging out now J afk 15 min . . .*

Alex leaned over her shoulder, scrolled down a few hours. "Here."

Yes, they had actually found him. She had begun to lose hope. The whole idea of finding a person with the help of a fuzzy photo had started to seem unlikely to her, like something out of a Bond film, but she hadn't wanted to say that to Greger. She laughed. In front of her on the screen she could see them discussing addresses, alternative names, checking records.

"Bernier," she read aloud. "He's named Jean Bernier."

The weakness that had been dripping through her body like a heavy molten metal, pushing her into the ground, was gone. Instead she felt a tough determination filling her to the brim. She would never give up. Never.

For one, prolonged, wavering moment, they sat in silence and looked at the screen, surrounded by the pulsing music.

"Why are you looking for him?"

"Jean Bernier? It's his fault. If he hadn't contacted me then none of this would have happened. I need him to prove that I'm not guilty."

Alex sat quietly for a moment. She had pulled up her legs underneath her and was sitting cross-legged on the sofa, which made her look even more like a backpacker in India, with her baggy pants and long hair, which she pushed to one side.

"What did he want, then? I mean, why did he choose you?"

"I think . . ." Carina said and then stopped herself. She thought about how he had caught up with her after the meeting. Everyone had been so repulsive. She remembered how much the French representative had provoked her with his usual, well-formulated way of arguing for the review of border controls in the Union. They had talked about migration flows, about security—as if it was about swarms of locusts. "He gave me the report because I had a conscience. That's what he said."

Alex looked at her thoughtfully, took a final drag on the cigarette, and stubbed it out on the foot of a lamp. "So do you have one?"

"I guess so."

She had always been proud to work in the Foreign Service. She had never doubted Swedish foreign policy, not really. She had always believed that, if you did a good job, things would be okay. And yet, here she was, in hiding.

Greger turned up at around seven, along with the enormous, shaven-headed guy who introduced himself as Victor. "Great party yesterday," said Greger, grinning knowingly. "You really came alive." Apparently she had been completely impossible to wake up, even when they had tried to carry her to a mattress in the study. Did she feel better? Victor smirked when he thought she wasn't looking.

They sat around the coffee table, each with a cup of coffee. Greger pulled out a notepad filled with handwritten numbers, jottings, and a grainy black-and-white printout of the photo. It was very pixelated but she could still see clearly that it was the face of the man in Brussels.

"It took a few days, we had to double check a few things, but I'm pretty sure we've got the right guy."

"Jean Bernier."

"Exactly." Greger turned the pages of his notepad. "French citizen, lives in Brussels. The thing is, there were five Jean Berniers in the Brussels area. But there was only one who matched the photo—the one you said you met." Greger tapped the printout. "He works at the EU Commission, in something called . . . GD Home. He's a lawyer. Although perhaps you already knew that."

It seemed right. GD Home, or the Directorate General for Home Affairs, as its full designation ran, was the part of the EU Commission that dealt with matters concerning police cooperation, terrorism and organized crime, and border controls.

Greger cast an eye at her briefly before continuing. "He often turned up in connection with departments . . ."

"A2 and A3," said Victor, who was half reclined in one corner of the sofa.

"Exactly. Victor managed to get on to an EU server," said Greger with a grin.

"Okay." She kept her mouth shut, tried not to think about what that actually meant. It was illegal.

"We acquired an extremely informative list," Greger continued and passed her a piece of paper.

She glanced down it: a list of names, roles, titles. "What is this?"

"Employees at A2."

Someone called Markus had found a page on LinkedIn and, through that, they had been able to compare the information with the Belgian motor-vehicle register, Victor explained in a satisfied tone. Then they had run the picture through various recognition software before managing to hack into an EU server. "That solved most of it. I put a Trojan on it . . ."

Greger and the others keenly discussed various technical issues, which very quickly became incomprehensible to Carina. She half-listened while reading the list. There were around one hundred names and, in amongst many others, it said, *Bernier, Jean.*

GD Home had legislative powers for anything to do with migration, law enforcement, which data could be stored and for how long, as well as hundreds of other areas. Their reports shaped thinking in the capitals of the Union.

The EU Commission consisted of eighteen Directorate Generals and each Directorate was fighting to survive. As one-eyed giants, those working on competitive matters saw competition in everything; GD Home probably saw the world as nothing but a matter of interior security. The Directorate General always tried to expand

its influence through repackaging politics and recovering important issues to its own corridors, winning over member states, winning over the EU parliament. It employed cadres of researchers and
experts, courted capitals and their governments, and then made
proposals. Its reports landed on the tables of governments and told
ministers what was good and what would never fly. It shaped European politics. It had the power to change the lives of millions. It was
from those corridors that Jean Bernier had come. He had sought
her out. But what had he expected? She flipped through the list
again. Did he think he would be able to go against a giant like the
EU Commission? Perhaps he was just crazy. She sighed.

"Here are the addresses." Greger tore a page out of his notepad:
a list of telephone numbers and addresses. They had been forced to
check all Berniers in Brussels to be sure, he explained. There were
eight; five of them were called Jean. It was hard to say which of the
addresses was right, but it was probably this one—he tapped his
finger on the one at the top; it was circled—an address in Waterloo,
in the southern quarter of Brussels. She nodded. Waterloo: that was
the right area. Affluent, prosperous, lots of diplomats and civil servants in the EU bureaucracy lived there.

"This is great. I'm so, so grateful . . ."

"No problem." Greger laughed. The pleasure had been all theirs.

Carina took the notepad and slowly turned through the pages;
she looked at the photograph of Jean Bernier for a long time. She
hadn't thought that it was possible to find out so much information
about one person, but they had been thorough. Here was everything she needed. It was possible.

29

Stockholm, Wednesday, October 5

Bente was in the backseat of the patrol car and looked across the small, suburban square as they rolled past. A few teenagers were smoking on a bench. A man with a walker was coming out of the grocery store. Otherwise, there were just some normal shops where very little was happening: a video store and a hairdresser, a liquor store.

A phone call from Dymek to Badawi had come in the evening before. The address had been traced to a pizzeria. The investigators at Counterterrorism had already interviewed the employees during the morning. They had been able to identify Dymek and recalled that she had come in at around six o'clock and made the call from their phone, before leaving on foot. Counterterrorism was working on the hypothesis that she was within walking distance, no more than two kilometers radius. There were around five thousand households within that area. A person could hide for a long time in an environment like that.

The car slowed down. The police officers in the front seat looked to the side and studied the two young individuals on the bench. Then they moved on. The faux leather seats squeaked. No one said anything. They were ordinary police and knew nothing about the investigation, didn't know who Bente was, only knew she was in the Security Service and that she was to accompany them on a search of the area. They were curious, but reserved. That suited her just fine. She had no desire to engage in small talk.

The residential areas opened out into an expanse on either side of the road: black-green shrubbery, tower blocks, and parked cars. They passed a playground. A group of children were running around the enclosed area; they stood out like colorful stains against the dark asphalt.

Everyone left traces. It was unavoidable. Dymek might have left the suburban area, might not even be in the Stockholm region, it didn't matter. The IRC channel had provided hundreds of digital footprints and Counterterrorism was now following them, connecting them to physical addresses. Of the approximately fifty people who had visited the discussion thread, around forty had unprotected IP numbers. They had been identified by Counterterrorism and checked against records; they were not of interest and had been ruled out of the investigation. That was how it worked: identify, sift, prioritize. Five or ten people were left.

Two days of signals intelligence had begun to provide results. The British netspionage had closed in on the IP addresses of three of the usernames using the IRC channel. One of these was in Malmö and two were in the Stockholm area. Early that morning, they had implemented intrusive measures against the individual in Malmö and were now able to follow their traffic and discern patterns, behavior, which pages were visited. The people were young, clever programmers and had no previous criminal records. No extreme views—they were not jihadists—just supporters of Internet liberalism. What was emerging was a loose group on the IRC channel who knew each other, who socialized. The individuals were spread across northern Europe, Canada and the USA. There was nothing that tied them to any crime, but the interceptions were productive, the footprints led on.

The police driver turned around. Did she want to see more? They could do another lap. She shook her head: no, that was enough. There was nothing else to see here. They headed toward the arterial road.

At Globe City, they turned off and stopped in front of a corner shop. One of the officers asked if she wanted anything. The driver went in and returned with a bottle of water and three cups of coffee. She thanked him and strolled away with her coffee, checked her cell and looked in the window of a clothes shop. The two police officers remained by the car and chatted, glancing at her when they thought she wasn't looking.

The office was full of people when she returned to the Counterterrorism department at the Security Service building. She sat down at a free computer and logged in. Masses of new e-mails had flooded in during the morning, and she almost missed what Hamrén had sent her and the heads at Counterterrorism at nine thirty-five—he had also copied in management. It was short—only a few sentences. Hamrén informed everyone that an agreement had been struck with British signals intelligence, Government Communications Headquarters. It was a temporary reinforcement of the investigation. They would now be able to draw on GCHQ's significant resources, he wrote. Everyone was encouraged to cooperate in full.

Hamrén was happy to work with Brits and liked to move quickly. But bring in GCHQ? Was it even allowed to use British signals intelligence against targets on Swedish soil? GCHQ had processors strong enough to penetrate any encryption out there. They had entire departments filled with mathematicians who could pull apart civilian algorithms in a matter of days. From their headquarters in Cheltenham, the British followed the behavioral patterns of over fifty million people online every day, via their signals intelligence. Their supercomputers could, at any given moment, process billions of phone calls, e-mails, and transactions. She had visited the facility, together with the Head of the FRA and a select group of people from the northern European security services, where they had spent two days discussing how best to track terror suspects who had left Schengen, how to target signals intelligence against third countries. GCHQ was the crown jewel of the British intelligence service. It was from Cheltenham, through their network of over fifty offices worldwide, that British signals intelligence was managed. The headquarters was three hours from London, in the midst of grassy hills and small, picturesque villages filled with stone cottages and rose gardens, with names like Bishop's Cleeve and Minsterworth. She would never forget the way in which GCHQ looked like an enormous gray doughnut in the middle of the soft landscape—an alien body.

She found Hamrén in his office. Wilson was there too. She had really wanted to talk to Hamrén alone and was close to leaving, but Hamrén had already seen her.

"So we're bringing in GCHQ?" She spoke Swedish. Wilson looked at her cautiously. It was clear he didn't understand—that was just fine.

"Yes, that's right."

"A bit dramatic, don't you think?"

"Oh?" Hamrén turned his back to her and put some papers in a file.

"I don't understand why you're involving the Brits. The Section has sufficient resources."

"The Section has nowhere near enough resources, Bente. We need to move forward more quickly. The summit is next week. We need to act in the next few days."

"Sorry," Wilson interrupted. "Are you talking about GCHQ?"

Hamrén nodded.

"Is there a problem?"

"No, not at all," said Hamrén with wooden smile.

"This isn't how we normally work," Bente said to Wilson.

"With GCHQ?"

"In investigations."

"So how do you work?" Wilson looked at her in amusement.

Hamrén tried to interrupt her, but she beat him to it. "It's not in proportion to what's going on."

Wilson looked at her in surprise. "I don't think you're taking it seriously enough," he said without dropping his gaze from her. "We're facing a terror attack against the EU."

Hamrén nodded emphatically. "We're taking the threat seriously, Roger."

"Clearly not all of you."

Bente had intended to tell Wilson that she was probably the one who took things the most seriously around here, but Hamrén interrupted her. He clicked his fingers—a hard little explosion in the middle of the room. "That's enough, Bente," he muttered. "We'll talk later."

She sat back down at her seat and worked for an hour, but she was angry, found it difficult to concentrate. All the voices, all the people moving around her—it all annoyed her. Just before lunch, a situation report arrived. She read the e-mail slowly. So-called intrusions were being made into the IRC channel with support from British resources, apparently. With the help of GCHQ, data was being sorted, automated searches of relations and patterns were being carried out, parameters compared. Targets could quickly be distinguished. A further sixty-five targets had been localized and tagged with physical addresses. Two more encryptions had been penetrated. One of the usernames, Frontline, had been tracked down to a residential address south of Stockholm, another to an address in Berlin. It was pointed out in the report that GCHQ had huge databanks that gave them the ability to test data against a large volume of stored phone and web traffic, transactions, and state records. The prospect of being able to identify all suspects was considered good.

She went to the IRC channel and scrolled slowly through the discussion. Hundreds of new posts had been added in the last twelve hours. The tone was disciplined, but easygoing. They were discussing practical things. Someone had now found Jean Bernier's home address. *Have you checked the car?* wrote Redstripe at one point, and got a *yup* from Frontline just minutes later, together with an extract from the Belgian motor vehicle register.

Hamrén irritated her a great deal. He was wrong, she thought. The tone wasn't at all typical of what extremist websites normally sounded like, not even among autonomous communities. Extremists had a completely different tone. There was something naïve here, as if the people involved were basically playing a game. They were joking. She knew that Counterterrorism was convinced that this was some kind of attack planning—she had thought that herself, initially—but it didn't make sense. If this was attack planning, why choose Jean Bernier in particular? She had never heard the name before. A normal lawyer at the EU Commission.

She read on and noted that the username *Redstripe* was the one leading the discussion. Perhaps Dymek was hiding behind a username like this one? Redstripe. She opened Dymek's profile and brought up the photograph provided by the MFA. Set against a gray-white background was a young woman with determined features. Dark blond, longish hair. Serious gaze. Desk officer Dymek. This woman was a diplomat, a trained lawyer. Her bosses had described her as clever, ambitious. Would she have friends on a website for programmers? Would she socialize online with hackers and the generally antisocial? It didn't make sense.

Hamrén came toward her along the corridor. She stood to meet him and he came right up to her, forcing her against a frosted-glass wall.

"What the fuck are you doing?" he said in a low voice. He was furious.

"Jesus! What's up with you?"

He had surprised her. If she had been a man, he would have physically shoved her, she was sure.

"You've crossed the line."

"Surely justified criticism should be voiced?"

He stared at her. People nearby were looking at them, she noticed.

"You're welcome to contribute to the investigation. But take care not to piss off our partners. Understand?"

"I have to be able to discuss the investigation with you—what shape it is going to take—surely?"

"That's wasn't what you were doing. You crossed the line."

She looked at him and decided, quite calmly, that she would no longer take him into consideration. Hamrén thought he had the right to lay down the law with her; she would beat that out of him soon enough.

"My dear Roland," she said sweetly. "You will not tell me where the line is. You're letting the Brits make far too many decisions."

He looked at her, his face quite empty. "You know that we need them. Their intelligence is world class. Coming into my office and insulting Wilson is completely unacceptable. If you carry on like that then you have no business being here. Is that clear?"

Bente met his gaze. She could have bitten his head off, the little twit. But she was canny enough to know not to, not now, not while surrounded by curious onlookers. She nodded slowly.

30

Stockholm, Thursday, October 6

Everyone's gaze turned toward Bente as she entered the room. Wilson smiled with exaggerated friendliness toward her. His assistant, Sarah, stared. Hamrén merely glanced briefly at her and looked back down at his papers. She was not welcome. The Head of Directed Surveillance had stopped when the door had opened and turned toward Hamrén. Bente pulled out a chair and sat down, without saying a word.

"It's okay. Go on, Peter."

The Head of Directed Surveillance cleared his throat uncomfortably.

"Yes. As I was saying, all we have to go on is the phone call. We still have no definite information about where the meeting between Badawi and Dymek will take place, only that they agreed to eat dinner at Badawi's some time during the evening. We'll still be able to retain reasonably good control of the situation. If they take a walk, it may be across a large area, but no more than a few kilometers in radius. A team will follow them, ready to provide coordinates for where Badawi and Dymek are. We'll be near Badawi's apartment—here." He pointed at a map, spread out on the table. Others leaned forward. "There is a building site near his address; the first team will gather there. The second team will follow them on foot. If they take the nearby Tvärbanan light-rail system, then the second team will follow. We also have a small team up by the station, here." He pointed.

Wilson was looking at Bente, right across the table. He had a puzzled, thoughtful expression, as if wondering what to do with her. The others noticed this and fell quiet. It became so quiet in the room that she could hear the murmur of traffic outside the building. The woman from MI6 was the only person to continue taking notes in her notebook, before she too glanced up and looked at Bente, expressionlessly.

They didn't dare drive her away. However much they wanted to, they couldn't ignore her, despite her questioning of their investigation. She was from the Section. They needed her; Security Service management listened to her. The sun streamed through a gap between the faded curtains, lighting up the projector screen that was still on the opposite wall. Bente concentrated on relaxing her face completely and meeting their gazes.

This was the third meeting since yesterday of the operation's command group; she had missed the two previous ones. She hadn't been told. They had changed the times, moved venue, and not told her. It was pure chance that she had caught sight of Hamrén's assistant an hour ago; Bente had waylaid her, forced her to go to her computer, log in, and give her the meeting times. Hamrén was sitting diagonally across the table, twirling a pen between his fingers and looking at her with no particular facial expression, as if he was waiting. She met his eyes. He blinked and looked away.

"Well then," Hamrén said, turning to Wilson, who hadn't moved an inch. Everyone was waiting, even him. He wasn't in charge here, it struck her. Someone had told him that Bente Jensen was to be kept out of the loop. Or the decision had been taken after a discussion between those sitting at the table now. Perhaps Wilson had turned up in Hamrén's office, pulled the door shut, and said a few choice words. Hamrén listened to London.

"I think we're done," muttered Wilson.

"And Badawi?" Bente interjected.

Bugging of his phone and the rooms at his address was ongoing. They had been listening in to his apartment, his cell, and his e-mails. It wasn't giving them much. Since his return from Vienna earlier that day they had heard only music—classical—and the sound of Swedish TV. Even his work computer at the Ministry of Justice was being watched. There was little activity, nothing unusual. The hypothesis that Counterterrorism was working off was that he was awaiting fresh orders from Cairo.

"He's under control," said Hamrén.

He truly was under control. The technical unit had intercepted a text message sent by Badawi to Dymek less than an hour ago; they had agreed to meet at the Skogskyrkogården subway station. They could arrest him whenever they liked. Wilson rapped his knuckles against the table, as if to emphasize what he was saying. He wanted to hear every word said. Every word. Hamrén nodded. They quickly ran through the evening's operation, step by step. A select group from the department would make up a cell team of two cars. A group of British specialists would participate. Positions— here and here. Wilson pointed at a map of the area. They briefly discussed communication procedures, wavelengths for radio contact. Instructions for effective fire.

"Do we have any more on Bernier?" Bente said to the room at large.

They had begun to rise. Hamrén had already thanked all present and closed the meeting when she posed the question through the scraping of chairs. Hamrén said nothing while Wilson pretended not to have heard.

"What do you mean?" The woman from MI6, Sarah, had turned her unmoving, narrow face toward her. London's analysis was that one of the EU Commission's employees was under threat, she explained rapidly. "That's our assessment. A targeted attack against that individual, probably to make an example of him."

That was the Swedish assessment of the situation too, added Hamrén.

Everyone vanished into the corridor and dispersed into the office. They tried to pretend she didn't exist. She watched Hamrén and Wilson leave together. The leadership team would presumably start to talk about her as soon as they resumed their conversation somewhere else in the building. She left the floor without looking around.

It was cold in the subterranean parking lot. She got into the car and turned the ignition key, switched on the radio and the heating, then drove out of the city center, to the west, across the Traneberg Bridge, and continued along the main road. She was in no hurry, and she needed time to think.

The arrow on her navigation system pointed straight ahead. The road ran north, alongside the subway line, past small suburban centers and expansive residential areas behind sound screens bordering the road.

Soon enough, she reached a leafy suburb filled with villas. She turned off at a crossroads, rolled on to a residential street, and stopped at a turning circle to check the address.

The Dymek couple lived on one of the side streets, in one of the smaller wooden villas. They had lived here since the middle of the eighties. This was where Carina Dymek had grown up.

Her mother was Swedish, born in Stockholm. Upper secondary school teacher, recently retired. The father was a Pole, born in Gdansk. Immigrated at the start of the seventies, Swedish citizen since 1988, employed at an upper secondary school in Blackeberg. He was a former officer of the Polish army and, unlike many Poles in exile from that period, not an outspoken opponent of the communist regime in Poland. There was a fuzzy, old note about that in the report from the archives. No hits on their criminal records. According to the Swedish Tax Agency, the couple also owned a house north of Norrtälje—probably a summer cottage.

They lived on a small plot with a lawn, shrubs, and a fruit tree in the corner, bare and gnarled. There was a slightly sour smell of brown, wet leaves and burning smoke. Someone was having a bonfire. Not a soul was in sight.

She parked the car at a sufficient distance from the house for the registration plates to be unreadable, pulled out her camera, and took around ten photos, mostly for the sake of it. Then she got out of the car and walked toward the house, moving past slowly and looking up at the windows, before continuing on a lap around the block. A peaceful area with no social problems, this was where teachers, bank clerks, and nurses lived: stable people who represented the median of the Swedish population. Back in the car, she got out her phone and dialed the Dymeks' number.

A woman answered. "Hello?"

"Is this Agneta Dymek?"

"Yes?"

Bente used a cheerful and friendly voice—light and lively. She said she was calling from the broadband company and wondered if she could ask a few questions about their Internet use.

"By the way, does Carina Dymek live at this address?" she said, as if in passing.

Carina? No, she didn't live there. She had moved out years ago. The woman reluctantly answered her questions.

Dymek's mother was telling the truth; her daughter wasn't in the house. Bente would have noticed if she had tried to hide that Dymek was staying with her parents. The mother's calm and slightly distracted tone also suggested that she knew nothing about what her daughter was involved in.

After the conversation, Bente drove around at random, as if in a dream, and finally ended up at Bromma airport. Next to the airport were two large supermarkets, old hangars that now housed their stock on kilometers of shelving. She parked the car in the middle of the parking lot. She looked across its expanse. It was a weekday afternoon and the cars were few and far between. She would be alone here. Sitting behind the wheel, she slowly turned the pages of Dymek's file.

Twenty years in the business had taught her when to listen to her gut—the weak signals that told her something wasn't right. A worry. About what, she didn't know. She had brought a bundle of reports and parts of Dymek's dossier in a file: e-mails, transcribed phone calls to Badawi—some items dated as recently as yesterday—and the list of what had been found in Dymek's apartment during the search. There were reports from GCHQ and other British intelligence reports on the Muslim Brotherhood, the Ahwa group, their structures.

She got out of the car and stretched her legs. A leaden gray bank of clouds towered above the supermarket. The storage units and office buildings around the airport cast dark shadows. Rain was in the air.

Why would someone like Carina Dymek be in contact with an extreme wing of the Muslim Brotherhood? The question suddenly formed in her head. Why?

British intelligence was convinced, and there was some sort of threat associated with the IRC channel, they had discovered. The British had shown a connection between Dymek and Badawi and the Ahwa network. Still, there was something that didn't make sense. She looked up at the dark, looming clouds. Empty plastic bags danced in the wind, swirling away across the tarmac. She couldn't work it out. An MFA civil servant, mixed up in the planning of an attack against a summit meeting? Bente had spent the last day focusing almost exclusively on the operation targeting Dymek and Badawi; she had barely had time to think, only time to manage the stream of details—thousands of pieces of information that could be combined endlessly. But did she actually understand what was going on? Could she see the threat? A lot suggested that there was a threat to the safety of the nation, yet she still didn't understand. Would a person like Dymek risk everything by collaborating with terrorists? Perhaps, out of loyalty to her boyfriend. But she was no convert. Was she being blackmailed? Perhaps. But blackmailed by the Muslim Brotherhood? It seemed so peculiar.

Badawi: the clear connection to the terrorist organization. He was compromised, involved—the only question was, how deep? The evidence for that was stronger; the intelligence provided by the British was convincing. But Carina? The lines ran in parallel and seemed to generate a true picture—but, paradoxically, something didn't add up. It was like an Escher print that tricked the eye.

And the photograph. The target.

She caught sight of her face in the angled car-door window, monstrously contorted.

On the way back into the city, she stopped at a gas station. She needed to think and was craving coffee. She got out of the car, twisted the gas cap off, and put in the nozzle. The pump began to whirr away at her side just as her cell rang. It was Mikael. Yes, she could talk.

"The man in the picture: Jean Bernier." Mikael's voice disappeared in the racket.

"Yes?" She took a few steps away from the car.

The Commission had confirmed the identity of everyone on the picture. The man in the middle was, just as Bente had thought, the Director General, Manservisi, the Italian. The two young girls next to him were both administrators in the department that dealt with migration policy—completely uninteresting. The man in the background, staring straight into the camera just as the picture was taken, was Jean Bernier. He was a lawyer. Worked at GD Home reviewing EU Commission proposals concerning police and intelligence matters. Mikael had his CV. French citizen. Educated at the Sorbonne and Harvard Law School. Fifteen years as a human rights lawyer at the UN in Geneva, four years in New York and, as of six years ago, working at the EU Commission. He had been involved in the review of the European Intelligence Service proposal.

"But, Mikael, we know this. Why is he of interest to an IRC channel? Why is he a target?"

"Yes, but listen: we checked him out with the Belgian police. He's dead."

"What?"

She stopped.

"They found him about a week ago, next to a lake in northern Belgium. He and his wife had a hideaway there. A neighbor found him in the garden."

She looked around to make sure no one was listening, which of course no one was. In the eyes of others, she was just a middle-aged woman on her cell at a gas station.

"Is it confirmed?"

"Yes. He had diabetes. The first preliminary examination showed insulin shock, apparently."

"No signs of violence?"

"No. Nothing. He had been there for a while. Not seen since Thursday, two weeks ago. They're going to attribute the death to natural causes."

Dead since Thursday a fortnight ago. She got out her pocket calendar. The 22nd of September: the same day Dymek left Brussels.

"He must have died shortly after Dymek got the report."

That a person like Jean Bernier was dead was no coincidence. All her professional experience had taught her to distrust chance. His death looked like a coincidence, and it was precisely that which convinced her it wasn't. Real coincidences were stragglier, more abrupt. But here was a perfect coincidence, and perfect coincidences were normally the result of well-planned and carefully executed human actions.

"I can check with the Brits."

"No," she said. "Hold off on that."

"Okay."

Mikael fell silent.

"What does the EU Commission say?"

"They were shocked and so on. But one of our sources in their HR department checked the records for us. Bernier had been disconnected from his work for the last few months—signed off on sick leave several times." Mikael leafed through some papers at his desk in Brussels. "And he had received warnings. There's a note here that says he was going to be reassigned."

"Good. Carry on looking into his background. See if you can find a colleague willing to talk."

Mikael was quick. That was why she liked him—for his ability to read situations, to see potential ways to access new information. He had already let one of the signals intelligence operatives at the Section discreetly hack into the EU Commission's server to search Bernier's e-mail account. There was probably a colleague, someone Bernier had worked with a lot. But it would take a little time. They had tried to build a timeline of Jean Bernier's last week alive, but it was slow work. The Belgian police were suspicious of organizations like SSI. Mikael would get in touch when he had more.

Dead for two weeks. She went inside to pay for her gas and bought a coffee that was so hot she could barely keep hold of the paper cup as she came back out to the car. A heavy raindrop hit the windshield with a loud, hollow thud as she got behind the wheel. Then another a second later.

The rain hammered on the car roof, ran down the windows. The windshield wipers didn't have time to shovel aside all the water. She got stuck in a jam a few hundred meters from the Security Service building. While she slowly crept closer, the downpour got worse and rattled furiously against the window. Water ran across the pavements in wide rivers and formed huge pools at the congested crossroads. All traffic was at a standstill; all people had turned into crouching, hurrying figures.

Bente leaned against the steering wheel. She knew there was no point getting worked up by the traffic; it was, just like the weather, a power over which no one could prevail. She had called Hamrén on his cell but he hadn't answered. The nauseating anxiety was back, stronger now. The car crept through the traffic. Jean Bernier was dead, so why was he a target for a planned terror attack? Why was he being mentioned at all in the chatter? Once again, she was blind.

The office was deserted. Tables everywhere were empty, desks tidied. It occurred to her that the department was going to have a big meeting this afternoon: a complete review of the situation. Presumably they were all behind the closed double doors at the other end of the floor. Counterterrorism was preparing for a major operation against Dymek and Badawi, she knew that. During the last twenty-four hours they had identified the Swedish network of people with connections to the Brotherhood. They were on high alert. All physical addresses were established; the targets were under surveillance; Counterterrorism was ready to strike. Ironically enough, the only thing missing was Dymek. Neither Hamrén's people nor the Brits had managed to locate her since she had disappeared.

Bente crossed the floor and stopped in front of the door. Voices were audible as a subdued murmur. She ought to be there, but it couldn't be helped. The meeting had already begun. It would look wrong. It would be stupid to provoke Hamrén again by entering now, when she wasn't welcome, anyway. Better to keep a low profile. For a second, she missed Brussels, her colleagues at the Section.

It probably benefited Hamrén and Counterterrorism to keep her and all the others outside, so that they could take all the credit for the collaboration with the British and show the top bosses that they mattered, that they needed more resources next year too. Counterterrorism had almost quadrupled in size in the last few years. Hamrén was an ambitious bastard, but a skillful one too. He would probably go far.

She sat down at a computer, logged in and brought up the files, quickly searching through the file structure: Dymek, Brussels, Ahwa. Somewhere, there had to be more about Bernier. The only thing related to Bernier was a British intelligence report and the MFA's record of their conversation with Dymek when they suspended her. Bente flicked through the documents; the Ministry paper she had read, but the British intelligence report was new. She printed them, gathered together her papers and left the silent floor without having been seen by anyone.

The guest apartment was absorbed in darkness. She still hadn't had time to unpack. Her suitcase was lying open in the middle of the floor, a curious-looking beast in the darkness. She turned on the lights and put down the papers on the coffee table. It was still raining. Water ran down the tall panes of glass, gushing in sloping vertical lines from a hazy, gray sky. There were around thirty meters between where she stood at the window and the building opposite. No one was visible in any of the windows. The Section's temporary apartment looked good, but was sparsely furnished. It was better than staying at a hotel, and safer—safe connections, all rooms swept for microphones and other hostile installations—but you couldn't be too careful with your conversations; there were other apartments surrounding it and the walls hadn't been reinforced. This was no place to receive visitors or talk about things of a sensitive nature. It was an apartment for eating and sleeping in, for being alone in.

She went back into the hallway and found an umbrella by the coat stand. It was time to work, but first she needed something to eat—she was starving. She was dreaming of a glass of wine—a glass of red, and the chance to see some normal people. She needed to get out, let some air into her head.

A few blocks from the apartment, close to Östermalmstorg, she remembered that there was an Italian restaurant. Just as she was opening the door and about to move into the stairwell, she heard someone coming up the stairs and quickly closed the door. She didn't want to be seen here; the apartment couldn't be connected to a face. She waited until the steps had faded away and she heard the rattle of a door being opened and closed a few stories higher in the building, before opening the door again.

The rain bounced against the pavement and the empty street was transformed into a glittering, hazy surface of splashing water. She jogged, but got wet anyway, in spite of the umbrella. The restaurant was unexpectedly busy. Sitting around circular tables with flickering candles, there were families eating and watching the rain; children ran between the tables and got in the way of the servers hurrying to and fro with large pizzas between the kitchen and the various parties. Behind her, a young couple tumbled through the door, tittering with laughter, their hair dripping with rainwater. Bente had really only intended to buy a pizza to take out, meaning to eat it in the apartment, but the restaurant was pleasant and lively, and she decided to stay. Sometimes it was better to take a break from work and come back to it later, when thoughts had had time to rest.

After a short time, a waiter spotted her and secured one of the last tables for her. Perhaps it was a risk, eating dinner like this, so close to the secure apartment. She couldn't help but think like that, but couldn't say why it would be risky. She was just so used to thinking in that way. She constantly tried not to be noticed, not to leave traces in the consciousness of others—even eating dinner in a pizza restaurant set off a small alarm somewhere inside her. Regulations said that one should avoid habits that made it easy to recognize and track employees of the Section. But she knew she was unnecessarily cautious. Presumably, no one would notice her here. She ordered a glass of red and a *quattro stagioni*, then sat nibbling on the grissini sticks left by the server in a small basket, while she amused herself by observing those around her. A young couple. Some business-men. At the table furthest from the door, a family.

The young couple in their early twenties were celebrating something, judging by the expensive sparkling wine they had ordered and the way in which they clinked glasses. The man was in high spirits and talked constantly while the woman listened with small smiles and nods. The businessmen weren't as inter-esting; they seemed mostly to be conducting polite conversa-tion while cautiously eating their pasta. The family comprised a couple in their forties, their three children romping around the room and an older couple who looked like maternal grandpar-ents. The grandfather was happily joking with the grandchildren, which made his daughter, who was trying to get the children to calm down, annoyed. Bente couldn't help but observe people like this, at a distance. It was one of the reasons she had started out at Counterterrorism almost twenty years ago. There was rest to be had in watching others without having to get involved. People's behavior revealed their inner selves. For a long period, she silently followed what was going on around her in the restaurant, and was so engrossed that she almost jumped when the server discreetly placed her pizza before her.

While she ate, she went through the Dymek case. Even if she accepted that Badawi really had recruited Dymek, there was still this business with Jean Bernier. If Jean Bernier had been dead for two weeks, it meant that the time of death had been around the end of September. They had found him at his cottage that he and his wife had rented for many years. That his death was being written off as natural causes meant nothing. There were a number of ways to make death appear natural.

Back in the apartment, she sat down with the papers again and leafed through the MFA's notes from the last conversation they had held with Dymek, rereading it. At the end of the short memo, she found a chronology of events: *September 22nd—desk officer Dymek participates in the COSEC council working-group meeting.*

That was the day that she said she had met a person who had given her the report. Dymek claimed not to know who the man was—that she didn't even know his surname—just that a man called Jean had given her the EIS report. Bente stopped herself: Jean. Dymek had been very certain that he had been called Jean, which was all she had really been able to say about the man she said had given her the report. Jean Bernier. Naturally, it was him; it made sense. He "just appeared" after the meeting. He had given her a report.

Bente got out her diary. She belonged to the shrinking number of people who still didn't use digital calendars. At the Section, they were careful about things like that. Digital notes were vulnerable to hacking; old paper diaries just needed to be locked in a safe. The 22nd of September was a Thursday. Jean Bernier had, in that case, still been alive at lunchtime.

If Carina Dymek had told the truth. If there really had been a Jean, and if he had really been Jean Bernier. She tested the idea. Until now, she hadn't deemed Dymek to be believable, but there was something in the way she expressed herself, so naïvely and stubbornly, that wasn't rational if she was truly hiding something. On the other hand, people who withheld the truth often tried to protect themselves by telling the part of the truth they couldn't deny, while denying all else till blue in the face, lying if necessary. But Dymek didn't give that impression. She hadn't been afraid, hadn't tried to humor her bosses. She could have dodged questions and explained things away. But she hadn't changed her story, even when she found out she was being suspended. If Dymek had told the truth, she had met Jean Bernier that Thursday, the 22nd, after the meeting in Brussels. She received the report, whereupon they went their separate ways.

Perhaps Jean Bernier had gone to his cottage afterward, on the same day, possibly, or a day or so later, and died there shortly afterward. Had Dymek accompanied him there? Could Dymek be his killer? No, nothing suggested that was the case. She had caught a flight home to Stockholm on Thursday evening, just two hours after the meeting. There were even minutes from the meeting that clearly showed Sweden had made several contributions to discussions during the afternoon session. Dymek hadn't left the meeting. She wouldn't have had time to get to the cottage in northern Belgium and then back to Brussels in time to catch her flight, even if she had gone straight there and back, stopping for no more than a minute or two. Mikael had texted a link to a map of where Bernier had been found, in the middle of a nature reserve north of Ghent.

She got up and wandered around the apartment, before coming to a stop in front of the window. If Dymek was telling the truth, then Jean Bernier was completely unknown to her, someone who had appeared completely unexpectedly—a stranger.

She reached for the British intelligence reports and slowly read through the one about the Muslim Brotherhood and the Ahwa group again. Here they were, talking about an Islamist network within the Brotherhood, its structure and its key persons. The British intelligence services had clearly had them under observation for some time, since they suspected they posed a threat to Europe. The report was long—over fifty pages—and described, among other things, persons in the Badawi family living in Cairo and London, which made it clear they had used wiretaps, e-mail intercepts. The Brits had carefully documented regular contact between people in the circle surrounding Jamal Badawi's uncle and Jamal Badawi himself. According to the report, there were e-mails that they considered to be coded messages. Jamal Badawi, said the report, had worked systematically for a long time to get inside the Swedish administration, into the Government Offices and the Ministry of Justice, in order to wait, like a sleeper agent, until the right moment. Carina Dymek, stated the report, had been that opportunity.

It said it there, in black and white. According to the report, Badawi had contacted Carina Dymek and started a relationship in conjunction with beginning to plan an attack against a summit meeting. MI6 noted in the report that Dymek was probably well suited for the needs of the Ahwa group. She was tied to Badawi, the nephew of a well-respected figure in the Ahwa group, by their relationship. Her name was clean, no one knew who she was: she was the perfect *clean skin*. Badawi had won Dymek through courting her. He had then built up a close relationship with her through sexual contact and, in that way, kept Dymek close to him. The relationship had been built over a longer period of time, following the Russian method, said the report. Ensuring she was compromised by asking her to leak classified material was a step toward making her dependent on Jamal Badawi and therefore more useful to the group in Cairo. Getting her to become an accomplice to the planning of the attack was also not difficult, as her bond to Jamal Badawi had grown strong. She was probably unaware of the Ahwa group's ultimate plans. The report suggested that Dymek had probably been chosen carefully by the group in Cairo. The British had, in some unfathomable way, managed to find out that she had strong opinions about EU policies toward Europe's southern neighbors. At several EU meetings she had voiced strong criticism of "the EU's colonial overtones in relation to the Arab nations." An anonymous source in Brussels was cited.

MI6's assessment was that Jamal Badawi had cultivated Dymek as a fresh resource: a messenger, a mole. A tool for Islamist attack planning.

But if Badawi had been part of a terrorist network, then why hadn't the Brits raised the alarm earlier? Why hadn't they spoken up about their suspicions, if they were so clear? The report Bente held in her hand seemed to be based on intelligence gathered over several months, if not years. How was it possible that Swedish Counterespionage had not perceived the slightest threat? Kempell was competent; he would have smelled that kind of infiltration within the ministry. A planned attack against an EU summit wouldn't have escaped the notice of the Section. The Swedish Security Service had been fumbling in the dark for a long time, but now they had SSI. They had signals intelligence, they had sources, they had the ability to carry out long-term surveillance and spot the threats. Even if Stockholm hadn't spotted the threat, SSI should have discovered it. So why had no one—not the Section, not Stockholm, not Interpol, nor the German, French, or Spanish security services—seen this threat that the Brits were able to describe in such detail?

She put her fingers to her forehead and massaged it slowly, as if to try and wake up her brain from a deep sleep as it lay beneath her skull.

If Dymek wasn't lying . . . She tested the idea again. Then she had met Jean Bernier in Brussels that Thursday two weeks ago. It explained how she had gotten hold of the report. But it didn't explain why an entire IRC channel was looking for one and the same Jean Bernier. It didn't explain why Dymek would take part in the planning of an attack.

Unless there was no attack being planned. Unless there were no terrorists.

The thought reared its head, slowly, without any warning. It was just possible . . . If Dymek wasn't lying.

Was it all just her imagination? She looked at the cold walls of the living room as if they might give her clues. But the walls were quiet; the apartment was quiet and seemed to be airtight. It had gotten dark around her. Only the lamp by the sofa spread a soft light. If Dymek really had met Jean Bernier in Brussels on that one occasion on the 22nd of September, then the British analysis was wrong. Something else was going on.

She got up and turned on the ceiling light in the kitchen; she wanted the apartment to be light. Was she wrong? Had they been moving around like fish in a pond, like blind carp, swimming around and around in the belief that they were getting closer to the sea? Perhaps.

All the material that MI6 had provided, all the analyses—where had they got it from? Where, where, where? She needed to call someone: Hamrén. She reached for her cell, but stopped herself.

What would she say to make him believe her? She had nothing—nothing concrete that would change his views at this stage. The summit was four days away; the response team was on high alert; Swedish Counterterrorism was ready to respond within minutes at the first sign that the group was gathering for an attack. Hamrén wouldn't listen to her now.

She sat down heavily on the sofa and looked at the papers that lay spread across the coffee table. If her suspicions were proven right, nothing was true.

Once again, they were blind.

She gathered together the documents, knocked the bundle against the table to straighten them out, and put the stack in front of her. There was nothing further to gain here, she thought bitterly.

She went into the kitchen and in one of the cupboards she found a bottle of Famous Grouse with a drop left. She poured it into a glass and drank as she slowly wandered around the apartment. There was nothing left to do in Stockholm. The answers weren't here.

At first, all she noticed was a buzzing sound, but she didn't understand what it was. She put down her glass and went into the living room. Her cell was on silent, lying there, vibrating on the coffee table.

It was Mikael.

"We've found a guy at the Commission who's prepared to talk to us."

"Good." Her voice sounded odd, she noticed. She cleared her throat. "That's very good."

"How are you?"

She was fine, she replied. Mikael really was like a barometer: he noticed the slightest shift in people. She was grateful that he didn't ask more; she couldn't say anymore on the phone. Could he arrange a ticket to Brussels for tomorrow morning? she said. For the first flight out.

31

Stockholm, Thursday, October 6

It was beginning to get dark when Carina reached Skogskyrk-ogården, the woodland cemetery. She had spent the entire day in Alex's apartment. Alex hadn't been home; the apartment had been quiet and peaceful. The only person she had seen was Greger, who had stopped by late in the afternoon with a few borrowed clothes and a suitcase. She had bought a ticket to Brussels and packed, just like she would before any normal trip for work. When everything was ready, she felt so nervous that she couldn't sit still and had instead wandered around the unfamiliar rooms, turned on the TV, and flipped between various afternoon shows before turning it off when she found herself watching a repeat of a nature film about gazelles. She got dressed and went out.

She had called Jamal from the pizzeria again; they had agreed to meet at the ticket gate at Skogskyrkogården subway station. To pass the time, she had then walked all the way there through the suburbs. She could already see his thin, upright figure from a dis-tance as he stood waiting for her in the harshly lit ticketing area. She was so happy to see him again. He was fiddling with his cell and looked up and smiled at her when she appeared. She hugged him, hard, pulled him close to her. They kissed for a long time before she slowly and unwillingly let go.

"How are you, darling?"

She shrugged her shoulders. "I'm okay."

The weather had cleared up and a glowing evening light that would soon turn into darkness lay across the trees. The chapel and the edge of the woods on the ridge came alive momentarily in a blaze of light before quickly darkening. They aimed for the large cross that towered up toward the purple sky.

Jamal looked tired and haggard; he had dark circles under his eyes. He had probably been working around the clock for the last few days; the kind of negotiations he had been involved with in Vienna could go on all night.

As they walked toward the chapel, she told him in detail about what had happened. How the police had turned up, how she had fled the apartment, and that she had stayed at Alex's.

They passed the bare chapel building and were soon in among the pine trees. The woods rose around them like a columned hall filled with straight, dark trunks. Rows of older graves ran through the lines of trees. They walked along the gravel path that led through the woods while she told him about how Greger's friends had helped her to find Jean. Jamal walked silently alongside her, listening.

A hundred meters ahead, the track twisted. Low barracks could be glimpsed, dark and barred up. Not a soul was visible. But, by one of the barracks, there was an SUV parked. She reacted to the expensive car being parked there, but couldn't say why and let go of the thought.

They turned off the track and began to walk along a small gravel path that led between the trees, past a number of family graves.

"My God, Carina," Jamal said finally, when she had told him everything.

It upset her to hear him sound so skeptical. A chilling thought crossed her mind: what if he said he couldn't cope with her situation? What if she was going to lose him too?

"You don't think I'm doing the right thing, is that it? Be honest."

"I don't know. I really don't know," he said in a low voice. "By doing what you're doing, you just risk complicating things. It's one thing to try and work out what happened and quite another to flee the police. And tracking people down on the Internet . . . That's . . . hacking. I mean, wouldn't it be better to talk to the police, explain what happened?"

"And what would I say to them? No one believes what I'm saying. I have to get hold of the man who gave me the report, otherwise there's no point in going to the police. Surely you understand that? I have to go to Brussels."

He shrugged his shoulders as if he didn't know what to say and stared off between the trees.

She felt the anger welling up and said sharply, "I've fought for eight years to get to where I am today, and there's no fucking way I'm going to let them consign me to the scrapheap just because it suits them. I haven't done anything wrong. I was just doing my job. And I'm going to prove it to them. I won't back down."

"I know. I understand that," said Jamal in a conciliatory tone. "But you shouldn't have started trying to trace this man," he added. "I think, if you talked to the police, things would sort themselves out."

"How can you know that?" she said abruptly. "I tried, didn't I? I did everything by the book. And what did I get in return?"

He spread out his hands. Naturally, he didn't know. He kicked a root that was sticking out of the ground.

"Don't you care?" she said.

"Yes, I do care," he said. "I care about us. About *us*, Carina."

"Then help me."

"Can't you try talking to the MFA?" he said.

"I *have* tried! There's no point!"

The air went out of her. Perhaps he was right. Perhaps she had been wrong, despite having tried to do the right thing all along. Maybe she should never have accepted the report and maybe she shouldn't have asked Greger for help. She was so tired of it all and she was very close to tears. They were standing here, opposite one another, like any old quarreling couple. That wasn't how it was meant to be, not with Jamal.

She reached for him. "Say something—please."

He shook his head and gave her a hug, but it was a brief and edgy embrace, a placatory gesture. Neither of them knew how to continue the conversation, every word had become so overwrought with meaning.

They had reached the outer edges of the cemetery and continued walking between more recent graves. The ground had leveled off here. It was beginning to get dark. High above them, the treetops bristled.

When the wind turned and carried sound toward them, she heard tires on gravel and, for a second, she thought she saw something moving on the gravel road—two or three darker shadows moving between the trees and breaking off into the shelter of the motionless trunks, a shift in the horizon that caught her attention.

"What is it?"

"There's someone there."

"Where?" He squinted.

"Over there. On the road."

Jamal stood still and looked in the same direction. He couldn't see anything. Perhaps she had imagined it. The darkness between the trees was so dense that it created its own shapes, darker patches in the dark of night. Maybe there was nothing to see.

They left the cemetery via one of the small roads that led through the wall, and came out next to two ochre-red wooden houses with white trim, lying there like a dreamy postcard in the darkness. The main road carrying traffic into Stockholm was just a few hundred meters away.

They walked along the road and came to a twenty-four-hour burger joint, sat enthroned in the middle of a deserted parking lot like an illuminated temple.

Jamal had been quietly walking a few paces behind her since they left Skogskyrkogården, but asked her now whether she wanted to come back to his place. She could stay there, then go to Arlanda from his. She had hoped he would ask. A taxi picked them up them ten minutes later and drove them to Fruängen.

Alex was still out. The apartment was dark. Carina quickly gathered together her clothes and emptied the contents of her bag into the suitcase Greger had brought for her earlier. There was still a creased copy of the report in the bag, as well as the other documents, along with the USB memory stick. That damn report. What

should she do with it? She couldn't take it to Brussels; if she was discovered carrying sensitive material like that, she would be charged
with breach of secrecy. But the papers couldn't be allowed to disappear, although right now she felt like throwing the whole lot down
the garbarge chute. She looked around the apartment.

There was a small gap under the fridge, just a few centimeters
high, where the electronics of the fridge were located. An oblong
plastic grill covered it. She gently coaxed it off and pushed the
report and other documents into the gap. They just fit. Then she
put the USB stick in as well, before replacing the plastic grill. When
she stood up, nothing was visible. To discover the hiding place, you
would have to be on all fours, peering under the fridge.

She wrote a short note for Alex, thanking her, and promising to
let her know when she was back in Sweden. Then she left the apartment, locked the door, and pushed the key through the mailbox.

It felt like a huge exhalation to arrive at Jamal's place. The quiet,
tidy two-room apartment was just as it always was. Jamal turned on
some music and went into the kitchen to make tea and sandwiches.
She lay stretched out on the sofa and closed her eyes. The phone
rang. She could hear the mumble of Jamal's reply in Arabic and saw
him go into the bedroom.

She watched Jamal as he sat huddled up on the edge of the bed
with his cell pressed to his ear. She didn't understand what he was
saying, but it was clear he didn't want to talk to whoever was at the
other end and was trying to end the conversation. He looked so
anguished. Who was it that kept calling him all the time? Perhaps
she was just tired and worried, perhaps she just wanted to be left in
peace with Jamal, but the call annoyed her.

Finally, Jamal flipped his cell shut and came out to her, sitting
down heavily on the sofa.

"How are things, darling?"

He sighed, just shook his head.

"Who was on the phone?" she said.

"You don't want to know," he mumbled.

"Yes," she said with emphasis. "I do."

He looked dead tired. "It's like this," he said in a low voice. "My mother . . . isn't well. She's sick. She imagines lots of things." The words came out slowly, as if getting them out of his mouth was a huge struggle. "She thinks she's being watched by the police—things like that. Then she calls me, says a lot of stuff." He sighed deeply and slumped slightly.

"I didn't know . . ."

"It's okay. It's just me who knows. Me and a quack," he said with a sad smile.

"Oh, love." She stretched out her hand.

They sat quietly beside one another on the edge of the bed.

"Are you getting any help?" she said after a while. "I mean . . . is anyone taking care of her?"

"No." He shrugged his shoulders. "They prescribe her medication. She takes it for a while, and then she stops and gets ill again. That's when she starts calling me."

Carina stroked his neck. He was alone, it occurred to her. She wanted to hold him until that loneliness went away, but something in his manner made her hold back.

"I'm used to it," he said slowly after a long time, during which she thought he had decided to say nothing more. "It's been like this for years—ever since we came to Sweden. My father was never happy here. He missed home. What was he supposed to do in Sweden? In Egypt, he was a lawyer, had all his friends and family. But here? Nothing." He spread his hands out. "When Dad died, Mom lost it completely. She had been getting by while he was alive. It goes up and down. It's been a long time, but she's getting sick again."

He got up and went into the kitchen.

While they were eating their sandwiches on the sofa, Jamal said, "The report . . . I didn't mean that you weren't doing the best you could. I understand that you are."

"It's okay, Jamal," she said. "You're entitled to be worried. *I'm* fucking worried."

"Things will work out."

"I hope so."

She looked at him and stroked his arm. Here they were, sat together like an old couple, full of troubles. Why couldn't they just live their lives in peace and be happy together? Her vision became blurry. Angrily, she brushed the tears out of her eyes.

Later, when the apartment was dark and still, Jamal lay close beside her in bed. They were quiet. She felt his breath on her neck. She needed to get up in five hours' time, but that didn't matter; she didn't feel like sleeping.

"Are you asleep?"

Jamal was awake too. She turned over and shuffled closer. Their naked bodies were soft and warm, fragile in a way that was completely different from the hardness of their bodies when they made love. She carefully slipped her arms around him and kissed him.

In less than a month they would be in Egypt. Just the two of them, in Cairo. She saw it through the darkness: the cafés, the bazaars. She imagined how they would wander the city during the day, returning to the hotel for the hottest hours of the afternoon, and at night, when they had visited various restaurants, they would lie together, just like this, but with the nocturnal sounds of a metropolis murmuring through an open window. She leaned toward Jamal. "I love you," she whispered. But Jamal didn't answer; he was asleep.

32

Brussels, Friday, October 7

Bente took the car to Arlanda on the gray and dreary autumn morning. She was leaving Sweden without telling anyone. On the plane, she allowed herself to relax. She had slept badly during the night. Thoughts about the investigation had floated around, uninterrupted, until, at three in the morning, she had realized that there was no point in trying to fall asleep and, instead, she had gotten up to read through the papers again. She had gone through all the documents one more time. The suspicion, the doubt she had felt during the evening, had at first seemed exaggerated, and that had calmed her down. Perhaps she was unnecessarily disbelieving of people; there was always that risk, in her line of work; disbelief became part of your vision and, in the end, you didn't believe anything, didn't trust anyone, and didn't know what was real. But the more she reread the material, the more convinced she was that she was right. She didn't want to be right. She didn't want to discover what she had discovered.

She woke up with a jolt as the plane landed.

Daylight streamed through the enormous windows in the gate area at Brussels airport. The runways gleamed following the early morning rainfall. She took a taxi home and dropped off her bags. She knew that Fredrik would be at work and the children at school. The rooms of the house were resting in the morning sunshine— all was quiet and familiar. It felt good to be home. She would have liked to lie down on the sofa and nap for an hour, but there was no time for that. She wrote a note to say she was home and left it on the kitchen table before taking the taxi into the city center.

Mikael was standing by one of the steel tables outside a little café in Schaerbeek. He was smoking. Just this morning, that struck her as odd. During the year or so they had worked together, she had never seen him holding a cigarette. Presumably he smoked in his private life, but not at the office; she didn't know much about his life beyond SSI. At the Section, no one knew much about anyone at all; you left that life outside when you entered the office through the security doors. She was careful about involving herself in the private lives of her employees—work was stressful enough. Perhaps her number two had completely different habits when he wasn't at work, perhaps he was a completely different person compared to the tidy, efficient, sharp Mikael who turned up at the Section every weekday morning. The thought made her smile.

Mikael caught sight of her; he returned her smile, stretched, and stubbed out his cigarette. "Good morning."

"Good morning."

"Everything okay?"

She nodded: yes.

She ordered a double espresso from the waiter clearing the next table along. It was morning in Brussels. People had left the surrounding offices and shops to drink their coffee in the glorious weather at one of the many small bars and bistros in the area. It was rare that she visited this part of the city, but Schaerbeek was a pleasant area. She smiled, listening for a while to the lively hubbub around them. Then she reminded herself why they were there. They had to do this first. She couldn't tell Mikael yet, she decided. Not everything. She wanted to think things through first, needed to sure that her doubts were well founded.

"This . . . colleague. He lives here?"

"Yes. Around the corner. We agreed to meet at eleven o'clock. He wanted us to visit him at home."

She drank her espresso. The strong, sugared coffee had an immediate impact: she felt more alert right away. It would be a day filled with lots of coffee. Mikael looked at the time and lit another cigarette. He looked at her as if he really wanted to ask a lot of questions, but said nothing. This wasn't the right place for a discussion about what he was probably wondering—they both knew that. They chatted for a while. Mikael had found a new Taiwanese restaurant and told her about their fantastic noodle soups while she finished her coffee and paid. They had ten minutes left. Rodriguez, the head of the Section's cell team, and his people were already in place. They began to walk. A block from the café, they turned off the busy boulevard.

"So we have a problem?"

"Yes." She hesitated. "I think so."

Mikael nodded and looked calmly over his shoulder while they kept walking. A sparse flow of people moved around them but no one caught Bente's attention. A garbage truck thundered past them; shortly thereafter a sedan slowed down and pulled into an empty parking space about ten meters in front of them.

"I'm not sure what's going on," she said. "Kempell was right. We're relying too much on the British."

"The British?"

"They knew Bernier was dead. I don't understand why they didn't say."

"Are you sure? London seems just as surprised as we are."

She shrugged her shoulders. "I think they knew he was dead. And that worries me."

They said nothing and carried on another two blocks along the boulevard until Mikael dropped his pace. They were getting close to the address, a modern residential building squeezed between two older brick buildings.

"The guy we're meeting is called Florian Klause. He works in the same department as Jean Bernier. He's a *stagiaire*."

"An apprentice?"

Mikael shrugged his shoulders and passed her an ID card, dangling in a frame.

"You're Maria Lundvall. I'm Eric Smith. We're from the HR department at the EU Commission—that's all he knows. We're carrying out an internal investigation following the death of Jean Bernier in order to close his personnel file, close his accounts, and make sure all personal possessions are retrieved on behalf of the estate. Routine procedure."

The Section had found Florian Klause by chance. He had contacted the police and said he had something that belonged to Bernier. The Belgian police suspected no crime and provided his cell number when one of the Section's employees turned up and claimed to be from the EU Commission.

They had reached the main door. Mikael pressed a button beside the name KLAUSE. A moment later, the door buzzed.

A pale young man opened the door to the apartment on the fourteenth floor. He had a small, round, childish face with freckles on his nose, where there perched a pair of steel-rimmed spectacles. He was wearing a light blue shirt and chinos. According to the records of the EU Commission, he was twenty-eight years old, but the neatly buttoned shirt and his gentle face made him look much younger. He shook hands energetically. He was nervous; Bente could feel his hands sweating.

"Come in. Come in," he said in English with a strong German accent.

They were admitted to a small attic apartment with a sloping ceiling and a window that had a panoramic view across all of Brussels. It looked like he had just moved in, which couldn't be the case; he was probably just one of those young civil servants who mainly ate, slept, and worked. The only furniture was a small bed, an ugly sofa, and an enormous flat-screen TV. Piles of books were stacked along a wall; lots of law and study books, she noted. Typical bachelor pad. In the tiny kitchen, clean dishes were still dripping. He must have been cleaning for their visit.

"Do you want something to drink? Water, tea . . . ?"

She shook her head. Mikael sat down on the sofa.

Their presence clearly made him nervous. He stared at them, cleared his throat and didn't seem to have a clue how to handle the situation. He stood, rubbing his hands, as if trying to rub something off, before pulling a chair up to the coffee table and sitting down.

On the table there was a brown envelope. She recognized the type—for secret correspondence, with a black lining on the inside to prevent any transparency. She stopped an impulse to pick it up.

"It's great that you could meet with us," said Mikael.

"Of course." Florian Klause smiled stiffly and fell silent. Then he burst out, "I know that you must be wondering how this all happened. And, of course, I'll tell you. I just want to say that I'm terribly sorry about what has happened."

The words came tumbling out of the young man, as if they had been stuck somewhere inside before gushing from his mouth in an irregular torrent. His face was very tense. He looked eagerly at Mikael, then at Bente. She adjusted her expression to a warm smile—the motherly smile. She didn't understand a word of his little outburst, but was careful not to show that. There was no point in pushing this boy; he was upset. A vein had begun to throb in his forehead underneath his blond locks.

"I know that I shouldn't have taken this." He sighed and looked at the envelope.

"Is this what you wanted to give the police?"

"Yes," he said. "It was so stupid of me. But I didn't know what to do. I should have given it to the Head of Department, or you. But when Jean died . . ."

"Yes?"

"I . . ." He shrugged his shoulders dejectedly. "It went wrong," he mumbled.

Mikael glanced at her. He seemed just as unsure as she was about what the young man was actually talking about.

"You should have given this to your boss," said Mikael.

"Yes."

"But you didn't."

"No. I didn't." He sighed deeply.

"You took it home instead."

"Yes."

With a small movement he pulled off his glasses and hid his head in his hands. She could hear him whispering to himself: *"Mein Gott."* Neither of them moved or said a word. Silence reigned in the apartment.

"I made a mistake," he said, finally, with a thick voice.

They waited for him to pull himself together. Cumbersomely, he put his glasses back on. His eyes were red rimmed. He pointed at the envelope as if it was an enemy.

"I know it was completely crazy. These documents—they're top secret. I know it was wrong to take them home. It's completely against the rules. I would never normally have done something like this. I shouldn't have accepted them. I know it's a crime; you don't have to tell me. I understand if you'll need to take . . . certain measures." He looked glumly at them.

"But why did you keep them?" she said. "Why didn't you give them to your boss?"

"Jean asked me not to."

"He asked you?"

"Yes."

"Why?"

Florian Klause sighed and stared into space. "He didn't trust anyone at the Directorate General. Everyone was against him, you know? But I worked with Jean"—he quickly corrected himself—"with Monsieur Bernier. I know what he was like. He was a good person."

They said nothing.

Bente's cell rang. The sound made Florian Klause shudder. She swore, got out her phone, and quickly turned it to silent. It was Rodriguez calling.

Klause continued: "Monsieur Bernier was reviewing a proposal concerning a new organization within the EU—an intelligence organization." He looked at them carefully. "I was helping him with research and so on. I really liked working for him. He used to give me legal texts or extracts from the EIS report and say things like, 'Florian, read this and tell me what you think.' You could discuss things with him. I mean, he was the sharpest lawyer in the department. But I know a lot of people didn't like him."

"How do you mean?"

He paused to think. "There was a conflict with the primary authors of the proposal. They hated him, actually—couldn't stand him. But they were wrong." He smiled.

"What do you mean—that he was right?"

"His criticism was justified. The proposal was poorly written."

"So they were arguing about that. Him and your colleagues."

He nodded.

"Then what happened, more precisely?"

"Things escalated, you might say. Some people at the department accused him of being biased, unprofessional, and wanting to destroy the work. They spread rumors, sent e-mails that said terrible things about him."

"Like what?"

"Like that he was sick, that he had started to lose his sense of judgment because of illness. They claimed he posed a risk to security. Things like that."

"Didn't he?"

"No!" He stared at them. "Never. It was all lies. They wanted to get rid of him. You have to understand this, Monsieur Bernier was quite well—and totally devoted to his work. All he cared about was the law."

They nodded.

"After that, it was open war at the department. That was back in the spring. It was as if there were two teams: those who agreed with Bernier and those who thought he was ruining everything. Finally, the case was brought up with Manservisi, our director general. And apparently Bernier was a problem, in his eyes. I remember that some external people came in and had several chats with Bernier. I guess they were trying to make him change his mind. But he refused. Then they took him off the job."

"Which external people—do you remember?"

He creased his forehead in concentration and thought. "They were from the British delegation to the EU."

"The British?"

"Yes, the British were involved in the proposal from an early stage. We often received messages from them with drafts for parts of the report. They were the ones who brought the annex."

She was a fraction of a second away from asking what annex he was talking about, but stopped herself at the last moment; she cleared her throat instead.

He pointed at the envelope. "They wrote the annex," the apprentice continued. "They demanded that it be added to the report. That was the final straw for Bernier. He refused to approve it. He was furious. They were crazy, he said. Barbarians destroying the EU. Things like that."

"And then he gave you this document?"

"Yes." He fell silent; his gaze wavered.

Bente's cell rang again. It buzzed in her inside pocked. She got it out and glanced at it. Rodriguez again.

"It's a very secret document, I guess."

Klause nodded. "Yes. Red level." He blushed fiercely and looked down at his lap.

They sat in silence for a while.

"Why did he give it to you? You don't have the necessary clearance."

He sighed. "He trusted me, I suppose. He said he couldn't keep it himself. I know that only a few people at the department knew of its existence. Apparently it wasn't going to be shown to the EU parliament, or any politicians. They were completely in the dark. I never got to read it, but Monsieur Bernier had read it, of course. He refused to accept it. One day, he came to me and said he was going away. He asked if I could look after it. He said I couldn't give it to the boss or anyone else. I didn't want to refuse. I liked him, and, to be quite honest, I think they treated him unfairly. So I took it."

"You looked after the document. How long had he planned for you to do so?"

"He asked me to distribute it." He sniffed.

"Distribute?"

"Yes. Send it to all EU embassies in Brussels if he didn't contact me before the summit."

If he didn't get in touch. She stopped for a second. Mikael pulled a pack of tissues out of his jacket pocket and passed it over to the apprentice, who was sitting quietly, tears running down his cheeks.

"Does the name Carina Dymek mean anything to you?" Bente said after a while.

Klause turned his bloated face toward her and looked at her quizzically, shaking his head.

"A Swedish diplomat."

"No. Nothing."

"Are you sure?"

"I've never heard the name." He blew his nose loudly, staring at her and then Mikael. The worry shone in his eyes.

She leaned forward, plucked the envelope from the table without any apparent urgency and gave it to Mikael. Without even stopping to reflect, she slid into her role.

"We'll have to report what's happened. But," she added quickly when she saw the unhappy grimace that covered his face, "given the unusual circumstances and the fact that you contacted the police about this, and that you've helped us to establish the facts of the matter, you don't have to worry. We'll recommend that you remain in your post."

"Thank you," he said, dabbing his face. "Thank you. I'm so sorry about all of this. It's my first year at the Commission; I didn't know it would be like this. It won't happen again, I promise." He looked at them, teary eyed.

She leaned forward and patted him on the shoulder.

"It'll be all right, Florian."

One of the guys from the cell team was in the stairwell. He appeared to have been waiting outside the door. When he caught sight of them, he angled his head toward the microphone wire and called to them in a low voice.

"What is it?"

"We've got company."

They began to run down the stairs, silently. On the first floor they paused, waited a few seconds until they heard an all-clear signal through his earpiece, and continued running all the way to the ground floor.

Bente was panting heavily; it was a long time since she had needed to move like this. They passed through a fire door into the basement, went down a narrow corridor, back up some stairs, and into a messy inner courtyard, filled with humming fans. Rodriguez was there.

"I called. Why didn't you answer?"

They had a problem. At least three people had followed them on the way to Klause's apartment. They hadn't managed to discover them in time. Presumably there were more of them nearby.

Another member of the cell team came out of the rusty fire door at the other end of the yard and waved. She and Mikael ran after Rodriguez, stumbling down some dark stairs into a boiler room and hurrying through a doorway into a small basement corridor that ended by a narrow stairway twisting up toward gray daylight. She caught a glimpse of yet another member of the cell team, his automatic weapon drawn, following them.

If they had been found . . .

The thought flashed through her head. She swore silently. All their security arrangements to hide the Section, protect the identities of operatives, the networks of sources and informants, to cover up the traces of their electronic intrusions and tracking, all of it was vulnerable. They were all in danger. Her stomach dropped when she thought about Fredrik and the kids.

They crossed yet another inner courtyard, continued through a wooden door and into another stairwell, where Rodriguez abruptly stopped, holding up his hand, signaling to them to stay by the wall. They waited, panting, while he listened in concentration with his index finger against his earpiece.

"Now."

They hit the street at the same time as one of the Section's black BMW SUVs came out of a side street and slammed on its brakes in the middle of the road. The passenger side doors were flung open.

"Go! Go! Go!"

Rodriguez pushed them in front of him. They hurried across the pavement. Some passersby stopped in surprise and watched them. Bente narrowly avoided rushing straight into a woman pushing a stroller, before squeezing between the parked cars and into the SUV. With a hard jolt, the car made a flying start.

33

Brussels, Friday, October 7

The thick cloud cover opened up without warning just before they landed. Carina managed to catch sight of the gray Belgian suburbs spread out below like dark fields—industrial areas, tower blocks, villas—all sweeping by, and, for a moment, she saw the freeway to Brussels, like a scar across the landscape. At the scheduled time, a few minutes before ten, the Scandinavian Airlines morning flight descended into Zaventem.

When she had been in the early morning hustle and bustle at Arlanda, she had almost hoped that they would stop her at security, take her to one side, and that it would all be over. But no one had stopped her. She had checked in, the same as usual, handed over her bag, and the uniformed clerk had even wished her a pleasant trip. Then she had passed through security, along with all the other sleepy business travelers, and no one had reacted when they checked her passport and boarding pass, or when she was lining up at the gate. She knew almost nothing about how the police worked, and even less about how Säpo worked, but she knew enough to know that, if you were able to fly out of Arlanda without being stopped, then you weren't on a wanted list. Perhaps the woman who had called her from Säpo had actually meant it when she said she just wanted to talk. For a second, she regretted not going to the meeting at Säpo; perhaps it would have solved everything. But it wasn't that simple, she knew that.

A few minutes left until they landed. Everything was so familiar. How many times had she flown into Brussels? Hundreds, probably.

She watched the business travelers around her: two of them were talking cheerfully to each other across the aisle, a gray-haired man closed his laptop in preparation for landing. She hadn't had time to think about the MFA, but here, surrounded by the people who would have been her traveling companions on a normal trip to Brussels, it struck her how far away from the Ministry and her normal job she was. While the plane rushed toward the airport, she realized that she might never be able to return to her normal life. If it had been an ordinary working day, she would have been on the way to a council meeting by now. She would have been going through the Swedish positions and preparing for the usual race through the arrivals hall to get to a taxi first, to get to Justus Lipsius in time for the meeting. She pressed her forehead against the cold pane of glass in the small oval window. It vibrated against her temples. The ground was rapidly getting closer beneath her, taking shape and becoming more detailed.

"Are you all right, madame?" A stewardess leaned forward.

Carina nodded.

"Please return your seat to the upright position." The stewardess gave her a friendly, professional smile and said in quite another tone, as if a friend, "Are you sure you're okay?"

"I'm fine."

Once off the plane, she felt calm and safe again. The oblong arrivals gate was packed with people. She joined the flock of businessmen hurrying away with their briefcases and travel bags, and already felt better when she reached the baggage conveyor belt. She really knew this airport—she could find her way around it with more ease than she could central Stockholm—the air-conditioned halls, echoing announcements, advertisements; the well-known Brussels feeling of hurrying out through the arrivals gate.

Planes from Paris, Munich, and Moscow had arrived at the same time; out by the taxis, there was a long, snaking queue. She did what she usually did: went up one floor and caught a taxi before it headed down the ramp to join the taxi rank. The success of her old trick put her in a good mood. The rush-hour traffic, the chatter of the radio, and the driver's way of changing lanes on the freeway at the risk of life and limb cheered her up. She was in Brussels. This was her hunting ground.

While in the taxi, she booked a room at the Radisson Blu on Rue d'Idalie. Maybe she ought to be careful and stay at a smaller bed and breakfast in case the police were looking for her. The thought flashed through her mind in a flutter of anxiety. She waved it to one side. Säpo, she reasoned, only operated on Swedish territory. For them to have contacted the Belgian police when they hadn't even put an alert out on her at Arlanda seemed unlikely. She concluded that she was in Brussels, one of thousands of morning travelers who had just arrived, one of the masses, and she had no reason to worry. The Radisson Blu was really a little too expensive, but she was only going to stay for a few days. She might as well do what she wanted, and the prospect of staying at the Radisson Blu lifted her spirits. She always stayed there when she went to Brussels with work. Some weeks she had spent as many nights there as she had at home in her apartment. It was part of her Brussels.

The hotel was as it always was: the same minimalist lobby with a restaurant and bar with subdued lighting just inside the entrance. She couldn't help but smile at the sensation that she was home.

At the reception, the same man always checked her in: an older, very proper gentleman of Indian appearance with a well-groomed, gray mustache. He was behind the counter and greeted her exuberantly when he caught sight of her, as if he had actually been waiting for just her to appear.

"*Voilà, madame.*"

In the hotel room, she threw off her coat and unpacked her small notebook. It was a good room, peaceful and quiet, with a large TV and a soft bed with extra pillows. She picked up her oilcloth notebook, the same one she always used at the MFA. The covers were black with a red border, and it was the right size to fit in a handbag or an inside jacket pocket. Everyone in the Ministry used them. Her notes from the last COSEC meeting were still there. But she wasn't representing Sweden now; she didn't represent anyone at all.

She ate lunch at the hotel. The restaurant was teeming with cheerful employees of a global audit firm. She had no idea what a controller did, but a sign in the lobby welcomed all senior controllers to a two-day conference at the hotel. She looked at them and felt downhearted. There was something ridiculous about adults with name badges, as if some guardian had put the badge on them in order to easily include them in a count of beef cattle. Her mood wasn't improved by the slow delivery of her Caesar salad. For some reason a silly little thing like the kitchen forgetting her salad made her question the entire idea of coming to Brussels. Somehow she had imagined that everything would sort itself, if only she came here, but now she had arrived, things were just as complicated as they had been in Stockholm.

After lunch, she wandered around the city. She was in the heart of central Brussels, among the EU offices, banks, and international organizations. She turned down Rue du Trône and began to walk toward Parc de Bruxelles. It was unusually mild weather. Clusters of civil servants with pass cards fluttering on lanyards around their necks passed her. The Swedish Brussels delegation was only a few blocks away. If everything had been as usual, she would have gone there to check her e-mail, say hello to some colleagues. But nothing was as usual and it would be a long time before it was again.

At Regentlaan, she went into a shop that sold cell phones. She needed a new one; the kind of handset she had lost was of course not available, but would also have been very expensive. She listened, stony faced, to the assistant who showed her different models. Finally, she chose the cheapest available phone on pay-as-you-go. She had promised herself not to be bothered by her lost cell, yet she was grieving for it and in an unusually bad mood when she approached the Royal Palace. She walked up along one of the gravel paths and ended up in the wake of guided tour. The tourists stepped on to the lawns and took photos of each other with the heavyset palace in the background, despite the small signs that strictly stated that walking on the grass was not permitted. The palace, with its expansive parks and pompous statues, had once been the center of a great power, ruling over the heart of Africa. In annoyance, Carina pushed past the tourists taking photos of a statue of Leopold II on horseback; they were seemingly quite unaware that the king had devastated an entire continent.

She crossed the avenue and entered the larger park next to it. At its northern end, she found a bench that was set to one side. It felt restful to sit alone. She looked across the empty lawns and the dark green avenues of trees. In the middle of the park was a noisy stone fountain. A jogger ran past at a slow pace and there was a woman pushing a stroller along one of the gravel paths. Parc de Bruxelles at lunchtime on a Friday. She was left in peace.

She turned the pages of her notes. At the top of the first page, she had written, *Bernier*. Beneath that, a list of phone numbers.

There was no point in delaying things; she would just get more nervous. She got out her phone and gathered her thoughts for a second. Then she dialed the first number. She almost knew it by memory.

Hold music.

An operator broke in, in French. "*La Commission Européenne, bonjour.*"

"I'm looking for Jean Bernier," she said with the professional tone she had spent years practicing while working at the Ministry, and which she could produce at a moment's notice.

After a few seconds, the operator said that Jean Bernier wasn't in the office.

"That's strange. I'm calling from the Swedish representation and had agreed a telephone meeting for now," she said.

It was important to keep talking, not to seem crestfallen. She turned to the page in her notebook where she had written down a few names from the personnel list for GD Home, department A3.

"Perhaps you can connect me to one of his colleagues?"

She knew how it worked; if you sounded sure enough and could give a name that matched one in their phone database, you could get past the exchange. She was connected. For a second, the turgid hold music returned, then a woman answered.

"Bonjour, how can I help you?"

"I'd like to speak to Jean Bernier."

"But you've called Mr. Steigl." She had presumably been connected to a secretary. "Who is speaking?"

"Anna Svensson, at the Swedish delegation. I'm looking for Mr. Bernier—Jean Bernier. It's concerning a matter he's discussed with the delegation. I was connected here by the operator," she said with a tone of certainty, as if she didn't have time for this kind of nonsense. Plausibility was important; she needed to sound reasonably stressed, but not obstinate. If she was lucky, the secretary would connect her internally within the department just to get rid of her.

"But Mr. Bernier isn't in," said the secretary, already doubtful.

"Oh." She maintained the stressed tone, implying that this was very inconvenient in her hectic working day. "That's strange—I was asked to call today."

"What was it concerning?"

She said it was about a report from the directorate. A proposal that would be appearing under agenda item five at the summit the following week.

"Oh." She could hear the secretary had become noticeably stressed. "Yes, I understand . . . I'm sorry; Mr. Steigl is in a meeting. I can ask him to call you back." Carina said that wasn't necessary and asked to be reconnected to the exchange.

A new operator was connected. That was correct, Jean Bernier was not available. No, he hadn't left any message about his absence.

Carina thanked her and hung up.

Not available. That could mean anything—that he was just somewhere else in the building and would be back soon, or that he was away from work for a week—what did she know? She would have to try again later under a different name; she didn't dare use her own. There was always the risk that a warning had gone out about her name and that some alert individual would note her calls and send a message to Stockholm. Then the EU Commission would pull down the shutters—she couldn't let that happen.

The city spread out in all directions around her. She had never really thought of Brussels as a city. For her, Brussels was carpeted corridors, conference rooms, quick lunches, and long meetings about European security policy. The city itself was something she had mostly glimpsed from the back seat of a taxi on the way to or from the airport. Brussels was a place of work that you got home from on the seven-thirty flight. But now she was here in this city with millions of people, of which she was looking for just one. She needed to think through what she was going to do.

She navigated her way through the streets around the park and came out by the Grote Markt. The City Hall, with its jagged pinnacles, stretched into the clear sky.

After a few hours of brisk walking, she found herself somewhere in south Ixelles, where she stopped for a coffee. She was in one of those small local places with organic teas and a girl with Rasta dreads who made the coffee. There were FC Brussels scarves pinned above the bar and a large flat-screen TV was on the wall, showing Formula One cars racing soundlessly around a track somewhere in Europe. She ordered a double espresso and a small brandy and asked for a phone book.

Greger had said the name was one hundred percent right, that the guy who called himself Jean had the surname Bernier. But she wanted to be sure of the address. She turned to the page with surnames beginning with B and found the column of Berniers.

There were three Jean Berniers. One lived in a suburb, in Schaerbeek. That couldn't be right. The second was Professor Emeritus Jean Bernier and lived in the city center, near Grote Markt. That sounded wrong; the Jean Bernier she was looking for was unlikely to be a Professor Emeritus. But the third one . . . She smiled. Greger was right—the phonebook said that the third Bernier lived in the south of Brussels, in Waterloo.

34

Brussels, Friday, October 7

Some kind of monitoring, a form of hostile activity, was being directed against them. SSI's leadership team was sitting around Bente in her office, listening to Rodriguez. There was no doubt that she and Mikael had been followed on the way to Florian Klause's apartment after they had left the café. The question was whether SSI was the primary target or whether they had gotten caught up in a reconnaissance operation against Klause, or someone else. They had discovered three men and a woman following her and Mikael after they had left the café, said Rodriguez. It was standard procedure to reconnoiter before the Head of SSI had scheduled meetings. The café at Rue Vifquin had been deemed secure; there had been nothing there to raise suspicion. It was when she and Mikael had left the café that they had noticed something was wrong. A man had followed them.

Bente couldn't remember anyone following, but Rodriguez was certain. During the walk to Klause's apartment, they had spotted four people—there were probably more. They were, without doubt, professionals; based on their patterns of movement and the way in which they were coordinated, these people were probably well trained in intelligence work. It had all gone so fast, Rodriguez hadn't had time to contact her or Mikael before they reached the apartment. She hadn't answered her phone either, said Rodriguez with a tired expression. The pursuers had positioned themselves in the area surrounding Klause's apartment. They had probably noticed that the Section had discovered them and chose to abort.

"Did we intercept any radio traffic?" She turned to the Head of Signals Intelligence.

There hadn't been time to locate them. It had all gone so quickly; they were gone before they had managed to contact the cell team to search frequencies, let alone crack encryptions.

"But we have photographs."

Rodriguez brought up around thirty photos on his laptop. They were taken from the surveillance team's van using a telephoto lens. In one picture, she could see herself and Mikael on the street. Twenty meters behind them was a man in a hoodie. Then another series of pictures of a woman buying a newspaper at a street kiosk that Bente remembered had been opposite the main door to Florian Klause's building. She was thin, dark-haired, wearing a polo shirt and leather jacket. She was standing so that her face was visible in profile. No one that Bente knew, of course. Then photos of a young guy in a denim jacket, wearing headphones, walking along the pavement, presumably on the other side of the street from where Bente and Mikael had been. He was turning his head, as if casting a glance across the street.

"Try to identify them," said Bente and nodded at the screen. "I want to know who is watching us. Name, employer—whatever we can find. Check with other services. The French. Interpol."

Mikael nodded and made a note.

They discussed the level of threat against SSI. According to their signals intelligence, there had been nothing to previously suggest that the Section was a target. The physical plant was intact: no tampering with code locks or doors, no intrusions recorded, no unauthorized persons had been into the Section. The premises had been swept just a month ago—no microphones or other hostile equipment had been found in the building or in their server room to the south of the city—and no hostile code in the computer equipment either. No members of staff had shown any signs that could be deemed threatening. It was terrible even to contemplate that someone in the Section might be in pay of another power; Bente knew how loyal everyone was. But she was in charge and the security of

SSI was her top priority. She ordered Mikael to run security checks on all personnel—their e-mails, their phone calls and meetings for the last three months. A tense atmosphere filled the room.

"Do we need to evacuate the office?" She looked at them.

Rodriguez was certain that they had managed to disrupt whatever operation was currently being undertaken against them. The hostile monitoring was also unlikely to have traced them back to the office. No one had followed when they had driven back toward the Section after evacuating from Florian Klause's. She nodded. They had driven at breakneck speed through the city, following a route that Rodriguez had designated for rapid extractions. Three fast car changes, for safety's sake, then back to SSI the long way around. Their address had not been revealed.

But some form of monitoring *had* been ongoing against SSI—or against her, to be more specific. It was entirely possible she had been under surveillance since landing at Brussels airport in the morning. It was entirely possible that they had been waiting for her at the airport and then shadowed her from there, followed her taxi home and then to meet Mikael. The question was—who? She had her suspicions, but said nothing.

Signals Intelligence was going to send the photos to Stockholm and run them through the FRA's databases. Perhaps they might get a hit on something. Apart from that, Bente wanted all staff to minimize their movements. No meetings around the city for the next forty-eight hours unless there were crucial operational reasons to do so. No movements on foot. Contact by cell with family members and other outsiders was forbidden as of now, for two days. Then they would conduct a review. With regard to radio communications, they were to be kept to a minimum: no more talk on the Section's wavelengths than was absolutely necessary. An additional security check of the premises would be carried out. She turned to the Head of Liaison and asked him to contact the Belgian police to try to secure surveillance footage and other material where the hostile operatives might have been caught. She also instructed him to see whether Belgium's security service had any hits on the people photographed by Rodriguez. As they went through the motions, she began to feel calm. They were safe, for now.

The meeting broke up. Mikael stayed behind while the others left the room. Once they were alone, he got out the rumpled envelope and put it on her desk. She sat quietly for a while and thought. So someone was watching them. That poor young apprentice probably needed police protection, it occurred to her. But that couldn't be helped; they couldn't look after him. She looked slowly through the pictures Rodriguez had left.

"I think we've been very naïve, Mikael."

She told him how she had begun to have a clear sense that things were not right while she was in Stockholm, and that feeling had only grown. She explained, without being certain whether Mikael believed her. It didn't matter right now. She needed to say what she was thinking to someone she trusted, needed to get the thoughts out, hear the words so that they became real, and then get Mikael's assessment.

Fact one: the British knew about Jean Bernier. They knew about him from the start. He was a problem for them, just like Klause said. He was a cog in the machinery, pulling the wrong way, and over time had come to pose a real problem for them. Jean Bernier contacted Carina Dymek, by methods unknown, and they met.

"On the 22nd of September, here in Brussels," Mikael interrupted.

"Yes. And I think Dymek is telling the truth. Jean Bernier gave her the EIS report."

"And she shared it with a few people in the Ministry of Justice," said Mikael promptly. "With her partner, among others, who has been shown to have close links to the Muslim Brotherhood."

"Yes. So they say."

He looked sharply at her. "What do you mean?"

"Mikael, how do you know that?"

"What? How do I know what?" he said in hard tone of voice, as if he didn't really want to continue this conversation. He was close to switching off, ceasing to listen to her.

She said lightly, "How do you know it's true?"

He flinched and looked at her with an austere expression around his mouth. "Well, among other things, thanks to the British intelligence we've received—"

"Not among other things," she interrupted him. "*Only* thanks to the British intelligence. Do we have any other source that points in the same direction? Even one? Have the Germans or the Danes got any information like that? Have the French? We don't actually know anything except what the Brits have told us."

"But . . . why would . . ." He stared at her, open-mouthed. "MI6 are reliable. We've evaluated their information."

"Mikael, listen to me."

She explained that, when they had found the IRC channel, MI6 had said they didn't know anything about Jean Bernier—didn't know who he was. When it turned out he was a civil servant at the Commission, directly involved in the work on the EIS report, she had become suspicious. She had begun to wonder. The Brits were deeply involved in the EIS proposal; they knew every single official at the EU Commission who was working on the proposal, and naturally they must have known who Jean Bernier was—so why had they claimed they didn't?

"He was problem for them," she said. "Klause confirmed that. And yet the Brits said that Bernier was unknown to them. Then, just after we found the IRC channel, they used that to suggest Jean Bernier was a target for terrorists. Convenient, don't you think? But odd at the same time. Why just him—a normal civil servant at the Commission? Why would he be a target for terrorism? And why did we find out that he was a target, precisely when we did?"

"Because they didn't know before."

"No. Because they hadn't had to invent it before then."

"So you're saying they're lying—the British are lying?"

"I don't believe their intelligence."

Mikael looked at her as if she were crazy. His slightly condescending, slightly amused expression irritated her and made her want to hurt him.

"Do you remember when we found out that Dymek had leaked the report? I met Green that day," she said, with a sense of cruel satisfaction as she saw Mikael's surprised expression, which he quickly tried to hide. He didn't know about the meeting.

"Oh?"

"Green was angry—or more like pissed off—and he said nothing about terrorist threats. He was pissed off about the *leak*, Mikael. He wanted us to stop it, as fast as we fucking could."

"The leak was a problem—we thought that too," said Mikael with a shrug of his shoulders.

"That's not the point," she said and wished for a second that she didn't have to say another word, that she didn't have to explain, that she could just transfer the contents of her brain to him, wordlessly, through some kind of telepathy. "They were worried about the leak, because the leak was the real problem. And still is."

Mikael looked at her. She had his attention now.

"Green was worried about the leak—genuinely concerned. Then Wilson turns up in Stockholm and suddenly we have a terrorist threat on our hands. I think . . ." she said and stopped herself. What she was about to say surprised even her.

"I think," she said slowly, "that the Brits began to invent a story after my meeting with Green. They were worried about the report. Bernier was a vocal opponent of EIS and the entire report prepared by the Commission. He gave it to Dymek. Then something happened, something that forced them to change tactics. So they began inventing. You know they're the masters of deceptive operations, Mikael. They can do disinformation—they're almost as good as the Russians at it. And a rule of thumb is that, once you've begun to make up a lie, you have to stick to it. The Brits invented something and now they have to keep going with it. Think, Mikael," she said with emphasis. "Apart from the letter from Akim Badawi, what intelligence do we actually have about this mythical movement within the Muslim Brotherhood? What do we actually have that we didn't hear from the British first?"

"We've got lots of data," Mikael burst out. "I don't understand what you're talking about."

"But apart from the letter?" she said calmly. "Do we have *anything* that stands up by itself, without the Brits?"

Mikael made an attempt to protest. His face was tense; he was staring out of the window, as if he was looking for something to say that would fob her off. She knew he appreciated the British and the mere thought that they had provided them with intelligence that had been fabricated was humiliating. They were SSI; they ought to be in control. No one wanted to feel cheated. She knew Mikael—he hated losing.

"I just meant the British are controlling our analysis," she continued. "I don't trust them. They're holding things back."

"So does everyone."

"They're lying to us."

"How do we know?" he exclaimed. "Their intelligence makes sense."

"You know it doesn't, Mikael."

"It's plausible . . ."

"We only have what the British have told us. Nothing else," she hissed. "We don't have a chance of checking whether what they have said is actually true."

He raised his hands in a gesture: I give up.

"Listen," she said. "Our entire case is built on British intelligence. We're being drip-fed, constantly. And we acknowledge that they're running the investigation. We had a case together with Kempell. A leak—a job for Counterespionage. But then Wilson turned up, gave us the letter, gave us an elegant analysis and directed the investigation to Counterterrorism. Then we found Bernier, and—abracadabra—they suddenly declare that Bernier, about whom they had initially told us they knew nothing, must be a target for a terrorist attack. The IRC channel is linked to the Ahwa group—a link which no one else can confirm. It comes at a convenient moment and explains everything. They're filling in our horizon, Mikael. They don't want us to see anything."

"Yes, but what would that be?" he burst out. "What?"

"I don't know. It's normally you who is the skeptic. They're lying about Jean Bernier. And I wonder which other facts they have adjusted. It's something you should be asking too."

"I have asked myself that."

"Oh, really?"

She regretted her quip and fell silent. He was listening now, she noticed. He was thinking outside the box, saw what she saw. Some of what she had said was slowly sinking in. Mikael continued to stare out of the window, as if focusing on a small dot far away across the roofs. She looked at him. He had clearly not given any thought to the things she had just brought up. Presumably it was all too much, even for an analytical and quick-witted person like Mikael. He was defensive because he couldn't bear to rip apart his assessments, see everything through fresh eyes. She waited while he stood motionless, looking through the window.

Finally he said, "And Badawi?"

"He's a question mark."

A question mark. Yes, that was right. She wasn't sure about him. There was evidence—e-mails between him and the uncle in Cairo. There was a connection to the Muslim Brotherhood there, just like the British had said. It couldn't be denied. At the same time, the Ministry of Justice had checked him out when he had been appointed. His background was spotless; he was a talented civil servant. But, as the Brits said, an Arab background . . . There might be a loyalty to militant groups they hadn't discovered.

Mikael looked at her. "And Dymek—the leak. Is that made up too?"

"No, I don't think so."

"So what do you think?"

She pretended not to hear his sharp tone—didn't let him provoke her. "The leak is genuine."

Dymek received the report and had distributed it: that was true; it was proven; it was real. But how much of that was down to Badawi, or to do with a radical element of the Muslim Brotherhood was unclear. Perhaps there was a connection; perhaps there was nothing there at all.

Mikael began to pace up and down the room. He tried to protest. She interrupted him.

"Of course, of course. MI6 had intelligence that clearly indicated they were all nodes in a terrorist network. But they had lied about Jean Bernier. And why would someone like Dymek have anything to do with an Islamist group? It didn't make sense. So the question instead was . . ." She stopped herself, because she hadn't had time to pose it to herself yet.

"The question is, what aren't they telling us? What do they want us to believe?"

"But . . ." He stopped short, shook his head and began to laugh. He looked at her with an odd smile, as if trying to say that she was amusing him with her madcap theories, but now she had gone too far. A weak ray of sun struck through the cloud cover that lay across the city outside.

She said quietly, "So how do you explain this annex?"

He shrugged his shoulders. He didn't understand what she meant.

"Jean Bernier gave this document to his most junior colleague," she said, as she pulled the papers out of the envelope. She hadn't even had time to look at them. "A *stagiaire*, for God's sake. Completely wet behind the ears. He can't have trusted any of his other colleagues. He was quite clearly an opponent of the annex. The British wanted it included in the EIS proposal, but he was against it. Perhaps he was the only one who really was. And now he's dead."

"Due to natural causes."

She smiled coolly at him. "Not even you believe that."

Mikael shrugged his shoulders.

She remained seated while Mikael left the office. He seemed depressed and anxious. She had thought better of him, that he might be able to suffer greater disappointments. It was at times like this that you saw what made people tick, and Mikael was clearly a little too impressed by the British. Admiration like that shook your judgment. The British weren't friends; they were an old imperial power trying to remain in pole position. She had no illusions about Her Majesty's Government, as they liked to call themselves. That Mikael didn't see things as she did disappointed her.

Out in the large command room, everyone had fallen silent. She heard Mikael hand out orders, assignments. All British material connected to the Dymek/Ahwa case was to be reviewed. As far as possible, they were to trace all sources, verify and test all data one more time. There was no other way. They needed to know. Counterterrorism in Stockholm needed to be certain before sending in a task force, before Wilson and his hunters got an order from London, before lives were destroyed. It was her responsibility as Head of SSI to present a clear picture of reality.

Three days until the summit meeting. Verifying intelligence of this kind in such a short period was an almost hopeless task. But that was the situation. They would contact the other services, the Danes, the German Verfassungsschutz, the French DGSE, the various Spanish services. Something would turn up.

She opened the envelope they had been given by Florian Klause, pulled out the papers and glanced through them. The document was just five pages long, but written in impenetrable EU Commission prose. It was a draft legal text. It was about security, about some form of judicial cooperation between countries, but it was so dense and technically written that she kept stumbling over the sentences. She quickly reread the text, but still didn't manage to work out what it actually said; she couldn't understand the contents of the text. The margins were full of notes written in red ink—probably Jean Bernier's notes. In several places there were just question marks or exclamation marks. *Completely unacceptable!* Jean Bernier had written next to one paragraph.

She got up heavily. She could sleep for a week. She rooted around for her car keys and cell and stretched so much that her back creaked. She put the annex document back into the envelope, folded it in half and put it in her inside pocket, reaching for her coat as she left the room and headed to the exit. Mikael watched her go. Perhaps he was wondering where she going, but that was none of his business. She nodded at him, as if in benediction. It was time for her to meet an old friend.

35

Leiden–Brussels, Friday, October 7

Leiden was just a two-hour drive north on the E19, but Bente hadn't been there for over a year. She used to come here more often, before she and Fredrik had children. She loved the old-world atmosphere the Dutch university town exuded, the beautiful professors' houses along the canal, and the pleasant, winding streets and squares, with their old-fashioned stone-built houses. She could still remember when she had been there as an exchange student, decades ago. Leiden had a tranquil, carefree air about it, as if the town really was a haven from the stupidity and narrow-mindedness of the world. The university had been there since the sixteenth century and was proud of its heritage as a defender of religious freedoms and the freedom of thought. *Presidium Libertatis*—the stronghold of liberty. It was fortunate that there were any left in the world.

Students swarmed past her on the wide stone steps. The Faculty of Law was located in a heavy, beautiful building in classical style, with marble pillars and symmetrical rows of white mullioned windows. Perhaps she should have become an academic. Or perhaps not, given how often she had fallen asleep during lectures. But she had enjoyed the courses in international law. She had thought about becoming a lawyer and working on the big questions surrounding international law, working at the International Criminal Court in The Hague. She could smile about it now. Reality had demanded other things of her, an income for her children. She probably wouldn't have enjoyed the academic environment; she was no theoretician.

Afternoon lectures had just ended and young people streamed through the corridors. She found her way to the room where Professor Willem De Vries had just delivered a lecture about international humanitarian law. The students were on their way out and passed her in small groups with their notebooks and cell phones. She peeked through the doorway. By the podium was a tall, blond man surrounded by a group of students, lingering to speak to their lecturer. She recognized his rich, friendly laugh. She had heard it many times before and knew how it could grow into a roar when he thought something was especially funny or uncommonly stupid. She watched him while he finished talking to his students. He was a handsome man.

"Hello, Willem."

The last students had squeezed past her in the doorway. Professor De Vries was alone at the lectern, lost in thought. When she entered the room, he looked up from his papers absently. It actually seemed as though he didn't recognize her. Then he laughed and boomed, "Bente! What a pleasant surprise!"

He came to her and kissed her on both cheeks.

"What are you doing in Leiden? I thought you were in Stockholm."

"I've moved. I'm in Brussels these days."

"And still defending our open, democratic society, I take it."

She smiled. "Something like that. That's actually partly why I've come here."

He nodded, became slightly more serious.

"The fact is that I came to see you."

"Well, it's been a long time since we met," he said and smiled at her warmly. "I have no more lectures today. If you have no objection, we can go back to my place. I live nearby."

They left the room together and walked out toward a side entrance while talking about what had happened since they last met. She had moved to Brussels, got a job there. He was tactful enough not to ask what it was. He knew how it worked in her business. He had worked in the Hague for several years as a legal expert at the ICC, but now he was back in Leiden and had a professorial chair.

"It's nice. A little sleepy, though." He laughed.

Willem De Vries was one of the world's leading experts on the rules of war—or international humanitarian law, as it was called in his circles. He had been Head of the Legal Secretariat at the UN in New York, one of the big hitters inside the UN that had spoken out against the US invasion of Iraq. He still looked good—the same easygoing, intelligent man she had fallen in love with as he lectured over twenty years ago as young, brilliant PhD researcher. They had stayed in touch. He was one of the few men she sometimes wondered what it would have been like to share her life with. Naturally, nothing had ever happened between them. But when she started at Counterterrorism, she had gotten in touch with him when she needed an independent assessment of certain complex legal matters. Willem De Vries had an instinctive feel for the nuances of international law, and he was incorruptible. She had never met a person with such integrity, such an ability to see the letter of the law.

They walked together through the heart of the town, along the winding pedestrian mall alongside the canal, until they reached one of the larger villas—a big, beautiful brick-built house with views over a small park, situated in the bend of the watercourse. He opened the gate to a messy garden, overgrown with scrubby rose bushes, honeysuckle, and vines behind a dense box hedge that prevented anyone from seeing in. She followed him up the garden path and into the house.

She waited in the living room while he moved around the house, turning on lights and preparing coffee. The walls were covered in bookcases; thousands upon thousands of book spines faced toward her. There was something impressive about this quantity of different titles that she had never heard of. Here and there were books she recognized, a few classics, and an almost exhausting amount of specialist literature. So much knowledge gathered between the covers of books, probably already dated. As a practitioner, she had never had any great need for legal textbooks after her studies.

Willem reappeared holding a tray with a pot of coffee, cups, cream, and a plate of small chocolates. Was she was hungry? he inquired. He could make some sandwiches. No, she wasn't hungry.

The aroma of the strong, well-brewed coffee filled the room. Here, among all these books, she relaxed. It was good to see him again. She wished she was here for a more pleasant reason.

"It's been a long time," he said.

"Yes. You haven't changed a bit."

He smiled.

She drank the coffee and looked around the room. It was so peaceful here. She really wanted to talk to him—as Bente. Ask about his research, how his years in New York had been. But there was no point postponing the real reason she had looked him up. She got out the envelope, straightened it, and pulled out the papers. He looked calmly at her and then the envelope. This, she said slowly, was top secret material. She had come here unbeknownst to anyone else because she needed his assessment.

"I want you to read this and tell me what you think the text means."

She passed over the five pages. No, she couldn't tell him what it was about. She just wanted him to read it and give his interpretation of the text. He shrugged his shoulders and took the document with an amused but quizzical expression. He got out a small pair of spectacles and leaned back.

While Willem read, she went outside. The weather was mild and it felt pleasant to wander around the unkempt garden. Apparently her former lecturer liked to cultivate herbs because there was a small corner filled with fragrant shrubs. She rubbed a few silver-white leaves between her fingers: sage. Then it occurred to her that perhaps it was De Vries's wife who gardened; Bente didn't even know if he was married. She looked over her shoulder: Willem was hunched over the document, reading in concentration.

Her cell vibrated in her pocket.

Carina Dymek is in Brussels. Landed 09:51. Staying at Radisson, Rue d'Idalie. Action?

So she was in Brussels. Why hadn't she found out about that? Hamrén should have notified her. She looked at her watch: almost four. Nearly six hours. She swore silently and wrote a quick reply: *Follow her. No intervention. Keep me informed.*

She stood for a brief moment and stared into space while gathering her thoughts, so she didn't notice that Willem had finished reading and was looking at her seriously.

"Bente."

She put away her cell and returned inside. "Yes?"

"I'm just wondering, does this exist? I mean, is this going to become reality?" He tapped the paper with his finger. Then, when he noticed her hesitation, he made a dismissive gesture. "You don't have to answer. It's just that . . ." He shook his head as if he couldn't quite believe what he had just read. "If this is an excerpt from an EU decision, which it appears to be, then it's . . . extremely radical."

"In what way?"

He wasn't listening. He had picked up the annex and was grimly rereading it.

"What is a 'strike team'?"

"Where does it say that?"

"Here." He pointed at a footnote.

She knew what a strike team was. It was what the Americans called their special forces, used to eliminate high-value targets—like bin Laden. Since the American administration had forced the CIA to close its secret prisons, American counterterrorism had moved into targeted operations, using lethal force. Of course, some prisons were still left, but there were fewer of them and the ones that remained were more secret than ever. She leaned over his shoulder and read the document.

"Willem, tell me what it says."

"To put it simply, it's like this." He adjusted his glasses. "This document is an agreement between the EU and the USA, giving the American authorities the right to run independent operations on European soil. It also gives them the right to act in accordance with American law, without any consideration for differing national legislation. This would only be allowed in certain circumstances . . ." He read silently for a second. "They mention various criteria here. One of them is that everything should only occur after approval by a particular body—the European Intelligence Service. They call it a 'window.' This kind of window can only be open for a short period and must be connected to a specific operation or action, may only be used as part of the fight against terrorism and within the framework of the international agreements and conventions that govern the fight against terror. Blah, blah, blah. As far as I can tell, the agreement gives the Americans carte blanche to do whatever they fucking want on European soil, as long as they inform us first."

"And all they have to do is follow US law."

"Yes . . . That's my interpretation. There are similar examples of this kind of cooperation. The Americans always want an exemption—an exemption so they can have armed civilian security staff on transat-lantic flights; an exemption from the Geneva Convention so they can torture captives; an exemption so they can invade nearby countries." He laughed. "They rarely allow themselves to actually be governed by international law."

"But, in layman's terms, you're saying that the Americans, with this agreement, will be able to operate on, for example, Swedish or Dutch soil, without adhering to the laws of the land. They'll be able to send in special units on operations—to fight terrorists."

"Yes." As if what he had read had only just struck him, he mumbled in an appalled tone, "It's completely crazy." He looked straight at her. "What the hell is this?"

"Willem, I can't talk to you about it."

"Is this a real proposal?" He looked at her. He pulled down the corners of his mouth and frowned, as if he had caught sight of a dark and twisted side of her face that frightened him.

"I can't talk to you about it."

"No, no. I understand."

He turned his gaze away and said nothing. A chilly silence lay between them. She wanted to say something, to explain. But there was nothing to say that didn't immediately threaten to reveal too much. Perhaps she had gone too far in showing him the annex; maybe she had trusted him too much. She glanced at him. She wanted to stretch out a hand and touch him, get him to look up with that smile again and see her, Bente, as the person she was. But who was she? In his eyes, she was probably part of the machinery that was formerly known as the war against terror, and which now went by alternative, more bureaucratic designations, like foreign contingency operations. A part of her conscience noted that it was good he had begun to dislike her. Their friendship was a burden for the Section. She needed to distance herself, and silence between them was a first step. Silence protected her. Willem got up, without a word, and disappeared into the garden. She stayed seated. She saw him outside, smoking.

Picking up the paper, she flipped through its pages. So this was what the British had wanted to keep secret. The politicians knew about the European Intelligence Service, but this annex was the little secret that the Brits had carefully introduced—a seemingly insignificant annex of an operational nature, and secret to all but those who supported it. A new transatlantic collaboration against terrorism. Good God.

She read the footnote that Willem had spotted. It was a short, dry note stating that the agreement also included "tactical measures, cooperation in surveillance, reconnaissance, and operations involving strike teams and other similar resources." That small sentence contained the entire war against terror. She couldn't help but shudder. Not that she was unused to such proposals, or believed that counterterrorism work didn't involve violence. It was the enormity of what that short, seemingly insignificant text opened up that made her dizzy. If this proposal were adopted at the summit, the Americans would, in principle, be able to operate on Swedish soil. It would be like Pakistan, which had to go along quietly with American operations and clean up after deadly shootouts. Man hunters like Wilson would set the agenda.

The British had consciously left the agreement outside of the report so as not to draw attention to it. An annex. She rubbed her eyes. What was it the apprentice had said? The text hadn't been shown to the EU parliament. It was completely unknown to all but a few. Jean Bernier had read the annex; his notes were on the document. And he was dead.

Willem came back in and flopped onto the sofa.

"I know I can't ask questions. But this text . . ." he said. He was subdued. "There must be something I can do. I mean, if this becomes EU law . . ." He shook his head.

"No, Willem." She looked him steadily in the eye. "There's nothing you can do. You have seen something that very few people have seen. I'm glad you were able to help me. But you should do nothing. Never mention this to anyone. You should forget we ever discussed it. Is that understood?"

He stared at her. Then he nodded, slowly. She put a hand on his knee and let it lie there for a second. They wouldn't see each other again. This was the last time. He couldn't be anymore involved than this; she had already taken a risk by showing him the annex, and things could quickly get worse if he betrayed her and their meeting. There was always a danger, with people like De Vries, that they might decide to use their academic freedom to write a long opinion piece about the subject. She didn't want him to end up like Jean Bernier; it would be so terribly unnecessary. She leaned forward and kissed him lightly on the mouth, got up quickly, and left him sitting on the sofa. She hurried out of the house, down the garden path and kept going.

Somewhere north of Antwerp, just ten minutes after she had crossed the Dutch-Belgian border, she spotted the other car—a silver Mercedes; a recent model—two hundred meters behind her in the other lane. When she increased her speed, she noticed how the other car softly followed, and probably had been doing so ever since she had left Leiden.

She raced along the freeway, junctions slipping past at a steady pace. The silver car remained behind her throughout.

She quickly began to approach Brussels. She now had two options. Either she could keep going and try to lose them by herself in the city center, or she could call the Section and notify them of the situation. She would get assistance. But, on the other hand, there was a risk that the Section would be exposed if the cell team carried out an operation to bring her home. Rodriguez would want to know what the hell she was doing out on the road when she herself had ordered all SSI staff to remain stationary and maintain radio silence.

She leaned forward and felt under the seat. Her Glock was where it should be.

There was more traffic. She was driving south, had just passed Mechelen and was on the way into Brussels from the north. She needed to get away from the freeway. She was rapidly approaching a bedroom community, around ten kilometers from the city perimeter, near Mechelen. She accelerated until she was doing one hundred and eighty kilometers an hour—before turning off on to the N211 at the last possible moment.

Fields raced by, a construction site passed by in just a few seconds. The rear wheels skidded. She came off the ramp and, as the road straightened out, she accelerated again. The other car had managed to exit at the junction as well and appeared a couple of hundred meters behind her. By leaving the freeway, she had avoided the jams that normally formed around the airport at this time of day, and instead she was heading at high speed toward the small suburban town of Machelen. She got stuck behind a truck for a few seconds at a traffic circle, before finding a gap and managing to overtake it, increasing her speed, crossing a railway line, and rushing through an avenue on the outskirts of the town in less than a minute. To the left were railway tracks, to the right, industrial units and low office buildings and workshops flickered by as the slanting sunshine streamed into the car. Finally, the avenue narrowed and became a local road. This provided opportunities to disappear, so long as she didn't end up in a cul-de-sac. The other car was still behind her.

Without any warning, she reached the town boundary. She almost drove into a field but, after braking heavily, she took a left, drove under a railway viaduct, and reached a residential area. People were in their gardens; she could sense heads turning, gazes watching her car. She couldn't draw too much attention to herself. She slowed down and drove as calmly as she could until she reached a thoroughfare. A sign said she was on the road to Vilvoorde. That wasn't good. She needed to shake the other car, but Vilvoorde was an old town, full of impassable, narrow streets where you could easily get stuck. At a crossroads with a larger avenue, she put her foot down, drove through a red light, and skidded into a left turn, just as the traffic in the other direction began to move. Drivers honked their horns. The car skidded hard. She passed a lamp post and regained control, and was through the crossroads. A glance in the rearview mirror confirmed what she had hoped: the other car had gotten stuck at the traffic lights. She increased her speed gradually and glided up to the next crossroads. No police nearby. She was on the way out of Machelen, away from these small towns. An industrial area opened up before her: large expanses, no people. She accelerated up to two hundred kilometers an hour on a straightaway and rushed between the low factory buildings and empty industrial plots, before stopping by a large, fenced area with a big windowless building, clearly the town's thermal power station; she turned off. Two enormous white chimneys rose out of the fields a few kilometers away.

She drove around the area until she found what she was looking for: a parking lot. There were around one hundred cars. Visibility was good. She parked in a space, turned off the engine, bent down, and pulled out her Glock. Clicking the safety off, she got out of the car, crouched next to the warm chassis, and waited.

A little while later, the silver Mercedes appeared. She saw it brake, before turning into the parking lot. She straightened the gun in her hands. If they discovered her, she would need to move quickly, before they had time to get out, and open fire on the driver. The car in pursuit was not armored—that was visible. Four or five shots. She would incapacitate whoever it was that was following her. She saw the car glide along the rows of parked vehicles at a leisurely pace, around and around, for what seemed like an eternity. Then it accelerated rapidly, drove back onto the road, and vanished. She waited for over twenty minutes before finally, stiff legged, she crept back behind the wheel and started the engine. The other car was nowhere to be seen. When she got back to the southbound road, she lowered her speed and began to breathe easier. Darkness fell as she passed through the suburbs of Brussels.

Mikael came toward her in the corridor of the Section. The floor was in partial darkness, but a lot of staff were still at their screens as they flickered in the dark. The surveillance against Dymek demanded resources; an entire team of signals intelligence operatives from the FRA and parts of the cell team were now following her movements through the city. At the same time, a group of analysts was working through the British intelligence, comparing and checking details with data gathered from other sources. They were in a hurry; they needed a clear picture of the situation before any arrests in Stockholm could take place—they would need enough material by then.

"Where have you been?"

"Out. I had to check something."

Mikael looked at her as if he was surprised that she hadn't said more, but merely nodded. He was so used to not asking questions that he let the subject go without another word.

"Has something happened? You look serious," he continued while following her down the corridor toward the conference room.

She shook her head. She had decided not to say anything about what had just happened—better to keep it to herself. But it worried her. Whoever had followed her had wanted to frighten her, to show their presence, that they were watching her and SSI.

As if he had somehow heard her thoughts, Mikael said, "We've ID'd one of the people from outside Florian Klause's apartment—the apprentice, you remember."

"Okay, good."

Mikael pulled out three photographs from a folder and handed them over. They were pictures of the woman in the leather jacket who had been by the kiosk buying a newspaper.

"Who is she?"

"She's CIA."

She stopped and looked at him. Was he serious? Sometimes security services watched the work of other security services, but the CIA? If the Americans were carrying out surveillance against them, it meant something was worrying them.

Mikael held out a piece of paper and interrupted her train of thought. "We ran a search using the images and got lucky. She was on a few diplomatic lists. We found an old piece of information stating she was a consular assistant at the US embassy in Indonesia in the early nineties. Then nothing. Vanished off the face of the earth."

She nodded. That was how the Americans worked. The CIA often registered its agents as consular staff at the American embassies. If they then began to work in the operational part of the CIA, they were recalled to Washington, given a protected identity, and then disappeared.

So the CIA was interested in what the Section was up to as part of this case.

Her leadership team was waiting around the table in the conference room. She noticed that they were having a conversation that abruptly turned to silence as she entered the room. Things had probably happened while she had been gone. She knew that Rodriguez's group had worked all afternoon on the surveillance against Dymek. He looked tired but alert in the way she had seen many police look during ongoing operations. It had been an intensive day.

She opened the meeting without any ceremony. "Okay, friends. What's the situation?" She turned to Rodriguez.

For the last eight hours the cell team had been following Carina Dymek, ever since she arrived by taxi at her hotel at half past ten in the morning. She had gone to the same hotel that she had stayed at several times while traveling on business for the MFA, in central Brussels—they had established this after discreetly hacking into the hotel customer database. After checking in under her own name, she had begun to move around the city, had made a few cash withdrawals, then bought a cell phone with a credit card.

"Do we have the number?"

"Yes, we're listening in on that phone," said Rodriguez. "We've got Dymek in check." He looked anxiously at her. It wasn't Dymek who was the problem. There had been others at the hotel. Other operatives. "It all went to hell."

One of their technicians had gone in to install a bug on the phone and broadband connection in Dymek's room, Rodriguez explained. He discovered that there was already a bug there and raised the alarm. Parts of the cell team were already in the hotel, but had pulled out rapidly to avoid discovery. Once they understood that they weren't alone, they placed two men in the lobby.

"Continue."

"We regrouped and waited. Olof went up to Dymek's room and there, outside her room, he spotted one of them, dressed as hotel staff."

Olof was one of the more experienced spotters on the cell team; she knew she could rely on his judgment. He was one of those she had personally managed to recruit from Stockholm when SSI was founded. He had happened to come across the other operative, who was clearly keeping an eye on the floor. Nothing should have raised Olof's suspicions because the man was dressed in the hotel's uniform and had passed him calmly before disappearing into the elevator. But his shoes were too expensive: black hybrid shoes with soft, shock-absorbent soles—made for sprinting.

Then the man was gone. But one of Rodriguez's team had caught sight of him from a window as he had hurried away across a rear courtyard.

"Then we saw another one in the lobby. He turned up just as a large group of guests was checking in. Dressed like a businessman—suit, briefcase. Black guy; tall. Maybe it was because he looked too fit."

This man had checked in and they had cornered the receptionist and coaxed out of her which room he was staying in; it transpired

he had checked into a room on the same floor as Dymek, two rooms
down the hall. Two others had been spotted on the upper floors and
one had been posted on the street by the entrance.

"Presumably there were more of them. I aborted—it was too
risky to stay."

An hour later, Rodriguez had gone in with a false warrant from
the Belgian police and demanded the videotapes from the surveillance cameras in the lobby. The man in reception had been caught
on camera.

Rodriguez opened a file on the computer: a grainy picture of a
hotel lobby. Bente could see suitcases spread across a large, oriental
carpet, people by the reception counter and in small groups around
the room.

"There." A tall man, dressed in a suit with a coat over his arm,
stood by the reception counter, a little apart from the others. Only
his back was visible, seen diagonally from above. When he turned
around, his face was only visible for a second. Rodriguez froze the
picture.

"We checked him out," said Mikael. "The passport he showed
to the hotel was fake: it's not in SIS or any Schengen systems. He
probably has a protected identity. The receptionist said he spoke
British English. I did a little fishing and it transpired the Germans
recognize his face. They say he's ex–Special Air Service. According
to the Germans, he was involved in an operation in Hamburg three
years ago."

"Hamburg?" She looked up. "That's Wilson's team."

Five years earlier, Roger Wilson had led an operation in Hamburg against a group of individuals with connections to al-Qaida.
The German Bundesverfassungsschutz and MI6 had, for several
years, been tracking German targets—radical persons who moved
in circles around the al-Quds mosque in Hamburg. The individuals had been part of an Islamist network for a long time; several
of them had been connected to the apartment on Marienstrasse
where Mohamed Atta, the pilot in the World Trade Center attack,
had lived; names that had come up in interrogations of captured

al-Qaida members. For the operation in Hamburg, the British had sent an elite force from the SAS which stormed an apartment. All five individuals inside were killed. Another two people were later arrested, but found innocent. The operation was kept dark; relatives' silence was bought. The operation became notorious throughout the industry.

At once, the situation became clearer. Wilson had followed the target, Dymek. Naturally, he wasn't letting her out of his sight. They knew that Counterterrorism in Stockholm could look after Jamal Badawi, but Dymek had left the country. They wanted to keep her under control and weren't planning to hand that task over to the Section or anyone else.

Wilson had Dymek in his sights. Why, Bente asked again, had the British sent him to Stockholm? A man hunter; a British counterterrorism expert. Why had they put the toughest resource the British intelligence service had, a man who was used to tracking battle-hardy al-Qaida members in northern Pakistan, up against a soft target like Dymek?

If it was Wilson's team that had dealt with Jean Bernier, then Carina Dymek only had a day or so left to live. But for what? For a report? Or were the British actually stopping an attack against the summit meeting? While, simultaneously, an American team was watching her own SSI. Uncertainty flickered through her, an unfamiliar feeling that she found surprising. The truth was there, but she couldn't see it. It was like looking down into pitch-black water.

The others sat quietly in their chairs, waiting for her.

"Where is Dymek now?"

"At the hotel."

So no one had yet intervened, tried to arrest her or take her away.

Dymek had sat in Parc de Bruxelles just after lunchtime, added Rodriguez. She'd made a string of calls—several to the EU Commission. Then she had returned to the hotel. He made a small, tired gesture.

"We're trying to get as close as we can, but we have to be careful not to run into Wilson's group. It's harder to follow her." Ordinarily they would have been able to follow the target closely in the urban environment, but now they were being forced to observe her from a distance.

"Continue following her. See what the Brits are doing, but avoid confrontation. No contact before I say so. Mikael, let me see the pictures again."

Mikael got out the photographs of the woman outside Florian Klause's home. Why would the Americans turn up there?—that was the question. Bente concentrated, looked down at the table and followed the winding grain of the wood. The Americans' operation outside Klause's bore none of the hallmarks of a CIA counterterrorism operation. If it had been them, they would already have carried out a rapid strike against Dymek and everyone who had any connection to the case. They would have gone in with or without the Belgian police, with a completely different level of firepower. But Klause's name was not to be found anywhere in the ongoing terrorism investigation being conducted with the British. If the CIA saw a terrorist threat, then there was no reason to watch the poor German apprentice. Unless they had been at the address for completely different reasons. Mikael tried to say something but she raised her hand.

"Wait."

She saw the silver car in front of her. What was it Willem had said to her in Leiden—about the annex? That it was a crazy proposal. That it would give the Americans unlimited opportunities to operate on European soil.

They were watching SSI. The CIA wanted to know what SSI was up to, but not because they were concerned about the ongoing terrorism investigation.

She smiled. That was how it was.

"Have we been able to verify the British information yet?" she asked him. "Akim Badawi, the Ahwa group—all that stuff?"

Mikael cleared his throat. He and a liaison officer had been in touch with other services. Neither the French, nor German, Danish, or Israeli services had seen any indications of the threat MI6 believed was in existence. Interpol had been curious. He hadn't been able to verify any of the British data.

"Nothing."

"Nothing at all?"

Mikael shook his head. "No one has heard of Dymek."

"And Badawi? What about Akim?"

"No, neither Dymek nor Jamal Badawi was in any records. Nor was Akim Badawi. No one was at all interested." He threw out his hands.

"So they didn't see a threat at all? What did they say about the possibility that there was an attack being planned?"

He shook his head helplessly. "They were very surprised by what I had to say. They seemed to have no similar indications whatsoever and wondered how I had found out all of this information."

"And you explained the situation."

"*Of course* I did," he burst out passionately. "I got the DGS in Paris to call their people in Cairo. I made such a fuss that Interpol ran the names through their records twice. Nothing came up. I came across as a complete idiot."

She nodded. "Okay. And the foundations? Did you ask about the foundations managed by Akim Badawi?"

"The French knew about Akim Badawi, but only as one of the old men in the Muslim Brotherhood. Apparently he looks after some funds and foundations, but the French consider them to be of no interest whatsoever—small academic projects. They checked him out five years ago in connection with a larger sweep, a purely routine check, and found nothing." There were radical elements in the Muslim Brotherhood—individuals with Islamist, anti-Western views—everyone knew that. But Akim Badawi was not part of that faction, said the French. "They wondered what the hell I was up to. Akim Badawi is just an old guy in a book club."

They sat in silence for a moment as Bente took this in.

"Good," she said. She couldn't help but smile. "Excellent."

The others looked at her quizzically and probably thought she had misunderstood what Mikael had just said. But she hadn't misunderstood anything—quite the opposite. For the first time, things were beginning to fall into place. The CIA was shadowing the Section. The reason, she realized—with an insight that came so naturally and with such ease that she was surprised—was the annex. The annex to the report. De Vries had pointed out the enormous potential of the opportunities opened up by the agreement for the American intelligence machine to operate on European soil, just as long as the Commission's proposal was adopted by the EU members. The EIS was real to them—Washington's focus was the report. And yet, all the Brits talked about was the terrorist threat—but, interestingly enough, a terrorist threat no one else appeared to have perceived. But the radically differing perception of the situation was no misunderstanding; it wasn't because Interpol and the French and the Germans and every other European security service were worse at spotting threats than the British.

"Okay," she said. "So we have two completely opposite assessments of the situation. Personally, I doubt that everyone apart from the Brits has missed a serious terrorist threat against an EU summit. And if we work off that, then . . ."

She stopped herself one last time to think through what she was saying. MI6's assessment of the situation differed completely from how the other services perceived the situation. Or, more accurately, the threat scenario that MI6 claimed to have identified *did not exist* in the analyses of the other services.

She felt a kind of relief and, at the same time, the situation made her gasp. It was so brazen, so damn daring, and the worst thing was that the British had succeeded.

"If we assume that it is the British who are claiming there is a terrorist threat," she said slowly, "and not a single other service sees that threat . . . then my conclusion is that we have been the subject of British disinformation."

The word made the Head of Directed Surveillance groan loudly. Rodriguez and the Head of Security protested, talking over one another. She couldn't be serious, surely? She said nothing and waited for them to calm down. Way above them were organizations with far greater influence than the Swedish Security Service, controlled by people to whom the Section, the Security Service, and Sweden in general were nothing more than appropriate tools to reach certain strategic targets. She hated the thought as much as they did, but she wasn't in denial.

Disinformation: every person in the industry hated that word. They stared at her. Mikael didn't protest, he just sat quietly looking down at the table. He agreed with her now. He hadn't seen this coming until he saw it in black and white from other sources, but now he agreed with her.

"It's possible that I'm wrong," she said, "that there still is a threat to the summit meeting. But if it is as you say, Mikael, the most likely scenario is that we are the subjects of a British operation to mislead our counterterrorism efforts. Most probably all the other services are correct and there is no terrorist threat."

Mikael nodded emptily.

"And in that case," she continued, her voice echoing in the now silent conference room, "this is not a matter for Counterterrorism. It is about a hostile power trying to disrupt our operational capabilities."

"But why?" exclaimed the Head of Directed Surveillance. "What the fuck do they want?"

She didn't like the emotional, shouty tone that some of the leadership team sometimes adopted. But now wasn't the right time to point that out. She suppressed a harsh comment and said calmly, "I think the British intelligence service wants to draw Sweden's attention in the wrong direction. They have created a situation that we are reading as a terrorist threat; they want to give the *impression* that it is about terrorism. And they have gotten us to behave just as they intended. The difference is that we know about it now. That's a small advantage."

She reflected. Then: "I met Green last week. MI6's chief in Brussels. He was concerned that a Swedish diplomat had come across the EIS report. I think he was telling the truth. He told it as it was, before London realized that was a mistake and began to cover everything up—sending in Wilson, ensuring it was all about terrorism."

She was adamant now. They needed to act. If they could get the Brits to believe that SSI still trusted their intelligence, they would get a little breathing space. She thought. The situation was clearer than before, yet also more complex. They could, with a little luck, play a game of doubles—behaving as expected with a focus on counterterrorism, while also trying to establish what the British were actually up to, with a view to intervening. They had to act before the British reached their goal. They had to get there in time.

"Mikael, get in touch with the liaison officer in London and ask him to contact MI6 to request additional intelligence on the Ahwa group. Send a convincing request so that they believe we're really on the ball." She quickly handed out orders to the others. An operative was to contact the Head of Security at the EU Council secretariat. "Say that we believe there is a threat. Sweden believes there is a terrorist threat against the meeting. Be convincing. Make them worried. Get them to react; that way they'll call around and the Brits will get to hear about it."

Mikael looked up from his papers with a puzzled expression, as if he only now truly realized the extent of it all. "Bente, are you sure about this?" he said.

"What do you mean?"

They were quiet.

"The British." His eyes flickered. "I mean, what if we're moving too quickly? What if Badawi actually is dangerous? What if they actually are planning an attack? Then it'll all go to hell."

"The Brits are lying, Mikael."

"Are we completely certain about that?"

"No, not *completely* certain," she snapped. "You can't be completely certain in these situations. You know that too, Mikael. But my assessment," she said and turned to the others, who had all been listening downheartedly, "is that Interpol and our other partners are right. There is no threat against the summit meeting. The British are bluffing." The only people with a threat against them right now, she thought quietly, were Carina Dymek and Jamal Badawi.

"Okay, let's say that it's all British disinformation," said Mikael with a tense, somewhat sarcastic tone. "Why is Wilson hunting Dymek and Badawi? If what we have seen online isn't attack planning and there is no terrorist threat, if everything the Brits have said is lies, as you now claim—what is Wilson doing?"

She was going to say something about the EIS report, but stopped. Mikael was right. What was Wilson up to? Ever since he had joined the investigation, he had been acting as if there really was a terrorist threat, and he didn't do bluffing. He really believed that Bernier was a target, when in reality he was dead long before MI6 had sent Wilson in. Once again, she recalled his puzzled expression from their first meeting, with Kempell, when he had tried to smooth over the fact that he knew nothing about the report.

She stopped herself and concentrated. For a second, all these questions writhed before her like a threatening darkness. Wilson, she thought. Then she saw the pattern—how it was all connected.

"Wilson believes there is a terrorist threat," she said, while clarifying her thoughts. "He's convinced of it. Because that's what London has told him. He's lost track. Don't you think?" She laughed. She hadn't seen it like that previously, but now it was obvious. "London is using Wilson. They've fed him the same lies that he's feeding us. Right?"

Mikael didn't answer. He stared straight out of the dark windows, visibly struggling with his own thoughts.

"I don't think Wilson has a clue about MI6's true intentions," she continued. "London just wants to stop the leak. It was the leak that Green was worried about when I met him. As I said, he mentioned nothing at all about a terrorist threat. It's still the leak and the report worrying them. The focus on counterterrorism is just a way of misleading us, of getting to Dymek and everyone who has come into contact with the EIS report. If you're going to lie then you have to do so truthfully—so they sent Wilson: the terrorist hunter. No one questions his motives. And to make Wilson seem plausible, they lied to him too." The cynicism of it all was so simple, so brilliant, that she couldn't stop herself from feeling strangely elated. London had fooled them all, even its own. "Wilson believes there is a terrorist threat."

Mikael met her gaze: he understood.

After the meeting had ended, Bente shut herself in her office. It was night; outside the window, the lights of Brussels city center glittered. She turned on the desk lamp and sat down to briefly gather her thoughts. She needed to think. Roland Hamrén trusted the British completely—he wouldn't see any disinformation. There was also no safe way to convey what she had just arrived at without the British finding out. She put her hand on the phone and, after a slight hesitation, dialed the number.

It took a moment for the ring to start. It was that tiny second of silence, that small latency in the connection that, back in the day, before digital connections, might have meant someone was listening to your telephone line. Perhaps they had already been exposed, she thought with a grim smile. Perhaps the British had managed to put clamps on the phone lines, connect to their servers. So let them hear this. She waited while it rang.

Hamrén answered as if he knew she was going to call.

"She's in Brussels," Bente said.

"We know."

"Roland."

"Yes?"

She stopped herself. She wanted to tell it as it was, but knew that would be madness. She would destroy the small, almost microscopic chances they still had of influencing the situation. If she told Hamrén what they had discovered, he would, firstly, not believe her, and secondly, the British would find out and launch a full counterattack. She would probably have to close SSI, and Swedish intelligence would be carved up with a cleaver.

"Bente? Hello?"

"Sorry, I was distracted. Do the Brits have anything more on Dymek?"

"They're bugging her hotel. She's on the move."

"What do the Brits say?"

"She's carrying out reconnaissance."

"Okay. Before an attack?"

"Yes. She's calling her contacts. Presumably, the final preparations." A lie that came so easily out of the mouth of he who thought it was true. Hamrén was completely convinced by everything the British had said.

"Good that you've gotten things under control," she said.

"We've gotten things under control," he said tersely.

"But do you have sufficient cause?" She couldn't help but say it. "I mean, for a prosecution?"

Hamrén was immediately pointed, defensive. "That's not for me to decide, Bente. I have a terrorist threat against the government and against an EU summit meeting, and we're acting based on that. Quite honestly, I don't give a shit whether there are grounds for a prosecution right now. We can work that out later, right?"

"Of course," she said guardedly. She hated it when people were vulgar. "When do you go in?"

"Tomorrow."

"Against Badawi?"

"Against Badawi, and against Dymek. The British will take care of Dymek. Bente"—he stopped himself—"I can't talk now. We need to keep going. Call me tomorrow, at nine."

Hamrén hung up.

She got out the annex. She understood what it was all about now. An operation against Jamal Badawi would take place tomorrow, whether she wanted it to or not. An operation against Carina Dymek was going to happen, and she couldn't stop it. A network of actions had been set in motion and—once it had started, the decision had been made—it couldn't be stopped.

36

Brussels, Friday, October 7

It wasn't hard to work out when Jean Bernier ought to be at home. The life of a normal civil servant at the EU Commission followed a regular pattern. He got to work at nine in the morning and worked until seven, or perhaps sometimes eight in the evening. Jean Bernier was married, Carina remembered, so he probably rarely ate out—possibly he stopped for a quick beer with colleagues before the journey home to Waterloo and dinner with his wife. Since it was Friday, he might have been invited out. But he might just as well be on a business trip or on vacation. There were many reasons why Jean Bernier might not be at home, but she had to try.

She leaned back in the dark back seat of the taxi and tried to think through what she would say to Jean Bernier, because, on closer reflection, she only had a vague hope that he would understand the situation and help her. She hadn't thought any further than that, not in any detail. Should she ask him to contact the Ministry? Write an e-mail and explain what had happened? And then . . . What would happen then? Should she ask him to come to Stockholm to testify? To whom? She had assumed it would all work itself out as long as they met again. Perhaps it would; perhaps things would solve themselves when she met him. He would probably have some idea of how to solve the situation. She took a deep breath and watched the evening rush-hour traffic racing by.

After traveling south for twenty-five minutes on the N5 toward Charleroi, the taxi left the freeway and turned into Waterloo.

They rolled through a leafy neighborhood filled with villas. Rows of large houses were visible, discreetly hidden behind shrubberies and whitewashed walls. This was where the Brussels elite lived, at a comfortable distance from the city. Waterloo was known as a calm and child-friendly area with large green spaces, good schools, reliable neighbors and high security. She knew that several of the bosses from the Swedish representation in Brussels lived here.

The taxi stopped at the bottom of the drive of a house that looked like a large Tyrolean villa. This was Avenue Wellington 15, said the taxi driver. She was so nervous that she fumbled as she tried to open the door to get out. Calm down, she said to herself. He'll recognize you; he'll understand. When the taxi had disappeared from sight, she was the only person on the street. Around her, the villas brooded.

She had hoped that at least someone would be home, but she immediately realized that was a mistake. The lights inside the house were off, the windows dark. Standing at the foot of the wide stone path that led between two large fir trees to the front door, she felt uncertain about what she should do. Perhaps they were at a dinner, or—worse—away.

She went up the path to the front door and listened, before crouching and pressing her face against the dark glass bricks in the wall beside the door. A dark hall and possibly a room further inside the house were just about discernible.

She rang the bell, waited, and then rang again, but there was no movement on the other side of the warped glass; no lights came on.

Between the house and the drive there was a gravel path that ran around the side in the shelter of an enormous bougainvillea bush. She went around the corner and discovered a surprisingly large garden that spread out before her in the evening darkness like a silver-gray rectangle. The lawn was surrounded by tall hedges and some large fir trees, which effectively prevented anyone from overlooking the terrace that ran along the length of the back of the house, neatly furnished with garden furniture and a barbecue. She was right outside Jean Bernier's house and yet she had gotten nowhere. It annoyed her. She couldn't just leave, not yet.

There were sliding doors into the house from the terrace and she pressed her face against the glass, screening off light with her hands. She could just about see a darkened living room on the other side.

The sliding door was unlocked. Someone had apparently just pulled it shut and forgotten to turn the small key that was still in the lock. She gripped the frame of the door and opened it a meter or so. It emitted a low squeak and slid open, offering a dark gap, sufficiently wide for her to step through. She poked her head in.

"Hello?"

No answer. The silence immediately enveloped the alien sound.

She had come here to get answers; she wasn't going to leave until she had them. She wiped her feet and took a step in, held her breath, and listened. She carefully entered the living room, rounded a flowery sofa suite and peeked into a narrow hall. There was the front door at the other end. There were two doors and stairs to the floor above. She looked up the stairs.

"Hello?" she shouted again, a little louder. The silence struck against her. No, definitely no one at home.

She ought to leave now; she had no right to be here. She went back to the living room and was about to step out through the terrace door when she spotted another door at the far end of the room and stopped. Perhaps it was stupid, but she couldn't help herself. She moved quickly to the door and discovered what appeared to be a study behind it. She looked along the shelves filled with books and files. Abstract paintings hung on the dark walls. By the window, with a garden view, was a large, beautiful desk. It was more or less cleared, apart from a few tidily stacked pieces of paper. On a whim, she turned on the desk lamp and caught sight of the framed photograph next to it. The picture was of a dark-haired woman standing on a lawn. There was a lake in the background. She was middle-aged and suntanned, laughing at the camera. Her hair had a careless elegance, held back by a white hairband. Next to her, with an arm around her waist, was Jean Bernier.

Next to the lamp was a Rolodex of business cards. She flipped through a few. There were hundreds of cards from EU civil servants, ambassadors, ministers—even a few names that she recognized. Many of the cards were from people at a high level: DIRECTEUR . . . PRESIDENT OF . . . H. E. AMBASSADOR . . . Many bore the logo of the EU Commission, other flags, state emblems. The usual assortment of contacts for someone who moved through the upper echelons of Brussels.

On top of the pile of papers was a small book with tabs in worn, green leather: an address book. She glanced quickly through the pages filled with scribbled handwriting and put it in her inside pocket.

The muffled sound of a car engine outside the house startled her. She turned off the light and moved back into the dark living room. She listened. Now she could hear the sound of a car door being shut and, shortly afterward, a faint, rasping sound at the front door. A key was put into the lock.

She squeezed out of the terrace door and rushed across the yard. Panic took over. She ran across the grass, threw herself over the hedge, and found herself on a small side street off Avenue Wellington, before veering off and carrying on until she reached a larger street, where she forced herself to walk while she caught her breath.

She could go back and ring the doorbell; it occurred to her that it could have been Jean Bernier returning home. But she didn't know if she could keep her composure; she needed to calm down. This hadn't gone exactly the way she had expected—it was best she acknowledged that. Better to try again the next day, when she was a little more composed.

In a small park with a fenced tennis court, she sat down on a bench and brushed her hair, straightened her clothes, and breathed out. She had a vague sense of which way the city was. She had been here on one occasion a long time ago, at some reception at the home of the Polish ambassador, but she didn't remember what the area looked like and she spent a while wandering around the winding streets before reaching a small, picturesque square on which there lay a hotel and a large supermarket, and finally she found the suburban railway station.

When she got back, her hotel room had been cleaned; the bed was perfectly made. She sank down into the soft mattress and lay completely still for a while. But the anxiety wouldn't let go. She sat up and saw herself in the mirror above the desk. She looked pale and tense. She leaned toward the minibar and took out one of the small bottles of whiskey and drank it. She showered and then watched TV, trying to switch off all her thoughts so she could drift into an empty present.

37

Brussels, Saturday, October 8

A narrow beam of daylight cut between the curtains. Carina remained lying down while a dream slowly dispersed. Then she remembered what had happened yesterday and gave an involuntary shudder. She cast off the duvet, got up, and drew apart the thick curtains in an attempt to shake the sticky sensation of anxiety that made her entire body ache. She shouldn't have done it—it was burglary. But Jean Bernier could only blame himself; it was his fault; if he hadn't given her the report then she wouldn't even be here.

The anger reinvigorated her. It felt good to be angry; it gave clarity to her thoughts. She called reception and ordered an English breakfast, and had just finished showering and dressing when there was a knock at the door. A man wearing the grayish beige hotel uniform wished her good morning and rolled a cart into the room, bearing a plate of scrambled eggs, fried tomatoes, and small sausages. She ate voraciously while she watched the TV news. The headlines were about Greece and the latest Euro crisis, the upcoming elections in Tunisia, and an Indonesian storm.

After breakfast, she pulled out the address book. She fingered the worn tabs and thumbed through it with a feeling of shame. She was not proud of having stolen something from a stranger's home, especially something as private as an address book, but it couldn't be helped now.

The book was full of names and numbers, written in angular handwriting. Some had then been struck out, names had gotten new addresses and numbers, and some pages were so closely written that the lines became minimal scrawls that were impossible to deci-pher; large parts of the book were completely filled. She turned to the letter *E*. Next to lines of unfamiliar names, she found certain series of numbers that she recognized—internal numbers from the EU Commission. Perhaps she could try calling some of them later. Throughout the book, she noticed, all the names were recorded by surname, apart from two. Those two names had only first names, and were listed under their corresponding letter: Suzanna and Syl-vie. Probably people that Jean Bernier knew well.

The number that belonged to Suzanna had a French prefix—a Paris number, if Carina had guessed correctly. A woman answered breathlessly, lively: "*Oui?*"

"Madame Bernier?"

The woman laughed and at once sounded as if she was on her guard. "It's a long time since anyone called me that. Who's calling?"

Carina said she was a colleague of Monsieur Bernier. "I need to speak to him on an urgent matter, but I haven't managed to get hold of him."

"Oh," she said with uninterest. "Why are you calling here, then?"

Carina cleared her throat; she could hear the barbed undertone in the voice at the other end. Did she possibly know how Jean Ber-nier could be reached? she began, but the woman interrupted her.

"Is this about André again?"

"No, I'm—"

"Why are you calling here?" said the woman, tersely. The voice had a sharp edge to it. Carina tried to say that she was looking for Jean Bernier in connection with a work-related matter, but the woman wasn't listening.

"I'm not going to play this game with Jean any longer. We've sorted it out, and if he wants to see his son—or whatever this is about—then he can call himself. Are you his lawyer, or what?" She did not pause, carrying on before Carina could answer. "You can tell him from me that there's nothing else to discuss, and I don't want you to call here again."

The line went dead.

Carina lay on the bed and groaned loudly; this was so embarrassing. She waited a few minutes, went into the bathroom, and drank some cold water to build her courage.

The second number, which belonged to Sylvie, was a Brussels number. An address was noted in minimalist handwriting. She fingered her cell and finally dialed the number and waited. It rang four times, and she was beginning to think there was no one home when a woman answered: "*Halo*?"

Carina introduced herself, said she was looking for Sylvie.

"That's me."

She hurried to say that she needed to speak to Jean Bernier, but that he was apparently absent from work, and she had been looking for him for several days. "It's important."

"Jean?" Silence fell at the other end of the line. For a moment she thought the line had been cut off, but then she heard a long, deep sigh at the other end. The silence grew. "I'm sorry, but—"

"I really need to speak to him," she interrupted. "I met him a couple of weeks ago and he gave me some material that"—she didn't know what to say; she didn't actually know who she was speaking to—"which I need to discuss with him."

"I'm afraid that won't be possible. I'm sorry." An abrupt silence fell again. Carina listened to the receiver and heard a weak, whispering sound. Was she crying? Then the line went dead. The woman had hung up.

This Sylvie had reacted completely differently; she knew something. She knew Jean Bernier, but who was she? Maybe a lover, or a relative. There was a Brussels address listed in the book: Avenue Saint-Augustin 8, Forest. Carina put on her shoes, grabbed her coat and hurried out of the hotel.

A crisp, elegant ringing sounded from what seemed like deep within the house when she pressed the doorbell. Avenue Saint-Augustin was a peaceful street and number eight was in a lovely red-brick residential building facing the monumental Saint-Augustin church. Heavy curtains prevented any glimpses through the house's crisscrossed windows. There was a brass plaque by the front door that said REIGNAULT.

Just half an hour earlier, someone named Sylvie had answered the phone at this address, so someone ought to be at home—if not her then perhaps someone else, if she didn't live alone. Carina rang the bell again and waited for a long time; when nothing happened, she had an almost unstoppable desire to start banging on the door. It wouldn't be that easy to shake her off; she had decided to talk to Jean Bernier and no one was going to stop her now. The doorbell's trill rang throughout the inside of the house; if no one opened this time, she would find a café nearby and wait there, she decided, and she would come back in a few hours' time.

A narrow face appeared in a gap between the curtains in an upstairs window; she only just saw the fluttering movement and a face, hovering momentarily behind the window, before it vanished.

Shortly after that, she heard steps and then the rattling of a bolt. A thin, elegant, middle-aged woman with red hair appeared in the doorway.

"*Bonjour?*" said the woman, making it sound like a question. She looked at Carina expectantly.

"Madame Reignault?"

"Yes?"

"Hello. It was me who called earlier," she said quickly. "I really do need to speak to Jean Bernier. Perhaps you can—"

"And who are you?" exclaimed the woman.

"I'm a . . . colleague. From Stockholm. It is of the utmost importance that I meet Monsieur Bernier. As I said on the phone, he contacted me at the end of September and gave me a document that has led to some problems."

The woman made no move to let her in. Indeed, it was quite the opposite; she remained standing in the doorway, looking at Carina, puzzled.

"So you met him. When, more precisely?"

"The 22nd of September, here in Brussels."

Madame Reignault nodded and seemed to decide something. "Wait here." She pushed the door shut and disappeared.

Carina could hear voices from inside the apartment. Carefully, she pushed open the front door a few centimeters and saw a large, light apartment and a hall with a checkered floor and an attractive wooden staircase leading to an upper floor. The woman was talking to someone in a low voice. Then there were steps again and the woman reappeared.

"Come in."

She was let into the hall. It was a lovely apartment, spread across three floors in typical Belgian fashion, with steep stairs and long, narrow rooms. The woman led her up the stairs to a light, airy room with a large, panoramic window to the rear of the building, and told Carina to take a seat. She sat down in the corner of the large, soft sofa in front of the window, still wearing her coat. Being in this quiet, unfamiliar home put her ill at ease. She said nothing and tried not to blink as she met the woman's gaze.

"So you know my brother?"

Her brother? "I . . ." Nerves tangled her French; the words wouldn't come out the way she wanted them to. "No, not really. We met in Brussels. He contacted me," she managed to splutter.

"Oh."

Carina was grateful when the oppressive silence was broken as the door to an adjoining room opened and another woman entered, also in her fifties. Carina vaguely recognized her—from the photograph in the Berniers' home, it struck her. She looked down at the floor. Madame Bernier greeted her cautiously and turned questioningly to the other woman, Sylvie, who shrugged her shoulders.

"She's one of Jean's colleagues, apparently. She met him in September."

"That's right, Madame," Carina added quickly. "I met him a couple of weeks ago, and . . ." She hesitated, uncertain about how to continue, before saying, clumsily, "It caused problems."

Madame Bernier nodded absentmindedly and slowly sat down on the sofa opposite Carina and lit a cigarette with small, smooth movements. She looked haggard.

"So you don't know what's happened," she said in a low voice, a statement of regret. "My husband," she blew smoke toward the ceiling, "passed away recently."

Dead?

Carina tried to form a sentence, but the words wouldn't come. Her French came to a sudden end. Jean Bernier was dead? Her mouth was dry; she sat there quietly trying to swallow.

"I'm sorry," she finally squeezed out, and felt everything within her sinking.

Madame Bernier nodded curtly, dragged on the cigarette again, and looked out the large window for a long time while she and Sylvie sat silently. Then she turned back to Carina. Her eyes were moist. With a slightly over-cheerful tone of voice she said, "So you said you met my husband?"

"Yes, in September—the 22nd. He contacted me in connection with a meeting and gave me a report. It was sensitive material that—well—it caused problems," she added, before falling silent again.

"The 22nd of September." Madame Bernier looked at her. "You're sure about that?"

"Yes."

"How did he seem?"

"How do you mean?"

"Well, when you met?"

"He was . . ." Carina tried to find the right words in French. She wasn't used to this kind of situation; she usually took part in negotiations and used diplomatic French, negotiation French—she didn't normally have to describe a dead civil servant to his widow. "He seemed stressed. He really wanted to talk to me about a report he didn't like."

"I understand," said Madame Bernier, who seemed lost in her own thoughts.

Carina got up. "I'm sorry for your loss. I'm very sorry, I probably ought to—"

"No, no—sit." Madame Bernier made a vague gesture.

Carina sat down again, on the edge of the sofa.

"So you talked?"

"Yes, we went to a restaurant near the EU Commission. We were there for about half an hour, then he left."

"And you don't know where he went?"

"No."

"Jean disappeared that day," Sylvie added. "They found him a few days later at Marie and Jean's place in the country. It's close to Assenede. He didn't mention Assenede? That he was going to meet someone there?"

"Not that I remember."

Madame Bernier stubbed out her cigarette with a rapid movement and promptly lit another. "You're sure that he didn't mention Assenede to you?" she said and looked straight at Carina.

Yes, she was sure. She couldn't remember him mentioning it. She shook her head and carefully tried to stand up.

"He didn't tell Marie that he was going there. We think he met someone there," said Sylvie seriously, and she turned quickly to Marie and put a hand on her knee, as if to calm her. Madame Bernier had turned away. "We don't know. These are just guesses."

Madame Bernier nodded silently.

"They found him out by the house four days later. The police said it was insulin shock. They say he must have died on the 22nd or 23rd of September."

"Jean was careful with his medication," Madame Bernier hissed angrily. Her mascara had streaked a little. "Jean would never have made a mistake like that. Do you know how much insulin you have to take to cause a shock?" She didn't wait for a reply, because it was clear she didn't need one. She merely shook her head and reached for the cigarette packet. "The police say that he killed himself, but that's just wrong," she continued. "I know my husband." She fumbled with the lighter and blew out smoke in a hard exhalation.

Carina nodded without knowing why. She felt numb. There was no longer a Jean Bernier to solve the situation for her. That possibility had never existed, because Jean Bernier had died, perhaps just hours after they had met.

"Do you think that someone killed him?"

"I spoke to the neighbor's wife out there. She's certain that she saw people in the garden. But the police didn't care about that," said Madame Bernier coolly, with a piercing gaze toward her.

"I understand," Carina said quietly and stood up again. Madame Bernier was sitting with her back turned, smoking, and seemed to have lost all interest in Carina. It was probably time to leave.

"I hope it works out for you," said Sylvie, without moving an inch.

"I'm sure it will," she replied.

She went down the stairs and, after the front door had closed behind her, she hurried as fast as she could to get away from that gloomy, suffocating apartment and the two women wrapped up in their grief. She reached a large crossroads and continued along a boulevard, gradually calming down and walking slower. She was alone in Brussels; there was no reason for her to stay here. She brushed a hand across her face and tried to stand up in the face of the soft hopelessness that had found its way into her thoughts. Jean Bernier was dead. And someone had killed him? Every step she put between herself and that crypt of an apartment made it seem more unlikely. He had probably committed suicide. He was stressed, had crossed the line. She swore aloud. What was *she* meant to do now? No one would ever believe her; no one would listen to her. Without a plan, she wandered from block to block, surrounded by a sunny Brussels, full of people having lunch and hectic traffic, while dismal thoughts whirled within her.

"Madame!"

Carina was on the way through the lobby, past a large group of auditors who seemed to have gathered to go to lunch together. They filled the entrance with their lively voices, so at first she didn't hear the concierge calling after her.

"Madame!" The concierge passed an envelope to her with a smile. "A message for you."

She thanked her and stayed where she was, holding the envelope. Inside was a folded note; on the front it said, in rapid blue ballpoint handwriting, *Ms. Carina Dymek*. She unfolded it. The message was in English; three lines written on the hotel's notepaper:

> *Ms. Dymek,*
> *We need to meet. Be at Gare du Midi, south entrance. Today, Saturday,*
> *17:00.*
> *A friend of Jean Bernier.*

She scrunched up the note. Goosebumps appeared on her arms. It was almost too good to be true. A friend of Jean Bernier? It could be anyone, but it was probably a colleague. Perhaps her calls to the Commission had borne fruit, in spite of everything. It had to be someone who was careful and didn't want to be seen with her openly; Gare du Midi was Brussels' large southern train station, a place where it was easy to disappear into the crowd. The person who had written the message clearly knew where she was staying in Brussels—that was strange. She couldn't remember having mentioned that to anyone; not even Jamal knew she was there.

Who had left it? No, the concierge, a young woman who was fully occupied checking in two new guests, shook her head. She didn't know who had left the note; it had been there when she had arrived.

Carina went up to her room, got out a tourist map, and spread it out on the bed. She found the Midi station. Her hands fluttered as she bent over her suitcase; a faint nausea rippled through her stomach; she was nervous and found it difficult to choose what to wear. She didn't want to be too sloppily dressed if she was going to meet someone from the EU Commission. Eventually, she changed into a pair of new jeans, a T-shirt, and a black turtleneck, then she checked that she had her cell, wallet, and the map.

Jean Bernier was dead, so the question was, what could a friend of his do? But she had no other option. Now she would at least find out more about what had actually happened—the true story.

Dazzlingly sharp autumn sunshine met her as she came out into the street and began to walk to Midi. She had caught the subway from

De Brouckère station to Gare de l'Ouest and changed on to a south-bound train, alighting at Clemenceau, where she had reemerged into the sunshine. She had very little cash, and withdrew two hundred euros from an ATM. She was ravenous and stopped at a café to buy two *croque-monsieurs* and a coffee, which she consumed quickly, standing by one of the small bar tables, before continuing. The beautiful weather had tempted people into the streets; people were in the outdoor seating areas of restaurants and the streets in Ixelles were full of life. She passed a small market where the typical blend of Ixelles residents and tourists wandered between the stands of organic bath products and batik-dyed sweaters, but she couldn't stop to look, restlessness drew her onward.

A few hundred meters from the station, she found an Internet café. It was shadowy and deserted. She was assigned a computer and sat down for a while to read her e-mails. Nothing from Jamal or Greger, just one from British Airways that she almost deleted.

Egypt: she had completely forgotten that she and Jamal had booked tickets. She smiled to herself; it was unreal to think that in a few weeks they would be on vacation together, in the sun, just the two of them. She still had Jamal. That thought made her calm. She glanced through her friends' and colleagues' updates on Facebook and went to Jamal's profile. But he posted rarely; the page hadn't been updated for over a month. She would call him later in the evening, she decided.

Out in the autumnal sun, she followed the street that led into the hustle and bustle of Rue Bara. The Midi Tower's glittering mirrors rose above the rooftops. Rattling streetcars traveled past her as she stood on a street corner and tried to work out at which end of the station the south entrance was located. She was close to Place Victor Hortaplein and, if she wasn't mistaken, the meeting place ought to be on the other side of the station. In which case, she had to hurry. She jogged past the bus stops around the Midi Tower and scattered a cloud of dirty gray pigeons, which took off as she bounded across the deserted square outside the station as the clock struck five.

Thousands of people passed through Gare du Midi in Brussels every hour; it was one of the three large railway hubs of the city. From here, people were distributed to the whole of the Brussels region and throughout Europe. A group of newly arrived travelers blocked the entire entrance with their suitcases. She hurried up to a taxi driver. Yes, this was the north entrance. "Go through the concourse," he said in a stressed tone and waved his arm toward the grubby, glass façade of the station building. "The exit for Fonsnylaan."

Inside the station building, it took a moment for her eyes to adjust to the pallid light. She slowed down, took in her surroundings. The entire train station was a rundown, clattering passageway. A swarm of people were moving beneath the low ceiling. An arrow pointed straight ahead for Avenue Fonsny.

It was two minutes past five, according to a clock suspended from the ceiling. She was late, but made an effort not to walk too fast.

When she was close to the Fonsnylaan exit, she caught sight of an older, graying man who appeared to be waiting for someone. He was wearing a thin coat over a gray suit; a typical civil servant, unperturbed by the crush of people around him, splaying across the concourse. It was clear he was waiting for someone; he looked at his watch with a small grimace and began to pace to and fro, swinging his laptop bag.

She raised her hand in greeting and began to make her way toward the man, but he didn't see her—a group of young people with enormous rucksacks obscured her. She was only a few paces away from him when he fished his cell phone out of a pocket and, with a smile, looked at the screen before disappearing through the exit, swallowed by the city. Clearly she wasn't meeting him, she noted with disappointment. She stood in the throng of people. It was five past. She had arrived a little late, but only by a few minutes; surely that didn't mean the meeting was off? There was a constant stream of people flowing toward her like black shadows in the glare, forcing their way past her. She moved to the side and followed the faces passing by. Whom she was waiting for she did not know, but, among all these people, the person she did want to meet would surely appear at any moment.

Out of the corner of her eye, she spotted a man with a shaved head moving toward her on the concourse. He was young and wearing a hoodie and a padded jacket—not the appearance she had expected of the person she was meeting. But she was not mistaken: the man was on his way toward her, forcing his way through a group of travelers. But something in the way he was moving wasn't right. He was walking too quickly, too purposefully.

About ten meters to the right, she spotted yet another man approaching in the same rapid, purposeful manner. Their grimaces were directed at *her*, among all the crowds of people. She swallowed; her mouth was dry. Something was very wrong. Or was she imagining it? For a second, they vanished from sight. The loud clatter of the concourse and the station loudspeaker pounded against her; her pulse beat against her head. She gazed through the crowds and quickly spotted another, then two, then four men—all moving straight toward her. She backed into a souvenir shop window. Her insides became a sucking, corrosive emptiness. She should never have come here. It was a mistake. Obviously no friend of Jean Bernier would have been able to find her at her hotel.

She stumbled on her feet and regained her balance. The rubber soles of her shoes gripped the surface. Her legs didn't obey her at first. Her feet were heavy like lead; each step sucked her down to the flat, hard surface and it felt like she was running in slow motion. All she could hear in her head was that she had to run, faster, had to get out—off the concourse. For a second, she saw the man in the hoodie, and the other one in the leather jacket, close beside her in the crowd. She collided with an elderly man, who spun one hundred and eighty degrees and fell headlong against a billboard, and then, for some reason, the crippling sensation disappeared—her legs were carrying her again. Astonished, angry faces appeared right in front of her, but she barely noticed them; the entire concourse had narrowed to a long, black tunnel. Everywhere, strangers were in the way—sluggish bodies that she bumped into. Without knowing where she was going, she ducked to the side, into a passageway.

She had a small head start of twenty or thirty meters when she reached some stairs, slipped, fumbled for the handrail, and heaved herself up through the throng that was pouring down the steps. She just managed to glimpse a pink school bag and a girl falling over. Someone shouted at her.

She reached a platform where a commuter train was standing, ready to depart. The door-closing warning signal had already begun as she threw herself up the final steps and rushed toward the nearest car, tackling the half-closed doors and pressing her body between them. She fell into the car. One foot was still sticking out; she pulled it in and fell, panting against the wall by the door. Go, for fuck's sake! And, as if she were able to control the train by the power of thought alone, it began its endless and soft acceleration out of the station.

She got up and looked around the car. Three teenage girls, who had been sitting with their heads close together over a cell phone, stared silently at her. Faces looked at her anxiously, with caution. The commuters around her were probably wondering why a woman had come crashing in like that, and trying to work out whether she was drunk, dangerous, or psychologically disturbed, before slowly losing interest.

They were already on the way into the tunnel. None of her pursuers seemed to be in the car. Who were those bastards? She leaned against her knees and struggled to control her breathing. Had the Belgian police tricked her into going to Gare du Midi in order to arrest her? That was completely sick. Why would the police set a trap for her? She didn't know much about police work, but it wasn't difficult to work out that it was a pretty major operation to track her down, leave a message at her hotel, and then lure her to a train station to arrest her. It didn't make sense. Even if the Security Service was interested in her because of that damn report, it was still completely crazy.

At the next station, she stood by the door, ready to rush out, and popped her head out as soon as the doors opened. But no one moved between the cars; no one seemed to be looking for her on the platform.

She went another two stops, got off at Noordstation and stuck close to a group of girls in headscarves as she left the platform. She descended into a long underground passageway with small shops and eateries to the sides. No one in the stream of people seemed to care about her one bit.

She had been tricked. It was all just a trap; there was no friend of Jean Bernier. She had to think clearly. The hotel, it struck her—she couldn't go back; they knew she was staying there and would probably be waiting for her. But her passport, her bag, all her things were still in the room. For a second, a sob quivered in her throat. She couldn't stay in Brussels, either; the people looking for her would find her again. Thoughts chattered inside her head.

She found herself on a narrow street just outside Noordstation. A long row of worn buildings faced the railway tracks. Pink neon, red signs, and flickers of electric blue glowed along the street in the afternoon gloom. Large shop windows housed restless, moving silhouettes: women for sale. She had come to the red-light district, the north of the city. It was deserted, but in a few hours, when the shiny banking houses turned off their lights, the sordid trade would begin in earnest.

She hurried over the pedestrian crossing and continued at random along a rundown street. She didn't really know what to do, whether to try and find a hotel or boarding house nearby, try to hide and wait, or take a chance and go straight back to the hotel. Wandering around the city all night was not a possibility. Maybe it was best to try and leave the city. But how would she get back to Stockholm without her passport? She was probably wanted and would be caught at the first border control she reached. Maybe she could cross the border by night, hitch-hike with a truck. For a second, that seemed like a completely reasonable idea. She had only seen it in films but had never considered that she might do it in reality. It was dangerous, but a possibility.

At first, she couldn't tell where the sound was coming from: a sharp engine noise that made her turn her head. The blank surfaces of the skyscrapers rose into the afternoon sky and had become pillars of velvety, shimmering light. The brick station-building was in shadow; it was only possible to discern people as small, dark figures. Then she caught sight of them: two figures on motorbikes by the station. Shiny helmets.

For a brief moment, she wanted to believe she was wrong. But then the motorbikes turned, crossed the crossing, and accelerated toward her with a sharp roar.

She ran like a four-hundred-meter sprinter on the home stretch, down a small and deserted side street, and had just reached a crossroads when the roar of the motorbikes came right up beside her. In a desperate attempt to escape, she threw herself right into the road and only just managed to jump out of the path of a van, before taking aim at a fence, throwing herself against the splintery wood, pulling herself up, and tumbling over the edge. She fell hard onto a pile of cement bags. The pain radiated up through her shoulder.

A demolition site: piles of mortar and brick, and a backhoe enthroned in the middle of the plot like a sleeping, prehistoric beast. At the other end of the pitted site was a decimated residential building—a ruin. On each floor there were gaping holes where rooms that had been torn apart stared into the abyss. Fear made her teeth chatter. Reality was flickering; she was struggling to take in and comprehend what she could see around her. It was definitely not the police chasing her; it couldn't be—the police didn't try to run people over with motorbikes.

There was a scrape on the other side of the fence. One of them seemed to be climbing over. She stumbled across the plot and ran along a tumbledown wall with reinforcing iron sprawling above her in the air. At the other end of the site there was a new fence. She had just managed to climb over the palisade when she heard panting on the other side. She didn't know where it was coming from, but she felt how the fear receded when she saw the pursuer's face: an ugly, oblong face, which appeared at the top of the fence. A violent rage rushed through her. Before she had time to think, she had picked up a large, sharp rock that filled the palm of her hand and had thrown herself up at the fence with a roar, brandishing the stone toward the face of the pursuer, striking him in a sweeping, crunching movement, right on the nose. He screamed and tumbled backward.

In the dirty, enclosed backyard she had ended up in, there was a door standing ajar. She stepped into a kitchenette and then into a narrow corridor. Adrenaline made her feel nauseous, and she leaned against the wall for a second, gasping. At the end of the corridor she could discern a woman's curvaceous silhouette, surrounded by a glowing aura of red light, and then the woman's alarmed face.

"*Putain!*" she screamed. "What the fuck are you doing here?"

"*Pardon, pardon,*" Carina mumbled. Sorry, sorry. That was all she could say as she forced her way past the woman and discovered she was in a sex shop. It was hard to get her bearings in the purple-red light and she knocked over a stand filled with pornographic magazines and bumped into a customer who was reading. Then she found the way out and threw herself into the street, crossed over, and began to run as fast as she could up a new side street.

All around her, there were people moving. She no longer had any idea where she was, only that it was somewhere in the northern part of Brussels city center. If she was right, she ought to head south to reach a subway station. Without dropping pace, she ran several blocks through a rundown residential district. The crowds on the pavement began to increase. She had reached a lively area with small, ordinary shops, cafés, and takeout places. The streets here were clogged with traffic; the throng of people forced her to slow down.

On the corner of two streets, in a small building, was a grocery store with garishly illuminated sign on its façade: ALIMENTATION GÉNÉRALE. She forced her way through the piles of fruit and vegetables to the back, where she could hide among the shelves. The shop was not large. If they thought to come in and look, they would find her right away, but she didn't have the strength to run anymore.

She withdrew into the rear of the shop and stood there, panting, her hands on her knees, next to a shelf filled with canned food. An elderly Arab couple looked at her suspiciously and quickly pushed each other to the other half of the shop.

They were still out there; through the murmur and the French folk music blaring inside the shop, she could now hear the clatter of the motorbikes in the distance. They were presumably circling the area and searching. Then she heard another sound; she didn't understand what it was until she felt her cell in her pocket. It was ringing.

38

Brussels, Saturday, October 8

Bente grabbed a headset. "Call her," she ordered abruptly. "Now. Give me her position."

One of the technicians shouted across the room: Dymek was one hundred meters east of Rue Royale.

The cell team had been at Midi station, just ten or so meters behind Dymek, but had still been taken by surprise when a group of six people had thrown themselves forward and tried to apprehend Dymek. It had gone so fast, they hadn't been able to follow, but had had to wait and watch them disappear toward one of the platforms. Wilson's people specialized in this kind of hunt: manhunts. One of the pursuers had been identified as the British elite soldier from Dymek's hotel. Minutes had passed during which they had no idea what was going on. Then: Noordstation; Dymek on foot, alive, in flight. The Section's other cell team was en route, but would arrive too late. Bente knew the next few minutes were critical. It was hard to melt away into the streets around Noordstation. The pursuers would find Dymek, if they didn't already have her in their sights, and, if that was the case, she only had minutes left to live—if the Section couldn't bring her in first, make her disappear off the street.

Mikael ordered silence. The command room went dead quiet. Gazes turned to Bente. The phone rang clearly through the speakers, then another ring.

"Hello?" Noise, rustling. Dymek panting.

"Carina. My name is Bente Jensen. I can help you."

"Who?" she said through the gasps. "Who are you?"

"Bente Jensen. You're in danger. Listen to me."

"Who the hell are you?" screamed Dymek.

"Listen to me." She raised her voice, turned it into a steel blade. She gripped the microphone between her fingers. "Your only chance to get away is to listen to me."

The speakers were filled with Dymek's gasping. "Okay," she panted.

"Good. Two hundred meters straight ahead is Rue Royale. A tram, the number ninety-four, will stop there in two minutes; it's coming down Rue Royale now. Take it. You have to catch it. Sit at the very back. A woman will pick you up. She's blond—her name is Beatrice. Two minutes. Can you do that?"

"I don't know if I'll make it. They have motorbikes."

"Try. Run."

"Okay."

Bente met Mikael's gaze and saw that he was thinking the same thing she was: this could all go very wrong. She looked at the time. Rodriguez's group would soon be there.

A fierce noise penetrated through the speakers. Then the sound of traffic, distant voices, and the wind whistling, and through all of that the quick, rhythmic sound of steps on the pavement. Dymek was running.

Everyone in the Section's command room sat in complete silence, listening to the speakers. A technician pointed at the screen. Dymek ought to be there by now. It was taking time. Perhaps she was having trouble crossing the road; Rue Royale was packed with traffic at this time of day. All they could here was noise, fragments of voices, and the city at large. After waiting for what seemed an eternity, Dymek reemerged.

"I'm here," she shouted. "Where's the tram?"

"It should be there now." Bente looked at the technician, who nodded emphatically. "Number ninety-four."

"No, no. Where is it?" Her voice cracked. Dymek's panicked breathing filled the speakers.

"It's there. The platform closest to you."

Bente made an effort to remain calm. People in stressful situations often lost the ability to read their surroundings. The ability to comprehend was reduced; all one saw was basic structures—buildings, roads, light, dark.

"Number ninety-four."

They heard Dymek's agitated breaths, the sound of the wind, a passing motorbike. She shuddered. That could have been it. Dymek's pursuers were probably very close by. She couldn't stay at the tram stop; she was completely in the open there. Now they heard her moving again.

Dymek returned. "I'm on the tram."

"Good. Very good."

The background noise had indeed changed. The sound of the wind was gone. Now Dymek's voice was quite audible against a background of other voices and the characteristic clattering and squeaking of the tram.

"Okay, I'm sitting here."

"Good. Stay there. Look around. Is there anyone looking at you?"

There was a pause. "No, no one."

"The motorbikes—do you see them? Look out of the window carefully."

Another pause. A pinging sound was audible, followed by a recorded voice announcing the next station: *Botanique.*

"No."

"Good. Stay there. We're sending someone in to bring you to safety." She made a sign at Mikael. "Do nothing before that. Do you understand?"

"Okay," they heard Dymek say.

Dymek was now just following orders. She sounded a little numb. Her voice was muted, as if she was in a room filled with fabric. The tram was probably busy, other people standing close by her. That was good. Bente told Dymek to breathe and just listen to her. She was Bente Jensen, she said. She was from the Swedish Security Service—Säpo. They had spoken once before. That time, Dymek had hung up, but this time she should listen to her and trust her. They would help her out of this situation. She was in danger. But, if she remained calm and did exactly as Bente said, everything would be fine. She said nothing about terrorism, nothing about the summit meeting, nothing that would agitate Dymek. Dymek listened.

Mikael held up a hand with three fingers raised.

"Okay. In three stops' time, one of our people will get off the tram—at Treurenberg. A blond woman, wearing a red leather jacket. You will follow her. Just take it easy and be ready to move. Don't hang up; keep listening to me. It'll all be okay."

Everyone in the command room listened breathlessly. Dymek was quiet. They could hear the muffled sounds of the inside of the tram. Voices and individual words from people who were presumably right next to Dymek were audible, conversations in French blended into a buzz. It was evening; people were on the way home from work. They heard the tram begin to brake before it stopped completely. The doors opened with a hiss and let in the sound of the evening rush-hour traffic. Then there was a long tone as the doors closed, followed by the rising, humming sound of the tram accelerating. Two stops to go.

Dymek's voice came back. She whispered, "There's a man here. He's looking at me."

"Ignore him," said Bente calmly, as if it was nothing out of ordinary. Dymek was jittery; all that mattered now was that they kept her calm until the pickup was complete.

"He's shaven"—She didn't finish the sentence. She sounded breathless.

"Carina," Bente said. "Breathe in and out. Only two more stops to go."

She stared straight at Mikael, who bent down and spoke into his headset before turning to her and nodding: next stop. Beatrice would get on at the next stop.

"He's getting up," Carina said in a suppressed exclamation. "I think he's coming toward me."

"Take it easy, Carina. You're worried and I understand that. But he isn't an enemy. Don't look at him. Breathe and listen to me. Don't hang up. We're almost with you."

Where the hell was the team? She gesticulated at Mikael; he made a silent grimace and spread his arms out. All they could do was wait for the tram to arrive at the next stop.

"It's them." Dymek gasped. "They're coming."

"Carina," she said loudly and clearly, with an emphasis on each word, as if by the power of words alone she might get Dymek to listen. "Wait. Calm down."

Silence.

"Hello?"

They heard the tram braking for the next stop. The sounds changed. Thumps, noise, unclear fizz. Traffic. The sound of wind was coming out of the speakers; the city. She was getting off.

"No, Carina!" Bente shouted at the room in general.

But it was too late. There was no one at the other end.

Carina got off the tram and turned around. The man was there, watching her from inside the tram. Or perhaps he was looking at his cell, she couldn't tell. The tram glided away over the crossroads.

She was at Rogier, the glittering center of the city. In front of her flowed a slow river of evening traffic heading down Rue Rogier. She looked around: no motorbikes. But they could appear again, she was certain. She hurried toward the wide pedestrian crossing and stood, surrounded by traffic for a moment, before spotting a gap between two cars and throwing herself across to the other side, joining the stream of people crossing the main road.

She was in the shopping district just north of the central station. Less than a kilometer away was Grote Markt and the Parc du Bruxelles, and her hotel couldn't be more than fifteen, twenty minutes' walk from here. Perhaps she should go back, get her things, and disappear. But they were probably watching her hotel. How would she get to the airport? she thought as she choked on a sob.

How would she leave the country? A group of guys in suits walked around her; they probably worked in one of the skyscrapers in the financial quarter and were heading for some after-work drinks. She kept close to them and calmed down a little. Perhaps she could ask the hotel to send her luggage to the airport. She could leave quickly using a minor airline; some of them didn't always manage their passenger lists properly. Or she could travel by bus to Holland and then fly from Schiphol. If she was wanted, it might only be in Belgium. Good God, this was completely absurd! Two dressed-up couples got out of a taxi and crossed the pavement so close in front of her that one of women brushed her arm without even noticing her.

The Security Service. She looked around and stopped in front of the large shop window of an American designer label. Where were they? Maybe one of the many people passing her on the pavement was an agent, or one of those standing at the bus stop further away. The people chasing her weren't Belgian police; they were from a different kind of organization. But what the hell was going on, in that case? Were they trying to kill her? It was as if she only now realized what she had gotten caught up in, and the weight of it almost made her sink into the pavement. It was incomprehensible. She began to jog, fear driving her forward; she moved through the crowd on the street and had never before felt so alone.

She had gotten as far as Place de Brouckère when she heard the sharp sound of a motorbike. She stopped and looked across the intersection. At first she saw nothing apart from the gleaming lines of cars at a red light, then a dark figure shot across the crossroads and was followed a second later by another. Two motorbikes turned on to the avenue in amongst a mass of cars and accelerated.

The glass façade of the Finance Tower vanished up toward the cloudy evening sky before coming to life and pulsing in purple, blue, and red neon. Carina pressed herself into the side of the building. For a moment, she thought of trying to cross the street—running across the middle, to the other pavement—but there was too much traffic; she might get stuck in the middle—an easy target. She rushed behind the skyscraper.

An expanse opened up in front of her. The city had withdrawn and left a dead and deserted area the size of a runway. She tripped over the cracked concrete flagstones and continued between scrubby, low bushes and rows of streetlights. Around the open space lay large, dilapidated office buildings. She couldn't stop here; she was far too visible.

Halfway across the open space, she heard the growl of the motorbikes bouncing between the buildings. She ducked into a bush and looked around. The white light from their headlights flickered between the buildings, up at the Finance Tower. They would find her. They would find her and kill her. This insight flew through her in an ice-cold sensation, like plasma through blood. How did they know where she was all the time? They circled on a ramp and then rolled down on to the expanse of asphalt. They stopped, turned off their engines and dismounted.

In the shelter of a low stone wall, Carina ran toward the far end of the area and crept under a bush in the shrubbery.

A sharp ping came from her pocket. The small, everyday sound was like an explosion in the silence; for a moment, she was convinced that her pursuers had also heard it. She swore silently and pulled out her cell. A text message: *Best Western Hotel, Rue Royale 160. Room 513. Go to it. You will be safe there.*

Then it occurred to her—it was so obvious—they were tracking her via her phone. The whole time she had been walking around with it and they had been able to see exactly what she was doing. That was how they had found her; that was how they had followed her. She caught sight of a drain about a meter away and, when the two bikers were out of sight, she stretched toward it and dropped the cell through the grate.

Now she could see them. Three figures had appeared from between the buildings, then more: five—six. They came out of the dark from a side street and spread wordlessly across the open space. She could see them clearly now—see their alert faces, hear the rustle of their windbreakers. Something in their behavior and way of moving told her they were trained for this. She shuddered. They were hunting, moving like a pack across the area to the place where she had just been hiding. A lanky man in a cap appeared.

Further away, to the right, an SUV came to a stop on a side street. She hardly dared to move, but still managed to see a large man step out of the car. The man spoke to several of the others in a low voice; she couldn't hear what he said, but he spoke English. They began looking among the trees, the benches, toward the Finance Tower. They moved calmly and methodically across the space, as if looking for a lost object. Some of them had flashlights and shone them into bushes, before switching them off again. She shook. The bush she had crawled into was dense and thorny; she could feel the small barbs on the branches pricking her back. She was lying on her front, so she wouldn't be able to escape quickly if they found her. She could only wait. For a short, dangerous second, she felt panicked, and a wild impulse to just stand up and scream took hold of her. She bit her lip until she could feel the sweet taste of copper in her mouth.

A man in a cap came walking toward the place where she was lying. The cone of light from his flashlight pierced through the bush. He moved a few steps closer, shone the light at the shrubs and surrounding ground. Adrenaline was coursing through her entire body as she braced herself against the ground and prepared to fling herself up and flee. She knew that if he caught sight of her now it was over. Perhaps she could strike him to one side and escape from the square before they caught up with her . . . But they would catch her.

Please, go. For God's sake, go. Go. Go!

The man lowered his flashlight and shone it straight into the shrubbery, just a few meters from her face. She could see his white sneakers.

There was a rustle—the man swore quietly—a rat.

A low shout was heard from further away. After an unbearably long moment, the man turned around and left.

The group lingered, talking for a long time. The man in the cap pointed. As if on cue, she heard the two motorbikes start up in unison and saw them leave, heading back toward the Place de Brouckère. The large man got back into the car, which turned on to another side street and vanished. Just as suddenly as they had arrived, they were gone, swallowed by the darkness.

She lay there for half an hour, perhaps longer. It was an eternity before she dared to move, but finally she began to straighten up. Her joints were stiff; her hands and arms were ice cold when she crept out of the bush.

She was forced to stop and lean forward; she broke into a cold sweat as she battled to bring down her pulse, gasping as she tried to pull air into her lungs. What had just happened? She was just an ordinary civil servant; why were they hunting her? Her heart pounded inside her ribcage. Best Western, it had said in the text message— she should go there. She would be safe there. She was on the verge of tears; she really wanted to believe it was true, but she couldn't go there, they couldn't fool her again, the bastards. She had to get away from here fast—now.

39

Brussels, Saturday, October 8

Rodriguez and two members of the cell team were waiting in the hotel lobby, two men were on the same floor as room 513 and an operative was waiting in the room. But still no Dymek.

The last contact with her had been just before she had left the tram. Since then, there had been no signs of life. The text message had reached her cell phone, but the question was whether she had seen it. She hadn't answered when they had called ten minutes later. Bente stood completely still and looked across the command room. The other staff were sitting quietly and waiting, standing by for the next order. She was the Head of the Section, it was for her to make the operational decisions now, but for a moment she felt unable to do anything except stand there and feel their eyes searching her for a sign of what they should do. Dymek was gone. Contact had been broken, and they could only wait and hope that she would come to her senses and go to the hotel.

Bente knew when a situation could no longer be influenced, although she hated the sense of powerlessness that came with that knowledge. They had taken a risk and intervened to give Dymek a chance to get away, but Dymek hadn't taken it. With British operatives so close by, they could only hope she had been quick enough to get to safety on her own—sending Rodriguez's people out into the city to look for her was far too risky. In a worst-case scenario, they might end up in an acute situation with the Brits. A firefight with Wilson's team would result in casualties, maybe fatalities—and witnesses. There would be consequences that they couldn't control.

She wasn't going to risk SSI, national security, and their entire partnership with the European intelligence community. No one was worth that much—not Dymek, not any one else.

The rustling silence in her headset was broken by a crackling call sign. It was Rodriguez: "One, over. Nothing yet."

Bente looked at the clock on the wall. It had been twenty-one minutes. She turned to Mikael. "What do you think?"

Mikael pursed his lips. "Perhaps she's managed to hide."

Perhaps. There was certainly the possibility that Dymek had managed to hide somewhere in the area—if she was quick and smart. She might have taken shelter in a large group of people, maybe in the large shopping mall close to the Place de Brouckère. But Dymek wasn't trained and she was on her own; Bente didn't even want to contemplate how low the probability was of Dymek evading Wilson.

Restlessness crept into her. Many a time it had been she who sat waiting in a hotel room—for hours, days—for a person or a phone call, a signal that, to other people, seemed insignificant but which, for the initiated, could be a matter of life and death. She hated it.

Dymek was missing her chance, and Bente couldn't do anything to prevent it. If only Dymek would get in touch. The Section had a car standing by in the hotel car park and a safe house in northern Brussels where they could keep Dymek for a day or two while they got the Brits to calm down. Then they could hand her back to Stockholm, interview her, and sort it all out. And presumably—hopefully—they would rule her out of the investigation and close the case.

Thirty minutes now, she noted.

"Shit," she muttered to herself; Mikael, who was standing beside her, heard and nodded. She drank what was left in her water bottle with a few angry swigs before crushing it between her hands until white cracks appeared in the soft plastic.

"Incoming call."

The low shout across the command room made her flinch. An assistant signed that the call was being connected to her headset.

Finally. Dymek might still be in play; she had almost given up hope that she would call.

"Good evening, Bentie."

For a moment, she was perilously close to saying, "Hello, Carina," but she quickly swallowed those words. It was Jonathan Green. *Green*, she mouthed silently at Mikael and saw his face cloud with anxiety. She turned around and walked into an adjoining corridor; she didn't want to have this conversation in front of the entire command room.

"Jonathan," she said, and quickly added, to disguise her surprise, "so good to hear from you." She wanted to get a grip on him right away, put him off balance. "What's going on?"

"You know what's going on," he answered, irritated. "What the fuck are you playing at?"

"What do you mean?" She knew where he was going; she needed to buy time.

"Are we working for same thing, Bentie?"

"I truly hope so."

"Best Western Hotel. Room 513. What the hell was that?"

She closed her eyes and clenched her jaw. Of course the British had picked up the message to Dymek. She should have assumed they were monitoring Dymek's cell.

"We were trying to bring her in."

"Well"—Green laughed harshly—"it was a fucking clumsy attempt, if you'll excuse my saying so. Keep your hands to yourself. Understood? We have an ongoing operation and it simply won't do to have you walking in on it like this."

"We didn't mean to disturb you."

"Okay."

She said nothing.

"For a second, I thought you were trying to sabotage a live operation," he continued in an odd, easygoing tone. He was still angry. "But I must have been mistaken."

"Yes, you must have been mistaken."

The silence said everything. He didn't believe her.

"We're working toward the same objective, Jonathan," she added.

"I'm pleased to hear it." Then, as if he wanted to break through the tense silence, to talk to her like one colleague to another, he said, wearily, "She's a terrorist, Bente. She's a threat to our most vital interests."

"So you say."

"I'm sorry?"

"That she's a terrorist. Is that really your assessment?"

"Don't be stupid. She's a threat!" Green burst out. "She's a threat and that's that. I don't have time for academic discussions, Bente. Terrorist or not, that's not the main thing right now. She's in the spectrum. The Arab and his uncle, the letter, the poem—all that stuff—it's enough. I was just calling for some reassurance that we hadn't . . . misunderstood one another."

She heard something in his voice, the slightly lighter note, which could turn into a shrill tone of voice. It was barely noticeable, but she heard it again—the lie. He was lying. There was no doubt about it any longer: the Brits were doing nothing more than packaging the case as terrorism. They had gotten Stockholm on board so that they could reach their final objective—the EIS. A sudden weariness overcame her.

"So where is Dymek?" she asked.

"Oh, you know, out and about in central Brussels."

"I want to know what you'll do with her."

"Naturally, we'll keep you fully—"

"I want to *know*."

"Of course," he said, and added in an apologetic tone that wasn't even meant to sound genuine, "I understand this is sensitive. Damn precarious situation for you. Swedish diplomat and all that." Then, as if he had suddenly come up with a cheering idea: "Our American friends were kind enough to give us an hour on a Global Hawk that's just taken off from Ramstein. They rerouted for our sake, a small diversion before it heads to Peshawar and the usual hunt for the Taliban. It's in the air now. Providing remarkable pictures." She could hear his smile. "I'll send you a link—how about that?"

In the command room she ordered one of the technicians to connect to the link and put the footage on the big screen. In the gloom, they saw a gray, shimmering film: a high-resolution aerial picture of Brussels. It was streaming live, she realized when she saw the little digital time display furiously counting away tenths of a second, seconds, minutes, hours.

Mikael turned to her. "What's this?"

She looked at him. "They've got a Global Hawk over Brussels."

Streets, squares and the rooftops of skyscrapers and buildings formed a geometric pattern. The aircraft moved slowly across the city, the longitude and latitude numbers shifting incessantly. The city stood out clearly in gray-green digitally processed tones that gave Brussels-by-evening a surreal sharpness in its appearance; Congresplein, the Finance Tower, and Rue Royale—the area where Dymek had gotten off the tram. This was Brussels, as seen from one of the world's most powerful reconnaissance aircraft. Global Hawk was the type of unmanned combat aircraft that the Americans had used as tactical support in the wars in Afghanistan and Iraq; it had the capacity to distinguish moving targets from a distance of one hundred kilometers; its cameras had such strong resolution that they could identify objects as small as half a meter across within an area of ten square kilometers. It had night vision, infrared cameras, and built-in signals intelligence that processed everything into a collective situation overview, which was probably being streamed directly to a Californian airbase or the command center in Langley. Nothing escaped this hunting machine. She had seen footage from Global Hawks before, but she couldn't help but shudder when she saw central Brussels, as cars moved away from a red light at a leisurely pace, trams passed one another on an avenue, and small figures moved almost hesitantly among the structures of the city. Normal people. Then the picture zoomed in. Abruptly, as if it was just one breathtaking stride, Brussels rushed toward them. The picture stopped just above the rooftops.

"My God."

Congresplein filled the screen and the resolution was unbelievably sharp. The focus had been changed so that they could see the city from an altitude of just a few hundred meters. She could clearly see the fences around the dilapidated Congress building, and the rows of streetlights and bushes, could even discern the different patterns in the cracked concrete flagstones. And there, running across the open space, was a figure.

"What do we do?" Mikael came up to her.

"We do nothing."

"Nothing? But shouldn't we try to bring her in?"

"It's too late." She nodded at the screen. "Don't you see?"

Carina was running; she stumbled but immediately regained her footing and carried on across the square. For a second, the shimmering gray picture became a little grainy as the transmission jumped, then the surreal sharpness returned. By all indications, Dymek was moving in a southerly direction, toward central Brussels. She was visible as a soundless, dark shadow, bounding ahead of a handful of other, slower individuals. The camera, controlled by a US Air Force officer thousands of kilometers away, followed her calmly, smoothly, never letting her slip out of focus. Bente went to the screen and stood close to its shimmering surface and watched the small, person-like stain moving through the cityscape. Dymek had reached the very end of Congresplein and crossed a narrow street where the traffic was moving soundlessly; she was momentarily obscured by a truck before reappearing on the opposite pavement. According to the measurement instruments on the reconnaissance aircraft, Dymek was in block 0136, at coordinates latitude 50.849172 and longitude 4.363793, and was moving in a southwesterly direction at a speed of twelve kilometers per hour.

40

Brussels, Saturday, October 8

Music rumbled across the park. A pulsing red glow flashed over the audience and turned into a stroboscopic flicker.

It was a miracle they hadn't caught her. She had stayed in the bushes by the Finance Tower for a long time before she had finally crawled out of her hiding place. Congresplein was a war zone in the heart of Brussels, a wide and abandoned expanse, surrounded by fences around buildings and dilapidated office buildings. She had stumbled on the way across the open space and fallen over, head-long, hard. The air had been beaten out of her and her left foot had gotten stuck in some debris littering the area, a piece of copper wir-ing, but at the time she had barely noticed the deep scratch on her face or the pain that was now beginning to throb in her ankle. She had kicked herself free and continued to run, blind to everything; she'd rushed out on to an adjacent street and immediately heard the scream of a truck's horn as it brushed past her, just centimeters from her face.

She had wanted to hide among other people, but the city was so deserted. The office district north of the central station in Brussels was full of Belgian civil servants and bankers during the day, but in the evening it was just an assortment of empty buildings with blank façades, closed parking lots, and dimly lit entrances that were watched over, suspiciously, by surveillance cameras. It was as if the narrow streets had been made for her to be discovered at a distance. There wasn't a soul here; there was nothing here to hide her. She ran, like a hare across an open field.

But they hadn't stopped searching, as she had first thought. At a crossroads, the four-wheel drive had appeared, seemingly out of thin air, about one hundred meters away. She had thrown herself between some parked cars and seen the SUV dwell at the crossroads before calmly moving on. Then she had heard the fiery sound of the motorbikes echoing around the buildings. They were still looking. She had stayed hidden in the row of parked cars, curled up in a fetal position, until the noise had gone away.

The central station was nearby, she knew that. If she could just make it there, the crowds would protect her. That was all she could think about: a human shield. If something happened, she could scream for help and someone would surely come to her assistance—as long as she was in a crowd.

She had come into a small square, on the other side of which a cathedral towered above her, illuminated, with skeleton-like gothic spires reaching into the sky. It was then that she heard the music. Heavy, French hip-hop echoed around the area. On the far side of the cathedral was a grassy area where a large audience was standing in front of an outdoor stage. It was an answer to her prayers, better than she could ever have hoped for. Quickly, she forced her way into the warm, dancing mass of people.

She stood in the middle of the crowd, surrounded by hundreds of people moving in time, with their arms in the air. For a short while, she thought she had managed to get away, that they would never find here, protected by thousands of sweaty, dancing people. But then she caught sight of their faces in the pulsing light, just for a second: two pale stains, bathed in red.

If they hadn't gone against the crowd by standing still when everyone else was swaying in time to the music, she would never have spotted them in time. One was tall, with a furrowed face, and the other was powerful like a body builder. For a brief second their gazes met, then the men were obscured. She had dug herself a long way into the sea of people, who were dancing away frenetically, completely unaware of her. The crowd was dense. She moved backward, bumping into someone who pushed her back hard. As soon as she could, she began to push through the tight rows of dancing people. People around her gave way unwillingly, without taking their eyes off the stage.

Tous les quartiers défavorisés . . . LIBÉREZ . . . Tout ceux que l'on représente . . . LIBÉREZ . . .

A loud bass pounded across the audience. The music was so strong she could feel the pressure in her stomach as she wriggled through the throbbing mass. She kept bumping into hard, dancing bodies, which squeezed her in between them. She fought with her arms, grabbed someone's sweater and heaved her way forward through a tight passage that had momentarily opened up, before someone else's wide back pushed her backward into a woman, who staggered and fell forward. The throng was so dense that she was almost lifted off the ground. Panic fluttered through her body. She tried to move to the right where there were fewer people, but was pressed forward, toward the stage.

LIBÉREZ . . . LIBÉREZ . . .

With a violent final push, she managed to force her way to the picket fence by the speakers to the left of the stage. The music was so loud that it transcended into an overwhelming din. She was dangerously close to being crushed against the battens of the fence when the audience around her began to dance, but she held on, heaved herself up on to unfamiliar shoulders and tumbled over the barrier. When she got back to her feet, the men were gone—lost to the undulating forest of outstretched arms.

She found a grassy area by the stage. There were fewer audience members here, standing in small groups in the dark. She continued running down empty, unknown streets, until she began to recognize her surroundings. She had reached Arts-Loi and looked down across the Rue de la Loi. The EU district rose above the city like a series of dark sculptures.

She couldn't run anymore; her ankle hurt. At a pedestrian crossing, she stopped and massaged her foot. The ankle was sore and swollen, probably sprained. Around her was a scattering of people in the darkness, waiting to cross the avenue.

The hotel, it struck her—it wasn't far away; perhaps a kilometer or so from where she was. Maybe she could take a taxi there—she would be there in five minutes. Throw some things into her bag, maybe a quick shower before she left; it would take less than fifteen minutes. Just the thought of the hotel room brought her to the brink of tears, she so desperately wanted to lie down, even if only for a short while. Maybe there was no danger in going back and having a proper night's sleep before flying home to Stockholm. No, no, for God's sake. The thought was deceptively attractive, but she had to stop thinking about the hotel; she couldn't go back there.

The pedestrian silhouette turned green and, in a quiet, communal movement, everyone around her began to cross the road.

"Carina."

She was about to step off the pavement, but stopped herself. The car headlights blinded her; she couldn't see who had called her name. A woman came toward her, smiling. Carina didn't recognize her.

"Hi, Carina," she said in a clear, British accent. Perhaps it was a colleague, or some other acquaintance. She really needed someone to talk to, someone who could help her.

It was too late by the time she realized what was happening. The woman came up to her and pretended to give her a hug, pushed against her and locked her arms together with a rock-solid grip. As if out of nowhere, a man appeared; all Carina saw was a light brown suede jacket and then someone grabbed her wrists and twisted them so that pain radiated through her arms. This couldn't be possible, she thought, as if watching it all from the sidelines. It was surreal; it wasn't actually happening. Then she screamed. Out of the corner of her eye, she saw some people on the street turn around, just a few meters away. But they did nothing, just stood there; they didn't understand what they were seeing. Carina was lifted off the ground; she lost her footing.

41

Brussels, Saturday, October 8

A van skidded to a halt next to the row of parked cars; the side door flew open. They tried to drag her into the road but Carina managed to get a grip on two cars with her feet and braced herself, struggling wildly: it made the man and woman holding her momentarily lose their balance. She wanted to do everything she could to stay in this world, outside of the van, and for a second she almost seemed to be free. A man in overalls jumped out of the van and stepped toward her. He had a small object in his hand; it looked like a small rod. Reality vanished; everything shrank to a narrow edge. She was going to die now. She tried to emit a sound but only managed a muddled groan as he pressed the rod against her neck. The needle hurt as it was pushed into her jugular and suddenly she could sense such strange things, like the odor of a strong eau de cologne and solvents. Someone said, "Got her—I got her." Her body turned limp, as if she was dying in a violent exhalation. She felt herself being lifted. Hands grabbed hold of her, pulled her inexorably into the dark.

When she woke up, she was in a car, with a harness seat belt across her body. She had probably been unconscious for a minute or so, maybe longer, she didn't know. Through the dark, tinted windows, she could see distant neighborhoods rushing by. They were on the freeway. She felt unwell and vomited violently into a bucket between her legs, and just that little detail—that the bucket was already there; that someone had expected her to throw up and didn't want her to mess up the vehicle—left her scared stiff.

Her body felt alien and numb, like jelly. Struggling, she turned her head. In the seats beside her were the woman and the man who had tricked her into the vehicle; in the front seats, a clean-shaven man was at the wheel and, next to him, another person. She tried not to cry, but the tears flowed anyway.

"Let me go."

The words were difficult to form; she was frightened by how slurred they sounded as they came out of her mouth. The man in the suede jacket calmly dug into a bag and pulled out a blindfold. It looked like a large pair of skiing goggles. No, she wanted to scream. She couldn't fight back; she didn't even have the strength to turn away her head as he attached the blindfold around her face.

Everything became dark. And, at once, she understood there was no way out. They could do what they liked with her, and no one would ever find out. That thought made her so scared she began to shake. After that, she was no longer in control of herself; she screamed, pulling at the seat belt, tearing and wrenching with all her might. But she couldn't move an inch; the belts tightened around her body and made her gasp for air. "I'm choking!" she screamed. "I'm choking." Then she felt a stinging pain in her neck. An enormous void opened in the darkness and sucked her into it. All sense of time vanished.

The sounds around her changed. She had come to again. They were driving more slowly. The car occasionally jolted, slowing down before speeding back up again; it felt like they were driving along smaller streets, through built-up areas. All she could hear was the sound of the engine, because the people around her said nothing. They didn't need to talk, of course; they already knew where they were going and what was going to happen. She couldn't hold back any longer. She cried. The inside of the blindfold got wet and, after a while, it began to itch.

The car lurched and then braked to a halt. The engine was turned off and the door opened. Several people took her out of her seat and lifted her from the car. Her knees buckled and she fell forward, but firm hands grabbed hold of her, gripping her hard around her arms and waist. Someone pulled off her blindfold. She squinted, trying to orient herself in the blinding light of car headlights. Darkness; sharp light. They were on a narrow road outside a low, concrete building—maybe in an industrial area. She could barely see anything because of the light from the car and the dense darkness around them; she only briefly glimpsed patches of bright light far away, low buildings made from corrugated iron, a fence and, on the other side of the fence, a railway track that disappeared into the night.

They took her through a door and down a corridor. It was a building site. The walls were roughly sanded, brick was still visible here and there; tins of paint and tools were lying all over the place; electrical cables trailed out of the walls. It was cold.

They took her to an empty room where someone had put plastic sheeting on the floor. In a corner there were rolls of insulation. They put her on a chair and left.

It was silent. She was close to throwing up again, but managed to control herself.

There were no windows in the room, or they were covered; the only light came from a raw, glaring builder's lamp hanging from the ceiling. How strange, she thought; completely normal light bulbs, like at any normal building site. All sound was sucked up by the surroundings. The walls were probably soundproofed; no one would ever hear if she began to scream. Only now did she realize that, all along, there had been a video camera on a tripod, pointing at her. Why was she here? It was as if her entire brain was mired in molasses; thoughts were groggy and shapeless. She tried to concentrate but the room kept floating sideways.

She didn't know how long she sat there. The room was silent and cold. She ought to be able to hear traffic, she thought, a dog, voices—anything that showed there was life outside. But not a sound was audible, not a trace of life made it into the room. She wanted to shout out for someone, but this entire place told her that there was no point. She looked at the door and decided she had to get to it.

But she couldn't get up; her body was so weak that she barely had the strength to sit up straight. Maybe this was how she was going to die. The thought grew inside her head and paralyzed her.

The door opened and two men came in. One of them was younger than the other, wearing khakis and a green polo shirt, with muscular arms spilling out of the top: a soldier. The other man was older and so large that, when he lumbered through the door, the room seemed to shrink. It looked like he had just stopped by on the way to work; he was wearing chinos and a white, crumpled shirt, and seemed completely relaxed. He had a broad, weather-beaten face and looked at her completely calmly, without moving.

The men went to a small table at the side of the room and put on white latex gloves. She watched the large man's broad neck, his thick arms underneath the rolled-up shirtsleeves. What did they want with her? Something about his calm manner frightened her so much she could hardly breathe.

The big one turned around, a furrowed face with eyes that calmly glanced around before fixing their gaze on her. He scratched his head through his bristly, reddish hair, as if contemplating what to do now, before fetching a chair and sitting down in front of her.

"Say your name," he growled in British English.

She obeyed without thinking. He had a tone that didn't accept no for an answer. Her knees shook uncontrollably. Her legs trembled; she tried to get them to calm down.

"Why am I here?" she managed to say. "You have no right to do this."

The men watched her, wordlessly. The big one, with the reddish hair, leaned back with his hands in his pockets and looked at her with an attentive, sarcastic gaze. The soldier leaned against the wall with his arms crossed.

"What?" she exclaimed. Her voice cracked.

They didn't answer. She looked down at the floor. There was silence in the room; all she could hear were gasping breaths. She understood at once that it was her panting and tried to calm herself. Breathing was suffocating her. Finally, the giant-like man seemed to have made up his mind. He straightened up. He informed her calmly that she would be wise to cooperate. She should be aware that she risked prosecution under British and American law for crimes related to national security.

"I am going to ask you some questions and I want you to answer them truthfully," he said. "Nod if you understand."

She nodded quietly.

"What is your relationship to Jamal Badawi?"

She stared at him. Jamal? "What do you mean?"

"Answer the question," he said quickly. "I want to know how you know him. Your relationship."

For the first time, she met the man's gaze. She didn't understand how they knew about Jamal and why they cared about him. It had been her who had mishandled the report; she had made the mistake.

"We're in a relationship."

He wanted to know when they had first started seeing each other. She remembered the days they had spent strolling around together, the beautiful weather, and how they had sat outside, drinking coffee, down by Riddarfjärden. But she was dazed, couldn't manage to remember a date, or even a month; it was as if the question was extremely complex. Had it been the beginning of May? Why was he asking about Jamal? she wanted to say. Jamal had nothing to do with it all. They couldn't hurt him—not Jamal.

He leaned forward. "When did you meet for the first time?"

She understood nothing. Who were these people?

"Concentrate," said the man on the chair. "Look at me."

"I don't understand why you're asking about Jamal."

"Answer the question."

He looked at her calmly, as if assessing her, but there was something in that eerie calm that was so unpleasant she looked away. He asked the question again. Jamal.

Now she remembered: they had first met in May—the beginning of May. "I don't know what you're up to," she said, "but there must have been a misunderstanding. I don't understand . . ."

He raised his hand, shook his head. "Just answer the questions. Akim Badawi: does that name mean anything to you?"

At first she said no, but then stopped herself. Akim Badawi.

The man looked straight at her and asked again. So she didn't know who Akim Badawi was—was she sure? "Answer the question," he said. "Akim Badawi."

"He's Jamal's uncle."

"So you do know him."

"No. Jamal's told me about him."

And what had he told her about him? the man wanted to know. What did Jamal say about him?

She didn't really know what to say. She noticed how the questions took shape around her like silent accusations. He had told her about Cairo, she said, about how he had grown up. She felt sick; she was telling them things Jamal had told her, only her, late at night, in his apartment.

"But you and Jamal have planned a trip to Cairo. Is that right?"

She nodded.

"Who were you going to meet in Cairo?"

"I don't know," she whispered. "It's a vacation."

He leaned back and looked at her for a while.

"Carina, you would be wise to take this seriously. We know that you were going to borrow a house from Akim Badawi. You were going to meet him. You know Jamal Badawi well and you were going to meet Akim Badawi. Who else were you going to meet in Cairo?"

She stared at him. "No one."

He released a drawn out sigh and turned around. The man who had been standing quietly by the wall came forward and told her not to lie. He spoke with an American accent. They would check everything she said, he told her calmly, and a lie would go against her in a trial. She could expect the harshest punishments under the law for the crimes she was going to be charged with. Just so she knew.

"But it's true," she burst out. She tried her best to answer their questions, but noted that she wasn't at all saying what they wanted to hear. She knew vaguely that what they were trying to get her to say was completely crazy; it didn't make sense. What contacts were they talking about? She had no contacts in Cairo; she was just saying things as they were. But they weren't satisfied. They looked at her. The soldier began to pace back and forth.

The man in front of her shook his head and leaned forward. "You won't convince me that you weren't going to meet anyone in Cairo. We both know that's not true. We'll continue to hold you here until you tell us the facts. Answer truthfully."

She stared at him. Please, she thought, please leave me alone.

The men looked at each other. The man on the chair nodded at the soldier and said, "If my colleague over there had his way, we would start off dealing with you like the Americans usually do with terrorists."

"Please," she whispered.

He got out a piece of paper and held it up to her face, letting her read it. "What do these lines mean?"

She read them slowly. It was a poem. "I don't know."

"Your little boyfriend, Badawi, says he read it to you. What does it mean?"

"What?" A maelstrom of despair swirled through her.

She remembered: the poem—the poem that Jamal had read to her—was that what he meant? A sob forced its way up through her like a sharp knife. She groped for words. She wanted to bite back, to silence him, to stop him asking all his questions that were destroying everything, soiling it all.

"What have you done to Jamal?"

"Answer the question. The poem. What does it mean?"

She just shook her head and said she didn't know—it was all she could get out.

His voice took on a hard, metallic tone. "You're in a relationship with Jamal Badawi and have planned a trip to Cairo to meet Akim Badawi. These are people prepared to carry out acts of terror, ready to kill hundreds or thousands of people. Tell me exactly what Jamal has told you to do."

Everything inside her screamed that they were wrong. They were wrong. They didn't know Jamal.

"He's not a terrorist." The words came out of her in a whisper.

"The EU summit meeting next week is the target," he said. "Who else is in on the plan?"

"What plan?"

The punch landed just under her left eye, a firm strike that came as a surprise and hit her hard. She almost fell off the chair. The man who had been by the wall was now by her side, pushing her violently back on to the chair. Instinctively, she felt her nose: her hand came away smeared with blood. Tears filled her eyes and her cheek burned. The man stood, leaning over her, close to her face. The unexpectedly sharp, nauseating smell of his aftershave enveloped her.

"We're going to hurt you. Do you understand? We won't stop until you tell us who they are. Who is planning the attack?"

She struggled to breathe. "I don't know."

He grabbed her neck and squeezed her throat; the pain struck her like a cast-iron pan over the head. It felt like her head was going to explode. She lost her breath; for a few seconds, her entire body writhed. Finally, he let go; she gasped for air. Then she vomited with her hands on her knees, threw up so much that it splattered everywhere.

The man turned away and lit a cigarette. When it was all out, she felt a little better. Her head was clearer. She spat and emitted an odd, involuntary belching sound. A little saliva dripped to the floor; she dried her mouth.

The man turned back to her. "Names," he said, right in front of her face. "Give me names."

She just wanted him to stop, for him to understand that there was no point in continuing, and to leave her alone, but then the man grabbed her throat again. It hurt like crazy; it felt like he was going to crush her windpipe. She shrunk into herself, trying to get free of his grip, and pulled instinctively backward, away from his face—but he kept hold of her head with one hand around her neck and the other around her larynx, like a vice. Everything became a giant ball of pain and she screamed, but all that came out was a kind of snort. He asked the same thing over and over: *Who*? The low, serious voice penetrated her like an icy chill. The other, younger man appeared too—asking the same questions in a shrill voice, his angry face right against hers.

"Names. You have to give us names!" they shouted. "Who else is involved? Give us names. Who were you going to meet in Cairo?"

The big man groaned as he almost lifted her from the floor. She could smell his sweat, feel his rock-solid, hairy hands over her mouth, and she glimpsed his face, completely distorted. She couldn't breathe. He's killing me, she thought. I'm dying. The panic welled up inside her and she tried to break free. Now the other one—the soldier—was holding her too. He grabbed hold of her wrist and bent it, and a pain that felt as if her arm was going to break shot up to her head and made everything else in the room blurry.

She sat huddled in complete darkness. Perhaps this was how she was going to die. Maybe this was what it was like to approach your own death, to wait in the antechamber of your own annihilation, because she was now sure there was no way back. While she had been in the plastic-sheeted room, she had hoped for an opportunity to give some kind of explanation, to reason with them—until they hit her. Then she had realized that this wasn't the kind of place where there was mercy, where it was possible to reason. Here, she would vanish. She cried.

She sobbed loudly, without trying to hold it back. The dark was like a cold and deep body of water, out of which a menacing shadow rose up and came toward her. The fear washed through her body. There was nothing around her except darkness, and she was part of it.

They had led her down a corridor and down some steps before shoving her in here. A man and a woman in uniform had held her under the arms and dragged her. For the brief moment when they opened the door, and a wide angle of light from the corridor illuminated the room, she had seen a tiny, cold space, not bigger than a spacious wardrobe. When they closed the door behind her, the beam of light was ground down into a glimmer, and then it disappeared. She had crept to the door and hit it, screaming and hammering with her fists until her hands were sodden with blood.

Finally, she had managed to calm down. She focused her hearing, but all she could discern was the heavy beating of her own heart and the blood rushing through her ears. She heard her own rasping breaths pressing the dark air into and out of her lungs, the small gurgles of her stomach, humming noises; all the sounds inside her were amplified and filled the room.

She was too tired to sit up and instead lay down carefully on her side. Her neck twinged every time she moved; her body felt like a sack of water. The floor was inhospitable—covered in chipboard.

The dark around her was just as dense as before when she opened her eyes after a long time and painfully sat up. She would never get out of here. The thought crept through her. She was imprisoned in an eternal darkness. Panic gnawed through her thoughts and she began to count out loud so as not to lose her grip completely. She tried to concentrate and count to sixty at about the same pace as the flow of seconds on a clock. "One, two," she heard herself say in the dark. Her voice was hoarse and raspy. "That's a minute," she said to herself. Then she counted to sixty again, and then again. But, as soon as she stopped counting, she felt how time began to float around and lose its sense of direction. Every minute was the same minute; she couldn't tell them apart any longer, however much she tried. She groped for the door and hammered furiously on the flat surface that lacked a keyhole, and she screamed. She didn't want to die; she didn't even want to go crazy. The whole room was suspended in swaying stagnation.

Something told her it was nighttime. She had dropped off through sheer exhaustion and was woken up by a sudden pain in her neck that made her draw breath. She had dreamed that she had been at home in her apartment and that sunlight had been streaming through the windows, warming her skin—roasting her, in fact. She opened her eyes and, for a second, she saw nothing but dazzling darkness. For a vanishing moment, she forgot where she was and stretched out an arm toward Jamal, but all she found was a brick wall. She lay still and listened to the darkness. Perhaps it was morning out there. Maybe it was night. It felt like night, because a special kind of silence always accompanied it. Or perhaps she was just imagining it because she couldn't hear anything—not a whisper; not the slightest vibration of people moving or doors being slammed.

She could see nothing, so it was better to close her eyes—then the darkness was her own. She shut her eyes and touched her hands, her arms, her face—as if to check they were still there.

She was thirsty. Her mouth and tongue were like dry leather. She fantasized about cool wine, clementines, fresh salad, salty bacon. She tried to get up, but felt dizzy and sank back against the wall. After a while, she managed to pull herself together enough to stand on all fours. She felt the floor under the palms of her hands: untreated, coarse chipboard. Carefully, she crawled forward until she hit the door on the other side. She groped upward, found the door handle and pressed her ear against the cool surface, tensing her muscles to make sure that not even the slightest sound would escape her. She longed to hear something, anything; even the sound of someone coming to beat her again would be a relief. Maybe they had left her here. She might as well have been buried alive.

42

Brussels, Saturday, October 8

The Belliard Tunnel enveloped them. Bente leaned back. Mikael was sitting beside her in the back seat in silence, and that suited her; she didn't feel like talking right now; she needed to gather her thoughts before the meeting. The evening traffic raced ahead of them and rows of red lights surrounded them. She couldn't help but feel a certain pleasure when she was in the Section's custom-built BMW. Rodriguez was a good driver. She liked how he drove: fast, calm, and safe, like everyone who worked in Dignitary Protection.

The Section had received confirmation from MI6 two hours earlier. The Brits had accepted the Section's request for an immediate meeting. Twenty-three hundred hours, Avenue Cicéron. It was barely six kilometers from SSI's offices to Avenue Cicéron, but procedures to ensure they were not being followed meant the journey took a little longer. She looked at her watch; they had plenty of time.

They came out of the tunnel and carried on along Avenue de Cortenbergh. Somewhere behind and in front of them were the cell team in their cars. She yawned loudly. She hadn't slept for almost thirty-five hours and reclined in the comfortable leather seat in the velvety darkness; tiredness ebbed over her.

"Fifteen minutes."

"We'll make it."

The Evers branch of KBC Insurance claimed to administer insurance for exclusive corporate clients. They had a website and a switchboard that always picked up with a friendly greeting and the name of the company, if you called. Their head office in Brussels was a six-story office block on the edge of a business park, at a reasonable distance from the other complexes in the area. The building was surrounded by a wide lawn, had discreetly installed surveillance cameras and round-the-clock security. Behind its carefully constructed cover as a branch of a bank, lay MI6's operational center in Brussels, home to around two hundred employees, led by Jonathan Green.

The cover was, seemingly, successful; they had been working undisturbed for the last ten years without being discovered. Despite all her contact with the Brits, Bente had never previously visited their Brussels office.

The car came to a halt outside the entrance. The building was dark, the rows of windows black and glistening. They were alone, but watched by a dozen small cameras recording their arrival.

They were expected. Reception was manned: a woman in a suit sat behind the soberly lit counter and looked up from a magazine as they came in. She gave them her best customer-facing smile, as if their appearance, an hour before midnight, was a perfectly common occurrence at this bank.

The woman pushed forward a lined box. They put their cells in it and were each given a badge to wear around their necks. A man in a dark suit came through the security barriers and approached them. If they would be so good as to follow him.

They were escorted through the building, up two stories by elevator, then through dimly lit corridors. A dark, open-plan office lay behind glass partitions.

Jonathan Green was waiting for them in a windowless conference room. He wasn't alone; a man in a dark suit was also sat at the end of the conference table. When Bente and Mikael appeared, they fell silent, got up, and stood completely still beneath the pale fluorescent lights.

Green came forward. "Good evening, Bentie."

He was on his guard, but friendly; he greeted Mikael listlessly. A real pleasure to see you. He was himself—the same boyish face, same inscrutable smile and the same blue eyes, which were now studying them with cool curiosity. The other man was an American. He greeted them without introducing himself and it took a second for her to realize who he was: Bill Sherman, the CIA's Deputy Director for Counterterrorism—their coordinator for covert operations. She recognized him, but had never met him in person before. He was remarkably broad-shouldered, tall, and had a long face with a powerful chin. They sat down.

"It's rare that we get to see each other like this," Green said. "So I want to take the opportunity to thank you. It hasn't been easy, but I'm sure the situation is going to resolve itself now. Many thanks for your cooperation." He turned to her. "Together we have removed a threat against the heart of Europe. We can be proud of that."

He smiled straight at her. But that was expected. What really annoyed her was that he was talking to her like she was a clever school pupil who had been on her best behavior. But she wasn't so stupid that she didn't realize this was a conscious strategy to throw her off balance, to weaken her in comparison to them, to get her to say too much, to disrupt her ability to analyze the situation. Naturally, she wouldn't fall for it. She nodded reservedly. She wasn't just Bente now; she was Sweden's representative, and Sweden needed these two men and their expansive organizations. As Kempell had said, there was an old friendship with the UK, as well as with the US, friendships that had lasted for decades and would last long after the end of this case.

She looked at the American, who met her gaze without blinking. He was calm, she noted, calm for real—not like all the arrogant cocks she had met over the years who presented a cool façade in order to seem more stable than they were. This man knew exactly what he wanted and who he was. He looked tired, possibly after a long flight. This case was minor for him, one of thousands of ongoing operations that his organization was running in cooperation with partners around the world, and could now be logged as completed. Tomorrow he would probably be in a similar meeting somewhere else—in Berlin or Madrid, Riyadh, Nairobi, Kabul. He didn't move an inch. He looked bored, but then opened his mouth and said, in an unexpectedly soft, deep voice, "Yes. You've done a great job. I think we can call this one a day now."

"Yes," said Green. "Good work."

"So, there's no terrorist threat any longer," she said lightly.

Green smiled. "No, thank God."

"It's funny, all this talk of terrorist attacks. And then the threat is gone."

Green's smile shifted in a barely noticeable manner. It hardened. He looked at her in surprise. What did she mean?

"I'm just surprised at how quickly the terrorist threat disappeared."

"Everything suggested attack planning was underway."

"Oh, did it?" she said.

Bill Sherman sat up slowly in his chair and looked at her with eyes that had awoken from their dazed sleepiness and caught sight of something that amused and annoyed him in equal measure: a little Swede. Her heart was beating hard. Just one remark of dissatisfaction from either of the two men would ripple through the Security Service like a shock wave and be followed by anxious managerial meetings, grim conversations, in which her future would be decided at the drop of a hat, then a new charm offensive against Washington and London to repair any damage to the friendship. She was close to the line.

"When we last met, Jonathan," she continued, "you didn't mention anything about terrorist attacks."

He shrugged his shoulders. "The threat changed."

The threat hadn't changed whatsoever; it had never existed. The lie was quite obvious; he was defensive. Quickly, before he gathered himself, she darted in as lightly as she could to say, "You talked about a leak. The leak worried you. Carina Dymek, you remember? I assume Jean Bernier worried you before that. You took care of him. But then Carina Dymek turned up . . . What a shame."

The Brit looked coolly at her. "What do you mean?"

The conference room was completely silent. She looked at the American and then back at Green, focusing on his two, fish-like eyes. "Stop talking shit, Green. There is no terrorist threat. Is there?"

Maybe she imagined it, but she got the impression that he shuddered—a minimal movement in his facial muscles, which immediately became impassive again.

"Who claims that Europe doesn't face a terrorist threat—your friend in Leiden?" he said as sharply as the lash of a whip. He looked at her in amusement. "You should be more careful making outings like that, Bente."

For a second, she could see the silver car turning around and heading toward Leiden, late at night, stopping outside the home of De Vries. It would have been a quick job, made to look like a break-in gone wrong. She pushed the picture to one side; it was precisely that kind of anxiety that Green wanted her to feel in order to gain the upper hand.

"You created a terrorist threat."

Green snorted. "Bente, this is ridiculous."

He shook his head and looked at Sherman as if he wanted to say that he'd had enough of this silliness and it was the American's turn to rebuke the Swede, but Sherman wasn't playing along; he was sitting, lost in his thoughts. Good God—what theater! But she couldn't laugh in their faces; they still represented two of the world's largest intelligence services, so she waited for them.

The American, who had been leaning back in his seat, motion-less, for almost the entire meeting, heaved himself forward. "What the fuck is your problem?"

"I—"

"You know," he interrupted her, "we like Sweden. We like you because you cooperate—which is a smart move for a little country like yours. You've done a good job: you tracked down that Arab and his terrorist network; you prevented an attack. And stopped a dangerous leak. *That's* the truth. You should be proud. You're fighting to protect a free, democratic society, Mrs. Jensen—together with us. And sometimes people make small mistakes. But let me tell you something: that's completely okay, as long as our citizens can sleep at night. I thought you understood that."

"So was there a terrorist threat or not?" she said, after she and the American had stared at one another for several seconds.

"So what? You still don't get it?" He looked at her apologetically. "We save lives, Mrs. Jensen. The European Intelligence Service will provide the EU with the necessary tools to prevent another London, another Madrid. And we'll be with you every step of the way. We're saving lives here."

"And we fully support it," she said and gave her broadest smile. She had scrutinized them. She hadn't even criticized the EIS, just questioned if there had really been a threat, as the British had suggested, and, based on Sherman's rhetorical whipped cream, it was clear there had been no threat at all. "So what is Wilson actually up to?"

The American looked at her indifferently and turned to Green, who quickly interjected: "Wilson is doing his job."

"Yes, but is he really hunting for terrorists—or just civil servants in general?" She couldn't help the sarcasm, but regretted it immediately; it was futile. She couldn't go too far.

Green sighed and placed his hands on the table with his fingers splayed. He nodded thoughtfully, as if he had finally made a substantial decision of principle. "Okay, Bente. I hear what you're saying. We may not have been entirely honest with you."

She said nothing. Sherman sat quietly, studying his fingernails.

"But it was necessary," he continued. "We needed you to act."

"And Jean Bernier?"

"Things like that happen . . . regrettably," said Green quietly, lifting the palms of his hands in a gesture of resignation. "Bente, don't overdo this. There are hoards of terrorist-loving politicians around Europe just waiting for an excuse to destroy everything we've built up over decades—naïve people, who don't want to see reality. But when the bombs explode, they point the finger at us because we didn't stop the massacre. We have to be one step ahead of the terrorists. Right? It's them or us. And, naturally, we sometimes do things we don't want to do. Personally, I didn't like having to"—he searched for the word—"handle you. After all, we're partners."

They said nothing. Handled us. That was exactly what it had been. London had handled Stockholm, had maneuvered individuals and organizations to achieve certain predefined objectives. They had gotten what they wanted. She had an answer and she had no desire left to pursue it further. She wasn't even angry; she just felt a chilly admiration for the way the British had managed the whole thing.

"Where's the report now?" said Green mildly. "I mean, I assume all copies have been secured?"

"That work is ongoing. Where is Carina Dymek?"

The American looked calmly at her. "We're taking care of her."

"What do you mean, 'taking care of?' She's a Swedish diplomat."

The American shrugged his shoulders. "Not anymore."

"She's a Swedish citizen."

"And?"

She met their gazes. These two men in suits sat in front of her, so calm, waiting. They were so used to getting their way by controlling the weather when it suited them. Gods in their kingdoms. These men could change people's lives forever by making a short call on their cell phone.

"I want Carina Dymek."

"I can't guarantee"—the American began.

"If she disappears, you'll run into problems."

"Is that a threat?"

"It's a prediction. Think about it—she's a diplomat and a Swedish citizen. She can't just disappear. People will notice."

The American raised his eyebrows and looked at her like she was a funny insect. "So you want her. What's in it for us?"

She met the American's gaze.

"Badawi is interesting," Green interjected quietly.

Badawi. Yes, he was still of interest—Bente realized that. His contacts with the Ahwa group were undeniable. If there was an Ahwa group. If he was innocent and the threat portrayed by the British didn't exist, he would be acquitted. Sooner or later. A person with nothing to hide could be put through the justice system and come out the other end a free man or woman. She knew it didn't really work like that, but it made no difference. She couldn't save him. She couldn't stop these two men and their enormous organizations from getting their way. Dymek or Badawi: one of them had to be singled out. Dymek was almost certainly innocent; it was possible to argue for her release. Badawi, on the other hand, was still of interest; there was the connection to a terrorist threat. Whether the threat really existed didn't matter—there was a threat because the British said so and the CIA had confirmed MI6's assessment of the matter. Stockholm would never question their truths. If she pushed away Sweden's most important friends now, Stockholm would never forgive her—she knew that too. They would recall her and pull her to pieces, remove her from the Section and put her in quarantine in some financial department until everyone had forgotten she ever existed.

She turned to Mikael. She only needed a look, an imperceptible nod, anything that revealed he understood what she was about to do and that he supported her. But Mikael was looking down at his papers.

"Okay," she heard herself say. "You can have Badawi."

43

Brussels, Sunday, October 9

A bright light streamed into the small cell. After the dense darkness, the fluorescent lighting of the corridor was sharp and hurt her eyes. Carina shaded her face with her hand. Two men were in the doorway. One of them came in and stood by the wall, without looking at her; the other put down a bucket, a plastic bowl and a bottle of water on the floor. Then, wordlessly, they left the cell. The door closed and, for a moment, the total darkness was back. She crept over the floor, feeling her way forward, and found the tray. The bowl contained rice and beans. She ate with her hands and drank large gulps from the bottle, before lying down on the floor.

She must have fallen asleep because she awoke with a start and opened her eyes. But it was just as dark as before. It might only have been a minute, or a day. She had no idea.

She sat by one of the walls with her legs pulled up to her chest. She felt calmer; hunger was no longer tearing at her stomach. Her thoughts meandered. At some point, she got angry about something; it was as if she had opened a door and let something warm and raging rush out of her body. Her pulse beat harder and faster; it pounded against her temples; she felt a huge rush of adrenaline; rage swept her along. She had begun to think about work at the Security Policy Department and her office on the fifth floor. She had tried to remember what it looked like, tying her thoughts to that mental picture. But then it had struck her that it was probably no longer her office. Maybe they had gotten some boxes and gathered her things together; maybe there was someone else in there now, a complete stranger in *her* room, and that thought made her so angry. She fantasized for a long time about how she would return to the floor and walk down the corridor toward her office, and how some other bastard would be in there, a young arrogant guy who had never even once had to fight for anything in his life, and how she would ask him, ice cold, what he was doing there. She would stand there and make the guy sitting in her office cry, then force him out of the room, make him return the keys and, as he sobbed, he would beg her for forgiveness. And everyone would be standing around in the corridor agreeing with her—agreeing with *her*. Then her thoughts wandered on to the morning when she had been called into the Head of Department's office and how they had questioned and humiliated her. She saw the department head and Anders Wahlund in front of her, how they told her that she had made an error, that she was injudicious. She thought about this for a long while. She had just let it happen. She had just sat there on the sofa and barely said a thing, had let them be right, and now she couldn't understand how she had just taken all that shit. The more she thought about it and all the patronizing things they had said, the more agitated she became. The rage tensed all her muscles until her body was stiff. She replayed the scene over and over and, each time, she just got angrier and finally she began to see herself getting up and standing in front of the department head and saying what she had wanted to say for so long. She gave him proper comebacks; she spoke to him directly as an equal. He was an idiot. He should be damn careful what he said. She saw how he shrank back in the face of her ice-cold rage and transformed into the little, oppressive shit that he was. Now she knew exactly what she should have said to them, not like then, when it had actually happened and she had just given lame answers, or sat in silence. She should have defended herself better. She saw how she got up and interrupted the department head and Wahlund with a few choice words to put them in their place, once and for all. She thought it all through very slowly, formed the words carefully using her hatred, honing the sentences until they were razor sharp.

Then the fury was gone. She was back in the darkness and the rage that had been rushing around inside her like a demon was gone, as if blown away on a gust of wind. What did it matter? she thought. Wahlund meant nothing to her life, and now, sitting in the dark, she knew that the Ministry of Foreign Affairs also meant nothing to her. She couldn't explain it, but it felt dispensable. Everything that she had believed was important, everything she had thought was the core of her existence—being one of the best people at the Security Policy Department at the MFA and an integral part of the Swedish diplomatic core—that all appeared completely pointless. She thought for a long time about why she felt like that. It was an important job. Everyone around her was always so impressed that she worked in foreign policy and she had been proud to work there. But, when she thought about the Ministry, all she could feel was an indifference that surprised her; it was like looking at a dazzling machine, a kind of gray, glittering system of corridors; there were just scattered images; she could barely even remember what she had been doing there and it wasn't even a feeling, more a kind of emptiness that occurred when she tried to gather her thoughts. She had been completely dispensable. She had thought she was part of a community where she was allowed to be the committed, professional diplomat that she had always dreamed of becoming. She had thought that what she was doing meant something because it was *her* doing it. But, in reality, she had just been working as part of a machine that needed her labor, and she had been replaceable, at a moment's notice, as soon as any of her bosses decided it should be so. Someone else would come after her and take her place. She had been pushed away and, without understanding how it had happened, she had ended up here. She would never be able to go back to the MFA; there was nothing for her to return to.

Maybe she imagined it, but she thought she heard laughter: men laughing loudly. Another time she woke in the darkness to a drawn-out scream.

She thought about Jamal and missed him so much that tears came to her eyes. She wondered whether he missed her. Maybe he was also being held captive. Maybe they had already caught him and taken him away and tried to make him say things. *No*, she thought. No. Not Jamal. These thoughts overwhelmed her; the darkness around her pushed itself on to her and made her gasp for breath. Please, don't let them hurt him, she prayed silently. Please, she thought. Not Jamal. She had to believe that things would sort themselves out and that she would soon see him; just the possibility that it wouldn't happen was so unbearable that she quickly pushed it away. It couldn't be right. It wasn't allowed to be right because that would be the end—she might as well give up and die.

She closed her eyes and tried to see the apartment in Hammarby Sjöstad. It was hard to see him in front of her; the darkness was so enormous that it consumed everything. "Jamal," she said, "don't go. Jamal, my love, don't go." She wanted to be with him forever, to hold him, to wrap her arms around him and never let go, and for a second the feeling was so strong that she stretched out her arms in front of her and hugged the darkness. Then she opened her eyes. There were voices outside the door.

44

Brussels, Monday, October 10

Bente Jensen was alone in the conference room. It was almost nine and, behind the closed door to the open-plan office, another working day at the Section was beginning. The on-duty officers had reported earlier in the morning: surveillance against five Nordic followers of al-Shabaab was continuing; two Swedish-Moroccans who had traveled to Karachi had been under surveillance by the Pakistani security service as of twelve hours ago—it was thought they were on their way to a training camp; the Section was managing the signals intelligence against the neo-Nazi who had arranged a right-wing extremist conference in southern Sweden; then a string of other, smaller requests from Stockholm. Just a normal working day.

After the morning meeting, she got a cup of coffee and shut herself in the conference room. The coffee was hot and black, just as coffee in the morning should be, but she didn't drink any of it. She fingered the remote control.

Counterterrorism had sent a link to the recording early that morning. She had already watched it with Mikael and the leadership team, but now she needed to watch it again. She didn't want to, but she had to, for her own sake, to be completely certain. She looked at the time: five to nine. An hour or so, then it would be on the news.

The arrest had taken place at half past four on Saturday morning. They had found him at home in his apartment, sleeping. Everything had apparently been completely undramatic; he hadn't resisted. The first interview had taken place right away and Hamrén had shared a recording with the Section, management and a few other parts of the Security Service.

She turned on the wall-mounted TV screen. A black-and-white buzz, then the picture appeared. The camera was in the corner of a room, at the side, so that the person being interviewed was seen diagonally from the front, but wasn't tempted to look into the lens. It was one of the small, light interview rooms at the police station where Badawi was being held in custody. It was sparingly and anonymously furnished with an IKEA table, a few chairs with tubular steel legs, and a sober office light. In an attempt to give the room an air of normality, curtains had been hung in front of the square, bulletproof windows.

Jamal Badawi was sitting at the table, immobile, with his hands in his lap. Opposite him was the lead interrogator from Counterterrorism, one of the more experienced police chief inspectors. Next to the policeman was the female MI6 agent, Sarah. Badawi was wearing a white T-shirt and sweatpants, which he had presumably been given in custody. The operation had been fast; they probably hadn't let him get dressed when he was arrested.

Badawi looked tense and pale. He had the expression of surprise, of jitteriness that everyone but the toughest showed after an arrest. The lead interrogator asked if he wanted water. He shook his head and looked around the room as if he didn't really understand that this was happening to him.

"Can you state your full name, please."

"Jamal Abdulwaham Badawi."

The interview began with the lead interrogator asking Badawi to describe his duties at work for the Ministry of Justice. Badawi glanced furtively at the chief inspector and the MI6 agent. Dark, wandering eyes. He was very tense and didn't seem to understand the situation.

"Why am I here?"

They looked at him. No one replied.

"I really don't understand. This is completely sick."

He fell silent. They waited.

Finally, the lead interrogator said, "I want to you tell us where you were on Friday the 23rd of September."

"Friday the 23rd of September?" Jamal repeated. The firm question made him focus a little. He looked at the ceiling. Maybe he was playing for time; maybe he was gathering his thoughts. "I was at work," he said eventually. "And then I met my girlfriend—in the evening."

"What's your girlfriend named?"

"Why do you want to know that?"

"I want to know what your girlfriend is named."

"Carina Dymek," he said sullenly.

"Describe what you did that evening."

He shrugged his shoulders. "We met—at my place. Had dinner. Talked."

"What did you talk about?"

"All sorts of things. Why?"

"Your girlfriend had been in Brussels the day before."

"She was at a meeting. For work."

"And came to your place in the evening?"

Badawi nodded.

Bente fast-forwarded. Ten minutes later: Jamal Badawi had admitted he knew about the report. Now the lead interrogator was going through exactly how it had been handled, whom he had passed the report on to, when and how. Solid facts. Badawi was tense, cleared his throat—was close to breaking. The lead interrogator took Badawi through the questions carefully. Now they had an admission, they would get more out of him. Badawi resisted, as if he understood he was being led into an abyss. He was anxious. The lead interrogator tried to calm him, breaking down all the sensitive questions into small, technical, administrative details: a name, a phone number. The lead interrogator spoke calmly to Badawi, like a father to his son, a manager to a civil servant. The approach seemed to work. Badawi, used to talking to persons of authority, became more factual in his replies. The shrill, defensive, confused tone slowly began to dissipate.

"What did you say to her when she showed you the report?" the lead interrogator wanted to know.

"I said . . ." Badawi began to cry. "She shouldn't have accepted it," he burst out. "I knew it was dangerous."

"Why do you think she accepted it?"

"I don't know. She wanted to make a difference."

"She wanted to make a difference. Okay."

"Yes. Fight for something greater. Or something." Dymek had shown it to him, he said. He had told her to pass it on to others on Monday. "She wasn't in the wrong."

"What do you mean?"

"She was just given the report. I think it was mostly chance. She didn't do anything wrong, but no one listened to her. They were against her at the MFA—suspended her for no reason. I told her to be careful, but she was so stupid." He shook his head. "She thought she could go against her bosses."

"Okay. So you tried to persuade her to be careful."

"Yes, but she didn't listen. She didn't understand."

The lead interrogator fell silent. There was a pause—it was conscious; they wanted to let him catch his breath before they continued. Badawi's description tallied with the information about how the report had been spread. But she could see that the chief inspector wasn't really interested in the report. He didn't believe Badawi. He was waiting for the right moment to ask the questions that would lead them to the terrorist threat.

The lead interrogator poured a glass of water for Badawi. He drank it slowly.

"I want to talk a bit more about your relation to Carina Dymek," said the lead interrogator when Badawi had drunk a second glass of water. "Can you describe your relationship?"

Jamal sat quietly for a long time and looked straight ahead. Then he said in a low voice, "I love her."

The lead interrogator said nothing.

Badawi seemed to be fighting back tears and merely shook his head. "Where's Carina?"

The lead interrogator still said nothing.

"I want to know where she is," Badawi repeated. "I haven't heard from her in several days. Where is she?"

"There, there," the lead interrogator said drily.

Badawi stared at him and fell silent.

"Can you tell us how you met Carina?"

"We met four, five months ago. It was completely by chance. I was out with a few guys from work for a beer, and she was there with some people from the Ministry."

"Where was that?"

"At Pickwick's—a pub close to work."

"Okay. So you were there and met her there. Do you remember when that was?"

"It was a Friday—in May. The first Friday in May. I had never met her before; she was at the MFA and worked on completely different stuff. We got talking. We had fun. She was tough and warm at the same time." He smiled briefly.

The lead interrogator said nothing, waiting.

"I got her cell number and we saw each other a few days later. I remember calling her right away on the Monday because I had been thinking about her so much. And I noticed that she had been thinking about me. Then we saw each other again. And I knew right away that she was the one."

"What do you mean by 'she was the one'?"

"I thought about her all the time. And something happened when we saw each other; it was special. I told her things I've never told anyone else. And I don't really know why. I trusted her. I loved her right away."

"What things did you tell her?"

"Well, about my family." He stopped. "There are so many people in Sweden who don't comprehend that there is anything else in the world except their own little lives, keeping up with the Svenssons. They're not interested. And if you're an Arab like I am then they're always stunned that you've been to college, and they never understand how a Muslim can be a Swedish lawyer working for the Ministry of Justice." He laughed—it was a dry sound.

"So you feel misunderstood," said the lead interrogator.

Bente fast-forwarded thirty minutes through the interview. She knew what happened next: the lead interrogator continued drilling down into Badawi's relationship with Dymek to try and find out exactly how he related to her. Both Stockholm and London were still convinced that he had recruited Dymek to bring in the report, to work against Brussels and the EIS. Badawi answered, but didn't seem to understand what they wanted. An hour into the interview, Badawi was asked about people he knew. The lead interrogator got him to name friends, work contacts, and asked questions about the IRC channel, although not in as many words. Badawi was shown pictures of people who had been identified as members of the IRC channel. He didn't recognize any of them, he said. Didn't know who any of them were.

It was at this point that Sarah from MI6 took over. The conversation switched to English.

"I'm interested in your relations with some of your relatives in Cairo," said Sarah in a tone that made it sound like all she wanted to know was how he felt. "Can you describe your relationship with Akim Badawi?"

It was clear that he sensed something was amiss. Badawi looked at the British intelligence operative with a creased forehead. He pushed his chair back from the table slightly. The chair made a scraping sound.

"My uncle?"

"Yes."

"What about him?"

"I want you to describe your relationship with him."

Silence. Then, "Well . . . he's my uncle. I haven't seen him for several years, but I was going to visit him this autumn. He looked after me when I was little. When my father was in prison, that is. My father was a lawyer and was imprisoned for protesting against the regime; he was gone for three years. My uncle and his wife looked after my mother and me while he was gone. I often stayed with them in Cairo before we fled. But we're not in touch much these days. Sometimes we write; sometimes we talk on the phone."

"But you're close."

"Yes. Of course. I'm still in contact with him."

"He's the only one of your relatives in Cairo that you're in contact with," clarified the woman from MI6. "Isn't that true?"

Jamal looked at her helplessly. "Yes."

"You said your father was politically active. Was your uncle politically active too?"

"Everyone was. Everyone was against the regime. Against Mubarak."

"In what way was your uncle active?"

"He was . . . committed."

"Jamal, it's for the best if you're honest with us. He was in the Muslim Brotherhood, wasn't he?"

"Yes. But everyone I knew was. We were against Mubarak, and the Brotherhood was the only thing strong enough to stand against him. Is that a crime?"

"Is your uncle still active?"

Badawi hesitated, worried.

"I asked a question. Is he still active?"

"In a manner of speaking, yes. I don't know."

"You don't know whether your uncle is politically active?"

"It's different nowadays," he said through clenched teeth. "Egypt is different."

"You've known him your whole life and yet you don't know if he's still in the Muslim Brotherhood?" She looked at him, amused. "Don't lie to me."

"I'm not lying!" he exclaimed. "He's a member of the Muslim Brotherhood, but he's not interested in politics."

"The Ahwa group."

Bente leaned forward, paused the recording and rewound a few seconds. She wanted to see Jamal's reaction.

"The Ahwa group," said the MI6 woman again.

Jamal looked genuinely surprised. "What do you mean—the café group?"

Bente paused. Rewound again. Pause. Yes, he looked surprised, as if he hadn't understood the question. She pressed play.

"What is your assignment within the Ahwa group?"

"I don't understand what you're talking about."

The woman looked at him expressionlessly and gave an almost imperceptible nod. For her, this was just a game, in which Jamal was now playing the role of the reluctant interviewee. How many furiously silent people had sat in front of this woman before? Hundreds. Suspects brought in after rapid operations against scruffy apartments full of ammonium nitrate and the familiar, acrid smell of the diesel oil used in bomb making.

"You are in contact with Akim Badawi," she said calmly. "Akim Badawi is not only active in the Muslim Brotherhood, he's also part of the Ahwa network. He has been in contact with you and given you instructions. What has he told you? What are your instructions?"

"What instructions?" said Jamal in agitation. "What are you talking about?"

She got out a piece of paper. "'Their stations will be near. Their fire will loom before you,'" she read, "'kindling desire into a blazing rage.'"

Badawi listened and then he understood.

"How the hell did you get hold of that?" he said, his voice smothered. Then he exploded, screaming, "How the fuck did you get hold of that? That's private. You have no right to do that."

"What do the words mean?" said the British woman.

"You're completely crazy," Badawi hissed furiously.

"You're risking twenty to thirty years in prison," the woman said calmly. "If you're smart, you'll tell me what the words mean. We know you've been using the poem as code. What did Akim Badawi instruct you to do?"

Jamal Badawi stammered something that she didn't understand.

They had a grip on him now, Bente could see that clearly. The woman from MI6 was very professional; she had him exactly where she wanted him: surrounded, contradicting himself. Badawi was sat quite still, waiting. He looked horror-stricken.

"'Their stations will be near. Their fire will loom before you,'" the woman said slowly. "'Kindling desire into a blazing rage.' What does it mean?"

"I don't know," Badawi said faintly.

"What does it mean?"

"What do you mean? I don't understand. It's a poem. Just a poem." He was frightened; he was practically begging for mercy. He was exactly where they wanted him mentally. "What do you want me to say?" he hissed aggressively, as if attempting to escape. "My uncle likes poetry. He used to read it to me. It's a book. He gave it to me." Badawi spread out his arms. He was becoming incoherent, she noted. "It's poetry that he likes. Arabic poetry—"

"A book," the MI6 woman interrupted him. "This one?" She held up a small yellow-bound book—the same book that Bente had found at Badawi's apartment—and smiled sarcastically. When they had arrested him, they had presumably seized the contents of his home.

Badawi looked at the volume silently. He began to cry.

She opened it at a page. "Here. You've underlined this. These are the lines that Akim Badawi also wrote to you in an e-mail. It's an instruction to you. Tell me what these lines mean."

"It's not an instruction," said Badawi. "It's just poetry. Don't you understand that?" He was beside himself; he was crying.

Bente paused, rewound and watched the sequence again. Then she fast-forwarded. The agent had moved on, asking questions about his contacts. Badawi had pulled himself together. Someone had brought him a box of tissues.

"You met Carina Dymek."

"What's that got to do with anything?"

"How long did you work to build up your contacts, Jamal?"

"What contacts?"

"Redstripe, Sala82."

Silence.

"Frontline, Sabo, Darknite."

Badawi had shrunk a little into his chair and was staring at her. "I don't understand."

"Your contacts, Jamal."

"I . . ." He stopped himself.

"Who else have you recruited, Jamal?"

He shook his head.

"It's best you tell us now, before it's too late. Tell us what you've done."

He continued to shake his head.

"You met Carina Dymek barely two weeks after Akim Badawi sent you this e-mail. Right? Four months later—a few weeks before a summit meeting—you managed to get her to find the plans for the EIS, the European Intelligence Service. You probably know the name, you've read the Commission's proposal."

Badawi stayed quiet.

"A week later, a group of people are discussing how to infiltrate a summit meeting, how to find individual EU civil servants. And everyone is talking about the EIS. You probably know the person leading the discussion online. Was it you who told Carina to contact Greger Karlberg?"

"No . . ."

"Don't lie."

"I don't know him!" Badawi exclaimed in a shrill tone. "He's a friend of Carina's. He wanted to help her. She was suspended from work and he was just trying to help. I don't know him, I promise. And I don't understand what IRC channel you're talking about—or whatever the hell it is. I don't get what you're talking about."

The words came at a furious pace, as if spilling out of him in a spasmodic contraction. He wept quietly. They waited for a while, not out of pity but because they wanted him to regain some composure.

"Jamal, we also need to talk about the report. Where are the copies?"

Bente fast-forwarded. Two and a half hours into the interview, Badawi was sat on the chair, motionless and pale. He stammered, tried to correct himself. Now they were asking about Cairo, about his contact with Akim Badawi. They held up photographs of people that MI6 had under surveillance. He replied in a monotone. The fear shone on his face. He was crying. They let him dry his eyes and then carried on. He had dropped all his defenses—it was visible. His face was a mask of confusion. He was fighting for his life; he begged them to believe him, to listen to him. It was clear that he grasped the situation; everything hinged on what happened in this room, but he couldn't find a way of getting out. Sarah, the woman from MI6, asked a question, but he was no longer answering. She repeated the question, but he didn't seem to understand it, just sat there with his head bowed and his eyes shut.

The British woman stopped and waited. Badawi shook his head. "I . . ." he said with a thick voice, then broke off.

He was in a bad way, Bente could tell: on the verge of panic.

"What is this?" he said quietly, in Swedish. "Please."

He stared at them. The room was silent. He turned unexpectedly to the side and looked right into the camera, as if he had only now discovered its presence. He stared through the lens at her. He was innocent. Bente knew that, but what could she do? Washington had already requested his extradition; London had requested his extradition too. She couldn't change the rules. All she had done was her job. She reached across the table and turned off the TV. Hands, she thought. She had to wait for her hands to stop trembling before she rejoined the others.

45

Brussels, Monday, October 10

The darkness was broken again. They took her to a windowless bathroom and gave her a towel. It was the first time she had showered since she had arrived, and it felt wonderful. The sensation of water running over her body made her remember her apartment, Stockholm, Jamal. Everything felt so distant; would she ever see any of it again? She stood, hunched in the shower cubicle and ran the water as hard and hot as she could bear, letting it stream over her arms, legs, back, and head. For a second, she could feel her body again, feel the warmth against her skin. After a while, there was a bang on the door. A woman came in and told her to put on the clothes that were in there: a pair of soft sandals, a pair of baggy sweatpants, and a T-shirt. She got ready and opened the door; she didn't want to provoke them.

They took her up some stairs to a new room. It was large and cold. There was a bed, a table, and a chair. And a window. There were steel bars in front of the pane of glass, but for the first time she saw daylight again—a grainy, emerging light that forced its way between the bars. She couldn't take her eyes off it; they filled with tears in response to the unfamiliar light. Slowly, a soft pink was emerging outside.

So they wanted her to stay here now, instead of down in the pitch dark. A woman was sitting on the bed, watching her. They had put out a plate of food and a bottle of mineral water. She sat down and ate with her hands; she was famished. She glanced around. The men who had interrogated her weren't there; it was just her and the woman in the room. Her minder was wearing jeans and a khaki green T-shirt, and looked remarkably ordinary—they were about the same age.

"Who are you?" Carina heard her own voice; it sounded strange and hoarse. "You've got no right to keep me here."

The woman didn't reply.

"Where am I?"

The woman looked at her disapprovingly and at first didn't seem to want to reply. She had a stern face. Her mouth was tight. With an Irish accent, which surprised Carina, she said, "You're on the way to heaven, love. How's about that?"

The woman sat perfectly motionless on the bed with her gaze fixed on a point somewhere on the floor. What did she mean, 'on the way to heaven'? Carina drank from the bottle of water and felt sick. She looked at the woman, but her face gave away nothing.

The door opened. Two men came in toward her. It was time, they said to the woman.

"Stand up."

They quickly escorted Carina out of the room. They walked faster than they had done before; they seemed stressed. They gave her back her own clothes and told her to change into them. None of them made the slightest move to leave her alone; they remained where they were and watched, stony-faced, as she changed. They wanted her to brush her hair and wash her face after eating: they threw wet wipes and a comb at her. She tidied herself up. But for what? She could barely stand; she shook with fear. Something was going to happen. Please, she thought, please, please, please let me live.

They put a blindfold over her eyes and took her down the stairs and along a corridor. She heard steps around her. Then a door opened and, without any warning, she was outside. It was cold. The chilly morning air swept around her and gave her goosebumps. At once she could smell damp grass covered in dew, cold night air, and the burned smell of electricity in power lines. She gasped and filled her lungs full to bursting. Wait, she wanted to say to them, just a second. She had never before found the smells of early morning to be so intense. She stumbled on the gravel and felt hard hands holding her up, quickly leading her on, away from the building.

A car started. They put her inside and fastened the straps around her so tightly she could barely turn her head. Then she heard the car door close. They set off and rolled down the driveway from the building, bumping along a crunchy gravel road before beginning to move faster and more smoothly.

"Where are we going?"

No one answered.

"Where are we going?" she screamed shrilly.

"Shut your mouth, for God's sake," said a dark voice right beside her, in English.

She said nothing. She knew there was no point in asking questions, demanding her rights. There was no mercy, no justice. She couldn't do anything except let herself be carried. She began to cry quietly. Perhaps this was how her life was going to end.

They drove for what felt like hours before she noticed the noise from the road had changed. She felt the increase in speed, heard the drone of trucks whizzing past in the next lane: a freeway.

A sense of confusion filled her. Just a few meters from her were ordinary people in their cars—on the way to work, on the way to their everyday lives—and yet no one could do anything to rescue her.

They turned off somewhere. The speed changed. They were getting close. She was breathing through her mouth, her heart beating like a drum.

Without warning, they took off her blindfold as the car stopped. There were three people—two men and a woman—all dressed in the same windbreakers. One of the men got out, opened the door, and took her out of the car.

They were in a warehouse, surrounded by boxes and containers. A goods warehouse. It was cold and windy.

They quickly took her into a freight elevator and went up one story. The men leading her seemed to be Americans. They spoke to one another briefly. She didn't catch what they were saying; it was just a few short commands.

They came out into an even larger warehouse area. Around them there were men working in overalls, carrying bags, and throwing them on to rattling luggage belts. No one batted an eyelid as she was hustled past them.

They led her to a door where one of the men produced a pass card and swiped them in, then led her down a narrow corridor. Carpets absorbed the sound of every step. Not a soul was visible, just empty meeting rooms. They reached a room with frosted windows, a table with metal legs, and a few plastic chairs. They pushed her on to one of the chairs.

On the wall was a poster advertising an airline's trips to the Maldives. She stared at the picture; it showed an atoll in a turquoise ocean. She concentrated on the poster and avoided looking at her minders. They seemed restless. This was presumably a normal morning at the office for people like them. But where were they? She was going to be moved, or so it seemed, but where to? Would they make her disappear forever? She looked at the door. She wanted to cast herself through it and run. One of the men looked sharply at her, as if he already knew what she was thinking. She looked down at the floor.

They waited like this for several minutes, until the woman stretched, listened to her earpiece, and nodded to the others.

"Okay. Let's go."

They moved down long, narrow corridors and exited through a perfectly ordinary, gray door. Suddenly they were in the hubbub of an airport. They walked past glittering tax-free stores, cafés, and row upon row of chairs in waiting areas, where people sat with their bags or stood queuing by their gate. She looked around, trying to ascertain which airport they were at. Above the enormous thoroughfares, an announcement rang out in French; the signs were in French. The men were walking on either side of her, with a firm grip on her arms. The woman wasn't visible, but Carina knew she was somewhere behind them, not in the masses. People moved around them all over the place, streaming toward them in a flood of voices and faces, colors, and flickering reflections. Carina managed to read a sign that flashed by: CHARLES DE GAULLE.

She was in France, and this was Charles de Gaulle airport on a normal morning. It was so overwhelming that she stopped. The men reacted immediately, pulled her arms and made her keep moving.

They passed the gate without even stopping, let alone showing a passport or boarding card; the woman at the counter seemed to pretend they didn't exist; she was reading some papers. Inside the aircraft, they showed her to an unoccupied seat. She groped her way forward and sank into it. She was last; everyone else was already settled. One of the men checked she was seated and put her bag in the overhead locker with a professional, helpful air that felt completely at odds with what had gone before. So they had gotten that back from the hotel in Brussels. Then they turned and vanished through the door.

Carina looked around the inside of the plane; the cabin was full of passengers. She didn't understand. No one came. No one pulled her away or strapped down her hands and arms so that she couldn't move. The cabin crew wandered around the plane, checking everyone was properly seated and then, smiling, performed the safety demonstration. She couldn't stop staring at them. She felt the plane begin to move. Was she free? The man next to her, a normal business traveler reading the newspaper, looked up for a second and smiled at her. And like that, without anyone noticing the slightest difference, she was just one of many travelers welcomed on board EgyptAir's morning flight to Cairo.

46

Brussels, Monday, October 10

Overnight, between Friday and Saturday, three people were arrested in Stockholm on suspicion of conspiring to commit terrorist offenses. Bente flipped between the channels; they were all saying the same thing: three people, Stockholm, terrorist offenses. Mikael came in with a coffee cup and stood by the TV. They watched the pictures for a while. The story was on all the news bulletins and was sharing media space with a tropical storm over Indonesia, a Russian passenger jet that had crashed on final approach, and reports from the EU summit meeting that had opened that morning. BBC World had it as a standing headline in its international broadcasts; CNN, Sky News, and France24 had all featured it in their lunchtime bulletins. The short segment featured the Security Service press officer, surrounded by journalists, outside the main entrance at Kungsholmen.

"All I can say," said the press officer, staring right into the camera lenses while brushing a strand of hair from her face, "is that we can confirm that three people were arrested with probable cause to suspect conspiracy to commit terrorist offenses."

A journalist asked an inaudible question.

"Yes. The arrests took place with the help of the national task force and the police in the county of Stockholm."

The press officer didn't want to go into any further detail on the reasons for the arrests, except that there had been a serious threat posed by a group of people and the decision had therefore been taken to execute the operation. Pre-investigation secrecy was now applicable and the Security Service was therefore unable to provide any further information. No, the press officer did not want to state where the people had been arrested. Nor did she want to state their sex or age. She didn't want to state whether they were Swedish citizens.

The news story had run all day; they wouldn't get anything new now. Bente turned off the TV.

The Head of the Security Service had called her in the morning and thanked her. He was happy and the British were also satisfied. He had personally received positive signals from London. Sweden could be counted on, the boss had said to her. Bente had said she was pleased to hear that. After she had hung up, she had sent an e-mail to the entire staff thanking them. They had worked hard, she wrote. The threat from the hostile intelligence operation against their office had been a strain on everyone. They had done a good job. They had shown that SSI was a top-notch resource and she thanked them all for it.

The leadership team meeting that morning was brief. The atmosphere was relaxed; the others were in high spirits. They had gone through their active cases and then discussed the threat against SSI. There were no indications that any surveillance was still ongoing against them. Rodriguez wanted them to remain in a high state of readiness for another week, just for safety's sake. She couldn't explain to him what had happened in Evers. Not even her colleagues would ever find out what had happened there. Without any further explanation, she decided that the Section would return to its normal level of readiness, despite Rodriguez's objections. Mikael understood, but he said nothing. That was how it should be; they were professionals and certain things could never be said aloud.

Really, she ought to contact her American counterpart in Brussels this afternoon. The Head of the Security Service was right. After the handling of this case, the Americans had begun to see them as a more attractive partner. They had already been in touch with the Section about the two Swedish-Moroccans in Pakistan. The Swedes were under observation by the Americans; they could bring them in at any time and were happy to cooperate with Sweden in this matter. The targets had a typical profile: both in their twenties, from deprived social backgrounds, and with several acquaintances among the three or four hundred individuals who were of interest to Stockholm. They had been in Pakistan for two weeks and the situation was developing. There was a report written by the CIA station in Islamabad that had arrived that morning, together with a request for signals intelligence against three addresses in Örebro. Counterterrorism was a restless activity. She had already received voice messages from the British liaison officer in Brussels and Green's deputy director. Sweden's friends didn't rest. There were always new threats.

She really should have called Green and the Americans back already, but she had kept on forgetting to, throughout the day. Standing by her desk, she realized that her entire being—her whole body—was against it. The thought of talking to them disgusted her. Not yet, not so soon. They had forced her to grovel at their feet, forced her to ask for Dymek's release. MI6 would keep Dymek under surveillance in Cairo, and probably for a long time thereafter; they wanted to be sure she was clean. Every security service preferred to be safe rather than sorry, and, once a threat had been perceived, it could take a long time before it was judged to have dissipated. Just as long as Dymek did nothing stupid . . . Bente had taken a risk getting the young diplomat back. The slightest sign that something was wrong—a suspicious contact, unexpected behavior—and Bente would be held personally responsible for having ensured her release.

But what was really burning inside her was that they had fed her all their lies and she had just swallowed them. It was her job and she couldn't have done otherwise, but it was hard to pretend that nothing had happened. She had chosen a job where silence reigned supreme, but now she didn't know if she could cope with it. She had never felt like that before; the silence weighed her body down like lead.

She gathered the papers on her desk and went to the safe, pushed the bundle inside and closed it. The combination lock emitted a beep. "I'm going home."

"Do." Mikael looked at her.

She stopped herself. "What's up?"

"What?"

She thought there was something accusatory in the way he looked at her, but when she glanced at him again it was gone. Maybe she had imagined it. She smiled at him and got her coat. He accompanied her into the hallway and waited for her to lock her office door. Was he doing anything nice this evening? He shrugged his shoulders. His wife was arriving in Brussels later. How lovely, she said. She knew that his wife was the sales director for a large tech company and traveled a lot—that had been evident in the security review carried out when he had joined the Section.

Out in the command room there was a group of FRA technicians working on the Pakistani case. They were in contact with the Americans. The two Swedes had been identified the day before in Islamabad. The Americans were counting on tracking them with unmanned aircraft as soon as they left the city. The Swedes would probably join one of the caravans traveling through the mountainous regions toward the northwestern border, and then across it into Afghanistan.

The traffic jam stretched all the way along Rue Montoyer. She should have anticipated this: security had been increased due to the terror threat. Naturally, there was no terror threat, but that didn't make any difference; a security apparatus was always needed to demonstrate that threats were taken seriously.

She didn't know how long she had been in traffic, but for once it didn't bother her. She was in no hurry to get home. It felt good to sit in the car and watch the stream of people passing by on the pavement. She could discern security personnel in plain clothes circulating around the area. They looked like normal civil servants in dark suits, but didn't seem to be on their way anywhere. In the entrance to an office building, there was a man looking through the window, watching passersby. At a street corner further ahead, she saw a woman, smoking. It was her baggy jacket that had drawn

Bente's attention; it was a little too large. She was probably carrying a concealed weapon underneath it. Helicopters rattled above the rooftops. The area around Justus Lipsius would be cordoned off throughout the week; anyone who wanted to get in had to pass three checkpoints.

The ministers had flown in from their capital cities that morning and now, at half past four, the first day of the meeting was drawing to a close. She turned on the radio. They were broadcasting from a press conference with the German and French home secretaries. Bente half-listened while the line of cars slowly began to move forward. Illegal immigration from the south had been one of the big issues during the day. The Schengen agreement was under the spotlight. All member states welcomed reform of the EU's border controls. This showed that the EU could respond to the challenges posed by the future, said the French home secretary. It was important to avoid a situation similar to the one during the Arab Spring this year, when thousands of Tunisians had landed on Lampedusa and then spread throughout Europe. A major review of all systems for border control and crime prevention was necessary. The German home secretary was satisfied with how the meeting had gone during the day; he said that talks had been constructive. He looked forward to creating a more cohesive policy for border control and crime prevention. It was true, he said, that they had also decided to step up cooperation in security matters within the EU. A new organization dedicated to this purpose would be established. Closer cooperation at an EU level to deal with future threats, in Europe and around the world, was necessary. The French home secretary said that he was happy with the decision; it was a first step and showed that the Union was united in the fight against terrorism. Criticism of the proposal had been heard from some Swedish politicians and EU parliamentarians, said the reporter, as the segment continued. According to a statement made at lunchtime, they were deeply concerned about the proposal. The reporter noted that the debate surrounding the balance between the security of the EU and the right of EU citizens to privacy was very likely to continue. The report, Bente thought. It was out there, in spite of everything. The European Intelligence Service had been launched and was part of the system.

She rapidly overtook a truck, passed the traffic lights before they turned red and, soon enough, she was in the tunnel. For a second she felt an impulse to switch lanes and carry on along the freeway—to head north instead of taking the exit for home. She could be in Leiden in two hours. It would have been so wonderful to sit on the sofa in De Vries's quiet living room, surrounded by his books. She thought about him. They would never see each other again, she knew that, but she still longed for him—or maybe it was the calm that surrounded him she longed for, she wasn't sure. His was a calm possessed only by those who knew they were doing the right thing. But what did he know about reality? She was in the middle of reality, it besmeared her, as was its nature—dirty and ugly, with no easy answers. He, however, floated in a world of truths. What did he actually know? Nothing.

Fredrik was already home. The other car, the small green one, was parked in the drive. She could already hear the boys' voices from the front door. She turned the key. When she came into the hall, she heard Fredrik shout to the living room, telling the boys to calm down. He appeared at the kitchen door with his cell pressed to his ear and looked at her in surprise, as if he was, for a moment, wondering why she was home so early. He mouthed a hello without taking the phone from his ear and disappeared back into the kitchen. She heard him talking about some PowerPoint presentation. Have you found it? he asked. The person at the other end was presumably still at the office. She kicked off her shoes and hung up her coat, and heard Fredrik shout to the living room, "Mom's here!"

The shouts and muffled, rhythmic thuds from the living room promptly stopped. The boys appeared in the hall, the eldest with a basketball under his arm.

"Hi, Mom."

The youngest waved as if he was far, far away. Then they vanished back into the living room; she heard them rush through the door on to the veranda and then heard the sound of their voices coming from outside the house. There was a shopping bag from one of the big out-of-town supermarkets on the kitchen floor. She picked it up and began to put the shopping in the fridge. Fredrik was in the living room and talking to his colleague when her own cell rang. She went into the hall and got it. It was Hamrén.

"We've interviewed Badawi again," he said.

"Okay?"

"The British want to extradite him as soon as possible. They're probably going to make the request soon. It's all gone very well."

"Yes."

"There's just one thing I'm wondering whether you can help us with." When she didn't reply, he continued with a barely noticeable tension in his voice. "They want us to verify some of their intelligence."

She said nothing.

"I know that your people did a great job. Extremely thorough." He cleared his throat. The flattery was so false that it made his throat dry; she could hear it. "It would be great if you could help us with this. We need you to verify some reports."

"Which reports?" she said quietly. What she really wanted to do was hang up, but that wouldn't help her.

"About Badawi—his contacts in Cairo."

"Okay. Can't you do it yourselves?"

"The Brits know you," said Hamrén. She could see him leaning back in his chair, in his office in Stockholm. "They trust you. Your word counts for a lot."

It was such an apparent lie that she was tempted to tell him to go to hell. If there was anything the Brits felt about her, it certainly wasn't trust. They needed her, wanted to use SSI's resources, but they saw her as a difficult partner. It would take years for the Section to rebuild trust with the Brits.

"Why should it be me who looks at the material? It's not my job. Surely the prosecutor—"

"Yes, yes. But it would be good to have your assessment before then. We've talked to management as well. Just an opinion. Confirmation, if you know what I mean."

"But I've made my assessment, Roland," she exclaimed in a low voice. "Everything the British have come up with is circumstantial."

"But if you look at their material again, maybe you'll see things differently," he said, "now that things have calmed down a bit. It would probably do the Section some good."

"What do you mean?"

"You don't have to worry. The Brits have nothing but good things to say about the Section. But, at the same time, they are stressing how important it is to close this case in a positive way," he said. hastily adding, "I just spoke to London; that's how I know this. It would obviously be very beneficial for the Section to show results, that you can deliver what the Brits ask for. You know how it is. Management in Stockholm looks at all the numbers. And, to be honest, there are some people back home who are raising questions about the Section, so a good result would set you up nicely for budget discussions, as I'm sure you understand," he said in a serious tone, as if he were on her side.

He had wanted to say it for so long, she could hear it in his voice. He was in a good mood and couldn't hide it, despite it not sitting well with the sympathetic tone. If Badawi really were innocent, he would be let go, Bente said to herself. It didn't matter if she confirmed the intelligence; all that would happen was it would be rejected at a later stage in court. Naturally, a court would poke holes in the British claims; there was no substance to them. They would realize who Badawi was—a normal civil servant—and find him innocent.

"Okay. I'll take a look. But I can't promise anything."

"Great, Bente. Many thanks."

He hung up.

She got out a bottle of white, opened it, and poured a glass. The taste unfurled through her mouth and made her eyes moist. It was a dry French wine, one of her favorites. She took another gulp—she couldn't resist it; it was truly delicious—yet it made her feel unwell. She swallowed. It was so desperately quiet around her.

Fredrik was in the living room, fiddling with his cell. He looked up quickly and continued writing on his BlackBerry. "Hello. So, you're back."

"Yes. I finished a bit earlier than usual."

He wasn't listening, was engrossed in his cell, presumably reading an e-mail. Then he put the phone in his pocket, came into the kitchen and gave her a dry, absentminded kiss on the cheek as he passed her. "You seem tired."

"I'm okay."

Fredrik nodded. She avoided looking at him. She didn't have the strength to explain and she didn't want him to ask more questions because she still wouldn't be able to say anything. She poured another glass of wine and passed it to him. She had spent half her life working in this silence, without wanting to break it. She had always believed in what she was doing. But she wasn't so sure any longer. Maybe it was all wrong.

She looked out the window. It was a long time since she had gotten back from the office this early; normally it was dark. The boys were moving around in the yard. They were chasing the basketball, running in circles on the lawn in some kind of contest. Their eldest stopped and whispered something to his little brother, who listened in earnest. The youngest seemed to do as he had been told and ran across the yard, vanishing from sight.

"It's funny that the boys . . ." she began to say, but broke off when she turned around and noticed that Fredrik was no longer there.

47

Cairo, Monday, October 10

An old car with rattling exhaust pipes had just swung in behind Carina when the call connected, so at first she couldn't tell whether anyone had answered. Two men were hanging through the windows and began to bandy words with the vendors perched on small camping stools outside the little shop where she had just bought the cell, now pressed to her ear.

"Hello?"

It sounded as if someone had picked up the phone and was still there at the other end of the line, but she wasn't sure; the line was bad. Sunlight cut sharp contours across the streets of Cairo. She wandered into a small side street where the midday heat was not as remorseless.

"Hello? This is Carina. Carina Dymek. Can you hear me?"

The poor phone line made it sound like Alex's voice was coming out of a mineshaft. "Carina!" she burst out, and then, as if she had really meant to say something else, she said, "Where are you?"

"In Cairo."

"*Cairo?*"

"Alex, I . . ."

Words were being delayed and Alex interrupted her. "Have you seen the news?"

"No."

". . . Greger, I think."

It was hard to hear Alex; the words were all fragmented. But she guessed what Alex had just said.

"... the hell? I've not fucking done anything!" she heard Alex say, as if she was at the end of an echoing tunnel. Then her voice was suddenly close by, shrill and whiney. She spoke quickly and breathlessly. She was frightened. "Greger said it was cool, that it was just something you needed help with. My site has been down since this morning and they've arrested Greger. I don't know what's happened to Victor—he's not answering his cell. No one's answering. What the fuck have you done? Who the fuck are you?"

Carina sank down on to the pavement and closed her eyes. Greger, arrested? A big bus rumbled past, dangerously close, but she didn't care. Her arms were numb; she could barely keep the phone to her ear. "Alex, listen," she said and tried to sound calm. "It's all a misunderstanding. It'll be all right."

"How—?"

Carina interrupted her. "I'm going to sort this out. You have to trust me."

"Fuck you!" exclaimed Alex, her voice cracking. "I don't want to go to prison. I haven't fucking done anything. I'm a computer programmer, for Christ's sake, and I just let you do what you wanted on my site. I wasn't in control—how the fuck could I have been? There must be—"

"Alex. Alex, listen," Carina said firmly in an attempt to break through the rattling stream of words. All she really wanted to do was cry. Everything had gone wrong—everything. She had to find a TV, she thought. As soon as she was done with the call. Only Alex could do what she was going to ask for. It was her last chance. With immense effort, she managed to soften her voice. "Alex, please. Listen to me."

There was silence at the other end of the line.

"I don't have time to explain everything," she continued rapidly, afraid of losing Alex's attention. She gathered her thoughts and spoke slowly, as if to a frightened child. "It's a misunderstanding. Whatever has happened, we have done nothing wrong. Okay?"

"Okay," she heard.

"I want to ask you for a favor." She took a breath. "Under your fridge there is a bundle of papers and a USB stick."

"Under my *fridge*?"

"Alex, listen!" she shouted and for a moment she was quite certain that Alex would hang up. But her tone of voice had the intended effect: Alex swallowed the questions that were probably on the tip of her tongue and abruptly fell silent. "You have to get the USB and the papers. Do you understand? It's very important. Can you do that for me?"

"Okay."

"Under the fridge, there's a small plastic grill. Take it off. The papers and USB are inside."

She waited impatiently while Alex went to the kitchen. It was so surreal to imagine the small apartment in the south of Stockholm, so infinitely far away from the lane where she was standing, sweating in the close heat. She heard a rattle and a scraping sound as Alex put the phone to one side.

After a frustratingly long time, Alex's voice returned, loud and clear: "There."

"Have you got it all?"

Yes. Alex had it all: the report, the secret documents and the memory stick. It was all still there.

"Was it you who put them all there?"

"Yes. I had to hide them."

". . . looks secret. What is it?"

"It's a report." She couldn't explain now, the line was too bad, but promised to explain everything later, even though she silently doubted whether such an opportunity would ever arise. "Three of the documents have green stamps on them. Do you see them?"

Yes, Alex had them.

Carina took a deep breath. For the first time in a very long time, she felt a weak, budding sense of hope. It might work. But they had to act quickly. If the police had shut down Alex's site and arrested Greger and the others, it was only a matter of time before they came looking for Alex too. But there was no point in telling her that, it would only scare the living daylights out of her.

"Hello? Alex, can you hear me?"

It seemed as if the line had been cut, and she swore aloud. But Alex was still there—her voice audible but delayed.

She had been right: Alex had a scanner. Carina quickly began to explain, and waited while she listened to Alex turning on her computer and then, page by page, scanning the short documents: the records from the secret meeting in The Hague, the grotesque instruction not to inform parliament about the EIS, and the annex. Finally, Alex copied the report on the memory stick.

Then: ". . . do I do now?"

Carina swallowed. What she was now going to ask Alex to do would irrevocably change their lives in ways she couldn't foresee. But that couldn't be helped. It had to be done.

"Go to my e-mail," she said, and spelled the password to her private e-mail account. She had to repeat it twice before Alex heard it properly. But now she did exactly as Carina told her to, quickly, without any objections.

"Okay."

Carina got out the crumpled note and read the e-mail address for the *Guardian*. She had considered other options, but had chosen the British daily newspaper. They understood British politics; they would take it seriously. If the *Guardian* made a big deal about the EIS and showed that the entire project had taken place without the knowledge of any elected politicians, there was still a chance that she and the others drawn into this would be exonerated.

"Also copy in these people," she continued, and read the names of the Swedish MPs on the Advisory Committee on EU Affairs. They were well-known politicians; over the years, Carina had become familiar with their debating techniques and their innermost beliefs. How many times had she prepared data for the foreign minister or other junior ministers so that they could provide watertight answers to all the razor-sharp, piercing questions about the government's EU policies? But now she was no longer a civil servant, she served no one. It was their right to know the truth and her damn democratic duty to inform them. She slowly dictated the short message that would be the first thing read by the recipients when they opened the e-mail, and waited. The heat beat down on her head. Sweat ran all over her body in small, sluggish rivulets.

"Send it now," she heard herself say. "Send all the files."

Shortly thereafter, Alex's voice penetrated through a wall of noise. There. Now it was sent.

"Good." But she doubted that "good" was really the right word. There was no triumph in her actions; this was just something that she had been forced to do, and now it was done. Hopefully, it would absolve her and all the others she had pulled into the case. She felt hopelessly tired. Without caring about the stares of the passersby, she squatted down to rest in front of a dirty yellow façade. "That's great," she repeated in a low voice.

". . . now?"

"What did you say?"

"What do we do now?" Alex repeated.

"I don't know, Alex." She just wanted to cry. She bit her lip and managed to say, "But thank you. You don't know what this means."

". . . problem."

The line crackled. It whistled and whined as if an electric storm was sweeping in between them. Alex's voice was subdued, the words indistinct.

"I can't hear you."

". . ."

"I'll be in touch, Alex. Speak soon. Okay?" Carina cupped her hand over the phone to hear better. But the line had already been cut off.

She got up laboriously, crossed the street and headed to a small café where, the whole time, there had been three elderly men watching her. She asked in English if there was a TV in the café. They looked at her, puzzled, as if she was a complete idiot, and said nothing. A young man came out and asked if he could help. He looked so eerily like Jamal that, at first, she was thrown. Of course he had a TV. With an amused expression, he led her inside the dark, cool room. The young man reluctantly changed channel to BBC World on the small flat-screen TV in the corner and indicated that she should sit.

She stayed there while some men stared at her from the next table, until, finally, the news she had been waiting for came on.

TERRORIST CELL IN STOCKHOLM UNCOVERED, was the headline. A probable terrorist attack had been averted, said the newscaster, after three people, suspected of planning attacks against targets in the EU, were arrested in Stockholm in the early hours of Saturday morning. According to anonymous sources, one of those arrested was a thirty-two-year-old Swedish civil servant with connections to Islamist networks. A grainy film sequence showed a task force moving around on the street outside the main door of an apartment building. Just as the segment ended, she recognized the building: it was Hammarby Sjöstad, outside Jamal's building.

"No!"

She flew up from her seat. The men at the next table had lost interest in her, but now fell silent and looked sideways at her in disapproval.

No. That couldn't be right. Not Jamal. She was tired; she must have been mistaken. But, naturally, she had not been mistaken; she had recognized the door, the gray exterior, the small sushi place. A sob swelled in her throat. It was all her fault. She fumbled with the remote control, which was still on the table. Her hands shook so much she could barely flick between the channels. Finally, she found another English-language news channel and waited. A similar report appeared. It was brief, but the same shaky images flicked past: heavily armed police moving in and out of Jamal's building.

She rushed out of the café, got out her cell, and called Jamal's number. But his phone was still turned off. The call was connected, crackling, and she went straight to his voicemail. For a few seconds his voice was so close, so soft, so familiar: "Hi. You've reached Jamal. Please leave a message. I promise to get back to you as soon as I can."

"Jamal, it's me!" she shouted through the din of the traffic hammering along the avenue. "Please call me. If you get this."

She blurted out the number for her new cell. Standing in the middle of the hubbub, she cried violently with the phone pressed to her breast, as if it contained the last remains of the man she loved. A boy playing nearby stopped and squinted at her curiously, occasional passersby glanced at her, but most people hurried past without even noticing her, occupied with their own lives.

48

Brussels, Tuesday, October 11

Bente was woken by a muffled sound from downstairs. The surrounding bedroom was dark and motionless. Fredrik was asleep, curled up on his side of the bed, barely visible under the duvet. She lifted her head from the pillow and listened. There it was again: a ringing sound. Their private landline phone was ringing, on the hall table. She got up quickly and reached for her dressing gown, which was on a chair. Another quavering noise came from the hall before she managed to find her slippers and sneak out of the room. Fredrik stirred in his sleep, but didn't wake up.

Her body felt heavy. The last few weeks of work were beginning to take their toll, and she had drunk rather more wine than she was used to last night. But not all evenings were alike. The Brits had made a laughing stock out of them, and that angered her. It was as if, only now, when it was all over, was she able to let out that anger. She had tried to be in the moment with Fredrik and the boys, but her thoughts had kept running away, anger had made her distracted and sullen, and she had poured herself another glass of wine. She was quiet at dinner and for most of the evening; she had wished the boys a distant good night after Fredrik had put them to bed. When she and Fredrik were alone, they had watched the news and then a silly French comedy on TV. She had noticed that her husband was hoping they would have sex, but he hadn't made a fuss and had gone to bed alone. She had stayed up until he was asleep and the house was silent. Sitting at the kitchen table, she had leafed through old magazines she hadn't had time to read, while her thoughts continued to grind away.

The phone kept ringing. She hurried through the house. The stairs creaked in the silence. She picked up the receiver just as it rang again.

"Hello?"

It was Mikael.

"Why are you calling this number?"

"Your cell is off."

It was true; she had turned it off last night. She normally kept her cell on, but for once, after speaking to Hamrén, she had decided not to take anymore work calls. Mikael sounded wide awake, as if it was ten in the morning and he had just had his second espresso.

"You need to come in. Things are afoot."

She didn't ask what, since they were on an open line. "I'll call from the car."

She reached the freeway quickly. The road to Brussels was almost deserted at that time of morning. Mikael answered right away when she called and she asked what had happened. While she listened, she noticed how she rapidly became more alert.

"We need to call people in," she said.

Mikael had called in a group of technicians; they were already conducting signals intelligence. They needed analysts too, she said. They briefly discussed a number of practical details. She would be there within quarter of an hour.

She gently increased her speed and swept along the empty highway. She smiled to herself. What Mikael had told her changed everything.

There were two hours left until dawn and the streets were desolate, like the abandoned architecture of lost civilizations. She let the car rush forth over roads on which she normally spent hours in traffic jams. A muted joy rippled through her. Maybe, it struck her, this was what they called schadenfreude. For the first time in many days, she felt strong and decisive, like the Head of SSI that she wanted to be.

A few minutes later, she reached the tunnel.

She slid along Rue du Trône. The streets were bathed in an inky blue darkness. Pedestrian lights changed without a soul crossing. It was as if the district had been evacuated.

She entered through the frosted doors of Integrated Systems, said good morning to the two men from the protection team sitting at reception (who were always ready to cheerfully answer the questions of anyone who had mistakenly ended up there, or answer fire in the case of an attack), passed through the perimeter security door lock arrangement, and entered the Section.

The command room was fully staffed. She stopped and looked at the screens on the wall for a second. TV images from news programs were running on several, and there, on the largest, was the *Guardian's* website. The news was the main headline on their site, unsurprisingly.

Mikael approached and handed her a coffee. "It's out now."

"I can see that."

The Brits had intercepted a conversation from an unknown Egyptian number yesterday afternoon, Swedish time, Mikael explained. MI6 had sent a flash to Stockholm and Counterterrorism, but Stockholm had forgotten to notify SSI.

Forgotten. She gave a crooked smile. She doubted that Hamrén had merely forgotten to tell her; after all, she had talked to him only twelve hours ago. But it didn't matter. What was now happening changed the situation entirely.

The conversation had been recorded by the British signals intelligence station in Cairo and also by the American systems. They had received a copy of the audio file, said Mikael. Bente nodded impatiently; they could deal with that later. She knew how it all worked. Within minutes, a transcription of the brief exchange was sent to Stockholm and London, the call was logged on British servers in Cheltenham, and the American signals intelligence center at Fort Gordon in Augusta, Georgia generated a flash to Langley before digital copies were forwarded to the NSA's servers in Utah and filed away as a microscopic particle among billions and billions of other pieces of data.

Carina's call had been to a certain Alexandra Gustavsson, a resident in the south of Stockholm.

"What exactly did she leak?"

"The Commission's EIS proposal and three memos from the Ministry of Justice—all green-stamped. Enough to uncover the lot."

No one had guessed that the EIS material was hidden in Alexandra Gustavsson's apartment, Mikael continued. It was now under surveillance. The National Criminal Police were preparing an operation to bring Gustavsson in within the hour for interview.

"That girl is the least of their problems right now," Bente said drily. That strange, gloomy joy made her smile. Mikael looked at her in surprise and then turned back to one of the screens where Bente was examining the *Guardian*'s website.

"The story went up an hour ago."

She nodded. It was a good story, a real scoop for a paper like the *Guardian*. ILLEGAL EU SPY ORGANIZATION REVEALED. It was a headline many editors would kill for, she thought quietly. The preamble told her that there was "a secret organization to fight terrorism established by the EU Commission and a number of EU member state governments." According to "documents from the Commission and the Swedish government," it said, "the organization would be kept secret from the EU parliament and elected politicians in member states." She skimmed through the story, which included phrases like "death patrols" and "extrajudicial arrests."

This news would spread like wildfire. There were probably already dozens of editors around the world preparing to splash the news, TV crews already on their way, right now, to lay siege to the homes of the politicians and civil servants responsible.

"Okay. What does Stockholm say?"

"The government will assemble for an extraordinary meeting. They're going into crisis mode now. The Junior Ministers' group meets at seven o'clock," said Mikael. "It's all about damage limitation, of course. We've received a request from the Government Offices for crisis management. They've asked us to listen in on what's being said unofficially at the Commission and how other EU countries are positioning themselves. They're providing the Prime Minister with updates every hour and need to be one step ahead. The justice minister also needs to be able to say the right things when she speaks to the media. She has a press conference at ten o'clock"—he looked at the time—"in precisely three hours and twenty minutes."

That wasn't much time to find anything of value through signals intelligence, but it couldn't be helped. She beckoned to the Head of Signals Intelligence. "Göran, you have three hours, then we have to report to Stockholm." She thought quickly. "Target key people in the Commission. Manservisi, and the heads of the various departments that handled the EIS proposal. Priebe, de Almeida. You know who I mean, Mikael."

Mikael mumbled a yes. Göran, the Head of Signals Intelligence, also nodded, although he probably didn't have a clue. He had a better idea of who the various underlings in Hezbollah, Hamas, and al-Qaida in the Sahel were, rather than who all the political commissars in the EU bureaucracy were.

"Try to get into their cells and iPads; we need to know what they're talking about. Then I want to get into the Brits' system. Their permanent delegation is vulnerable, so start there. We need to know what their military attaché is saying. They probably have some assistant with a crap password you can use. Priority number two is the French and Spanish EU reps, and the same goes for them: everything being said about intelligence collaboration is of interest. If we have time, try the Americans too—Kennard and his deputy, White. If that's heavily encrypted then forget it; we can check them out later. Okay, I think that's everything. Are there any prominent EU parliamentarians we ought to keep an eye on?" She turned to Mikael.

"Maybe some of the characters involved in intelligence matters, like the delegates on the LIBE Committee."

"Okay. Mikael has the names," she said to Göran. "Report back to me in an hour."

She went to one of the analysts and asked him to give her an overview of the media situation. The young man was new at the

Section, clever, had worked on open-source projects at MUST, the Swedish Military Intelligence and Security Service. He provided her with a situation report so quickly she couldn't help but smile. He was anxious to show her his abilities—she was his boss. Bente liked that.

The analyst brought up a number of windows on his screen and pointed. The news had, as they already knew, appeared on the *Guardian*'s website at four forty-five, and they were probably preparing a larger spread for their print edition. The BBC had been the first to pick up on it on TV. It was included in the first news roundup of their morning show, *BBC Breakfast*, which was currently going out live. The angle had been British: the British government had tried to establish a secret European CIA without the approval of parliament. That some of the documents were Swedish was mostly mentioned only in passing. Some of the larger blogs had already brought up EIS and described it as an enormous scandal; several stated that the home secretary, and possibly others, would have to resign. Around ten British parliamentarians, both Tory and Labor, had already tweeted about it.

"They're calling EIS"—the analyst brought up another page—"a monster . . . a grotesque violation . . . an idea worthy of a dictatorship. And so on."

Just a few minutes earlier, the British Home Office had released a statement to the press that emphasized the importance of increased cooperation with Europe in the fight against terror. He brought up the British website. Theresa May was to hold a press conference at twelve o'clock.

"She's a dead woman walking," Bente interrupted him. "Carry on, what do the others say?"

After the *Guardian*, several other British dailies had published the news on their websites: the *Daily Mail*, the *Daily Telegraph*, the *Sun*. More and longer articles could be expected to appear during the day. France24 already had a report about the leak. Deutsche Welle and several German radio stations had mentioned EIS in their early bulletins.

"And the Swedish media?"

"The *Daily Echo* radio show had it in their five o'clock bulletin, in brief, and will probably expand it for their seven o'clock bulletin. It's on their website." He showed her. *Secret spy network in Europe uncovered*. Out of the Swedish papers, *Expressen* had splashed the news first, surprisingly high up their homepage: DEATH PATROLS HUNTING TERRORISTS IN SWEDEN. GOVERNMENT HID SECRET PROGRAM. PARLIAMENT IN THE THE DARK. *"This is unheard of,"* Peter Eriksson, chairman of the standing committee on the constitution was quoted as saying—apparently, they had managed to get hold of him. Bente glanced through the article. It was basically a rehashed version of the *Guardian*'s story, but with a greater focus on the government giving the green light for foreign armies to fight terrorism in Sweden, while keeping parliament in the dark.

It was already a few minutes before seven. Everything was still in its infancy. But when the editorial and news teams sat down for their morning meetings at eight or nine European time, it would get going in earnest. In six hours' time, the American eastern seaboard would be waking up to a new day, and then the American news channels would also pick up the story. NBC, CBS, Fox, radio stations, political blogs. What was now a mere murmur would grow into an ear-deafening roar and spread around the globe as each continent began a new day. Perhaps the analyst had thought the same thing, because he brought up Al Jazeera. They had the story in their morning news bulletin and a short article was on their English-language website. CNN had also included a brief segment on *World Report* at six o'clock European time, and would probably develop the story for their eleven o'clock bulletin. Reuters, AP, and TT of Sweden had all had the story as their main headline for hours.

The government's website gave no indication of a crisis, apart from the dry press release about the Ministry of Justice press conference. However, the EIS leak was the fastest-spreading story of the day in the flood of Swedish tweets, said the analyst. Comments and links were beginning to gather under the hashtag #bigbrotherstate. The *Guardian*'s article and the *Expressen* article were spreading fast. It was worth noting that several Swedish MPs had already outlined their thoughts on the story in writing via their blogs. Bente read quickly, hanging over the analyst's shoulder while he brought up new pages. Several opposition politicians had commented on the leak, she saw. Someone demanded a vote of no confidence in the government; another wanted the resignation of the justice minister.

She stretched. "Good. Text me all the big stories for the rest of the day." She gave him her number. "Interviews with the government. Press conferences. Focus on TV and radio, and the big guns."

She looked around. A concentrated calm lay across the room. The analysts were at their desks around her. The technicians in Signals Intelligence had disappeared into the adjoining room to get to work. The rattle of keyboards and the murmur of voices from the news channels on the screens filled the room. The Section had started work. On this Tuesday, governments around Europe would be under attack, ministers would wake up to their last day in the job, civil servants' heads would roll, and an intelligence partnership, painstakingly worked toward for many years by the British and twenty or so other countries, would be torn to shreds. Yet Bente still felt remarkably calm and unaffected. EIS would die, as so many proposals like it had done before. It didn't bother her. There would be new proposals. But SSI would come out of this mess smelling of roses, unlike Counterterrorism back home in Stockholm, she reflected with a smile as she headed toward her office. Hamrén would have a lot of explaining to do.

She shut the door to her office and turned on the computer, glanced through her e-mails and saw that Hamrén had written to her. The tone was rushed and the message brief. He wanted to talk to her; could she call him as soon as possible? She snorted; she would leave him to sweat. She lifted the receiver, but didn't dial Hamrén's number— instead, she called the only person at the Security Service who would be in a good mood this morning.

A familiar, dry voice answered the phone: "Kempell."

"Good morning, Gustav. How are you?"

"Fine, thanks." Kempell was, of course, not in a good mood at all, but sounded his usual, reserved self. Since he was Gustav Kempell, he hadn't allowed himself to revel in the vain intoxication of having been right all along. "We have a big cleanup ahead of us."

Counterespionage had launched an investigation against the British to smoke out their operatives and discover what had really happened in their contact with Counterterrorism. They had to find out how deep MI6's disinformation had penetrated the Swedish system and then secure all sources: a major cleanup.

"What's Hamrén say?"

"I haven't spoken to him. I think he's rather preoccupied."

For a short moment, Bente thought she heard a tone of satisfaction in his voice, as if he was smiling. But maybe she was imagining it.

"I'm just wondering, given the turn things have now taken, what we should do about the investigation—the material. Hamrén asked me to go through everything we had on Badawi—"

"You can forget about that," Kempell interrupted her. "It's no longer relevant. There's nothing the Brits have given us that will support charges against Badawi."

"No; okay."

"We're going to release him today. Naturally, we'll continue to keep an eye on the young man, just for safety's sake. His name turned up in the margins when we looked into the leak to the *Guardian*, but nothing more than that. I'm mostly curious to see whether the British will contact him."

"What do the Brits say?"

"To be quite honest, I don't care what they say," said Kempell. "But MI6 informed the British prime minister yesterday evening, and elements of the MOD and home office have been in crisis meetings ever since. According to our sources, MI6 spent a number of hours considering whether to send in resources to—as they put it—neutralize Dymek."

"Seriously?"

"Apparently they had second thoughts," said Kempell, unperturbed. "Dymek has been ruled out of their inquiries. They don't need any more problems. They've also contacted us and stated that they would prefer it if the entire investigation was shut down. They presumably don't want to make a bad situation worse by having Dymek sing like a bird in court."

Bente snorted. No, obviously not. She thought about Green and what he had said about Jean Bernier, that things like that sometimes happened—regrettable things. Dymek would never know how close she had been to ending up a regrettable corpse in a ditch outside Cairo. But the last thing MI6 needed now was another dead body they'd have to explain away.

"Although, she's still a problem, Dymek."

"Yes . . . In what way?"

Kempell sighed. "I mean that she's likely to have committed a breach of secrecy—of the more serious kind. We could probably dig up proof that she was behind the leak to the *Guardian* . . ." He stopped.

"But?"

"The question is, Bente, do we want a trial?" He cleared his throat. "Do you understand where this is going? If it ends up in court, everything will come out. The Brits hoodwinked us—that's a fact—and we'll not be able to hide it if Dymek ends up in court. Believe you me, it won't be about a leak then; it'll be about how Sweden's Security Service let themselves be fooled like a bunch of village idiots. The service will be dragged through the mud."

"Probably, yes."

"Probability of one hundred percent, I reckon. Our partners will never look at us in the same way again. It would destroy our service. I'm not going to let that happen."

Kempell was right. A trial would be too public.

"So what do we do?"

"The Prosecution Authority wants our assessment about how much damage the leak has caused, and if there are grounds for a prosecution. We can formulate it so that there's insufficient technical evidence for the investigation to proceed."

"And that would be enough?" It almost sounded too easy.

"Perhaps. The fact is—it's true. We've got jack shit that will stand up in court. We have a bit more on Badawi; his name is tied to three of the leaked documents. There's a risk that the prosecutor will decide to go to trial. There's not much to go on, but you never know."

"We have to talk to Dymek."

"Yes. She's done enough damage. Can you talk to her?"

"Me?" Bente balked. She wanted to say no, but reluctantly realized that Kempell had a point. The Section was smaller and more secret than the Security Service; they could operate outside of Sweden without anyone noticing. Maybe they could reach Dymek before anyone else did. And the only person who had any chance of getting Dymek to listen was her. A minimal chance, but it was enough.

"Okay." She looked out of the window. The day was dawning; a pale golden glow hovered above the rooftops. "Give me an address."

"She's not in Cairo any longer."

"Then where is she?"

"Sorry, I thought you knew. She's on the way back to Sweden. Bought an expensive first-class ticket yesterday. I imagine she's probably in a hurry to get home." She heard Kempell turn some pages. "Dymek flew out of Cairo at ten past three this morning on Lufthansa. Landed at Frankfurt . . . not long ago. Fifteen minutes ago. Her flight to Arlanda is in four hours: five minutes past twelve. Flight LH2414."

49

Frankfurt, Tuesday, October 11

It was just a normal day at Frankfurt Airport. The expansive departing passenger areas in Terminal 1 were bathed in bright sunlight. Bente squinted; there were thousands of people passing through on their way to their final destinations, and somewhere among them was Carina Dymek. It would be difficult to find her in time.

She stopped by a television monitor and squinted at it. There: Stockholm, five past twelve, gate A16. Barely an hour until boarding.

She had received two text messages when she turned on her cell, both media updates from the analyst at the Section. The justice minister's press conference had gone badly. It had been short; the minister had been on the defensive and had aggressively defended the EIS and the government's decision to keep the entire process secret from the beginning because it affected national security. Everyone knew that didn't hold water. The assessment was that a bandwagon was rapidly gaining traction. There was a video clip from the press conference; Bente didn't have time to watch it now, but the first, frozen still from the video was a picture of the minister, staring into space, with a stressed expression on her face. She had probably been standing in front of a hundred journalists, gathered there as the fourth estate to pass judgment on her—an already-gone minister. The other text message contained statements from politicians. The opposition had demanded a vote of no confidence in the government. Several press releases had used the same language. Even some conservative politicians were strongly critical and wanted to see a review of the entire EIS project. The government was now fighting for its political life. At the bottom of the message was a list of URLs to foreign media, focusing on the British government; she didn't have time to look at those, either. She called Mikael.

"I'm here. How's it going?"

"We're working on it," said Mikael. "Maybe in half an hour . . ."

There hadn't been time to prepare the tactical support that was the norm during these kinds of operations. No targeted surveillance; no tracking of Dymek's phone; no resources in situ to locate and follow the target. At the Section, her technicians were currently frenetically trying to hack into Frankfurt's networks to access their closed-circuit cameras. But, even if everything went perfectly, intrusions like that could take a day to execute; an airport like Frankfurt had security on its computer systems that was practically up to military standards. One single mistake, one single careless attempt to introduce a virus or open a secret door might make the firewalls flare up. She knew that and couldn't demand the impossible. She would have liked to have the cell team with her, but the flights had all been full that morning. There had only been one available seat on a sufficiently early departure from Brussels. There was no point sending people in on later flights or leasing a private jet—by the time they arrived, Dymek would be in the air. Bente was on her own in one of the world's largest airports.

She had to be systematic. The airport was like a small city; the distances were enormous. If she made a bad decision and ended up in the wrong part of the airport, she wouldn't get a second chance to find Dymek. But this was what she was trained for and had spent a large part of her professional life doing: tracking and following people, gathering information about them, understanding their behavior and motives.

She would find Dymek.

She looked across the concourse. She was in Area B, a long pier stretching out from Terminal 1's main hub that tied together all the gates. Dymek's flight would depart from Area A. At least she was in the same terminal; she wouldn't have stood a chance if she had needed to take one of the shuttle buses between the terminal buildings. Bente tried to visualize Dymek's state of mind. She had flown out of Cairo late at night. She had probably seen the news and, as soon as she had found out what had happened, had thrown herself on the first plane she could to be close to Badawi. Now she had to wait at Frankfurt for four hours—undoubtedly an anxious wait. Getting home was all that mattered to her. She would have had to re-clear security before her next flight. It was unlikely she would have stayed at her arrival gate. Most probably she wasn't nearby the gate for the Stockholm flight, but she would turn up with plenty of time to spare.

On the other hand, Dymek had spoken to Alexandra Gustavsson and knew there had been arrests. Maybe she thought she was being looked for. Maybe she was afraid to be seen. In that case, she would keep a low profile, hanging around in the shops or hiding in some remote part of the terminal until just before departure, and then she would go right to the gate.

Bente began to walk toward the main concourse; she hurried past a large group of recently arrived passengers, who filled the passageway with their travel baggage and shopping bags, and upped her pace. After ten minutes, she was in the main part of the terminal building, where the shops and restaurants were. She got out her cell and brought up the picture: Carina Dymek. She studied the photo and memorized her facial features, her hair, her eyes, and then continued on, peered between the tables in a number of fast food joints, crossed two large tax-free stores, and wandered through some of the smaller shops. People everywhere, but no Dymek. She took the escalator down to the floor below and watched the crowds before hurrying back to the main concourse again.

Terminal 1, with its three stories, was large enough to house around one hundred shops and restaurants: far too wide an area for her to have time to search it on foot. She stopped and swore at herself for almost losing her temper. Forty minutes until departure.

Before Bente had left Brussels, the Section had arranged a ticket for a flight departing from the gate next to Dymek's, so she could follow Dymek through security, if necessary. She would be able to pass through security and stand by her gate, but if Dymek wasn't there then Bente would have no choice but to wait until she turned up to make contact with her. She needed at least ten minutes in private with Carina. To stop her from getting on the plane was pointless—it would draw too much attention. Dymek was probably dead set on catching her flight and wouldn't let anything get in her way. There would be an argument, and Bente couldn't draw the attention of the security personnel.

For safety's sake, she quickly looked in three or four other clothing stores and checked the changing rooms. In a luggage store, she waved away an assistant and tried to gather her thoughts.

Dymek had been in British captivity and had then ended up in Cairo, where she had gotten up in the middle of the night to catch her flight. She missed home. She was probably exhausted, frightened, possibly in shock, and paranoid that she was being pursued. In that state, it could be assumed that she didn't want to be surrounded by large crowds; she would prefer to be left alone.

Bente called Mikael. "I need you now."

"We're almost in. Hang in there."

She looked at the time. Twenty-five minutes.

Mikael called her back. They had stopped trying to access the airport's servers, he said; the security was too high. However, the technicians had found weaknesses in a system belonging to a security company, passing over an external server. "We have some surveillance cameras. About ten shops and restaurants . . ." he interrupted himself to issue rapid orders to someone in the background. "Run her face," she heard him tell someone. Facial recognition. Bente left the shop and stood in the middle of the main concourse where she could see everyone coming up the escalators and streaming in from the different gate areas.

"We're looking," said Mikael in a low voice.

Bente gritted her teeth. She could almost feel the minutes ticking away like a physical sensation. She wanted to scream. She was forced to control herself, to stand still and wait beneath the high ceiling of the terminal building, following the herds of passengers with her gaze.

"There!" shouted Mikael. "Asian restaurant. Coa—Cuisine of Asia. Where are you?"

"Area A, floor two, by the escalators."

Mikael stopped for a second; he seemed to be reading from a screen. Then: "Two hundred meters to your right, opposite side of the concourse, where the shops are, near security for the A gates. She's leaving the restaurant now."

Bente had already begun to run. The concourse was a wide thoroughfare right through the airport, with rows of shops on both sides. She zigzagged through a straggling flock of travelers on the way to their gates and squeezed past a tour group, oblivious to everything around them as they walked along the line of shops, pushing laden carts in front of them. She reached the end of the concourse and, on the left, separated from the shops, was a cluster of restaurants. She saw the sign: COA—CUISINE OF ASIA. She looked around, breathless.

The face—she was trying to spot it in the crowd.

Dymek was nowhere to be seen. But she couldn't be more than a minute away. Bente hurried toward the gates, still jogging, peering at the rows of seats by the counters. It was still deserted down by gate A16—the only person there was a woman from Lufthansa. A few passengers were sat there waiting, but Dymek was not one of them.

She swore. There wasn't long left now—fifteen minutes until boarding. Where could Dymek have gone? It shouldn't have been difficult to catch sight of her out here by the gates. Bente couldn't have missed her. She got out her cell and began to call Mikael.

Then it hit her: Dymek was flying first class. A first-class ticket.

She ran back along the gates toward security. She was right: there was the glass door. Lufthansa First-Class Lounge.

Steps inside the substantial door led up to a reception desk where a man in a dark suit looked up and greeted her with a professional, welcoming smile. No, she said at once, she didn't have a first-class ticket. The man made an attempt to explain with an apologetic smile that this was a lounge solely for Lufthansa's first-class passengers, but she interrupted him and held up her Security

Service ID. The man took it and examined it in silence with a frown. Wordlessly, he handed the card back and nodded.

A large, airy room opened up beyond the reception area. An entire wall made of glass offered panoramic views of the runways. The sun shone through pale panel curtains; there was a calm light across the room. Here and there, well-dressed men and women sat in the generous sofa suites, talking to each other, hunching over laptops, or leaning back and reading newspapers.

There.

A little apart from the other travelers, in a sofa by the glass wall: Carina Dymek.

Bente stopped, struggling to slow her breathing while pretending to select a newspaper from a nearby table. For a moment, she was unsure; Dymek looked so haggard. She was forced to double-check on her cell that it actually was her.

In no hurry, she meandered across the lounge and sat down next to Dymek.

Dymek was lost in thought and didn't take the slightest notice of her, just continued to stare emptily at the view. Bente could observe her slyly in peace and quiet.

Her face was taut, her eyes red-rimmed, as if she was sleep deprived—or as if she had been crying. There were ugly marks on her neck, Bente noted, and a yellowing bruise on her temple that she had tried to hide by wearing her hair down. She looked resolute, dogged. This wasn't a broken person, just a different one from the person smiling out at the world on the Government Offices ID card.

She followed Dymek's gaze, looking at an Airbus slowly lowering its vast body to the ground.

"It'll be good to get back to Sweden," she said slowly, "won't it?"

Dymek came to life and looked at her for the first time, surprised to have been addressed in Swedish.

"Bente Jensen." She reached across with her hand.

Dymek reluctantly took the hand, as a reflex. "Carina."

"I know. We've spoken before."

"Have we?" Dymek straightened up and looked at her intently, with a skeptical frown.

She held up her identification. Dymek lowered her eyes. She could see Dymek's breathing speed up as she read what it said on the small piece of plastic.

"I know you have a plane to catch. But I need a few minutes of your time."

Dymek didn't answer. Her gaze darkened and she turned away. At this moment, anything could happen. The worst-case scenario was that Dymek would try to escape or begin screaming and making a scene. That couldn't happen.

"We know that you leaked the EU Commission's report about the EIS. And a number of Swedish documents," Bente said calmly. "What you've done will cause a lot of damage to Sweden. And lots of other countries."

Dymek said nothing. She sat, staring at the runways with an austere, stony face.

"Your plane leaves in about half an hour. You're a wanted criminal in Sweden. You'll be arrested as soon as you arrive at Arlanda, and I think your chances of exoneration are pretty small. Do you understand?"

Dymek continued to look at the runways. Two planes were approaching the airport, one about to land, and the other still in the air. Sunlight glittered on their fusiform bodies.

She didn't have much time. It was important to quickly get Dymek to recognize the facts and remove the possibility of her denying the situation. It was just as likely that a trial would be dismissed, but she needed to exert pressure on Dymek, to force her to a point where she could only select the option offered by Bente. She could use threats, flattery—whatever it took to get there—so long as she didn't deprive her of hope, at least not too soon, especially not the hope that she could save herself. One of mankind's greatest driving forces was the desire to save himself.

"You're risking several years in prison," Bente continued. "Records that will follow you for the rest of your life. Believe me when I say—"

"Leave me alone." Dymek continued to stare straight ahead.

"I'm here to offer you an alternative."

Dymek turned around and cut her off. "Go to hell."

This kind of aggressive rejection was to be expected. Dymek was off balance, and struck out with the weapon of the powerless: the demand to be left alone.

"Do you have any other documents?" she said calmly. "Apart from the ones that the *Guardian* has?"

Dymek shook her head and muttered no.

"Sorry?"

"No," said Dymek loudly.

"Are you certain?"

"Do I look uncertain?"

Bente looked at her for a second and then smiled. "No." The woman sitting next to her was worn out and exhausted—scruffy, but not uncertain. Not with that harsh look. Bente recognized herself in her: the confidence in her own abilities, the unbending determination not to let herself down. She wouldn't get Dymek where she wanted her unless she at least pretended to lay her cards on the table.

"Let me be completely honest with you," she said. "We have no interest in charges being brought against you."

She waited. Carina was sat with her back to her, but seemed to be listening.

"Leaking those documents was very stupid. We don't want to have to deal with any other incidents like that; do you understand? All we ask is that you never breathe another word about the EIS for the rest of your life. Or about anything that has happened."

"You want to silence me." Carina laughed. "Isn't it a bit late for that?"

"That's not for you to decide. If you say as much as a word about something to do with the EIS, I can promise you that we'll do everything we can to stop you."

Dymek shuddered. She tried to hide it, but it was clear in the way she tensed her shoulders and back.

Bente leaned forward and adopted a more conciliatory tone: "On the other hand, if you keep up your end, we should be able to arrange for you to return to work at the MFA."

"The MFA?" Carina looked up. Her face was contorted with rage. "You think I want to go back there? They told me to leave and I've no intention of going back."

Bente had actually thought this would be sufficient bait to secure Carina.

"So you don't want to go back to the Ministry?"

"Never," said Carina sullenly. "I accepted the report and passed it on to my bosses. I did what any civil servant would have done. I didn't do anything wrong. They threw me out just because it suited them. And now they want me to come back nice and quietly—is that it? They can go to hell."

Carina wasn't anywhere near as broken as she had expected. Bente couldn't help but feel a certain tenderness for the furious young woman sitting there on the sofa.

"But do we have an agreement, Carina?"

"This isn't even about the EIS, is it?" Carina looked calmly at her, with a hard stare. "This is about Jean Bernier. It was you people that killed him, wasn't it?"

"No."

"It was you."

"No, Carina," she said quickly. "You're wrong, and I have no intention of discussing this with you. I'm sure you understand that."

"Because then you'll have to shoot me too, is that it?"

"You have no idea what you're talking about." She needed to bring this idiotic conversation to an end. It was so annoying how Carina, somehow, had managed to turn the tables and make her sit there defending herself. There was so little time; she needed to get them back on topic.

"What kind of people are you?" Carina asked.

"Just like you. Normal people."

"I don't believe that." She looked up as if a thought had just struck her. "It was you that called me in Brussels."

"Yes."

"Were you trying to rescue me?"

She hesitated. Rescue? "Yes. You could say that."

"You were trying to rescue me, but killed Jean Bernier. How can you live with yourself?"

"I'm doing my job."

"Your job." Carina shook her head with a smile. "Jean Bernier is dead. People like you killed him."

"Carina . . ."

But she wouldn't be interrupted. "He said I had a conscience. And I actually think he was right. I have a conscience. But you . . ." Dymek looked at her in disgust. "You're just empty."

"That's enough," said Bente sternly. She didn't want to hear anymore. "I've asked you a question and you still haven't given me an answer."

"I don't care about your questions."

"Maybe not," she said slowly. "But you do care about Jamal. We have his name connected to the three Swedish documents the *Guardian* received."

She waited; let the words do their work. She could see them taking hold. Carina stared at her; her eyes glazed over. Bente had guessed right. Carina would never betray Jamal. It was endearing, and useful.

"Leave him alone."

"That depends on you."

She met Carina's gaze.

"On me?"

"Yes."

"And how do I know you're not lying?"

"You'll have to trust me," Bente said lightly.

Carina snorted and looked out of the window. Then she got up, wordlessly. It was time to go to her gate. Bente followed silently as she left the lounge.

The noisy airport enveloped them. Droning announcements about different impending departures soared above the clamor

and clatter of thousands of feet and bags. The last call for boarding to Stockholm had been made; all remaining passengers were
requested to go to the gate immediately.

"I'll keep quiet," Carina said harshly. "If you release Jamal. You
have to let him go, and leave him alone. Forever. If he doesn't call
me when I get to Arlanda, then—"

"Okay." Bente met the raging eyes of Carina. "He'll call you."

"And you have to exonerate him; you have to leave him alone.
Forever. Get it?"

She nodded. Carina was, without a doubt, serious. She had
already inflicted serious damage upon Swedish and European intelligence operations and wouldn't hesitate to do so again if they didn't
keep up their side of the bargain. Right after this conversation,
Bente would call Kempell and get Badawi released from custody.

Carina glared at her as if she was going to say something so scath-
ing that it would cut into the deepest, most secret parts of Bente.
But she seemed to change her mind, merely shook her head and
wordlessly set off down the ramp toward the gates. Bente watched
her go. She felt sympathy for Carina Dymek, a kind of warmth that
aroused an impulse to catch up with her and continue the conversation. She knew the impulse was a weakness that occurred when
suspects managed to transfer their world view to an investigator.
She didn't grab hold of the feeling and it slowly faded away, just like
the tickle of an unfulfilled sneeze.

Dymek was no longer visible in the crowd. Slowly, Bente began
to walk to her own gate. She was in no hurry; the flight to Brussels
wasn't for another hour. They had now buried a truth. That didn't
bother her; secrets were necessary and good things. They were the
matter that made up her work—that filled her life. Modern existence would never function so well, so smoothly, if it didn't—to a
large extent—consist of secrets.

She lifted the phone to her ear. It rang. After their conversation, Kempell was going to contact Counterterrorism and then the
prison, and within a few hours Badawi would be driven to Arlanda
and released, thus contributing to a small, heartwarming reunion,

written and directed by the Security Service. They would conduct limited monitoring of the couple for a few months, until Counterespionage was convinced they would maintain their silence. In time, the media would also let go of the story, in accordance with the inexorable logic of the news hunters that even the biggest scoop ended up with the same number of column inches as an obituary. Then Carina Dymek would be on her way into obscurity. Dymek, someone would remind themselves. Oh, her, yes. She had to go. A shame. She was good, but she made a mistake—so they would say in the corridors of the Ministry. But eventually no one would remember what that mistake had been, and no one would be able to say what had actually happened.